The
SARACEN
Incident

An Adam Braxton Thriller

Jack Bowie

Visit the author's web site at www.JackBowie.com

ISBN: 1519696906

ISBN-13: 978-1519696908

Third Edition: April 2016

Cover design by Renee Barratt, www.TheCoverCounts.com

To my wife Sharon, and daughters Lisa and Jennifer,
with all my love.

CHAPTER 1

Washington, D.C.
Sunday, 7:00 p.m.

"GOTCHA, YOU BASTARD!"

It had taken thirty-five hours, two Pizza King super veggie pizzas, a box of Honey Nut Cheerios, a chicken parm grinder from Genoa's, two giant bags of hot and spicy Chex Mix, and fifteen caffeine-free Cokes, but he had finally caught the rogue.

The surface of his battered oak desk was invisible beneath a treacherous landscape of reference books, manila folders, and crumpled sheets of notebook paper. Only a precise pyramid of the crimson and white soda cans hinted at the true character of the detective. He really should have been studying for Tuesday's combinatorial math exam, but his quest was infinitely more exciting than computing Markov transition matrices.

He gazed bleary-eyed into the LCD monitor that stood on the back of the desk, scanning each line of output as his detector program reported the gateway's traffic profile. For the past three hours he had watched the status lines scroll hypnotically down the screen, showing nothing but the expected match between incoming and outgoing messages. All an Internet gateway was *supposed* to do was route and forward other computers' communications. It connected his university's internal network with the Internet backbone. Not unlike a local post office: a letter comes in, a letter goes out.

But now one of the comparisons was wrong; one more message was sent than was received. The post office had sent its own letter. He had first seen the anomaly the week before, but had accidentally destroyed the trace trying to analyze it. Now he had proof.

Exactly *what* the anomaly was, however, he couldn't determine.

It might just be a simple duplication of another message, perhaps caused by a transmission error or benign software bug. Or a maintenance message sent off to some anonymous network manager. But it could also be from a computer virus or worm. Something that could compromise the security and integrity of his network.

It wasn't really *his* network of course; it belonged to George Washington University. But ever since he had started on the network security project for Mendoza he couldn't help but think of the University's plexus of computers and communication lines personally. The network had taken on a life of its own; it was a dynamic, living entity feeding on the keystrokes of students, professors, and administrators, ingesting their notes and memos, files and reports to its invisible organs, and releasing their contents only to those authorized to view them. Yet there were always dangers; entities that would poison and drain the blood of the network, plagues that would disrupt the natural flows.

He was the guardian of this soul. And if something had invaded his ward he was determined to find out exactly what it was.

He had started programming the latest version of his detector early that morning. The bright, encouraging rays of sunlight that had filled his small apartment had now been replaced by darkness and the lonely, eerie glow from the monitor. Shadow companions of fatigue and despair had danced on the rough plaster walls of the room, coming ever closer as the hours drifted by. But he had fought off the apparitions and had caught his quarry.

Rubbing his eyes to clear the watery blur, he scribbled some final notes on a printout and clicked open the window to his electronic mail program. He had gone as far as he could; it was time to call for help.

The clock icon in the corner of his screen suddenly caught his eye. "Damn," he whispered. He had an appointment in less than an hour.

Absent-mindedly running his hand over his face another reality sunk in. He was hardly prepared to meet anyone. His face was a jumble of hair and whiskers, his clothes were covered with stains and crumbs, and his apartment had a . . . well, unique aroma. He badly needed a shave, shower, and clean clothes. And maybe an open window would clear the air.

He forced his attention back to the keyboard and pecked out the message, oblivious to a faint tapping echoing through the room. The tap turned into a rap, and the rap to a very insistent knock, finally breaking through his concentration. A knock? What was she doing here already?

After a final punch at the ENTER key, he slid his chair to the doorway, flipped the two deadbolts, and twisted the knob.

"Hey, why so early?" he asked with a grin as the door swung open. "I thought . . ."

His mouth froze in mid-sentence. Instead of seeing a smiling coed, two dark silhouettes were outlined in the glow from a bare bulb in the hallway. He groped around the jamb with his right hand and flipped the switch to the room's overhead.

Dirty yellow light filled the room and spilled out to the hall, illuminating the emotionless faces of two very imposing men. One was tall, he must have been at least six feet four, the other shorter, but with a neck like a professional wrestler. They were dressed alike, each wearing dark slacks and tan light-weight jackets. Dark aviator glasses covered their eyes. Their chiseled features and crew-cut hair reminded him of something out of *Men in Black*.

"Mohammed Ramal?" the taller man asked.

"Ah, yes," Ramal blurted out little too loudly as he bounced up from the seat and gave it a kick back across the room. The chair skidded across his threadbare oriental rug and struck the desk with a force that tumbled his aluminum monument and tossed most of his papers onto the floor.

"I'm Special Agent Harding and this is Special Agent Nathan, from the FBI." The men pulled small black leather wallets from their pockets and mechanically flipped them open so Ramal could read the ID cards. "We're doing a security check on one of your classmates and would like to ask you a few questions." The cards were quickly pocketed as Harding finished the familiar monologue. "Okay if we come in?"

Too surprised to debate the issue in the doorway, Ramal managed a curt "Sure" and stepped back from the entrance.

Despite the odd hour, the appearance of the agents was not that unusual. A number of his friends in the department had applied for jobs with the spooks and he knew that background checks were routine. The security agencies were always recruiting at GW; Langley and Fort Meade were nearly next door, and they both were major employers of comp-sci grads.

The two agents stepped slowly into the room and Ramal couldn't help but be intimidated by their watchful, measured bearing. He'd never thought about being a spook, but they did interesting work and had really cool toys. The cavernous underground computing facility at NSA was said to contain more processing power than that in most countries. He was bright, spoke Farsi pretty well, and had a good understanding of Islamic history. It couldn't hurt to ask a few suggestive questions could it?

As he turned to close the door, he noticed that the shorter agent was carrying a large plastic grocery bag. Why hadn't he noticed that before?

Harding wasted no time, delivering the *shuto* swiftly and accurately. The blow fractured the spinous process of the axis, or second cervical vertebra, just at the base of the neck. It drove the process into the arch of the smaller third vertebra, crushing it, the resulting bone shards easily slicing through Ramal's cheese-soft cervical spinal nerves. There was little blood and this particular injury would later be unrecognizable.

Instantly paralyzed from the neck down, Ramal collapsed like a severed marionette onto the ragged oriental. Unable to move or breathe but still conscious, he felt his heart pound like a jackhammer trying to push life-giving blood to the rest of his body. But without functioning lungs, the anoxic fluid only caused increased screams from his dying muscles. He watched, powerless, as the visitors went through his apartment while his consciousness, and life, slowly dissolved into darkness.

* * *

Ramal had been connected through his cable modem to *trumpet*, the main computer science server for George Washington University. His email program queued his outgoing message to *outmail.gwu.edu*, the outgoing SMTP server for the University. *outmail.gwu.edu* released it at 7:17 to the nearest Internet router, *gwu-gate*. After six seconds, *gwu-gate* forwarded the message to the next stop on its journey, *cmu-common*, on the Carnegie Mellon campus. Forty-five seconds later, *cmu-common* successfully sent the single block of computer data to the input network driver on *certcc*, the incoming server for the

CERT Coordination Center at the Software Engineering Institute in Pittsburg.

Bob Bennett was the response operator for the evening shift. This was Bennett's second year working part-time at the Center. It wasn't a bad gig; basically, he got paid for the time he spent doing his homework. Usually there weren't very many interruptions; which was a good thing tonight since he had a killer exam in number theory the next day.

It took him sixty-eight seconds to open and read the new email. It was 7:19 p.m. Eastern Standard Time. The message was sufficiently vague, and promised further detail, so Bennett classified it as a Grade Three, low priority. He saved the message into the designated electronic folder, and went back to figuring out why Riemann manifolds didn't belong on Jeff Gordon's NASCAR racer.

*   *   *

After circling the block twice, Susan Goddard finally found a parking spot on Colburn Street, slipping her BMW in the space as a rust-infested chartreuse Beetle lurched out. Pleased with her success, she set her car alarm, walked to the corner, and turned down Grady Avenue toward her friend's apartment.

Street traffic was light this Sunday evening and only a few couples, they looked like undergrads, strolled the sidewalk. She was fifteen minutes early but had gotten a cool new idea for their simulation while reviewing some journal articles and couldn't wait to tell Mohammed about it. Besides, it had been another weekend spent by herself. She badly needed some human interaction.

Goddard had spent Saturday cloistered in the stacks of the Library of Congress excavating articles on the geo-political development of the Malay Peninsula, and today staring into her web browser searching the literature on computer-aided instruction for some nugget useful to their project. All part of the unbridled excitement of being an overworked grad student. She really had to get a social life. Unfortunately, this evening's "study date" was as close as she was going to get.

She was only half a block away when a blinding flash of light froze her in place. Less than a second later, a high-pressure shock wave slapped her back to life, nearly knocking her down onto the cracked concrete sidewalk. She straightened up and saw a cloud of smoke and debris surround her destination like a dark cocoon, while fragments of glass, wood, and metal rained down onto the street.

Her book bag fell to the ground as she raised her hands to her face and let out a terrified scream.

CHAPTER 2

Washington, D.C.
Sunday, 9:45 p.m.

DETECTIVE SAM FOWLER, District of Columbia Investigative Services Bureau, Second District, double-parked his faded blue Taurus a block from the crime scene. It was a sultry spring evening in D.C., temperature in the mid-sixties, humidity about one hundred fifty percent, and dead calm. Fowler peeled his sweat-soaked back from the vinyl-covered seat and headed into a haze of smoke, guided only by spears of red and blue light shooting from the light bars on two patrol cars parked further up the street.

He emerged from the haze into a confusion of activity. Debris from the blast spread all the way across the narrow two lane pavement. Three patrolmen were trying their best to keep the press and other civilians away from the evidence as they wrapped the area in bright yellow "Crime Scene" tape.

The neighborhood was typical for this part of the northwest quadrant of the District of Columbia. Both sides of the street were lined with three-decker row houses, most built in the 1940's. Decades of paint hung thick on the clapboards blurring the lines of the siding and making the homes look like over-frosted birthday cakes. Cracked brickwork had been repaired and repointed so many times there was more mortar than masonry remaining. Still, the small lawns were clipped, and the litter was down to a manageable level. Overall, the houses were livable and in reasonable repair, the structures standing the test of time better than those in other parts of his District.

The full force of inner-city D.C. crime had not yet come out this far, and the owners of the tri-levels, most of whom were residents as well, were trying to slow the relentless invasion. The Second had its slums and its mansions; Fowler had seen them all. He hoped they could hold on. Still, it was hard to believe that there was anyone or anything in this neighborhood that was worth blowing up.

Fowler trudged forward, awkwardly ducking under the tape, then carefully stepping over the glass, wood and metal littering the ground. His eyes burned from the smoke and the throbbing that had begun in the back of his head was starting its forced march to his temples. This was his second murder of the shift and he hadn't had anything to eat since lunch, a long ten hours ago.

He stopped in front of number 94 and stared up to where the third floor apartment used to be. The two six-over-six windows had been completely blown out and black smoke still swirled through the ragged holes. Shards of glass, splinters of window frame, and sections of shingles littered the ground. Damage to the rest of the building seemed minimal so it couldn't have been all that big a charge. But from what the dispatcher had said, the scene inside was pretty ugly.

Two more blue and white patrol cars were parked in front of the row house alongside an unmarked he assumed was from forensics. Looking down the street, he saw the Bomb Squad van parked at the corner. They always did know enough to stay out of the way.

Fowler flashed his shield at the patrolman guarding the upstairs entry, and headed up. The detective was a big man, six foot three and 230 pounds, and found himself angling his body sideways as he trudged up the narrow staircase. His wife had given up nagging him about his weight, but climbing two flights of stairs at the end of a shift was almost enough to put him back on his diet. Almost.

The smell of gunpowder bit at his nostrils as he neared the third floor landing. He hadn't had a bombing case for a couple of years now, but the memory helped brace him for the chaos inside.

Fowler walked into what must have been the living room of the apartment and was again reminded of what even a small amount of explosive could do. The destruction was nearly total. Two portable floodlights glared into the apartment illuminating what was left of the tenant's belongings.

The furniture had been completely shredded, pieces blown into every corner. Fowler could make out the remains of an old sofa and at least two chairs. The frames of what looked like two television monitors were scattered on the floor. Dark red stains covered the carpet and dotted the bare plaster walls. The stench attacked him again, this time a mix of smoke, cordite, and human remains. One member of the forensics team knelt on the side of the room, picking up and cataloging debris. Lying in the middle of the room was Fowler's reason for being there: a blood-stained white sheet covering what was left of a human being. He tried not to think about the state of that piece of evidence.

He was about to check out the rest of the apartment when a familiar face appeared in the doorway. Rick Thomassini was a rookie, barely on the job a year, but Fowler had already worked with him on a couple of cases and liked the young cop. He gave straight answers and didn't try to play junior detective, a welcome change from most of the other rookies he'd met.

"How are you, Rick?" Fowler asked stepping around the rubble.

"Doing fine, sir."

Thomassini always said "sir" to a superior, even when he was off duty. Fowler was sure he'd get over it soon enough, but the salutation was a welcome change from the greetings he usually received.

The rookie was a touch under six feet tall with a thick neck and muscular arms. His slicked brown hair and dark eyes made him look more like his Italian longshoremen ancestors than a D.C. cop.

"Wes and I got the call about 7:50," he recited. "'Big blast over on Grady', they said. Called the Bomb Squad right after we got here. Then Captain Rodgers after we found the body. Or what's left of it. That was about 8:15. The Captain said to call you. I put a request in for the M.E. but they said he's had a busy night."

"So I heard. Any identification yet?"

Thomassini pulled a small spiral notebook from his shirt pocket. "The apartment's rented to a Mohammed Ramal. Dark skinned male, early twenties, probably an Arab. Student at GW." He paused and glanced back to the body. "It'll take a while to be sure of any identification though. The owner and his wife are downstairs if you want to speak with them."

"Thanks. I'll get to them later." Experience told him the owner and neighbors would be of little help. Nobody wanted to "get involved" anymore. He would be on his own, as usual.

"Was anyone on the second floor?" he asked.

"Apartment's empty. The tenant's been out of town according to the owner."

"Check it out anyway. I'm gonna look around then we can go downstairs."

Thomassini disappeared down the stairs and Fowler continued his survey. It was a small, one bedroom apartment. The blast had taken out most of the living room. There were books and papers all over, mixed with occasional pieces of furniture and who knows what body parts. He hated bombings. It would take days to find and catalog all the remains.

Fowler rubbed his fingers across the wall. The grit of explosive residue felt like a piece of number 20 sandpaper. He brought his hand up to his nose, tested the sample, then wiped his fingers on his trouser leg.

He made his way across the living room and into the bedroom. Spartan hardly described it: a single bed, small end table, and a tall five drawer dresser. Nothing matched. Same kind of junk Fowler had in his first apartment. The blast had tossed the furniture around but the pieces were still intact. Clothes from the small closet were stacked in piles on the floor. A third portable light had been set up for the other forensic specialist who was logging the room's contents.

"Got anything for me?" Fowler asked.

The specialist looked up from his work. "Yeah. You might find this interesting."

Fowler walked over to the bed. The specialist was using it as a sorting area; it was covered with papers and evidence bags.

"Found a bunch of these in the dresser. Similar stuff in the closet and around the living room." The specialist picked up a sack from the bed that was filled with sheets of paper. He carefully pinched one leaf between his gloved fingers and brought it up to the light. Most of the writing was Arabic but the pictures made the message evident: raised hands with fists and machine guns. "We also found a box in the hall closet with wire, timers, and electronics tools. Bomb Squad guys said they were consistent with explosives hookups. Looks like our friend got a little clumsy." He dropped the flyer back into the bag. "So much for amateur terrorists."

Apparently forensics had already made their analysis of the crime. It was a wonder they bothered to call ISB at all. The damn technicians were going to write this one off tonight if he didn't do something quickly.

"Yeah, that's great. Get every piece of this shit catalogued by location," he barked at the tech. "And I want the name of every book in the place, including the cookbooks. Especially any address books or calendars." The specialist flashed an angry look and turned back to the bed.

That should keep the asshole busy for a while. Hopefully long enough to see what else this poor bastard left behind.

*   *   *

Fifteen minutes later, Fowler had found nothing of value in the rest of the apartment. The real damage had been confined to the living room, substantiating forensics' call.

When he made it back to the living room a Bomb Squad officer was still there picking particles off the wall.

"What do you make of it, Pete?" Fowler asked.

Peter Jacobson was a colleague Fowler remembered from the Navy yard bombing three years ago. He was a serious cop and another department old-timer. Skinny as a railroad tie, he never seemed to gain any weight, the bastard.

Jacobson finished retrieving what looked like a small wire from a pile of debris and turned to the detective.

"Good to see *you* again, Sam." Jacobson smiled, exposing a mouth full of yellow-stained teeth. Fowler had never figured why explosives' experts always seemed to be smokers. Away from a scene, Jacobson was a chimney. "A few traces of cordite. Looks like standard powder, not plastic. Small charge, probably only about half a pound. He could have been putting together a tester when it went off."

Fowler nodded in agreement. "Okay. But how come his tools were in the hall?"

"Good question," Jacobson said as he wrinkled his brow. "Beats me. But that's your job anyway, remember?"

"Yeah, thanks." He turned to head out the door. "Oh, good to see you too, Pete."

Thomassini was waiting on the landing when Fowler left the apartment.

"Let's go talk to the owner, Rick. Anything else I should know?"

"One thing sir." Thomassini thumbed through the pages of his pad. "We have this girl downstairs. She was outside when the apartment blew. Says she's a friend of Ramal's from school and was supposed to meet him here tonight. She's pretty shook up but I thought you'd want to talk to her."

Fowler weighed his options. "We'll do the owner first then see her."

CHAPTER 3

Fowler followed Thomassini down to the first floor and knocked on the main entrance. The door pulled back against a steel chain and an aged black face peered through the narrow opening.

"Excuse me, Mr. Brown," Thomassini said into the space. "Detective Fowler would like to have a few words with you and your wife. Could we come in?"

Brown hesitated, then released the chain and let the officers into a clean but cluttered living room. A green tufted sofa filled one wall, facing a flat-panel Sony television on a plastic credenza. A carved pine mantle surrounded a badly chipped brick fireplace. Three other chairs and a Boston rocker completed the furnishings. Pictures of young children were placed prominently on the fireplace mantle and end tables. The apartment smelled of cooking oil and garlic as if the couple had just finished dinner.

Brown was short, about five foot seven, and seemingly frail. A long-sleeved denim shirt hung loosely at his shoulders, tucked into a pair of baggy dark blue cotton slacks. The skin on his face hung loosely from prominent cheekbones and jaw. He was nearly bald, only a few threads of gray still remaining on the sides of his liver-spotted scalp. He motioned for them to sit on the sofa under the front window.

"My wife's restin' in the other room," he said. "It's been a hard night on her. You don't need to talk to her do ya?"

"No, that'll be okay," Fowler replied as he took out his note-book. Despite the obvious physical weakness of Brown's body,

Fowler noticed his eyes were clear and bright. "Can you tell me what happened tonight?"

"Frances, that's my wife, she and I was sittin' here watching television when we heard this awful boom. Came from right above us. Sounded like a cannon shot. I looked outside and saw all this glass and stuff coming off the house. I went out and see'd it was from the apartment. I told Frances to call the police and went upstairs. It was horrible. I didn't think he was there but when I saw the body, I came right back down and waited for y'all."

"What time was that?"

"It was 7:45. We checked our clock." He pointed to an ornate bell-jar clock on the fireplace mantle. Fowler compared it to his watch and continued.

"You said you didn't think that Mr. Ramal was home. Did you see anyone going in or out this evening?"

"Didn't see or hear nothin' earlier. We were eating dinner. A little after seven we did hear somebody comin' down the stairs. Thought it might be him."

"You mean Mr. Ramal."

"Yep."

"Did you see who it was?"

"Didn't pay no attention."

Fowler closed his note pad and sat back in the sofa. The pain was now firmly encamped at his temples, pounding like a jackhammer. Between the headache, the acid in his stomach, and this all too forget-ful witness, he'd be lucky to get back to the office before midnight.

"How long had Mr. Ramal been renting here?" he finally asked.

"Came about two years ago. He wasn't no trouble so we kept him on."

"What kind a tenant has he been?"

"Like I said, no trouble. He don't throw no wild parties and keeps to himself. He's gone most days, to school I guess, and comes back in the evenings. Doesn't say much to nobody, just as fine with me, him being an Arab and all. Stays up kinda late though, we see his light from our bedroom."

Fowler sat forward. "How late does he stay up?"

"Don't know for sure," Brown said with a shrug. "Sometimes all night, sometimes not. We've had a lot of students over the years, he's pretty much the same as the rest."

"Did he have many friends visit?"

"We don't make a point outa looking at visitors. He didn't get very many though."

Fowler heard police traffic on the stairs from where he was sitting. He looked out the window and could clearly see the steps up to the front landing. "I'm sure you don't pry Mr. Brown, but did Ramal have anyone that came regularly, maybe other students?"

Brown glanced toward his hallway and then back to Fowler. "No real regulars. And not many, well you know, foreigners like him either. We didn't want no trouble after 9-11 and all." His eyes wandered off to the window. "This one gal has been by pretty regular the last few months."

"Did she come by this evening?"

"That's her out there." He motioned to a figure standing outside between two patrolmen.

"That's the girl I mentioned, sir," Thomassini added.

Fowler ignored the interruption and returned to Brown. "Does she stay very long?"

Brown stared back at Fowler before replying. "Don't stay the night if that's what you mean. Always leaves after a few hours."

"You said you thought Ramal may have left tonight. What time was that?"

"We heard 'em comin' down about 7:25."

"There was more than one?"

The old man raised his eyebrows at the cop. The creases spread half-way over his head. He wasn't so senile he didn't recognize his slip. "Yeah. I guess I did see two folks leavin'. A tall guy and a shorter one. I thought the tall one was Ramal. It was dark and we only saw their backs."

Brown clasped his hands and rubbed his palms together. "They were carryin' something though. Looked like garbage bags. I thought maybe he was takin' out the trash but tomorrow ain't pickup day. That's Wednesday."

"Did they drop the bags anywhere?"

"Didn't see where they went. Just down the street I guess. Didn't hear no car either."

Fowler was exhausted. His shift had ended an hour ago, and he still had to write up his reports. Between the late hour and the effort of dragging anything of value out of Brown, he was about to collapse. "Is there anything else you could tell us about Mr. Ramal?"

"Nope, nothing else I can think of. What was the explosion? Some kinda bomb?"

"We're really not sure yet, Mr. Brown. We'll keep you updated as we find out."

Fowler stood up from the sofa, pulled a wrinkled card from his pants pocket, and handed it to the old man. "Thanks for your help. We'll try to get all this cleared up as soon as possible. If you or your wife think of anything else, please give me a call."

Fowler left the apartment shaking his head. Who the hell were Ramal's visitors? And what was in those bags?

When they reached the street, Fowler turned back to Thomassini. "Rick, have a couple of the patrolmen look up and down the street for any garbage bags. Maybe our visitors left something behind. But first take me over to talk with our witness."

Thomassini walked him over to a pair of patrolmen standing by a lamp pole. The woman wedged between them must be attractive; it didn't usually take two of D.C.'s finest to watch a prospective witness. The patrolmen wandered back to their cars as the pair approached.

"This is Susan Goddard," Thomassini explained. "She came to see Ramal about 7:45."

Goddard turned to face him. She was young, mid to late twenties, dressed in standard student garb: powder-blue George Washington University sweatshirt, designer black jeans, and white Nike sneakers. About five feet eight, and slim, maybe a hundred and forty pounds. Wavy blond hair bounced above her shoulders as she turned and Fowler caught just a hint of perfume.

She was probably very pretty, but tonight her face was pale and tears from her deep blue eyes had left dark mascara tracks down her cheeks. She hugged a blue nylon knapsack as if it would shield her from the night's terrors.

"Miss Goddard, I'm Detective Sam Fowler. I'd like to ask you a few questions if you're up to it. Then you can go."

"I told the other policeman all I knew about the . . . explosion. I still don't believe he's dead." Her voice quivered as she fought back the emotion.

"You're a classmate of Mr. Ramal at George Washington?"

"Yes, sort of. I go to Georgetown but take some courses at GW. We're . . . we were," she corrected, "working on a project this semester."

"How long had you known him?"

"About seven months. I met him in a class last semester. We got to know each other and he helped me with computer assignments."

"Did you meet any of his other friends?"

"Mohammed didn't have many friends. Just other students he'd met in classes. He was a sort of loner like me. I guess that's why we got along."

"Had you two been dating long?" Fowler asked flatly.

She paused and managed a small smile. Even in the dim light of the streetlamp it lit up her whole face. "Oh no. We didn't date. It was just a friendship. 'Two lost souls' we used to say. Mohammed was busy with his thesis and I had my other classes. We just helped each other out."

"What were you going to do tonight?"

The smile quickly disappeared. "We had a project for a course. Interactive media. We were working on a training system for CPR. Mohammed was doing the programming and I was writing the script. We got together a couple times a week to sync up."

Why the hell would a terrorist be playing with a bomb when he had a visitor on the way? Unless the visitor was part of what he was doing. But this coed hardly looked like your typical national security threat.

"So you had been to his apartment before?" Fowler asked hoping to validate the forensic finding.

"Yes, a few times. Sometimes we met at the library but Mohammed wanted to show me what he put together so far. What difference did that make?"

"I'd just like to get a feeling of what his apartment looked like. Did he have a lot of posters or pictures?"

"Not really. Except for a big Albert Einstein poster. You know, the one with all the curly hair?" Fowler nodded to be polite but didn't have a clue what she was talking about. "Mohammed thought he was great."

"How about any favorite books or authors? Any particular reading style?"

"Just a lot of computer books. He really wanted to be the best in his field. He worked very hard. I don't believe what you're saying about him."

"What's that Miss Goddard?" Fowler gave a withering look to Thomassini.

"That Mohammed was some kind of terrorist. That he was making bombs." Goddard's voice became increasingly strident. "He wasn't involved in that kind of thing. I never saw any revolutionary books or pictures. Mohammed never talked about those things and I don't believe he could ever have been a terrorist." She paused to take a breath. When she continued, her tone was cold. "May I go now?"

Fowler couldn't tell if she was hiding something or had just erected a wall of protection from the strangers interrogating her. In either case, her new-found strength surprised him.

"Just a few more things. When did you last talk to Mr. Ramal?"

"Yesterday on the phone. We talked about getting together tonight."

"Did he say anything about having any other visitors today? Did you see anyone out of the ordinary? Around the building or on the street?"

"I'm sorry Detective . . ."

"Fowler," he added.

"Oh." The detective saw something flash in her eyes, then disappear. She continued her original thought. "Detective Fowler. Mohammed didn't say that he was going to see anyone and I didn't see anything strange tonight, except the explosion and all of you. I have no idea who would want to hurt him. I just hope you find who killed him."

"Yes, ma'am. That's what we intend to do." He handed her his card and made the same request he had of Brown. "Rick, please see if you can coerce one of these busy officers to see Miss Goddard home."

"My car's just around the corner," Goddard replied. "I'm quite capable of taking myself home."

"How about if we have one of the officers take it back for you anyway? I'd just as soon not have you on the roads tonight."

Goddard frowned as if she was insulted but didn't resist. Thomassini led her back to the waiting patrolmen.

"Ms. Goddard," Fowler called as they walked away. "We haven't met before have we?"

Goddard turn back to face Fowler. "No," she said firmly. "I'm sure we haven't, Detective."

"Of course. Thank you for your time."

Fowler watched as Thomassini gave his instructions to the patrolmen and they escorted Goddard to her car.

"Thanks for the help, Rick," he said when Thomassini had returned. "I'll check with the neighbors tomorrow and see if we can pick up anything else. You'll wrap up here?"

"Yes sir. Sorry about the slip."

"Forget it. It's been a tough night for everyone."

Fowler walked back to his car and tried to put the evening in perspective. No use in making the case any more complicated than it needed to be. Maybe it was just a dumb accident; a screwed-up college student in over his head. The damn Internet was full of stories of kids being converted into lone-wolf terrorists. At least there hadn't been any other casualties. The guy made his choice and got caught. These days no one was going to lose any sleep over him.

He called in at 10:35 and headed back toward headquarters. There were still two preliminary reports to enter before he could go home.

Driving slowly back M Street, he couldn't shake the feeling that he'd seen the Goddard lady before. The name didn't ring a bell but there was something about her face.

Easy to check her out. He hated loose ends.

CHAPTER 4

Carnegie Mellon University, Pittsburgh, Pennsylvania
Monday, 7:30 a.m.

"DID YOU SEE the UConn game last night? That Husky freshman center was unstoppable!"

Rachel Flanagan exhaled a frustrated sigh, leaned back in her chair and dropped a stubby, well-gnawed Faber pencil on the conference table. It was bad enough that Rydell had to have his weekly staff meeting at 7:30 Monday mornings, but having to sit through her colleagues' inane recaps of the previous weekend's college basketball results was worse than dinner with her ex's parents.

Flanagan was Deputy Director, Operations for the CERT Coordination Center. She had important work to do. Why the hell did she have to endure this crap?

CERT was one of the country's most important organizations in the war on cyber-terrorism. It had been born in the aftermath of the Internet Worm Affair. On November 2, 1988, Robert Tappan Morris, a student at Cornell, sent a new type of computer program into the Arpanet, a then-limited network of government agencies and federally-funded university research laboratories. By invoking hidden, so-called "trapdoor", capabilities in key Arpanet programs, taking advantage of accidental bugs in other routines and intelligently guessing user passwords, Morris' program gained access to other user accounts on his computer. It copied itself into those accounts and uncovered pointers to related accounts on other machines in the network. The program then sent itself to those machines, where it repeated the process, burrowing into the fledgling network "like a worm". A day later, over six thousand systems in the Arpanet had been infected, spending all their cycles running the worm program and grinding the network to a halt. Although not called that at the time, a new kind of terrorism had been created.

The danger portended by the release of the Morris Worm forced the Defense Advanced Research Projects Agency, funder of Arpanet, to seriously consider how to deal with security on the nation's burgeoning computer networks. Along with NSA's National Computer Security Committee, the Agency created a Computer Emergency Response Team as part of the Software Engineering Institute at Carnegie Mellon University in Pittsburgh. This team, eventually simply called CERT, was to watch over Arpanet. The Arpanet grew, eventually being consumed by the Internet, and CERT's role, and visibility, expanded in kind. A few well-orchestrated articles in the popular press had assured the organization's position as a major player in the global information debate.

By the mid-nineties, CERT had changed its name to the CERT Coordination Center, or CERT/CC, in recognition of their evolving role in an ever more complex computer security community. CERT/CC now gave workshops and training courses in system management, network security, and disaster survivability. But their most critical mission was still the analysis and identification of network vulnerabilities, or incidents. This was where Flanagan had come to make her mark.

"Gentleman," Rydell suddenly barked, oblivious to the female sitting across the table from him, "can we please get on with the meeting? I for one have a full day today."

Standard Rydell management style, thought Flanagan.

Dr. J. Timothy Rydell was a poster child for CMU: computer science grad, Associate Professor of Computer Science, Assistant Dean of the School of Engineering and now Director of CERT. He was tall, just over six feet, with broad shoulders and only a slightly bulging waist line. His dark brown hair was neatly styled with just a touch of gray at the temples and his signature half-lens reading glasses perched perilously on the end of an aquiline nose. He was a bit too arrogant and autocratic for Flanagan's tastes, but he did keep the academics at bay and the federal funding flowing.

Half an hour later the managing staff had rolled through a pain-fully-long list of standing items, none of which had caused Flanagan to even pick up her pencil. But they were getting close to the item that was the reason a plain manila folder sat on the table in front of her.

"There's only one item left on the agenda," the short, rotund man on Rydell's right announced. Edward Candela was the Center's chief administrator. "Rachel, it's your topic. What's this about?"

"We received this on Sunday evening." Flanagan opened the folder and handed a single page of printout to each member of the staff. "It suggests that the sender identified a threat in one of George Washington University's gateways."

```
From: saracen@gwu.edu

To: cert@cert.org

Subject: Network Anomaly

Have located network anomaly in GW gateway. SNMP
analysis performed. Found consistent independent
transmissions unrelated to incoming traffic. Possi-
ble rogue process present. Additional information
to follow.

Saracen
```

Flanagan waited for the team to digest the message. "The email was originally classified Grade Three. I found it this morning when I reviewed the weekend message log. We have received no additional communication."

The first to react was Walter Eisenkranz, head of External Research Projects. "I don't recognize the address as one of our researchers. Who is this Saracen? Does the message have any credibility?"

"We have been unable to identify the sender so far," Flanagan replied. "We have tried to confirm via email, but have gotten no response."

"Rachel, we get a lot of these claims and most are just red herrings," Candela said. "Have there been any problems at George Washington?"

"Nothing has been reported recently and all of our tests say the gateway is clean. Still, I'm hesitant to ignore the message. The description fits a pattern we have seen before from an occasional security audit. It may be that this is a new type of disturbance."

This was the critical moment. She couldn't run with this one alone; she was still the outsider at the table and had moved ahead independently on too many projects already.

"So what's the problem?" Rydell finally asked. "Just have one of your people follow up directly with GW."

"Timothy, you know that we have to get the security advisory on the Eastern European virus out this week, and we're finishing testing on the new firewall validation utilities. Between these projects and standard operations I just don't have the resources. This will take more time than we have. Unless you want to reprioritize the other work?" She tossed the gauntlet.

"You're the operations expert, Rachel. I don't understand why your ops staff cannot handle this as a standard request. It's not like we have had any major network threats lately."

She glared back across the table, locking her eyes on her boss. He knew her staff had pulled three all-nighters over the past week tracking down a new credit card threat that had surfaced at Toys-R-Us. And Rydell had been the one who had added security certification of network programs to their responsibilities, without adding any new people. She wasn't going to let him bully her on this one. It was time to tell him what it really took to run the Center.

Just as she was about to release this flood of emotion, Candela interceded. "Larry, do we have any contractors that we could put on this?"

It took a moment for Larry Grenacher to respond. Grenacher was head of personnel and human relations. With five years' worth of job applicants in their pipeline, Flanagan couldn't understand why they even needed an HR manager. And when the conversation turned too technical, Grenacher's eyes glazed over.

Candela's question finally fought its way into his consciousness, and Grenacher looked around the table to see all eyes waiting for his response. He pulled a report from the neat stack in front of him and scanned down it with his finger. "Yes, we do have one contractor that could be used. He's in Boston."

"How about it, Rachel?" Candela asked.

"We could probably do that." Flanagan broke her gaze from Rydell. "Boston's not that far from Washington. I'll check on his background after the meeting."

"Great. Thanks, Larry. We'll review status next week. If there's nothing else . . ." Candela glanced around the table, "then we're done."

*   *   *

Flanagan sat in her office reviewing the consultant's file for the third time. The staff meeting had gone even better than she had planned. She had made her point, and had gotten authorization to proceed with the investigation. It was a good thing she had reminded Grenacher about possible staffing questions earlier in the morning; at least he hadn't missed his cue. Maybe he wasn't completely useless.

What had surprised her was Candela's suggestion of the consultant. She had figured she'd have to do it herself. Candela was a queer duck. He spent most of his time being a pain in everyone's ass, but once a week he'd be sure to drop by her office and make a pass. So far she had been able to successfully divert the attention.

Not that coworkers hitting on her was a surprise. She worked in a world dominated by males. At five foot six and slim, with dark red hair softly framing her face, she certainly wasn't unattractive. An Irish heritage was right there for all to see, all the way to a dash of freckles over her cheekbones. As was a temper that was only slightly less fiery than her hair. But ever since a failed marriage while she was still an undergraduate at UPenn, men hadn't exactly been a priority in her life.

After graduation, and a relatively painless divorce, she had fled west and held a number of increasingly high-profile jobs in computer security. From Oracle to Microsoft to Google, she had honed her skills and eventually reached the top of that coveted application backlog.

She had only been at the CERT Coordination Center for six months now, and sensed her honeymoon period was rapidly coming to an end. She had been feeling more and more pressure from the Director and his administrator. Why did she think CERT would be any different?

The email had bothered her from the start. CERT/CC received over one hundred messages a day about network problems, but this one felt different. It could be the opportunity she had been waiting for.

This incident would get her personal attention.

CHAPTER 5

Cambridge, Massachusetts
Monday, 9:00 a.m.

THE NEEDLES STABBED at his naked body. His legs screamed with fatigue, the muscles in his back squeezed around his spine like a noose, and it hurt to even raise his arms. He tried to rub off the ground-in sweat and grime, but every wipe of the thin bar of soap brought throbs of pain from the open cuts on his forearms and hands. His body felt like it had been in a fight with a samurai warrior. Adam Braxton finally gave up on getting clean and simply let the steamy spray engulf him in warm relief.

No matter how hard he tried to keep in shape, rock climbing trips with Paul invariably resulted in sore muscles, bloody append-ages and a bruised ego. Why he continued to join his friend for these weekends of torture he didn't understand, except that Paul's companionship was the last vestige of what could be considered a social aspect to his very compartmentalized life.

The steam was finally bringing some relief, so Braxton let his thoughts wander. He had fought all the previous night to find a comfortable position in his bed. Finally falling asleep around 6:00 a.m., he had subsequently been awakened only two and one-half hours later by a telephone call. A rude "Hello?" had been all he had been able to utter.

The call from CERT/CC had caught him completely by surprise. A few months earlier a friend had suggested he submit his resume as a contractor, but he had heard nothing in the interim. Now their Operations Manager calls and offers him a contract.

A job with CERT could be high visibility and would definitely help his bank account. The timing couldn't have been better.

Finally feeling human again, he stepped out of the stall and grabbed a faded towel from the hook on the wall. As he dried himself off, he took stock of the image in the vanity's mirror. The sandy brown hair that Megan had found so attractive was still thick and curly, and his pale green eyes were alert and clear. His five-foot-eleven, one hundred sixty-five pound frame remained strong and taut. At least he had had the resolve to keep up his exercise regimen. More often than he would admit, jogging and climbing had been his only break from the anxiety of his professional life. The assorted bruises and scrapes merely added to his manly appearance, or so he told himself.

He brushed his teeth, shaved, and smeared another coat of anti-biotic over the angry red scratches on his arms and legs. Then he dressed and headed to the kitchen.

That was when a loud "Morning, Adam", echoed down the hall.

Braxton nearly tripped as he spun around to locate the intruder. Staring into his study, he saw his neighbor, Paul Terrel, huddled over an Apple MacBook.

Braxton let out a sigh and felt his adrenaline slowly dissipate. "Jesus, Paul. What are you doing here at this hour?"

"Told Wallace I'd be working at home today," Terrel explained, never once taking his eyes off the monitor. "Then I found my connection was down. You were in the shower so I didn't want to bother you. Figured you wouldn't mind."

Terrel was dressed in jeans and a plaid shirt, and his long black hair was pulled into a pony tail at the back of his head. He had moved into an apartment down the hall a year ago. Paul Terrel was young, less than 30, and worked as a programmer at Wallace Securities in Boston. Braxton guessed that the executives at Wallace were just as happy when he chose to work at home. He certainly didn't fit in a world of suspenders and power ties.

"Go right ahead, Paul," Braxton said with a smile. He had given his neighbor a key for emergencies, but hadn't expected morning visits. "What are you working on?"

"Oh, nothing too exotic. I coded up some new quants and need to test them out."

"What the hell are quants?"

"Quants. Quantitative analysis programs. The traders like to have different ways of evaluating market or stock trends. That helps them make the best selections for their clients' portfolios. The guys are insatiable. I can't keep up with all their ideas."

"I guess that's interesting. Good luck. Just don't be too long. I'll need the system in an hour or so."

"No sweat. I'll be outa' here by then. This stuff is my specialty." Terrel grabbed a notebook from a pile at his feet and proceeded to type furiously on the keyboard.

"What's with all the paper?" Braxton asked, shaking his head at the mess on his floor. "Don't you have all that in the Mac?"

"Most of it. But you know me, a real throw-back. Sometimes you just gotta have paper." Terrel turned and grinned. "But what's got you working all of a sudden?"

"CERT called this morning. They need help on an incident."

Terrel pulled himself away from the screen and looked genuinely pleased. "That's great, Adam. Anything really interesting?"

"It's too soon to tell. For now it's just a follow up on a message they received from George Washington University. I've got to track down the sender and check out a possible network problem."

"Doesn't sound too bad. You gonna get to arrest folks in this new job?"

"Afraid not, Paul. The Center's job is investigation of threats. Arrests and prosecution are up to the FBI. And that's fine with me."

"Too bad. With your background, you'd make a good cyber-cop. Guess you'll just have to stick with being a gunslinger."

Braxton cringed at the sobriquet. "Paul, please don't call me that."

"You should be proud," Terrel replied with another smile. "You're the guy the messed-up town calls in to shake things up and get rid of the bad guys. It's a noble and long-standing profession. And now-a-days you get to just use your smarts and don't even get shot."

At least literally, Braxton thought.

"Good luck anyway." Terrel returned to his Mac.

"Thanks, Paul." Braxton walked out to finally grab that cup of coffee.

* * *

After a quick breakfast, Braxton sat down in his dining room and peered out the bay windows to the scene below. It was a cloudy day in Cambridge, cool with the muggy feeling of impending rain. Looking down Brattle Street toward Harvard Square, he saw a couple of regulars from the neighborhood carrying grocery sacks and a cluster of Harvard students rushing to get to a mid-morning class. Life looked so normal on the street.

Braxton had been taken by the energy and youth of Cambridge when he had first come to the Boston area. Harvard Square especially was intellectually electric, constantly charged by an influx of students, professors, and business people. It fit the style Braxton had envisioned for himself. Cambridge living costs had put a dent in his reserves since Megan had left, but he had managed to keep the apartment. It was still his home.

He got up and moved into the living room. The inside wall of the room was one huge bookcase. He had had it custom built as soon as he moved in. When he was in school he would scatter books all over his apartments, but Megan had had a different decorating plan. He browsed the networking shelf, scanning early scholarly sources such as Quarterman's *The Matrix*, to references like *Applied Cryptography* and finally Mitnick's *Ghost in the Wires* and Stroll's *The Cuckoo's Egg*. Grabbing a few favorites, he dropped into the overstuffed sofa and leaned back.

Time for some basic research.

* * *

The hour went by quickly. He had taken notes on the latest intrusion threats, and come up with some ideas on how to validate the programs in the gateways. He was about to get up when he heard Terrel slam a book shut.

"Dammit."

Apparently things aren't going well.

His neighbor stormed into the living room, binders and laptop in hand. "Thanks, Adam. Looks like I've got to do a little more thinking. Damn series won't converge quickly enough to be useful. By the way, some of the guys at work are up for a trip north. You interested?"

"Sure, tell me when you get it set up. Your place again?" Braxton had quickly discovered that he and Terrel shared a number of interests besides computers. Both were hockey nuts, Braxton sticking with the Bruins and Terrel rooting for his hometown Red Wings. Terrel didn't run, a sight that Braxton knew would have been rather amusing, but did climb. The past weekend's excursion had been spent together in the White Mountains of New Hampshire.

Terrel headed for the door. "Works for me. I'll check everyone's schedules. See you later." He slammed the door as he left.

"Bye, Paul," Braxton commented to the empty room.

He picked up his notes and went back into the study. When they had turned the living room into a library, the second bedroom became his study. It was a small interior space, probably meant as a nursery, but they had been too busy to put the room to its intended use. *There would always be time later, wouldn't there?*

The room was a clutter of filing cabinets surrounding a battered wooden desk he had rescued from a Harvard dormitory sale. Two large monitors sat on the desktop behind a spot cleared by Terrel. Braxton's laptop lay to the side and an aging Unix server rested in a corner. Wires were strung in a maze underneath the desk, most by his own hands, a result of his impatience with Verizon's support team.

Flanagan had said that she would forward the suspicious message to his email account on the CERT/CC server. They had been unable to contact the sender directly and wanted him to try to track down the researcher and check out his claim.

Braxton connected to CERT's VPN, then logged into his email account. There were only two messages in his in-folder, an announcement for a CMU Blood Drive, and the note from Flanagan. He scanned the forwarded message quickly on the screen, then printed it out.

There didn't appear to be anything too extraordinary about the email, but the author sounded as if he knew what he was talking about. Also, Flanagan was very insistent about the incident. She had claimed that this was just a routine follow-up, but he had the sense that there was more to it. He'd worry about that later; for now he just needed to locate this Saracen and verify his claim.

He next checked the archive of security advisories on *www.cert.org*. He was fairly sure that Flanagan and her team would have cross-referenced the claim against known problems but there was no harm in doing his own checking. There were a couple of advisories that appeared related but nothing that met all of his criteria. He extracted the possibles and added them to his project file.

A check of the on-line network map showed there were two gateways into GW, *gw-gate* and *gw-gw*. He ran a quick scan of the gateways and found nothing out of the ordinary. He didn't really expect to find anything that quickly. Whatever it was would take some doing to track down.

The best approach would be to try to replicate Saracen's work. Going back to his notes, he started coding a custom monitor for the gateway. It only took a half hour to lay out the basics and paste together existing code from his archive to get it programmed and tested.

He loaded the GW gateway names into his program and started the monitor using the security codes CERT had given him. The monitor would periodically check the internal status of the gateway and send him a mail message with the results. He hoped to catch some evidence of the network problem while he was tracking down this Saracen.

Finally, he checked the status of Saracen's account on his home system at GW, *rdvax*. The account appeared to be real but the owner wasn't on-line. Any other time, he would simply call the school, but he had a trip scheduled to D.C. anyway and he could check in person. Some things were better done that way.

Braxton glanced at his watch and realized he only had a half hour to pack and catch the *T* to Logan. The *T*, the venerable Massachusetts Bay Transit Authority, or MBTA, which, among other less-positive milestones, boasted the oldest subway in the United States and the only system immortalized by its own folk song. It was old, dirty, crowded, and usually late, but still took half the time to get to Logan Airport compared to Boston's atrocious traffic. Traffic not the least bit improved by the obscenely expensive, and now leaking, Big Dig, and a tunnel named after Ted Williams. God, he loved this city.

The Red Line to South Station, then the new Silver Line to Logan. From there, the shuttle to D.C., another classic, if overly pretentious, American city. If he ever had to leave Boston, he actually might be able to live at the other end of the eastern megapolis. D.C. was like a big architect's model, carved out of a single piece of massive limestone. Classic design, straight streets, and logical names, it appealed to the left half of his brain. On the right side, it didn't have quite the richness of Boston's ethnic neighborhoods or the golden dome of the State House, but it was uniquely international and the aura of power was addictive. All told, not an unacceptable place to live.

He had scheduled a meeting with a friend at NASDAQ's D.C.-based IT group last week. They certainly had enough security worries to keep him gainfully employed. And now he would get the prospecting trip paid by CERT.

Feeling optimistic, he headed to his bedroom to grab his bag.

* * *

A small icon began blinking in the corner of the executive's monitor. He abruptly finished his telephone call and closed the door to his office.

Having safely isolated himself, he expanded the icon and read the status message.

```
Warning: Unexpected management queries

Node=gw-gate.gw.edu
```

Probably just a new SysOp, but the coincidence was troublesome. Shutting off the scanner might miss some important messages. He would just keep a closer watch on the traffic for the next few days.

CHAPTER 6

Theater Electronics, Reston, Virginia
Monday, 2:00 p.m.

"DON'T ANY OF you have anything positive to contribute to this company?" the man screamed. "What the hell do you spend your time doing?"

Robert Greystone, Senior Vice President of Sales and Marketing for Theater Electronics stalked the conference room like a starving lion. More precisely, the location was the company's "Board Room", a spotless, completely antiseptic chamber of glistening steel and polished woods. A room ideally suitable for boring financial presentations and subtle corporate executions.

A blazing afternoon Virginia sun had made the already humid and stifling habitat completely unbearable. And the mood of the Senior Vice President wasn't making it any easier on anyone.

Greystone was frustrated. Frustrated and angry over the incompetence of his subordinates seated around the table. In his view, nobody in the damn company seemed to care anything about the business.

And his business was command and control. As he always explained to new acquaintances, the "theater" in Theater Electronics didn't mean the sites of Broadway plays, but of battlefields. Outside of the big guys like Boeing and McDonnell Douglas, his company was the largest supplier of military communications systems in the world. In addition to the U.S. DoD, Theater had a major presence in NATO and Canada, and a growing business with our Middle East allies.

But the past few years had seen their market wither, as they missed opportunities in new encryption technologies, battlefield visualization and even remote drone control. They were behind and nobody seemed to give a damn, from Charles Keane, CEO and Greystone's boss, through product development and even his own sales staff. Well, that was about to change, despite his boss's ineptitude.

Last month, Keane had actually told him he was too hard on people. As if that was going to fix the company. An employee relations consultant had even been hired to "soften" Greystone's behavior. The consultant had told the SVP he would be much more effective if he used consensus rather than autocratic techniques. Didn't pace in front of his staff. Spoke more softly. Valued the differences in people.

Bull shit! What the hell did that over-educated, over-paid do-nothing know? When was the last time he had tried to keep a business afloat? Greystone *had* lasted almost twenty minutes into the meeting before he got up. That had to be a record.

He stopped behind a balding, middle-aged man with a painful-looking stoop to his shoulders. "Kern. How do you explain the drop in West Coast sales?"

Quentin Kern was a long-time Theater employee who had been a star sales executive for NATO before being moved up to manage all of Theater's civilian business: the non-military alphabet agencies like the CIA and NSA. Greystone's predecessor had had nothing but glowing praise for the man.

Well, the predecessor was gone and this over-the-hill parts pusher would soon be as well. With three kids in expensive private colleges, you'd think that he would want to keep his job. The sooner Greystone could get rid of these good 'ole boys the better.

"We've gone over this before, Robert," Kern pleaded. "Engineering just isn't giving us the right product. We're in all the key programs. I personally make sixty calls a month. We're not keeping up with the features the Navy needs. They want S8 encryption, integrated with their existing infrastructure and the new GPS algorithm. And when we loan them a beta product, the damn things break."

"Munson made *his* budget," Greystone barked back. "Just barely, but he made it. Maybe we ought to replace your folks with his?" The Senior Vice President walked two seats to his left. "How about it Guy? You want to move?"

A distinguished black man raised his eyes to his inquisitor. "Come on, Robert. We're all working as hard as we can. Business is just tough right now."

"What about that new Delta Force mission comm program you've been promising. COGNOS wasn't it? That still on track?"

Munson swallowed hard, but kept his eyes fixed on his boss. "Ah, they've put it on hold, Robert. Pending resolution of that new Bill in the Senate. They won't go ahead until there's proof of an escalation of the war effort. It'll turn around this summer."

Greystone put his head in his hands and rubbed his temples until his eyes watered. It was a good thing someone was watching this store; it certainly wasn't his staff.

"And maybe some of us will be around to see it, too," he growled. "Does anyone have any ideas to get us out of this mess?"

The heads around the table looked sheepishly at each other, each trying to think of any way to salve their boss. They shuffled papers, gulped bottles of water and twisted in their chairs, anything to avoid Greystone's toxic glare.

Then, incongruously, a "cocktail party moment" occurred. All the sounds in the room went silent at precisely the same moment; all except one.

"Well, a new Middle East war would be nice."

Fred Jamison, Sales Operations Manager, turned from what he had thought had been a private whisper to Jacqueline Garret, a singularly attractive, and available, manager to his left, and saw every eye in the room staring at him. His mouth gaped open and his face went ashen.

Greystone paused, letting the terror level rise, then calmly said, "At least Fred is trying. A bit overly optimistic, but a good suggestion. Since the rest of you don't seem to have any better ideas, why don't you all just think real hard about what you'd do if you lost your jobs.

"Now get out! You can call me when you think you have something of value to add to this company." Greystone strode back to his place at the head of the cherry conference table. His staff rapidly gathered up their papers and fled for the door.

"Lombard! You stay."

A short, well-dressed young man froze at the sound of his name. He turned and faced the executive.

"I just received this from Keane." Greystone tossed a half-inch stack of papers down the polished table. Lombard grabbed the package before they tumbled over the edge. "I don't have time to review another of his goddamn research reports. Go over this and give me an analysis."

Ted Lombard glanced down at the cover letter clipped to the report. "Uh, it says for your personal response, Robert."

"I don't care what it says. He's just trying to keep me busy while he runs the company into the ground. Find out what you can and write up a response. I need it for the Board meeting tomorrow."

"Yes sir," Lombard quickly responded. "Everything ready for your Congressional testimony?"

"I think so. Dumbing down the issues was harder than I had thought. But you can't present anything too complicated at these hearings. Not a bunch of insightful visionaries up there on the Hill."

"Just watch out for Senator Hastings. Somebody on his staff is giving him pretty good data."

Greystone squinted and shook his head. "He's a goddamn obstructionist if you ask me. A throwback to the twentieth century. Thinks diplomacy is going to save us from the terrorists. We can handle him. Potterfield's the key."

"The chairman of the Foreign Relations Committee? Can you get any time with him?"

"Of course," Greystone responded, as if the answer to the question was patently obvious. "I'm meeting with him over the luncheon break. Potterfield's definitely the key to getting our changes in the Bill. I think he'll play ball." Greystone carefully stacked up his papers and closed them in his folio.

"But that's not until Wednesday. First I have to get through the Board meeting. See what you can do with that damn report, then get the draft of the Board presentation together. I'll send you my notes tonight." He twisted his head toward the door. "Now get out of here."

Greystone watched as Lombard left the room, then slowly walked over to the room's panoramic windows overlooking the Virginia countryside. To any visitor, he seemed a man completely at peace with himself.

He was in his late fifties, but had neither the thinning hair nor the bulging paunch of most of his colleagues. His tanned face highlighted deep blue eyes, prominent cheekbones and a wide square chin. Thick dark hair was meticulously slicked back on his head and a custom Hong Kong silk suit wrapped his trim body. A starched white shirt and red paisley tie completed his official business attire. A persona carefully planned to project success and authority.

The tranquil setting outside Theater's offices sharply contrasted with the battle of wills waging within the executive suite. The next few days were critical to his plan and he needed to work through every detail. He could only push his efforts so far before they would become public. Exposed too early, they would cost him his job and his legacy.

He had gone much farther than his authority permitted, but someone had to do *something*. He would not let the doddering old fool destroy what Greystone had worked so hard to build. His plan was on track. There were a few legal obstacles, but his meeting with the Senator would hopefully put them to rest. The biggest problem was with Keane and the Board. He had to make sure they saw the inevitability of his plan.

His fingers dug into the soft leather of the folio. So much had led to this. He couldn't let it fail.

*   *   *

Theodore Lombard, Executive Assistant to Robert Greystone, took his time walking back through the maze of cubicles and secretarial areas. He wanted to make sure that everyone noticed that he was the one left discussing business with the Senior Vice President of Sales and Marketing.

Lombard was a small man, with a very boyish face, but he stood straight as a rod, stretching his five foot five inch frame to its maximum height. Moving through the office, he looked like a drill sergeant in a pin-stripe suit. He had been with Theater for five years, the last three as Greystone's assistant. It was a position of power and influence that he had long coveted. Unmarried, his reputation was as a hard-working, committed employee, but his first priority was always to himself.

When he finally settled down at his desk he reviewed the morning's activities. The most significant event was his boss's surprising behavior. Emotional outbursts were completely out of character. Sarcasm, yes.

Even anger. But he had never lost his temper. If anything, he was a control freak. Seeing him blow up was about as likely as Lombard's ex-fiancé passing up a diamond sale at Bailey, Banks, and Biddle. The situation at Theater must be a lot more serious than he had thought.

Charles Keane, the founder of Theater Electronics, had been a retired Motorola executive who just couldn't stay out of the game. He and some of his cronies had formed Theater to provide advanced, secure communication systems to the military. For many years, Theater had been a small, cliquish business, catering to highly classified black programs and Special Forces ops.

That business changed dramatically with the first Gulf War. Theater had expanded its products to cover standard squad operations and advanced intelligence data aggregation. The generals had only been too happy to outfit their troops with sophisticated equipment, including gear that would help connect them with their families on the other side of the world. It had been a different kind of a war with different rules and different objectives. Morale was a challenge, you never knew who was a friend and who was a suicide bomber, and if video chat and computer games helped with the long deployments, then that's what Theater supplied.

Then the engagement wound down, troops returned home, and equipment acquisitions were cancelled or postponed. Theater saw its growth stop, and its market share slowly dwindle. Lombard could see the pressure on the company's executives. He didn't understand all the issues, but it was common knowledge that his boss and Keane didn't agree on either the process or the strategy to get the business going again.

Greystone had the support of enough of Theater's directors so Keane couldn't simply fire him, but their animosity and divisiveness were strangling the life out of the company. Decisions dragged on indefinitely as study after study was consumed.

Lombard spread the papers his boss had given him over the desk. This report was another example of the stupidity. He sat down to work on the report from Greystone, but knew that the effort was wasted. He had to find out what was really going on.

He hoped tonight would get him the answers he needed.

CHAPTER 7

"How's it going Detective?"

Fowler looked up from the report and saw his boss, Captain Frank Rodgers, standing next to his desk.

"Ah, just fine, Captain," Fowler replied. "Reviewing forensics' analysis of the Grady Avenue bombing."

"Anything new on that one? Does it still look like an accident?"

"Well, that's what everybody thinks. We still haven't been able to identify the visitors this Ramal had, and there are some inconsistencies in the placement of the evidence."

"Anything new from the witnesses?" Rodgers continued.

"Not really. None of the neighbors can back up the landlord's description. And the girl friend was so shook up, she doesn't remember anything except the explosion. But she sure doesn't believe the closet revolutionary story." Fowler was as frustrated by the lack of progress as was his boss. He felt his case slipping away.

"I've had some calls, Sam," Rodgers said quietly. "Bombings make people real edgy. Do what you can to get this one wrapped up."

"Yes sir, Captain."

Fowler watched his boss walk silently back through the squad room and into his office. Rodgers was a young, well-spoken black who was just the representative the D.C. Police Department needed in turbulent times. He had quickly worked his way up the department chain of command, taking over command of Investigative Services a year ago. Rumor was he had well-placed friends in both headquarters and the mayor's office.

Fowler had never had any problems with him, and he hoped this visit wasn't a sign of changing times. The Captain had generally been fair and treated all his officers with respect, but Fowler had always wondered what the kid would do under pressure.

He figured he was about to find out.

* * *

Braxton opened the door to his room at the Dupont Circle Holiday Inn, tossed his bag on one bed and collapsed on the other. Boston fog had delayed the shuttle for an hour and then they had circled National for another half hour waiting on who knows what? US Airways certainly wasn't going to tell him.

After a few minutes of rest, he drifted into his regular on-the-road routine. First, he turned on CNN to find out what was happening in the world. Next, he grabbed the room service menu and ordered a pizza. It could be a long night and he was already starving.

Then he opened his laptop and connected to the Inn's Wi-Fi. Terrel had left a message that the climbing trip was on for the weekend after next. He made a note in his Outlook calendar and added an item to his action list to check out his hiking boots.

There were three messages from his monitor programs and another from Flanagan. Politely but firmly she was already asking for a status report. There certainly wasn't anything substantive he could report, so he marked the email for follow-up and moved on to the monitor updates.

He spent the next hour analyzing his program's results while simultaneously munching through the pizza. There was a clear pattern of anomalous transmissions appearing in the scans. They didn't seem to be correlated with time or activity, however, and only occurred on one of the two GW gateways. Not what he would have expected.

There weren't enough examples for any more sophisticated analyses so he saved the data in a working file and logged out. At least he had some hard data and a preliminary confirmation of this Saracen's claim. Hopefully he would be able to get more evidence tomorrow.

He was going to reply to Flanagan, but stretched back out on the bed for a few minutes first. It had been a long day and he still hadn't caught up from the weekend's excursion. Still, he couldn't stop thinking about the data from the gateway. As he fell off to sleep, he felt sure there was something familiar about the pattern.

* * *

The dinner had been excellent, but Lombard was more interested in the upcoming dessert. They had gone to her favorite Italian restaurant in Falls Church where she had selected a veal piccata and he had chosen a heavier marsala. They were both outstanding. For wine, he had picked a deep red Barolo, knowing it was her favorite and one that always put her into a talkative mood. The ride back to her apartment had been slow enough to build her anticipation even more. They were now relaxing on her sofa with an after-dinner *aperitif.*

She was not unattractive, tall and slim, with long dark brown hair she normally wore up but that somehow always started to fall by the end of an evening. She was older than Lombard but significantly less experienced in certain personal matters. A little flat-chested for his usual taste, but she was an apt and attentive pupil. All of which made for an acceptable relationship, to say nothing of the special extra benefit.

He had met her quite on purpose, of course, only two weeks after she had started at Theater. Keane's secretary of twenty years had died just after the New Year, and the President had been frantically searching for a replacement. The temp agency had sent four secretaries, each of whom Keane had burned out, stressed out, or thrown out in a day or less. Clarice Montonet had been their last chance and she had been perfect. She was even tempered, with exceptional clerical and organizational skills. She was effective enough to keep Keane happy, and dour enough to not alienate the other executive secretaries.

The relationship blossomed slowly, Lombard being careful to express the appropriate concerns and make the appropriate entreaties for propriety. But as affairs of the heart will do, they soon were involved in a steamy, if not public, affair.

Their desire to see each other as often as possible had reduced Montonet's overtime hours at Theater, and as a result, she was taking increasing amounts of work back to her apartment where she could complete briefings and reports between her lover's frequent visits. All of which was exactly what Lombard had been planning.

"Clarice, darling. You look tired. Has our boss been working you too hard?" Lombard leaned back on the soft leather sofa and sipped his brandy.

"Just the same old thing. Actually, Charles has been in a very good mood lately. He's been on the phone a lot. And smiling most of the time." Montonet had collapsed on the other end of the sofa and dropped her feet in Lombard's lap. The Barolo was definitely beginning to do its magic. "What I really need is one of your patented massages."

"If that's what you'd like." His smile was forced. This was not good news. Keane should have been worried about the Board and worried about Greystone. *What has he got up his sleeve?*

Montonet's oversized brown leather shoulder bag sat temptingly next to the hall table. Perhaps he could discover the answer to this riddle after all.

Lombard slipped off her pumps and began messaging her stockinged feet, starting at the ankle then moving down to each individual toe. His thumb made small, firm circles over her tired muscles.

Montonet softly moaned. "Your hands feel so good. How about working on my neck and back now?"

"And where after that?"

"That's for you to find out," she replied as she pulled herself up and took his hand.

"Now, now. You go ahead. I have to check my messages in case Robert called. I'll just be a minute."

"I'll be waiting," she said and carefully took off across the room, staggering only slightly between the pieces of furniture.

Lombard got up and walked to the hall. As Montonet vanished into the bedroom he took out his iPhone and punched the icon for his voice mail. No use in taking any chances. She could come back unexpectedly just to be cute.

Listening for his mail with one ear and for any unexpected movements with the other, he quickly reached down and snapped opened the bag. Rapidly scanning the contents, one document caught his eye.

"The old bastard," he whispered. "We never would have guessed."

Lombard replaced the document and closed the bag.

The sound of the shower echoed through the bedroom door. This *was* going to be an evening to remember.

CHAPTER 8

George Washington University, Washington, D.C.
Tuesday, 10:00 a.m.

BRAXTON'S MEETING AT NASDAQ had been a bust. If he had been a negative kinda guy, he would have sworn Sherman's only reason for agreeing to a meeting was to get a free breakfast. NASDAQ was completely satisfied that they had addressed any and all cyber threats, according to his friend. Well, Braxton wasn't one to wish ill of anyone, but he'd be waiting to read the inevitable article in the Times.

He grabbed a cab for GW. As the driver fought through the cross-town traffic to Foggy Bottom, Braxton leaned his head back and took a deep breath to fight off the agitation. Time to think about his next meeting.

He felt good about the job for CERT. The incident sounded like the kind of challenge he loved. Braxton had always been a problem solver. His father had been an engineer and had fed him a regular diet of broken toys, busted appliances and over-the-hill pieces of machinery. Braxton had a natural curiosity for the way things worked and an unrelenting single-mindedness to get to a solution. Have an actual Gordian's Knot of string? Braxton could sit quietly for hours until the cord was freed.

Professionally, tearing problems apart and creating solutions was both useful and profitable. When he was in his working zone, he could completely block distractions of any kind, including those of his co-workers, friends and family; a behavior that wreaked havoc with personal relationships.

Megan, his ex-wife, had called it his obsession complex. It was also a major contributor to her decision to terminate their marriage.

After she left, Braxton had taken stock of his relationships, both professional and interpersonal, and came to the conclusion that he was better off working for himself than for anyone else. Complaining about the incompetence of his managers and shutting out his colleagues wasn't getting him very far. If he was so damned smart, then he should be able to prove it. If he wasn't, then he wouldn't have anyone else to blame. Thus was Cerberus Consulting born.

Cerberus was a character from Greek and Roman mythology; a monstrous three-headed dog with a mane of snakes, the claws of a lion, and the tail of a serpent. It was supposedly the sentry that guarded the entrance to Hades to prevent the dead from escaping and the living from entering. Braxton had decided that this was just the personification of network security he wanted to portray.

Not coincidentally, MIT had called its Project Athena network authentication system Kerberos; software that Braxton had worked with in graduate school. The Cerberus name thus had the right provenance, and the name recognition was useful, especially in Boston's robust high-tech arena.

Cerberus was what the industry called a "boutique" consulting firm. Some believed this was because it specialized in very specific problems such as network intrusions, cyber-attacks and information theft. Early on, however, Braxton realized "boutique" meant you're a one-man operation and there's no one covering your back.

Parlaying connections from his previous position and positive references from new clients, he had managed a stable, but not opulent, stream of income. Sometimes the jobs were boring as hell, no more than adding a few documented checks and balances to an existing project plan, others even interesting, like ferreting out a major security flaw in eTrade's latest trading app, but the work had been enough to maintain his comfortable Cambridge lifestyle.

The gig with CERT could raise his industry visibility significantly. "White hats", as ethical Internet investigators and hackers were known, commanded premium rates and were in constant demand by major corporations, already paranoid from high-profile break-ins at Home Depot, Sears and even Sony Pictures. These benefits could, on the other hand, only be realized if he actually found a problem and then resolved it.

The cab slowed and turned down 22nd Street.

George Washington University filled twenty square blocks in the northwest quadrant of the District of Columbia, lying along the southern side of Pennsylvania Avenue between the White House and Washington Circle. Known primarily for excellent undergraduate and graduate programs in the Arts and Sciences, Braxton knew that another of its areas of expertise was Computer Science. He had hired a number of GW graduates over the years and they had become excellent developers.

The taxi stopped in front of a gleaming glass and steel cube at the corner of 22nd and H Street. This was GW's new Science and Engineering Hall. The building was home to the departments of the School of Engineering and Applied Science, and included the Dean's administrative office. Whatever he was going to find out about Saracen, it would be here.

Braxton had decided to start his investigation at the School's Computing Facility. CERT protocol dictated checking in with GW's administration before speaking with any university personnel, but in his experience this would be a frustrating and time-wasting experience; something he had no intention of inflicting on himself. Formal requests also made interviewees defensive and selectively forgetful. Better to see what a surprise appearance would uncover.

The Computing Facility was buried in the second basement level of Science and Engineering Hall. Braxton entered the lobby and walked down the spiral concrete staircase. At the bottom he saw two large arrows: the one pointing left was labeled "Resource Center/User Services", the one to the right read "Computing Center". The user services staff was unlikely to give him the information he wanted; he needed detailed account information. He turned right and headed down the hall.

A steady flow of students made their way through the corridor. D.C. diversity was everywhere: jeans and sweatshirts, coats and ties, dashikis and kaftans. All pecking at cell phones and stabbing on iPads. Not quite the way Braxton remembered his college years but he couldn't help but feel a bit of nostalgia.

He threaded his way through the crowd and paused in front of a Student Information bulletin board. The aging cork board, it must have been brought from the Center's previous location, displayed a rainbow of flyers ranging from the mundane, "Student Tutor - Windows, Linux, MS Word - Reasonable Rates", to the topical,

"African Student's Union - The Fate of South Africa", to the recreational, "Phi Delta Beta - Open Beer Blast". Social causes changed with the times, but a variety of thought and behavior was still alive and well.

Farther down the hall, he saw a window partially obscured with metal blinds. He peered through the tiers of metal into a sterile-looking machine room. The raised tile floor was dotted with colorful metal cabinets representing the wares of at least six major computer vendors. He could pick out most of the CPUs, disk arrays, printers, and communications hubs, although a few of the enclosures were unfamiliar. It was a typical academic computer center.

The computer room was devoid of human beings, so he continued down the hall and entered an office area. Straight ahead was a door labeled "Technical Services". Inside should be a number of System Operators, or "SysOps", the staff members who had access to the University's computer systems. They ran diagnostics, managed storage farms, and configured the networks. They also created, monitored, and deleted user access accounts. That's where he would start.

The door had a keypad electronic lock, but it was open slightly so he pressed it forward and walked through. University security procedures hadn't changed much. Inside, the walls of the room were covered with ceiling high cabinets and bookcases. Dog-eared reference books and three ring binders filled the shelves and overflowed onto four small desks that had been wedged into available corners. Two thoroughly preoccupied SysOps sat at the desks on his left. Plastic nameplates stuck to the ends of cabinets identified them as Stan Williams and Mona Levi. His entrance seemed to have no effect on either.

Williams' attention was fixed on typing something into his PC. He was dressed in jeans and a sweatshirt and his thinning sandy hair suggested he was a bit old to be a student. More likely a full-time employee of the computing center.

Levi was significantly younger than Williams, and leaned over her desk intently staring into a thick biochemistry textbook. Straight jet-black hair hung almost halfway down her back.

Braxton knocked on the side of a cabinet. "Excuse me, Mr. Williams," he said, "I'd like to get some information on a student."

Williams looked up. Braxton had been right about the SysOp's age; tufts of gray stood out at his temples and prominent wrinkles sprayed out from behind gold-rimmed glasses.

"I'm sorry, but this is the Computer Center," Williams said with obvious disdain. "Student Services is upstairs." He turned back to his keyboard ignoring the intrusion. Levi didn't move an inch.

"I'm Adam Braxton from the CERT Coordination Center," he announced with just a touch of bravado. "We're trying to reach one of your students to follow up on a message he sent us. We were hoping you could be of assistance." Both heads suddenly popped up.

"You're from CERT?" Williams asked as he jumped from his chair and thrust out his hand. "I'm Stan Williams, head of systems operations for the Center." The SysOp paused as if he wasn't quite sure what to do next. "Uh, please sit down." He grabbed a chair from another desk and pulled it into the middle of the aisle.

Levi waited for an introduction, then seeing that one wasn't forthcoming, took the initiative. "Mona Levi," she said standing and offering her hand. "I'm a student operator."

"Hello," Braxton replied, shaking their hands. He couldn't help but smile at their sudden attentiveness. It felt good to have at least the guise of authority. Since they all looked pretty awkward standing in the middle of the tiny room, he took the chair Williams offered and sat down. Williams and Levi followed.

"How did you say we can help you?" Williams finally asked excitedly. "We get all the Internet security advisories and such, of course. Always follow them. Are there any problems?"

Jesus, Braxton didn't have time for a paranoid operations manager out to cover his ass. "No, no. Nothing like that. We've just been trying to reply to one of your accounts and haven't gotten a response. I was in the area and thought I'd try to locate him in person."

"Okay." Williams seemed to calm down. "But I'm not supposed to give out student information without some authorization."

Braxton searched his wallet for the ID card the Center had sent him when he had returned his contract. It was a fancy laminated card with the CERT/CC logo, his picture, and "Adam Braxton" printed on the front. He never figured he'd really need to use the thing. He pulled it out of one of the discolored plastic pockets and handed it to Williams.

"I guess that's good enough," Williams said as he handed back the card.

"I've heard of CERT but I've never met anyone that worked there," Levi said. "It must be real exciting to be a cyber-cop."

Braxton winced. "Just mostly routine stuff," he replied flatly. He wanted to get on with this. "The name is Saracen," he said, turning back to Williams. He spelled it out.

"I'll look it up." Williams went back to his terminal and punched some keys. "I don't have any record of a user with that name. Are you sure you've got it right?"

"That's the name I have. How about as a user account? Saracen at *rdvax*."

Williams tried again. "Found it. The account is still active." More typing. "Name is . . . Mohammed Ramal." His jaw dropped and he became strangely silent.

"Oh!" Levi exclaimed.

The two SysOps exchanged a glance but Braxton couldn't understand why. "Is something wrong?" He asked.

Williams turned slowly toward him. "You're not from around here are you?"

"No, I just came down from Boston. Why?"

"Mohammed Ramal was killed on Sunday," Williams answered softly. "He blew himself up."

Braxton froze in surprise. He couldn't believe what he had just heard. Things like this didn't occur in real life. At least not *his* life. He finally recovered enough to mumble, "What happened?" It was all he could think to ask.

"Nobody has many details," Williams continued with a shrug. "I heard that the cops think he was a terrorist that got clumsy playing with a bomb in his apartment. At least that's the rumor that's going around. I hadn't thought to deactivate his account."

"This isn't related to your looking for him is it?" Levi asked.

"No, I'm sure it's just a coincidence." Braxton replied quickly. He didn't need to be part of a conspiracy theory spread all over the Internet. Flanagan would fire him for sure. "You wouldn't know any of his friends by any chance would you?"

"Sorry, I didn't really know him at all. Stan?"

"I didn't either. You might try his Department. Computer Science headquarters is up on the fourth floor."

Braxton put on his best calming smile. "Thanks anyway. We'll just call this closed. I appreciate your help." He stood up and headed for the door.

"You're welcome, Mr. Braxton," Williams called to Braxton's back. "If there's anything else we can do . . ."

After escaping the SysOps, Braxton stopped next to the stairway and leaned back against the tile wall.

Now what the hell do I do? He couldn't just call Flanagan and say, "Gee, I'm sorry but your contact's dead." He wouldn't hear from her again.

Ramal had died on Sunday. The same day he had sent the email. Why would a terrorist building a bomb bother to contact CERT? It didn't make any sense.

Maybe Williams did have the right idea. If Braxton could find out what the student was working on, he might get an idea of what happened. And at least he'd have something to give CERT.

He headed up the stairs.

CHAPTER 9

George Washington University, Washington, D.C.
Tuesday, 11:00 a.m.

THE ADMINISTRATIVE OFFICES of GW's Department of Computer Science occupied the south wing of the fourth floor. The Department Directory showed the chairman was a Professor Howard Wilkinson. Braxton went through a set of double doors and turned to a secretary on the right. The plate on her desk read "Naomi Abusan".

"Excuse me, Ms. Abusan. I'm Adam Braxton from the CERT Coordination Center. I'd like to speak to Professor Wilkinson about a network security issue."

Abusan looked up and considered the unfamiliar gentleman standing before her. Unfazed by Braxton's blunt approach, she turned to him and replied with a look of disdain and indifference. "Professor Wilkinson is not in at the moment. If you wish, I can try to schedule an appointment with the associate chair, Professor Cabot."

"I'm sorry, but I'm from out of town and it is very important that I speak to someone as soon as possible." He didn't have time for this bureaucratic run-around. "It's in regard to Mohammed Ramal."

The name of the student had its anticipated effect. Abusan blinked slightly and reached for the phone. "I see. Let me check if Professor Cabot is available." After she punched in a number he heard a ringing in one of the offices down the hall. "Where did you say you were from?"

"The CERT Coordination Center in Pittsburgh."

Abusan repeated the name into the phone. After another

whispered conversation, she replaced the handset. "Professor Cabot can see you for a few minutes. He's in the second office on your left."

As Braxton approached the office, a man appeared in the doorway. He looked about fifty, average in height and weight, but his wavy white hair was expertly styled and his double-breasted suit could have just come off a rack at Brooks Brothers. Braxton was sure he would have appeared just as cool if the fire department had rushed in.

"Good morning," the man said, extending his hand. "I'm Bob Cabot. Please come in. What can we do for you?" The smile on his face was about as natural as a papier-mâché mask. This was definitely someone you didn't warm up to.

"Adam Braxton from the CERT Coordination Center, Professor Cabot. We're investigating an alert sent to us from Mohammed Ramal."

Cabot motioned Braxton inside and to a seat in front of his ornate oak desk. The administrator's office was as impeccable as its occupant, down to the muted indirect lighting and scattered pieces of modern sculpture. The interior was a stark contrast to the bland, aseptic decor of the rest of the building. It was quite unlike any other that Braxton remembered in academia.

"Yes, Mr. Ramal." Cabot clasped his hands and laid them carefully on the desk. "A very unfortunate affair. You must understand, Mr. Braxton, that the University has had quite a bit of unwarranted attention as a result of the accident. We owe it to the rest of our students to exercise some amount of care regarding information on Mr. Ramal. I hope you don't mind if I ask for some identification?"

Braxton again produced his identification card and handed it across the desk. Cabot scribbled something on a pad and returned the ID. His smile was immediately replaced by an expression Braxton could only describe as frigid indifference.

"Thank you. Now, what is CERT's interest in Mr. Ramal?"

Braxton outlined the history of the email. He left out his discussion with Williams and Levi. Cabot looked like the kind that was not above recriminations. "I would like to understand if Ramal was working on any research projects? Anything that would help to explain his investigation of an Internet anomaly." He knew he was stretching the facts a bit, but was sure it was necessary to get any help at all from the reluctant administrator.

Cabot paused for a moment then lifted a file from the corner of his desk. He flipped a few pages then appeared to read from a report. "Mr. Ramal was a third year graduate student in the Department. His advisor was Professor Eric Mendoza who heads our research on inter-network traffic analysis. As I'm sure you are aware, we are a national leader in cyber-security and network profiling."

Cabot paused and Braxton nodded politely, which was apparently the academic's desired signal to continue. "He was a passable student, certainly not brilliant, but had not been any trouble. He had just started his dissertation research, so I would be surprised if he had any substantive results."

"What was his project's focus?"

"As I said Mr. Braxton, he had just started his research. I doubt he had developed any particular intentions as yet."

"And he had just started on his program?"

"Mr. Ramal had some remedial coursework that was required by the department. He was a transfer student."

"Where did he come from?"

"I believe he graduated from the University of Maryland."

"What courses was he taking?"

Cabot closed the folder and placed his hands together on the desk. "I don't have that information here. Only the note on remedial requirements. This is feeling a bit like an interrogation, Mr. Braxton. Is there anything else?"

This conversation was going nowhere. All Cabot cared about was protecting his University.

Braxton decided to try a different tack. "Did he have connections to any student groups?"

Cabot's expression became even more severe. "Mr. Braxton. As I'm sure you are aware, we cannot keep track of all of the extracurricular activities of our students. We were certainly not aware of any connection to extremist groups, however. Why is this of interest to CERT?"

"Just curiosity Professor." Braxton flashed a smile. Maybe his next question could rattle the administrator. "Who was supporting Ramal's research?"

Cabot paused, then replied without referring to the folder or taking his eyes off the visitor. "Professor Mendoza's research is primarily supported by Takagawa Communications. They have been very supportive of our work in telecommunications and inter-networking. I would hope that CERT will not find it necessary to bother them with this issue."

Braxton knew he had hit a nerve. He was vaguely familiar with Takagawa. They were a new Japanese entry into the global Internet market. Originally a portal and e-commerce company focused in Japan, they had started expanding internationally and were even building expertise in networking software and related equipment. Like Amazon, Google and Microsoft, their objective was to control as much of the flow of Internet information as possible. And like most Japanese companies, they did not like adverse publicity. An attribute that he could now use to his advantage.

"I hope that will not be necessary, Professor. But we do need some additional information on Mr. Ramal. I could simply review Mr. Ramal's notes for any background on his message. I trust there wouldn't be any problem contacting Professor Mendoza?"

Cabot hesitated, then the papier-mâché smile reappeared. "We will be happy to cooperate with CERT in every way. However, I'm afraid that Professor Mendoza will not be of much help. All of Mr. Ramal's files and papers were confiscated by the police. We have no access to them at the moment."

Braxton's heart skipped a beat as he again felt the assignment slipping away. "I see. And who is in charge of the police investigation?"

Cabot frowned, then returned to the file and pulled out a card. "A Detective Samuel Fowler. Second District. That is all the information I have." Cabot stood, making it clear the discussion was over. "Now if you will excuse me, I have a meeting to attend."

Braxton rose, then stopped briefly before turning to the door. Cabot didn't offer his hand, his face impassive, and Braxton felt no obligation for civility. As he left the office, he heard the click of a phone. He wondered who Cabot would call first.

Just because he knew it would bother her, Braxton smiled pleasantly and waved at Abusan as he passed her desk. Her look could have frozen the Potomac.

Once through the entrance doors, he pulled his cell, Googled the D.C. Metropolitan Police Department and called the main number, hoping to catch the detective in charge of the case. A curt operator forwarded his call.

"Fowler," came a muffled voice.

"Detective Fowler. My name is Adam Braxton. I understand you're working on the Mohammed Ramal case. I'm trying to get some information on Mr. Ramal and wondered if we could meet?"

"Braxton? You a reporter or something?"

"Oh, no. I'm, ah, a computer security specialist working for CERT. I'm trying to find out what Mr. Ramal was working on."

"What kind of information you looking for, Braxton? I'm kinda busy at the moment."

Braxton hadn't considered that the detective might not want to talk with him. From the sound over the phone it seemed as if all he was interested in was eating his lunch. He had to find a way to pique the cop's interest.

"I'm looking into some of Mr. Ramal's recent activities, Detective. Specifically his work at GW. I understand you have all of his records. Perhaps we could share some information? I'm at the University right now, but I'm free the rest of the afternoon."

There was a long silence on the phone. Finally, Fowler responded. "Okay. Meet me at department headquarters at two o'clock. 300 Indiana, third floor. The desk officer will give you directions."

"Two o'clock. I'll see you then, Detective."

"Sure."

As Braxton hung up the phone, the reality of his situation hit. He had bluffed and the detective called him on it. He certainly didn't have any information the cop hadn't already gotten from GW. Fowler probably didn't know about the email message to CERT/CC, but how was he going to explain that to some D.C. cop?

Well, he'd just have to play it by ear. It's not like he was going to get in any more trouble over it.

Now where was he going to get some lunch?

* * *

Greystone circled the small conference table in his office summarizing the changes he required. Then he stopped and dramatically laid his hands on his assistant's shoulders. "That's it, Ted. I think we're ready to go."

Lombard let out a visible sigh of relief. The two had been reviewing Greystone's Board of Directors presentation since 7:00 that morning. If

Greystone didn't let Lombard complete the modifications they'd never get done in time. The Board meeting started at 1:00 and Greystone still had other business to complete.

"Did you get any new information out of the Board members?" Lombard asked.

"Not a damn thing. They're going to play this as close to the chest as they can." Greystone stretched and rubbed his eyes. "The Chairman's a sly old codger. Sometimes I think he just enjoys seeing all the infighting play out. He won't commit himself until he gets a reading of the rest of the Board. Then he'll proclaim victory."

"They've got to see how important it is to follow this plan. We'll all be out of jobs if someone doesn't do something to move Keane out of the way."

Lombard's whining was pitiful. All he cared about was *his* precious job.

"I know that. But Charles still has a lot of support on the Board. And we don't know what he may be up to."

"Robert," Lombard whispered, "I did hear a rumor yesterday about what Charles might be planning."

So that was why his assistant had been so nervous all morning. Waiting to spring a surprise. "And?" Greystone challenged.

"He's been meeting with a team of executives from Hawthorne Systems. What do you think they'd be up to?"

"Hawthorne Systems! What the hell do you think?" Greystone slammed his hands on the table. "The bastard's going to give away the company. He's so hell bent in not following *my* partnership plan, he'd sell out to a defense conglomerate. No wonder I haven't been able to get Hawthorne to sit down and talk about working together. They've been trying to expand their electronics business for years. Charles is going to hand it to them."

"Couldn't he just be looking to sell off some of our assets?"

"Not a chance. They're not going to play second fiddle in this market. They want a major piece and we may be it. It won't take *them* long to build the products that we have planned." He looked squarely at Lombard. "But they'll surely do it without you and me."

Greystone wanted to make sure Lombard knew they were in this together. His assistant was a valuable asset but without scruples or loyalty. He had known that when he had hired him. Lombard would do anything to get ahead. He had been sleeping with that mousy new secretary of Keane's for months now and it was about time he picked up something useful. "Where did you get this?"

"I heard some of Charles' lawyers talking at lunch yesterday."

Greystone knew he was lying but it didn't matter. "Can we confirm it?"

"I don't know. I'll keep poking around. I did pull some data on Hawthorne this morning. I thought you might like to look at it." Lombard reached in his pocket and pulled out a flash drive.

Greystone took the drive, pushed it into his laptop and opened the file. It was a detailed summary on Hawthorne Systems' electronics capabilities, complete with charts, graphs and reference citations. Lombard must have spent all night on it.

"Finish the presentation," Greystone finally ordered. "I'll look at this and try to work out a counter strategy."

He turned and walked slowly back to his desk while Lombard gathered his notes and computer. By the time Greystone sat down, the assistant had disappeared.

CHAPTER 10

George Washington University, Washington, D.C.
Tuesday, 1:00 p.m.

AFTER LEAVING SCIENCE and Engineering Hall, Braxton looked for a friendlier environment for lunch. Fighting the surging lunch crowd on 23rd Street, he found the Rusty Nail, an eclectic Irish pub on a narrow side street. The sound level was only a few decibels short of a Stones' concert and every horizontal surface was covered in peanut shells. Just his kind of place.

All the booths were taken, so he grabbed a stool at the bar and managed to shout an order over the din.

While he was waiting, his cell phone shook at his waist. It was from Flanagan. He carefully considered his options and pressed "Ignore". If it was that important, she'd leave a message. He was sure he would never have been able to hear her anyway.

After waiting so long the cook must have had to cure the beef himself—he had been so bored he actually had started to count the peanut shells on the bar—his lunch finally arrived. With only fifteen minutes until his appointment, he wolfed down his Reuben and Coke, dropped some bills on the bar and hailed a cab for Metropolitan Police Headquarters.

Headquarters was in the Henry J. Daly Building on Indiana Center. It was a huge rectangular building, its stone facade stained from years of assault by rain and pollution. Inside was a swarm of citizens, administrators, and police officers, all trying to transact the business of local government. He squeezed past the line of unhappy citizens paying parking tickets and took the elevator to the third floor.

Asking for Detective Fowler at the first desk he saw, he was directed to the end of the hallway. There, painted across a set of double doors, was "Investigative Services Bureau, Authorized Employees Only".

Braxton walked up to the entrance, tugged to straighten his coat, and pushed one of the doors open. Ahead, a large open area was filled with gray metal desks, perhaps as many as fifty, but not in any regular pattern. The desks sat in groups, huddled together as in an elementary school classroom, but more likely to match case teams. Every desk had its apparently requisite computer monitor, stack of manila folders, stained coffee cup and assortment of candy wrappers and potato chip bags. A row of private offices ran along the wall to his right, light filtered through weather-etched and pitted windows to his left and file cabinets stood sentry-like on the remaining walls. Despite the clutter of the room, Braxton counted only eight inhabitants.

He navigated around the desks, focusing on an intense young detective to his left staring into his monitor. Braxton was drawn to the Boston Red Sox cap sitting on his head.

"Is Detective Fowler here?" he asked.

The officer silently stretched out his arm and pointed to his right. His attention never wavered from the screen.

The only person Braxton could see in that direction was sitting at an isolated desk pushed into the far corner. Apparently Fowler wasn't much of a team player. Braxton took a deep breath and headed as directed.

Walking through the squad room, Braxton could feel a growing anxiety. This was the first time he had been in a police station since he smashed Bobby Derrick's bicycle in eighth grade. His memories of that event and its aftermath were causing an uncomfortable churn in his stomach. Maybe the Reuben hadn't been such a great idea after all.

He pushed forward, determined not to let the discomfort show.

As Braxton approached the desk, he saw a burly black man with broad shoulders and a tree-stump neck seated at the desk. Maybe not big enough to be a Patriots' linebacker, but damn close. Wiry salt-and-pepper hair was shaved close to his scalp and his lined face suggested he had seen his share of D.C. crime.

He was dressed in a faded blue shirt and brown pants, visible because a pair of huge scuffed broughams were resting firmly on the top of his desk. He was leaning back in his chair, reading a file. Worn black circles shown through the soles of the shoes.

The desk was strewn with folders and papers, punctuated with an occasional plastic food wrapper. If this was his typical diet, it wasn't surprising the detective barely fit in his chair. There was a small family portrait, wife and two daughters, sitting prominently on a corner of the desk.

"Detective Fowler," he announced as boldly as he could muster. "Adam Braxton. Thanks for taking the time to see me." He stuck out his hand.

The cop glanced up from his reading. "Yeah, sure. Have a seat." He didn't bother to get up or acknowledge the extended arm. "Where did you say you were from?"

"I'm from the CERT Coordination Center. We're responsible for investigating security breaches of the Internet."

Fowler looked up from his reading and crossed thick arms over his barrel chest. He almost looked interested in what Braxton was saying. "Security breaches? What does that have to do with Mr. Ramal?"

"We received a mail message from him over the weekend. We tried to get back to him but got no response. I came down from Boston to try to talk to him."

"Long way to come for someone you didn't know."

"Well, I had another appointment here and it seemed like a good way to check out the incident."

Fowler's eyebrows rose. "What do you mean *incident*? I thought he just sent you some mail."

"He sent us *electronic* mail. He said he had been studying the George Washington University gateway, that's the computer that links all the other computers on the campus to the Internet, and found some messages that weren't supposed to be there. Standard procedure is to check it out. We call any report like that an incident." Braxton wasn't sure how much of all this Fowler was able to follow, but he'd give the cop the benefit of the doubt.

"What kind of messages did he find?" Fowler had now managed to put his feet down and turn to face his visitor. Braxton pushed back in his chair to distance himself from the detective's stare.

"We don't really know," Braxton replied. "All Ramal said was that the messages were unusual. I came down to try to find out what they were."

"And what have you been able to find out?"

"Not very much, unfortunately. Just that apparently Ramal blew himself up with some kind of explosive and that you think he was involved in terrorist activities."

Fowler leaned farther across his desk. "Who'd you hear that from?" he demanded.

"Ah, I spoke with a Professor Cabot at the University," Braxton replied. "He was the one who gave me your name." Fowler frowned and gave a nod of recognition. "He also told me you have Ramal's data files and records. I need to look at those materials and any other information you uncovered that might help us track down what he was doing."

It took less than a heartbeat for Braxton to realize he had made a mistake. Fowler leapt from his chair, slammed his hands on the desk and leaned over until there was only inches between his face and Braxton's.

"There's a couple things you *need to know*, Mr. Braxton. First, I would be very careful in believing anything that that fop Cabot says. All he cares about is protecting his precious research funds. Second, this is a criminal investigation. You have no goddamn authority to tell me what to do and I don't have to help you in any way. And without me you get shit."

Braxton's head snapped back and he felt glued to the chair. Now was not the time for a snappy retort. Best to take his punishment quietly.

Fowler paused to emphasize his point before continuing. "You got some identification?"

Braxton produced his now well-worn ID. Fowler grabbed a scrap of paper from his desk and scribbled some notes before returning it. Braxton's hand shook as he stuffed the card in his wallet.

The detective lowered back into his chair and Braxton managed to take a breath. This was actually worse than Bobby Derrick. He prayed he would never be across the table from this detective on a real interrogation.

When Fowler continued, his voice had dropped to a whisper. Now it was Braxton who had to lean forward. "On the other hand,

Mr. Braxton, we might be able to come to an understanding that could help us both. But this would be completely unofficial. Can you handle that?"

Braxton managed to push the words out of his throat. "I'd be happy to help in any way I can, Detective."

"Good. Let's take a walk." With that Fowler stood and took off across the room. Braxton was amazed how quickly the huge man could move. He was still five steps behind when Fowler entered a waiting elevator.

They left the headquarters, walked down 4th Street past the Court of Appeals, across E Street and into the quiet of Judiciary Square. Fowler continued his brisk pace.

"All right, Detective," Braxton asked after catching his breath. "Why the afternoon stroll?"

"Off the record, Braxton, I've got a problem. The department thinks Ramal was a terrorist. The physical evidence in his apartment is damned incriminating, but there is no link between your student and any known terrorist organization.

"The FBI wants him to be a terrorist, but even their whizzes couldn't find anything out of the ordinary in his computer.

"I don't buy the clumsy lone wolf theory, but I don't have any real evidence against it either. If you think you can find anything new looking at those files, I'll get it cleared. But whatever you uncover comes to me first. We talk about it and go from there. Deal?"

Deal? What was Braxton doing making a deal with a detective? And getting caught up in a criminal investigation?

Should he check with Flanagan back at CERT? If he did, how would it look?

He knew the answer to that. He had hired his own consultants in the past. It would look like he couldn't handle the job. He would get a polite thank you and never hear from them again.

Did he really think he could find anything the FBI couldn't? The answer to that was easy. He didn't have much respect for the computer expertise of any of the government agencies. Didn't they always go to industry to build their systems? NSA might give him a run for his money, but not the FBI.

And then there was his financial situation. Why pass up an opportunity to build some more clients? If he helped the D.C.

Police Department, it could mean more business in the future. *That* was thinking like a real consultant.

"Sure, let me take a look and I'll give you my best shot. But if I find something that's *not* related to your case, I get to take it back to CERT. Deal?"

Fowler turned and stared back at the consultant. If this was the cop's way of sealing an agreement, it was very effective.

"Okay," Fowler said. "Come back in the morning and I'll set you up. You can take a look at all the stuff then. Eight o'clock sharp."

Braxton glanced up and saw Fowler had taken him around the Square. They were back at E Street, headed toward Fowler's office.

He hadn't planned spending the night, but he had thrown a change of underwear and his toiletry kit in the carry-on bag just in case. It would be easier than fighting the airlines again.

"I'll be there," he said. "But one question first."

Fowler wrinkled his brow. "What now?" the detective growled.

"Why this case? I doubt you make a habit of going around your department, and the FBI."

"Despite what you may think about me, Braxton, I am a professional too, and I care about what happens in my city. And I really don't like anyone being railroaded, even some guy who may or may not have blown himself up. Now I have a question for you."

"Yes?"

"You said you were from Boston. I thought CERT was in Pittsburgh."

"It is. I'm just a contractor."

"I see." Fowler abruptly turned and walked across E Street. It was obvious he didn't intend for Braxton to follow.

He sat down on the grass of the Square and tried to shake off the tension of the encounter. The detective was a very strange fellow. First accusatory, then supportive. Stand-offish, then conspiratorial. That must be how the police get their information.

But Fowler was right. Braxton needed to see those files. And if he had to deal with the devil himself, he'd do it.

He had done everything he could today. A cool, damp wind blew across the Square and Braxton pulled his jacket tighter across his chest. Rain was coming.

Maybe some indoor sightseeing would take his mind off the frustrations of this case. He headed right on E, then south on 6th

Street toward the Mall. As he crossed Constitution Avenue, he realized just how much he had underestimated the cop.

CHAPTER 11

Theater Electronics, Reston, Virginia
Tuesday, 4:00 p.m.

"THIS PROPOSAL REPRESENTS a significant step forward for Theater Electronics as major player in the international command and control market," Greystone concluded. "To continue our legacy as an innovative leader in the industry we must shed our closed image and embrace strategic partnerships as the way to future success. I look for your support of this proposal and affirmation of its specific steps as our new operating plan."

Greystone finished his presentation with a characteristic flourish. He was again in the Board room, but cold, gray clouds had blown over as the afternoon passed, laying an ashen pall over the Virginia countryside. Try as he might, the somber scene outside had seeped into the meeting, darkening the moods of the participants.

He had stressed every key point and played to each of the special interests of the individuals sitting around the table. Their questions had been thoughtful and direct, although lacking in the long-term, strategic view he was hoping for. Even Keane had sat in his chair and listened intently to the presentation.

"Thank you Robert, you present a very persuasive argument," said a distinguished man at the end of the table. Julius Flitterman was a hard-nosed New York investment banker who had a long history in venture capital. Chairman of the Board, he had been with Keane since the founding of Theater, but lately Greystone had been sensing cracks in the relationship. With a little more pressure, the banker might come over.

"If you don't mind, Julius," Greystone interrupted, "I'd like to request the Board's approval to proceed with this plan. If we don't move ahead we will lose the momentum to build these relation-ships."

"You're asking a lot, Robert," came the harsh reply from a matronly woman seated to Flitterman's right. Despite her appearance, Meredith Hardesty was a cagey executive who controlled nearly ten billion dollars' worth of pension funds. She was not one to be pushed headlong into anything. Greystone feared he might have pushed too hard.

"We need to review all the other proposals thoroughly before any decision can be made. You're asking us to commit ten million dollars to this effort. Surely you understand our need for diligence."

"Of course, Meredith. I only want what is best for the company."

"Well, on that note let me give you an update on my plan." Keane rose slowly from his chair.

"Update, Charles? I thought you were ready with an alternate proposal." Greystone's voice cut a little too sharply for many around the table. Their eyes turned to Keane to see how he would respond.

"I've been busy with some other business, Robert." His voice maintained its calm, even temper. "We do need to look out for short term revenue as well as strategic issues you know."

Greystone considered a reply, but thought better and merely smiled. He closed his laptop, returned to his seat, and waited for Keane's presentation. Lying in front of him on the table was a folder he had prepared before lunch. Abstracted from Lombard's data, and adding some insights of his own, it was a scathing attack on Keane's Hawthorne Systems proposal. He placed his hand over the papers and felt another rush of the adrenaline. He was anxious to get on with the confrontation.

"I have also spent some time looking at major partnerships and divestments for the company. An analysis of our existing business plan and resulting cash flow requirements, quite before any addi-tional proposed expenditures," he slowly nodded at Greystone, "shows that . . ."

God how Keane could talk. Why can't he just get to the point? The tension grew inside the executive like an expanding shock wave. He ran through the Hawthorne arguments in preparation for the coming attack.

" . . . and despite insufficient time to prepare a full report, I can say confidently that this company will provide much needed cash resources as well as a broad technology base on which we can draw. In fact, it may be possible . . ."

Greystone drummed his fingers over the report. Each of Keane's words ratcheted the tension. Sweat broke out on his forehead as he tried to control the relentless pressure.

" . . . target will complement our efforts to produce a product that is both revolutionary and . . ."

Suddenly he just exploded. "Charles, I don't understand how you can think we won't be completely dominated by a cutthroat organization like Hawthorne Systems."

The room went silent. They had all been rendered mute. Eyes turned first to Greystone, then back to Keane.

"Hawthorne Systems?" Keane said in that same soft voice. "I'm sorry you misunderstood, Robert. I was not referring to Hawthorne, although they would be a rather interesting partner. I would prefer to refrain from getting into any further details until I can complete my analysis. Julius, could we continue this review at the Board meeting next month? I'd like to get off early today and head out to the cabin."

"Yes, yes, of course, Charles." Flitterman wasn't normally one to show surprise, but his halting speech gave him away. He had expected a deadly strike from the President. The other Board members seemed equally shocked. "Ah, if there are no additional items, I'll entertain a motion for adjournment."

Greystone slumped back in his chair. He had lost. Keane had played out the line and he had jumped for it; and there was nothing there but a shiny, deadly hook.

But Keane should have used the opportunity to destroy him completely in front of the Board. *Why would he let me off so easily?*

The old man fool left him an opening. Perhaps there was time for one more round.

* * *

Lombard sat dumbfounded at his desk staring into his CRT. He had been waiting all afternoon for any gossip on the Board meeting. One of the secretaries had said his boss had gotten in trouble, but no one could provide any details. And as usual, all the Board members had left the building quickly, paying no attention to the people that did all the real work.

Keane and Greystone had stopped briefly in their offices, probably to just gather up some papers, and then they had disappeared as well. He had tried to speak with his boss, but Greystone had abruptly waved him off.

The executive floor had slowly emptied out, as was typical when the masters were gone, and Lombard was left to do some clandestine research by rifling an occasional unoccupied desktop. He had finally returned to his desk and checked his mail, only to find an email from the President himself. Keane rarely sent electronic mail to his employees, except for the yearly Christmas greeting and the quarterly state-of-the-company reports, so to receive one sent directly to him was extraordinary. The contents were just as surprising:

```
From: Charles Keane

To: Theodore Lombard

Subject: Employment

Mr. Lombard, I am aware of your impropriety con-
cerning Miss Montonet and Hawthorne Systems. If you
would like to discuss your further employment by
Theater, please join me at my cabin this evening at
7:00. I have a proposal that may resurrect your
rapidly disappearing career.

CK
```

What could he do? Greystone had made it clear that he would take Lombard down with him if anything ever happened. But Keane still ran the company. And how would his boss ever find out about the meeting, anyway? Let the old gladiators fight it out. He was a survivor.

Over the past few months, he had kept detailed notes of Greystone's manipulations. These would be his bargaining chips. Keane certainly knew of Lombard's value. Why even bother to invite him if all he wanted to do was fire him? No, Keane wanted something and Lombard was ready to do whatever was necessary, for the right price.

He had only been to Keane's farm once before, when he had delivered some papers to Greystone at a corporate retreat, but the address was still in his email. He found the message, then called up Google Maps on his cell and copied in the address.

It would take him at least an hour and a half to get there from Reston, assuming traffic cooperated. But it was already 5:00 and the congestion on I-66 would add at least another half hour. He grabbed his jacket and raced to the parking garage.

CHAPTER 12

CHARLES KEANE'S "CABIN" was an estate in the Blue Ridge Mountains, just outside of Riverton, Virginia. The estate sat on one hundred acres nestled among the lush green foothills. The focal point of the property was the manor house, an overgrown English Tudor with great stone exterior walls and diamond-paned windows. It had been built in 1930 for a reigning labor leader who had lived in the house twenty years until he mysteriously disappeared during a Chicago union negotiation.

The property had next been purchased by a very well-heeled US Representative. As luck would have it, the Rep had later been implicated in a nasty conflict of interest investigation over the awarding of a defense contract. Keane had received a tip that the politician was trying to get out of the country before the FBI got involved. He had made a generous offer, in cash, and the property was his.

The home had fifteen rooms, including a huge library that took up one complete wing. The library was where Charles Keane "held court" as his friends described it; the place where he threw parties, convened meetings, and generally infuriated friends, business associates and government bureaucrats.

The walls of the room were covered in intricate oak panels, alternating with inset bookcases that rose to the edge of the soaring vaulted ceiling. Antique cast-iron rolling ladders ensured access to the eight foot high shelves that were filled with dusty first editions, collected from Keane's numerous excursions to the financial and political centers of the world. Only an occasional empty space could be found, and in these Keane had strategically placed an expensive *object d'art*.

A massive oak desk guarded the entrance to the room, sitting just to the right of the seven-foot double oak doors leading from the main hallway. It was a huge, ornately carved monument to the excesses of its owner. Save for a small lamp, telephone, and gold pen set, the top was clear; its polish a testament to the efforts of Keane's small house staff.

The far end of the room exposed the exterior stone including an elaborate six foot fireplace and mantle that drew attention to the significance of the area. Above the mantle hung a mammoth oil painting depicting a simpler time of riding and sport in Virginia Hunt Country.

A sitting area had been placed in front of the fireplace filled with deeply upholstered burgundy leather chairs arranged in a circle on a stunning deep blue Isphahan oriental rug. A small reading table sat next to one of the chairs; a rack of polished Meerschaum pipes and a humidor of tobacco rested comfortably on its top. Keane's wife, Margaret, had had but one rule as far has her husband was concerned: smoking was expressly forbidden in their home, except in the library. Despite her passing, Keane was unwilling to break this covenant. For most, the room had a stifling, oppressive, air but for Keane this was the one location in the world where he could truly relax.

Margaret had died three years earlier and his friends wondered why he continued to maintain the old house. It was much bigger than he needed and was sixty-five miles from Theater's Reston headquarters; quite a trek in northern Virginia traffic. He always replied that this was his home and he would stay here until he died; he intended to be a part of the continuing history of the estate. Margaret was buried in a small pre-Civil War cemetery at the top of a ridge overlooking the mansion and it was Keane's wish that he be buried alongside her when the time came.

The sun had already set behind the mountains, and the estate was bathed in the glow of twilight. The old house could still be a bit drafty, so Keane had started a fire as he waited for his visitor. He was sitting in his favorite chair reading the latest issue of Fortune when he looked up to see a familiar face standing before him.

"Robert, what are you doing here? How did you get in?"

"Now Charles, don't get excited," Greystone calmly replied. "I thought it was time for us to get together and talk things out." He selected the chair opposite Keane and leisurely sat down.

Keane felt a rush of adrenaline. His Senior Vice President was dressed completely in black: slacks, turtleneck, and even gloves. Whatever Greystone wanted, Keane knew it was not to just talk. He had humiliated his subordinate at the Board meeting. Had Greystone decided to get his revenge?

He also knew a physical confrontation was out of the question. Greystone was a regular at the fitness club across from their offices. He'd have to find another way to defeat this adversary.

Fear pressed in on him but he held it at bay, knowing his only chance was to stay calm.

How could he call for help? His alarm system! He had turned it on right after dinner. All he had to do was keep Greystone talking until the police arrived.

"Yes, I do think it's time to get our issues out in the open," he began, mustering a small smile at his intruder. "I know all about your little arrangements with our competitors too. The Board will be quite interested in hearing about the commitments you have made without their approval."

Greystone shook his head. "I doubt that will be coming to their attention, Charles. By the way, don't count on your alarm system saving you. Your telephone line seems to have gone out."

Keane was unable to hold back the look of surprise and despair. But there was still one other chance.

"I really can't let you proceed with the takeover plan, you know," Greystone continued calmly. "There are too many arrangements in place already."

Keane managed a weak smile. "There isn't any takeover plan, you fool. I planted three different sets of evidence with my staff. I knew who was behind the leak as soon as you mentioned Hawthorne Systems." Keane drew strength from his hatred of the underling. He refused to go down easily. "How did you turn Clarice?"

"I didn't. It was the work of my trusty assistant."

"Lombard?" Keane nodded in recognition. "He always was a weasel. I would have fired him, but thought you two deserved each other."

Greystone rose from the chair and strode to the fireplace. "If it's any consolation, Charles, she really didn't know. Lombard is quite good at what he does. I know he's on his way here, by the way."

"How could you? You weren't copied on his email."

"Come now, Charles. Lombard didn't send you anything, I did. And he thinks you invited him. It was time for the two of you to get together."

Keane furled his brow. What was Greystone planning? Was Lombard part of his plan?

Greystone draped his arm on the mantle and slowly gazed over the room. "This is a very nice place, Charles. I've always wanted a room like this." He returned his focus to Keane. "You look like you have another question."

"Why have Lombard come here?"

"To betray me. It was your idea."

Keane pushed himself up from the chair. He had to face Greystone and find a way to deal with this maniac. "I don't understand. Why would he . . ."

* * *

Greystone had had enough of the small talk. Listening to Keane's babbling just made him madder, reminding him of the indignity at the Board meeting.

He reached down and picked up a long iron poker hanging on the fireplace stand. He grabbed it with both hands and swung it like a baseball bat, striking Keane on the side of the head with all the force ·he could muster. Blood flew everywhere as the executive's skull split open exposing the raw tissue underneath.

The ear-splitting crack that accompanied the blow startled him. He had never broken a bone before and had not expected such an audible result. Another fact to remember.

Keane fell back onto the chair, then collapsed on the floor, a growing dark stain outlining his body on the priceless Isphahan.

Greystone wiped his hands on his jacket and calmly walked back to the entrance to the library. As he passed Keane's desk, he pulled two files from the pocket of his jacket. One he placed conspicuously on the top, being careful not to leave any blood stains. The other he slipped under one of the drawers, wedging it in the wooden frame.

He replayed all the steps, satisfied that there would be only one conclusion possible, and left the room.

CHAPTER 13

Riverton, Virginia
Tuesday, 7:00 p.m.

LOMBARD TURNED HIS Audi A4 onto the gravel road and checked the directions on his phone. This should be the place. He drove through the black iron gates and continued up the long driveway.

Storm clouds hung over the mountains like a shroud, and had become denser as the road had crept upward. He had had to turn on his headlights at Riverton to avoid dropping off into the voids next to the highway. At least the forecasted rain had held back.

Now his lights illuminated a winding trail that disappeared around each turn into the dense pine forest. He nearly missed the house, his attention so focused on the path. The house was completely dark, a huge ominous shadow in the woods. The darkness had been playing on Lombard's confidence ever since he left the highway. And that was probably just what Keane wanted.

It was 7:15 when he finally stopped his car by the front door and walked up the portico. When his knock went unanswered, he pushed on the door and watched it swing back into more darkness. Gingerly stepping in, he paused to let his eyes grow accustomed to the shadowy interior. The hall was long and narrow with doors lining each side for as far as he could see. A single slit of light knifed across the hardwood about twenty feet ahead.

Lombard called out Keane's name and heard it echo down the empty passage. Since the executive had invited him, he decided to go ahead into the house. As he approached the light, he saw that it was coming from a set of tall double doors, one of which was slightly pulled back. He knocked again, then pushed the door into the room and entered.

The huge room was empty. Light flickered from a wood fire at the far end of the space. A strange, sickly odor warned him of danger but curiosity drove him to explore further. He cautiously walked toward the light and the imposing stone fireplace. As soon as he saw the prone form on the floor he knew it was Keane. And the stain on the rug told him all he needed to know about the condition of his CEO.

His mind went into a frenzy. He had come to an isolated home to see an eccentric boss who had every right to hate him. The person he had been spying on was dead. This was not what was supposed to have happened. What was this going to do to his career?

He was about to run to his car and return to D.C. but hesitated. Keane couldn't say anything against him now. The message telling him to come was stored in who knows how many computers; that couldn't be denied. It would be safer to notify the authorities and tell the truth. Or at least part of the truth. He had arrived and found the body. He hadn't touched anything. Stick to his story and he'd be okay.

He glanced around the room and saw a telephone on Keane's desk. He raced over, grabbed the handset and started to dial 911 when he realized there wasn't any dial tone. The phone was dead. What was going on?

Lombard then reached for his cell phone, but stopped.

He remembered that Keane had had the local cell tower torn down. He demanded full attention at his conferences and this had been just another way to enforce his will. Lombard had always wondered who he had blackmailed for this little bit of public service.

"Dammit!" he whispered. There wasn't any way to contact the police.

He couldn't just wait there alone with a dead body. There had to be a phone down the mountain in Riverton. He'd drive there and call the police.

Stay calm, he told himself. *I can get through this. I haven't done anything wrong.*

As he turned to leave, he saw a folder sitting on the desk with his name on it. He flipped it open and scanned the pages. It was a report on his clandestine activities over the past five years. All of his contacts and payoffs. *How the hell did Keane get all this?*

He grabbed the folder and ran back to his car, now even more terrified of his precarious situation.

Lombard swerved down the driveway, gravel spitting in all directions, and skidded onto the paved road that headed back down the mountain. His heart pounded in his chest. Clouds had completely shrouded the road in darkness; he had only his headlights to guide him down the chicanes of the serpentine road.

At least there was no traffic to get in his way. Just a solitary pair of lights in his mirror. They would be far behind in a few minutes.

The road took a hard left and Lombard heard the tires squeal. He couldn't keep up this speed. He had to get to the police station to report his story, not fall off the mountain and be part of it.

He went to pump the brakes, but with each motion his foot pressed farther and farther. Then the pedal hit the floor board. He wasn't slowing down. He didn't have any brakes.

"Shit!" he exclaimed. The violent drumbeat of his heart throbbed down to his toes. He tightened his grip on the steering wheel and struggled to keep the vehicle steady.

A flash of lightning illuminated the road ahead; the next switchback was racing toward him. Droplets of rain appeared on his windshield. Just what he needed. There was no way he would stay on the road at this speed. What the hell could he do?

The emergency brake! He stomped on the pedal with his left foot. The car lurched, nearly throwing him over the steering wheel and through the windshield. The speedometer plummeted from ninety to seventy, then he heard what sounded like an explosion from the rear of the car. The emergency pedal went slack; the cable had snapped. His speedometer returned to its deadly creep upward.

Lombard pounded his hands on the steering wheel. Panic was taking over. His head throbbed and bile burned at the back of his throat. First Keane and now this. What was happening to him?

The rain became heavier. It was like looking at the road through underwater goggles.

The switchback was now only a mile away. He thought back to all those spy novels he was always reading. What would Jason Bourne do?

Look around! Think!

The rock face of the mountain was on his left; a shear drop into a granite valley below on his right. Could he rub off speed on the rocks? It would ruin his car but it just might save his life.

Could he really do that? If he hit too hard, he would bounce out of control and flip off the mountain. But he didn't want to die. It was his only option.

He mustered his courage and edged the Audi closer to the wall of stone.

Just a little bit farther.

There was a terrifying screech—the sound of metal scraping and buckling against the jagged, eternal mountain. The car lurched to the right and he was thrown hard into his seatbelt. He straightened the wheel and glanced at the speedometer. It was down to sixty. He could do this!

He lined up for another run then heard a roar from behind. It was the pair of lights he had seen. The damned car was coming up on his left. What was this idiot doing?

Lombard jammed his hand on the horn, but the car kept coming. He frantically waved his arm and screamed for the driver to get out of the way. But it moved faster, even coming alongside, leaving him no place to go. Was the driver trying to kill him?

He was going over eighty miles an hour. The guard posts on his right were a blur as they raced past, coming closer each second. He was wedged like a bull going to slaughter and there was nothing he could do about it.

The Audi ripped through the barrier cables just as another flash of lightning struck. Lombard took a final glance at the car's driver before going into the abyss. And everything became clear.

* * *

Greystone slammed on the brakes of the battered Trans Am and fishtailed through the turn, finally stopping at the rail on the other side. He watched as the Audi tumbled down into the mist of the valley. It disappeared into the darkness, then erupted in a ball of scarlet and yellow flame. At least that saved a slow and uncomfortable walk to the bottom for confirmation.

While Lombard had been inside Keane's home, Greystone had placed the bloody poker in his trunk, and a small remotely-activated explosive charge on his brake line. There would still be enough of the poker left for an identification, and the remnants of the charge would be lost in the debris.

His plan had gone as expected: with brake fluid gushing from the open line, Lombard had lost all control, careening back and forth across the highway.

Greystone had never thought that Lombard would try to slide onto the rock wall. It was a surprisingly brilliant idea and he had barely managed to intervene. That had been a bit too close.

He headed carefully back down the mountain, always under the speed limit, and pulled into a rest area just before rejoining I-66. Getting a summons for using a cell phone while driving would be the ultimate irony.

He took out the burner phone, dialed his home number and punched in the codes for the program he had written that afternoon. His computer monitored all the signals on that line and would handle everything else. He hadn't used some of the sequences for years, but a quick look in the TAP archive recalled them easily enough. It amused him that a cabal of teenagers would provide a key component of his evening's adventure. He ended the call and entered the Interstate.

The weather was getting worse. He had just enough time to dump the stolen Pontiac, change clothes and get to the dinner party in McLean.

                              *   *   *

The Phone Phreaks had been a unique phenomenon of the 1970's. Rejecting the social consciousness of the previous decade, they chose an alternate method of rebellion: electronic terrorism against the nation's telecommunications system. The Phreaks had been surprisingly innovative in their approaches, given that they were primarily asocial high school dropouts. They had started simply enough, using tenacity and wile to ferret out the secrets of the old mechanical telephone switching systems. They learned how to divert billing and place untraceable calls all over the world.

As the telephone companies updated their analog switching centers with digital technology, the Phreaks had evolved as well, learning the internal sequences of signals and tones used to control the new system. Their repertoire expanded significantly: they could disconnect lines, automatically bill calls to an unfriendly reporter, or access internal circuits to monitor lines and reroute calls.

The Phreaks eventually became victims of their own success. They began to enjoy the spotlight and notoriety, claiming credit for their increasingly public activities. They cultivated media attention, promoting childish ideas of information freedom and open access. During the late seventies and early eighties, Phreaks using the pseudonyms of Captain Crunch and the Cheshire Catalyst had been on the top of most-wanted lists from national law enforcement agencies and telephone security departments. Another Phreak, with the incongruous moniker of Tom Edison, documented their secrets in an underground New York newsletter published under the name of the Technological Assistance Program.

By 1983, the TAP began to unify their knowledge of the telephone and the computer and describe it to the public. Some organizations felt such disclosures could not be permitted. A sensational burglary and arson in a New Jersey condo destroyed all remnants of the TAP. The destruction was generally attributed to either ATT or the FBI.

By the mid-1980's, the social misfits of the next generation had found a new toy, the personal computer, and a new bureaucratic world to conquer. Hackers and Crackers replaced Phreaks in the anti-social hierarchy. All that remained of the Phreaks was their legacy of telephone arcana, much of which had been documented in the TAP newsletters. Greystone had, to his knowledge, the only complete set in existence.

* * *

At exactly 7:30 p.m., Greystone's computer accessed Verizon's main switching system and reinstated the dial tone at Keane's estate. Thirty-five seconds later, Keane's ProTec 7500 custom alarm system, still noting a zone violation, tried again to initiate an emergency call. Finally sensing a dial tone, it completed a call to Blue Ridge Protective Services, who immediately notified the Warren County Police. A squad car was dispatched, coincidentally the same one that was currently investigating a fatal auto accident on Scenic View Road.

Charles Keane's body was discovered at 7:53.

CHAPTER 14

Great Falls, Virginia
Wednesday, 12:05 a.m.

GREYSTONE'S ANSWERING MACHINE blinked three messages when he returned home. Each caller expressed an increasing level of concern and anxiety. The first was from an Agent Jefferson, Virginia State Police. He calmly explained that there had been some kind of accident and he would like Greystone to call him when he returned. The second was from Julius Flitterman. He sounded slightly agitated and wanted Greystone to return his call " . . . immediately. It's about Charles." Finally, Victor Sutherland, Theater's chief counsel, left a frantic, incoherent message about an accident, murder, and probable serious liability.

Greystone quickly triaged the calls.

"Robert, thank you for getting back to me so quickly," Flitterman began. The banker was as cool as ever. "There's been some kind of an accident and Charles has been killed."

Greystone paused appropriately then responded. "Killed! How did it happen?"

"I don't know the details, but apparently he died at his home earlier tonight. The police seem to believe that an employee, a Ted Lombard, had something to do with it. Do you know him?"

"Ted? Yes, I do. He's my assistant. How could he have been involved?"

"I certainly don't know. See what you can find out from the police." Flitterman had obviously recovered from any initial shock and was ready to take charge of the situation. "I'm flying back down in the morning. We can talk after I arrive. I'll also call a special

Board meeting for the afternoon so we can work this thing through. We have to protect the company as much as we can."

"Yes, Victor already called me."

"Victor's called everyone. I tried to calm the man down, he sounded completely unhinged. I sent him off to check some legal issues and stockholder precedents. We'll review those tomorrow as well. Find out everything you can from the police before we get together."

"Certainly, Julius. Should I cancel my testimony in D.C.? It's scheduled for eleven o'clock." He held his breath waiting for the banker's response. The meeting with Potterfield was crucial for his plan.

"No," Flitterman replied after a moment. "It's important we show that the company can still operate effectively. Just get back as soon as you can."

"Thank you, Julius. See you tomorrow."

Greystone's call to Jefferson was routed to the policeman's car phone.

"Agent Jefferson."

"This is Robert Greystone."

"Thank you for returning my call, Mr. Greystone. I'm afraid I have some bad news. Mr. Charles Keane was killed tonight."

Jefferson was certainly all business. "Yes, I heard that from our Chairman, Julius Flitterman. It was a tremendous shock. What can I do for you Agent?"

"It appears that a Mr. Theodore Lombard may be involved. I believe Mr. Lombard worked for you?"

"Yes, that's right."

"I was wondering if we could get together. As you can imagine, I have some questions that I would like to ask about Lombard."

"Certainly." Greystone visualized his morning schedule. It would certainly be an interesting day. "Tomorrow, say nine o'clock?"

"That would be fine, Mr. Greystone. At your headquarters in Reston?"

"Yes. I'll see you at the office, Agent Jefferson."

That was enough for tonight. He wouldn't bother with Sutherland, that was Flitterman's job. Greystone needed a good night's sleep for his next performance.

* * *

Braxton arrived at the Municipal Center promptly at 8:00. He called Fowler's number and was told to wait in the lobby. The Center was already crowded, with both cops and civilians roaming the halls, hunting for the right office to transact their business. It looked like opening day at Fenway Park.

He found an empty wooden bench by the front door and sat down.

Braxton was anxious to see the files. The FBI apparently hadn't discovered any evidence they cared about, but there had to be something to help with his investigation. He just hoped Fowler wouldn't get in his way.

After yesterday's meeting, he had spent the afternoon in the National Gallery's new Early Syrian Art exhibit. As he had wandered through the corridors filled with carvings, statues and drawings, the tensions of the incident melted away and he became mesmerized in the magnificence of the relics. He certainly wasn't an expert in antiquities, but he appreciated the skill and artistry required to create such beautiful, and long-lasting, artifacts of a civilization. He had wondered if anything created by his generation would stand this test of time.

After the Gallery, he had grabbed dinner at a Thai restaurant in Dupont Circle and finally arrived back at his room at 7:30. He had scanned his email, then reviewed the outputs from his monitor programs. The results had confirmed those of the previous days: suspicious messages were being sent by one of the gateways. But there was still no obvious explanation. Had Ramal discovered something he had missed?

In addition to a voice mail, Flanagan had sent another, more pointed request in email. Braxton had composed a very consultant-like, information-free response, promised more information soon and fired it off. Ten minutes later he had been sound asleep.

"Braxton?"

He looked up and saw Fowler glaring at him from across the lobby.

"Follow me," the detective ordered as he motioned Braxton down a well-travelled marble staircase. "I hope you're rested. I can only give you access for the morning. You gotta get done by noon."

"Thanks for the heads up," Braxton replied with a frown. *This was great. No pressure.*

One long story down was the building's basement. Its main purpose appeared to be storage; rusty file cabinets lined every available wall and loose folders were stacked on every available surface. After walking through a maze of the cabinets, seemingly positioned to disorient any unwanted visitor, they finally arrived at a large open area, the rear half of which was protected by a floor-to-ceiling wall of heavy chain link fencing.

"That's Charlie Waters," Fowler said, pointing to a cop sitting on the far side of the enclosure. "He'll pull the stuff for you."

Waters was an ancient black, thin and wizened, his uniform hanging on his body like it was meant for a cop twice his size. Sitting motionless behind a makeshift counter, he looked about seventy-five and much too feeble to still be on active duty.

"Charlie," Fowler said walking up to the man, "this here's Mr. Adam Braxton. He's a hotshot out-of-town investigator looking into that Ramal explosion. I'd sure appreciate it if you could set him up to take a look at the files. Just between us, okay?"

"Sure thing, Sam." The old man winked at the detective. "Just between us old-timers. How's Pat and the kids?"

"Doin' just fine, Charlie. How many grandkids you and Maggie got now?"

"Seventeen, Sam. And three great grandkids."

Fowler shook his head. "Don't know how you keep up with 'em."

Waters smiled, showing a mouth with as many empty spaces as teeth.

"I've got to go back upstairs, Braxton," Fowler said turning to the consultant. "Charlie here will take good care of you. When you're finished give me a call."

Fowler turned back into the maze and vanished.

Waters carefully pushed himself off his stool, unlocked a gate in the fence, and limped out toward Braxton. The old cop had a permanent list to the right, likely compensating for an arthritic hip. He waved for the consultant to follow him.

They continued into one corner of the open area where Waters pointed to a dusty, metal desk.

"Y'all sit down," he said. "I'll be right back."

"Can I help you?" Braxton asked. He was afraid the old man might get hurt carrying anything.

"Ain't no need," Waters replied with another toothy smile.

He disappeared into the evidence holding area, returning a few minutes later with two large cardboard boxes that he dropped on the desk. Braxton opened the first and found it filled with notebooks and files. He had no idea how the old man had hefted the load.

"Give a yell when you're done, sonny," Waters said, and slowly limped back to the cage.

CHAPTER 15

Theater Electronics, Reston, Virginia
Wednesday, 9:00 a.m.

GREYSTONE HAD PICKED up a *Washington Post* outside Theater's headquarters and now sat in his office reading the front page story.

Theater Electronics' CEO Murdered in Blue Ridge Estate

Charles Keane, Founder and President of Theater Electronics, a supplier of military electronics components, was found murdered last night in his home outside Riverton, Virginia. State troopers at the scene stated that they had responded to a silent security alarm at the Blue Ridge estate around 7:30. On arrival, they found Keane dead in his study, the apparent victim of an intruder. He had been fatally struck once on the head. There were no other occupants of the house at the time and no signs of any struggle. Police have been unable to determine if there was any property stolen.

Charles Keane founded the company in 1986, . . .

Sources close to the investigation are linking the murder with a fatal automobile accident on Scenic View Road, only two miles from Keane's estate. The driver, Theodore Lombard, 29, of Arlington, Virginia, was an employee of Theater Electronics. There are unconfirmed reports that a fireplace poker, matching a set in Keane's home, was found in the wreckage of Lombard's late model Audi. Residents near the scene placed the accident around the same time as Keane's security alarm. No motive for the attack on the well-known executive has been presented.

So far, so good.

Elizabeth, Greystone's secretary, called on the intercom and announced that Agent Jefferson had arrived. The executive made him wait an additional five minutes as he prepared for the interrogation. He knew he should be questioning, but not pushy; helpful, but not too much so; concerned, but not obsessive. And he couldn't volunteer answers that would imply too much knowledge. He'd let Jefferson take the lead and direct the conversation from there.

Elizabeth escorted the man into the office. Greystone motioned to the couch and the six foot four inch State Police officer sat down at one end. He was dressed comfortably in a herringbone sport jacket and khaki pants, but no amount of casual attire could hide the powerful neck and shoulders, huge leathery hands, and tell-tale bulge under his left arm.

Greystone sat in one of the adjacent chairs.

"Thank you for seeing me this morning, Mr. Greystone."

"Of course. Is it Agent Jefferson? I had expected someone in uniform."

"The Troopers are in uniform, sir. Agents from the Bureau of Criminal Investigation may wear civilian clothes." Jefferson pulled out his notebook. "I think we can keep this fairly short."

"That would be appreciated. As you would expect, things are a little upset this morning."

Jefferson nodded and began. "How long had you worked for Mr. Keane?"

"I joined Theater in 1998. I have worked for Charles since then."

"What kind of a man was he?"

"Charles Keane was the consummate business man. He was completely committed to this company. Since his wife died, he didn't take time for much else."

"Did he have any enemies that you knew of?"

"Charles had made his share of enemies in the business sense, but I can't think of anyone that would want to harm him." Time to get some information of his own. "How was he killed?"

"The coroner hasn't released an official cause of death, but it looked like a severe blow to the head."

Greystone puckered his face. "How awful."

"As I'm sure you know, Theodore Lombard was also killed last night in a car accident. I believe he worked for you?"

Greystone nodded. "Yes, Ted was my executive assistant. I hired him about three years ago."

"It appears that Mr. Lombard was at Mr. Keane's estate last night. Do you know why he would have gone out there?"

"No, I can't imagine. I thought he was doing some work for me last night."

"What work was that?" Jefferson flipped a page in his notebook and wrote something.

"I'm testifying at a Senate hearing later today. Ted was helping me with my testimony."

"You weren't working with him?"

"No. We had developed a final draft, but there was some background data that I needed. Ted was supposed to do the research while I polished the draft."

The Agent flipped another page. "It was rather late when you returned my call last night. Were you home all evening?"

Jefferson was finally getting to what Greystone knew was the point of the interview: his alibi. He paused, then began the script. "Actually, I had a dinner engagement in McLean at 8:30. I had just returned home when I got your message."

"And before that?"

"Home, working on my testimony. I started about 5:30. I checked some data on our corporate files, then did some additional Internet research. I was on until approximately 8:00." Greystone paused, letting the officer complete his notes. Then he added, "You should be able to check the access logs."

"I doubt that will be necessary, sir." Jefferson went back to the beginning of his notebook and continued in the same monotone. "I understand you and Mr. Keane were in a meeting yesterday?"

Greystone's heart beat a little faster. He was surprised Jefferson had found out about the meeting. *Who else had the cop already interviewed?*

"Ah, yes. Our Board of Directors met yesterday afternoon."

"Did anything unusual happen in the meeting?"

Greystone considered his response. There was no point in raising anything that would lead to further questions. Keep it simple. "Not that I remember. It was a fairly typical agenda."

Jefferson sat back in the chair, then looked directly into Greystone's eyes. "I understand you and Mr. Keane had a disagreement over a proposal."

Greystone managed to hold back his shock. Where had the cop gotten that detail? His pulse crept higher as he tried to put on a smile.

"Hardly a major disagreement, Agent Jefferson. Like most senior executives, Charles and I disagreed in some areas and agreed in others. I think we got along fairly well most of the time."

"I see," Jefferson replied with a slight nod. "Who will take over the company now that Mr. Keane is gone?"

"That's entirely up to the Board," Greystone replied confidently. This, at least, was a question he had anticipated. "I would expect Julius Flitterman will take the reins initially. He is already the Chairman. But, that's a topic that we will be discussing at our meeting this afternoon. There are a number of legal issues that we have to resolve."

Time to turn the discussion to a different direction. "When would you expect the investigation to be complete?"

"That's hard to say, sir. Probably only a week or so if everything falls into place. We would like to examine Mr. Keane's and Mr. Lombard's files. Hard copy and electronic. I trust that won't be a problem?"

"I don't believe so, but you'll have to contact Victor Sutherland, our lawyer, and he will get you everything you need. There is the matter of corporate confidentiality, of course."

"Yes, we understand that very well, Mr. Greystone. Thank you for your time."

Jefferson closed his notebook, straightened his coat and stood. Greystone relaxed slightly and rose to escort the officer out.

Pausing at the door, Jefferson said, "One last question, Mr. Greystone. Can you think of any reason why Ted Lombard would want to kill Mr. Keane?"

Greystone shook his head. "None whatsoever. Ted was always an excellent employee. I can't imagine why he might do something like that."

"Did Mr. Lombard have any close friends here?" Jefferson continued. "Anyone he might confide in?"

"Ted was a fairly private person. He didn't spend too much time

with others in the office. Except for . . ." Greystone hesitated and
waited for the expected reply.

"Yes, Mr. Greystone?"

"Well, there was a rumor he had . . . a friendship with Mr.
Keane's secretary, Clarice Montonet. Nothing I could confirm,
however. You will handle that confidentially, Agent Jefferson?" He
put on his best concerned look. "No use in upsetting Clarice any
further."

"Of course, Mr. Greystone. We handle these issues quite
frequently. I think that's about all for now. Thank you again for
your time." Jefferson offered his hand. "I may need to check back
with you in the next few days. You will be in the area?"

"Oh yes. I doubt any of us will be leaving the office for quite a
while."

Greystone watched as the huge State Police officer walked into
the secretarial area then turn and head for Keane's office.
Sutherland was pacing behind the glass. He hoped Victor was up to
the task.

He slumped back in the couch and wiped a few drops of
perspiration from his forehead.

That should take care of the police. Now back to more
important items. He rang Elizabeth to call for the limo.

*   *   *

Braxton rubbed his bloodshot eyes. The evidence area was dark and
dirty, and just trying to read the contents of Ramal's files had given
him a splitting headache. His primary illumination was a bare overhead bulb hanging over the desk from an electric cord. Cobwebs
arced gracefully from the light into the dark corners of the room,
testaments to the perseverance of the room's permanent inhabitants. Braxton peered up at the intricate pattern and concluded it
looked exactly like a map of the Internet backbone. It had been a
long four hours.

He was surrounded by piles of paper and notebooks, the legacy
of graduate student Mohammed Ramal. Fowler's team had gathered
what they could from the bombed apartment, added everything
from Ramal's desk at GW, and brought it to the station. A brief
report summarized the efforts of the FBI computer experts. It was
at best a cursory analysis. There were no indices or abstracts on the

computer files. Simple directory and text listings were somewhere in the stack on his left.

Braxton had only had time to scan the voluminous material. Ramal was a classic technology pack rat. He had kept old exams, writing assignments, and lab reports all catalogued and indexed in a homemade SQL data base. There were reviews from networking texts and a huge directory of what appeared to be small fragments of software programs. Braxton assumed that each fragment performed some specific network analysis or checked for a particular message state. It was a tool kit of routines for Ramal's research. All in all, quite a portfolio for a "passable" graduate student.

Just before 10:00, Braxton had pulled out his cell phone.

"Fowler," came the growl after Braxton had dialed.

"Good morning, Detective. Adam Braxton."

"Yeah, I know. What's the matter?"

"I've been going through Ramal's boxes. He was supposed to have a PC in his apartment, but I can't find any manuals or documentation. Is there any more evidence anywhere?"

"You got two boxes, right?"

"Yes."

"Then that's it."

"What about the FBI?"

"I said that was all. Us and the FBI."

"But there's also no disks or memory sticks. Ramal would have had to backup his system onto *something*. Are you sure this is everything?"

"That's all we found Braxton. Weren't there some documents there? I remember reading some kind of revolutionary crap."

"I did find a printout of the *Anarchist Cookbook*, but nobody with any sense would read it." The *Anarchist Cookbook* was a classic piece of Internet memorabilia: an anonymously written tome that contained recipes for bombs and explosives. Unfortunately, it was also dangerously inaccurate and hopelessly out-of-date. "If he was really a terrorist, he would have found better stuff on the Internet."

"Maybe that was his problem," Fowler offered. "Too lazy to look it up?"

"Possible but unlikely. He was a student for heaven's sake. He would have grown up on the Internet. You didn't find any other underground documents in either his apartment or at GW. Doesn't that seem strange to you?"

"Getting killed in an explosion seems strange to me, Braxton."
Fowler was sounding more frustrated. "You got anything else?"

He hadn't.

Braxton was supposed to track down Ramal and check out his
message. Well, he had found him, or what was left of him, and there
didn't seem to be any way of confirming his results. He couldn't
find any log of Ramal's actions and his mail file on the GW server
didn't show any related communications. It was probably time to
call this one quits.

Still, there was something about the search that kept pushing
him. He hadn't felt this driven about his work since his last project
at Century. He had solved some pretty bizarre puzzles in his career
and it felt good to be back at it. CERT/CC wouldn't care if he spent
a little longer on this one.

"Yes, one thing."

"What, Braxton?"

"Let's make that Adam, Detective. It's shorter. As I said, there's
nothing here that's out of place, but there's a lot not here that
should be. Do you really feel that this might not have been an
accident?"

"I told you all I had was a feeling. The forensic evidence
supports the bomb theory: there were no suspicious marks on the
body, just a shit load of busted bones and ripped-up tissue."

"What time was he killed?"

"The blast occurred about 7:45. We're assuming that was the
time of death. Why?"

"That's less than an hour after he sent CERT the email message.
A pretty quick change of activity. You're sure the body was Ramal?"

"Confirmed by fingerprints. You playing detective now?"

"Sorry, just curious. Did you talk to a roommate or any of
Ramal's friends that might suggest what he had been working on?"

"He lived alone and didn't seem to have any close friends."
There was a pause as if Fowler was considering something. "I did
talk with one other student who sounded like she knew him as well
as anyone. Why?"

Now he was going out on a very long limb. He hoped Fowler
wouldn't cut it off. "I'd like to find out where Ramal was working
on his projects; in his apartment or at the university. It might help
me figure out where he kept his most recent files."

The phone went silent. The request was a stretch, but if the cop wanted his help . . .

"I'll give you her name, but you didn't get it from me. You're on your own if you try to talk with her. And I want to know what you've found out. By tomorrow noon."

Fowler gave him Susan Goddard's name and address. Braxton made some final notes, re-boxed the evidence, and walked back to the evidence cage to find Waters. He hoped his next stop would fill in some crucial holes. If not, this was going to be a very short assignment.

CHAPTER 16

The Russell Building, Washington, D.C.
Wednesday, 12:30 p.m.

"PLEASE HAVE A seat, Mr. Greystone," the receptionist recited. A brass name plate proclaimed her to be Camille Johnson. She looked about seventy, was dressed in the finest Washington fashion and greeted constituents with gracious Southern hospitality. Greystone also knew she was as sharp as a rebel bayonet to Yankees. "The Senator will be with you in a moment."

He quickly scanned the reception area trying unsuccessfully to find a place to sit that didn't look like it had been designed by the Marquis de Sade. They were all cold, hard, and painful to sit in for any period longer than a few minutes. And he had no doubt that his wait would be carefully timed by Potterfield for maximum discomfort.

He, of course, had done precisely the same thing on any number of occasions.

Potterfield was Chairman of the Senate Committee on Foreign Relations. A frighteningly powerful position controlling a committee with jurisdiction over nearly all of the United States' relationships with other countries. The Committee oversees diplomatic policy, investigates breaches of international law, approves foreign assistance, and sanctions military interventions including declarations of war.

In the three years that he had chaired the Committee, Potterfield had led a strong pro-business agenda, implementing a new Republican-driven international industrial policy. Not a policy that positioned the government against the free-market, but one that increased international commerce based on strategic economic and humanitarian assistance. And one that greatly inflated the coffers of favored companies.

Potterfield's current focus was passage of the Senate's *Promoting Freedom and Democracy Bill*, or the *Potterfield Bill* as it was more commonly called after its principal author. The Bill would address the third leg of the Republicans' political stool: military assistance. It would open the doors to aggressive export of US military equipment and technology in support of regime defense, and potentially regime change, all in the name of promulgation of American democratic values.

To some, the policy would be a reaffirmation of the country's commitment to freeing the world of terrorism and tyranny, with the added benefit of not endangering American lives. To others, it was an excuse to rain death on today's political enemies, while ignoring the inevitable bite-in-the-ass from tomorrow's dictator that recent history guaranteed. To Greystone, it was simply the opportunity of a lifetime.

The Chairman had called a lunch recess to the hearing after Greystone's testimony ended and the executive had wandered the halls of the Russell Building for another ten minutes before discovering Potterfield's office. Ample time for the Senator to negotiate well-worn passages and disappear into his oak-paneled fortress.

Now, Potterfield's receptionist sat like a sentry behind her desk guarding the entrance to her sovereign's inner sanctum. The dour look on her face would be enough to stop anyone short of a Special Forces Drill Sergeant.

Overall, he had been pleased with his morning's effort. His prepared statement had gone smoothly and the questions he had fielded before the recess had been expectedly simplistic and easily handled. Still, even he had to admit it had sent a chill down his spine to be there. The Russell Caucus Room had been the scene of momentous events for the nation: the hearing on the sinking of the *HMS Titanic*, the infamous witch-hunts by Senator Joseph McCarthy, and the Watergate and Iran-Contra investigations. Greystone had been both awed and jealous of the unbridled power that had permeated the room. It was time to put some of that influence to his advantage.

Looking around the reception area, Greystone noted it had been appointed for maximum impact on visitors. Pictures of Potterfield with political leaders including Nixon, Reagan, Thatcher, both Bushes and even Khrushchev, hung prominently on the walls. These were interspersed with pieces of campaign memorabilia commemorating his years in public service and sappy letters from grateful constituents thanking him for interceding on their behalf. More likely, the Senator had simply ordered one of his aides to pressure some poor civil servant.

One particularly ugly object d'art was a garishly painted water buffalo that had been presented to Potterfield by the President of the Congo for "exemplary services rendered in support of the people of the Congo". As Greystone remembered it, Potterfield had supported an arms deal with Congolese rebels that had ultimately resulted in the deaths of 20,000 civilians.

"Mr. Greystone, the Senator will see you now," said the belle without glancing up from her work. "First door on your right."

* * *

While Greystone had been left to ponder the walls of the reception area, Senator David Potterfield, Senior Senator from Virginia and Chairman of the Senate Committee on Foreign Relations, had been reviewing his file on the executive.

Robert Greystone had come from a well-to-do New York family with homes in the City and the Connecticut shore. His father had been a financier and his mother a prominent socialite. The family philosophy was decidedly conservative Republican. He was an only child, and a late arrival at that, an obvious surprise to the middle-aged Mr. and Mrs. Greystone. They had given him the best education their money could buy, first at Andover Academy and then Harvard. Greystone had subsequently risen rapidly through a number of technology companies to his present position. He lived comfortably but had recently gone through a costly divorce. The report noted no known indiscretions.

Since Theater Electronics was based in Potterfield's home state, the two men had met on a few occasions, primarily fund raisers and lobbying events. Potterfield had pegged him as a slippery, ambitious businessman, just the kind to trade his company's support of the pending Bill for a few legislative favors. In a hastily added final sentence, Potterfield noted the recent death of Greystone's boss.

When Greystone had called the Senator's office and requested a meeting, Potterfield had graciously scheduled time over the noon recess. He was intrigued as to what the executive was looking for.

There was a knock on the door, and Potterfield replied with a homey, "C'mon in."

The Chairman's inner office was even more plush and ostentatious than the reception area. The walls were paneled in deep golden oak with intricately carved accents and the floor was covered in a rich gold broadloom. More photographs and memorabilia of the owner's political escapades decorated the walls and available cabinet tops. His desk was massive, taking up most of the back of the room. And behind the desk, huge windows offered a view of the Capitol dome rising over verdant trees and lawn, a proper reminder of the power held by the office's inhabitant. Off to the right a small sitting area had been created where informal conversations could be held, but Potterfield motioned Greystone to an elaborately-carved, and exceedingly uncomfortable, chair facing the Senator's desk.

"Senator Potterfield," Greystone began. "I very much appreciate you agreeing to see me on such short notice."

"It's nothin' son. I'm always happy to meet with representatives from the business community. But first, do let me express my condolences on the very untimely death of your CEO, Mr. Keane." Potterfield put on his best southern drawl and fatherly countenance.

"Thank you very much, Senator. I will convey your sentiment to our Board. Charles was a unique individual and he will certainly be missed. But I know he would not want his death to stand in the way of our small contribution to your important legislative efforts."

Potterfield's initial evaluation of the executive sounded spot-on. Time to toss the crap back. "The Committee does appreciate Theater's support of our Bill, Mr. Greystone. You received a very positive reaction, at least from most of the Committee." Potterfield attempted a smile but once it materialized on his craggy face it looked more like a sneer. "And I must say you handled Senator Hastings' inquisition very well."

"Thank you, Senator. I will pass along your kind comments to my research team. They were able to anticipate most of his arguments."

Donald Hastings, Senior Senator from Illinois, was a knowledgeable and influential member of the Committee. Unfortunately, the Democrat was also a lily-white dove, eschewing any form of military action or support. He and Potterfield had been at each other's throats for decades and the spectacle of the hearings on the *Potterfield Bill* were a perfect arena.

Potterfield shrugged. "My esteemed colleague does see things somewhat differently when it comes to supporting emerging democracies," he explained. "I believe we have to promote good old American values around the world."

"And we all appreciate your efforts, Senator. Our continuing support of your work is what I would like to discuss with you; how together we could achieve our common goals for eliminating terrorism and supporting true democracies across the globe."

"*My* goal is very simple, Mr. Greystone," Potterfield said, his eyes never leaving those of his visitor. "I want America to remain the beacon of hope for all people. To promote, and support, democracy and freedom everywhere. And to fight those that would enslave and oppress behind whatever flag. Do y'all have some ideas on how that might be accomplished?"

"As I outlined in my testimony this morning Senator, I believe the greatest impediment to adoption of your Bill is the concern by some parties, even members of your own party, that we would be releasing technology of critical importance to our national security. 'Opening the kimono too far', as they might say. These individuals adamantly support the existing ITAR 121 and Suite B restrictions."

Potterfield nodded politely while trying desperately to remember the last briefing his aides had given him. Military communication and intelligence systems were controlled by a bewildering set of regulations and classifications. ITAR 121 was Part 121 of the *International Traffic in Arms Regulations* document, better known as the *United States Munitions List*. This tome listed all the types of material under US export control. Included were guns, ammunition, tanks, aircraft carriers and encrypted communications equipment. State Department approval was needed for any distribution of listed equipment.

For communications equipment, the approved levels of encryption were further specified by Suite B, an encryption classification system developed by the NSA.

Passage of Potterfield's Bill was threatened by these two substantial constraints. Both doves and hawks were reticent to allow export of critical defense technologies even in the name of democracy.

That was the bad news. The good news was that the ITAR restrictions were enforced by the State Department. *His* State Department. They approved munition shipments. If the Bill could be passed, Potterfield could see that State toed the line.

"A concern you presented eloquently this morning," Potterfield finally offered. "Do you have any suggestions on how these obstacles could be removed?"

"Actually, not at all, Senator," Greystone replied calmly. "I believe we should embrace them."

Potterfield felt blood rushing to his face. *Why is this lunatic wasting my time?*

"What I mean, Senator," the executive continued with a conspiratorial grin, "is that we should use them to our advantage. Don't change the rules but add to them. Amend Part 121 to allow a new class of equipment to be exported while still limiting distribution of our most advanced technology. Our international friends get the assistance they need, and your political colleagues get the protection they demand."

Potterfield leaned back in his chair. *So the shark really does have something to offer.* It was a tempting idea. Use the existing policy structure to support his objectives. But could it really work?

"An interesting idea, son. But the issues involved are quite complex. Legally and technically. Involving difficult areas such as encryption methods and verifications." Potterfield paused and placed his hands on his desk. "Or so I understand. My office certainly doesn't have the expertise to dictate to the NSA on technology, or the State Department on verification and enforcement."

Greystone leaned forward and met Potterfield's cold stare. His voice was tense as he continued. "Let me be clear, Senator. I would not be here if I didn't have a specific proposal. It uses existing NSA evaluations and industry-standard protocols. It all depends on the way the pieces are put together.

"It is possible to define a new class of command-and-control equipment that relies on specific communication protocols. Protocols that are complementary to those DoD uses, but are not quite as advanced. The new equipment would still be far superior to anything our partners, or their enemies, have currently available."

Potterfield had been sitting quietly as the executive made his pitch. It was an arrogant proposal, but one that might resolve the deadlock in his Committee. He wondered how far Greystone had taken his thinking.

"So the modified equipment is exported and we keep the really good stuff, right Mr. Greystone?"

"I don't know that I would have quite phrased it that way, Senator, but yes. I believe such an amendment might appease some of your colleagues."

One of Potterfield's gifts was his ability to read people. It had served him well throughout his career in this snake pit of a city. Greystone was holding something back. And he thought he knew exactly what is was.

"And might that allow us to . . . perhaps *monitor* these pieces of equipment for proper operation?"

"An interesting observation, Senator." Potterfield saw the executive relax. He had guessed right. "I will need to check with my designers, but that might be possible. It would certainly assist us in supporting our allies."

And eavesdrop on their operations, Potterfield thought excitedly.

"There has been some discussion of new munition classes in the Committee, Mr. Greystone. But I will not wait for endless engineering studies and prototype development before we proceed. Y'all know that your beltway friends would bleed us dry in proposals and prototypes before one piece of equipment ever made it to our friends."

"We must protect democracy *today*, Mr. Greystone." Potterfield slapped his hands on the desk. His voice had lost it lazy twang. "Before these damn terrorists take over everything we hold dear."

The executive sat motionless, seemingly shocked by Potterfield's outburst. He finally took a breath and replied. "I understand Senator. You are right, of course. That is why Theater has invested in some, ah, preliminary research. I wanted to meet with you today to discuss our results. I must ask, however, that this be kept in confidence until appropriate arrangements can be made for its disclosure. Is that satisfactory?"

Well, the weasel does have something to sell. Potterfield sat back and crossed his arms over his chest. "This office will keep any such information private, Mr. Greystone. As long as it breaks no laws, of course."

"Certainly not, Senator." Greystone leaned forward and lowered his voice, apparently hoping to heighten the importance of his disclosure. "Over the past few months, I have built a coalition of companies to prototype a set of advanced command-and-control components. These components are built on a new architecture, implementing the vision we have been discussing.

"The results have been quite extraordinary. I can without any doubt confirm the viability of the specifications we have developed. Should a similar set of specifications become law, we will be able to deploy production units within the year. As permitted by your legislation, of course."

Potterfield sat poker-faced. Greystone was saying that he had already developed military-grade products based on a set of almost-state-of the-art specifications. If those specifications suddenly became law, he and his partners had an insurmountable lead in the market. The business potential was staggering.

"What other companies are involved in this coalition, son?"

"I'm not at liberty to give their names at this time, Senator. As I'm sure you're aware, this has been an expensive undertaking that no one company was able to take on themselves. Full production will incur even more cost. We would like to create a separate company to license the new technology and manufacture the product. We cannot take this step without legislative clarity around the details of the implementation strategy. Our risk would be too high. If that clarity could be secured, then there would be significant opportunities for forward-thinking investors."

So we finally get to the bottom line. But why would he have ever embarked on such a risky investment?

"You paint a very positive picture, Mr. Greystone. Perhaps we should re-evaluate our position on creating a new equipment class. As they say, 'the devil is in the details'. I would like to have a member of my staff review your technical specifications. It could be that we would need to make some changes before presenting to my committee. Would that be agreeable?"

"Certainly, Senator. I would be happy to work with your representative. We only want what is best for the country after all."

Of course you do, son. Potterfield was momentarily distracted by a flashing on his small computer screen. "If you'll excuse me, Mr. Greystone, I have a message in my private email account. It will only take a minute." He turned to the screen and his keyboard.

"Of course, Senator. I had no idea you were so familiar with the technology."

"Oh, it's really nothin'" Potterfield said with a plaster smile. "I do try to keep up with all the latest gadgets."

Actually, it had taken Potterfield's Chief of Staff three weeks to train him on the PC's operation and he could still only read his mail. But he liked showing off his expertise to visitors from the computer industry. It supported his image as a knowledgeable, progressive Senator.

Potterfield carefully clicked through the menus with his mouse. He stared transfixed as the message filled the screen, trying to stay calm despite the knife of fear slicing through his gut. Thankfully, the screen-saver finally blanked the image and he slowly turned back to his visitor. As he repositioned the chair, his finger slid along the bottom edge of his desk and touched a small button.

"Nothing urgent, Mr. Greystone. Now, you were saying?"

CHAPTER 17

The Russell Building, Washington, D.C.
Wednesday, 1:00 p.m.

BARCLAY "NICK" NICHOLSON heard the buzzer and again prepared
to save his boss from the latest national emergency. Last week it had
been an incredibly boring constituent from Charlottesville who had
wanted a noise ban on the fraternities at the University. Such were
the duties of a Senator's Chief of Staff.

Nicholson stood up and deftly slid two fingers down the crease on
each pants leg. Then he unhooked his jacket from behind the door,
slipped it on, and peered into the small mirror mounted there for
such occasions. The silk Armani suit hung lightly from his broad
shoulders. Only five foot ten, he kept in good physical condition
thanks to almost daily workouts at The Iron Body in Crystal City. His
features were what most would call ordinary, but he had never had
any trouble attracting the women he wanted. And one look from his
steel gray eyes was usually enough to discourage any other suitors.

Satisfied with the result of his preparations, he grabbed his iPad
and headed for the door.

* * *

Potterfield turned on hearing a knock on his door and watched as
an elegantly-dressed black man entered from the waiting room. The
man gave a quick glance toward the visitor and walked directly to
the desk.

"Excuse me, Senator," Nicholson said, "but you are due for
lunch with Representative Kantor. He's waiting for you now."

Looking surprised, Potterfield glanced at his watch then quickly
rose from his chair and moved toward Greystone.

"Mr. Greystone, this is my Chief of Staff, Barclay Nicholson. I'm afraid I simply must bring our conversation to a close. My counterpart in the House wants to discuss the progress of the Bill. Your ideas are quite interesting and I would definitely like to learn more. Please schedule some time with Barclay to bring him up to date. Camille can help with the details." He paused and then added, "I trust these new developments will remain between us for the moment?"

"Of course, Senator." Greystone rose and shook Potterfield's hand, then the newcomer's. "Mr. Nicholson. Pleased to meet you. Until next time, gentlemen." A slight nod and he disappeared out the door.

Nicholson pulled a more comfortable chair from the sitting area and sat down. "How did the meeting go, David? Did he have anything new to say?"

Potterfield winced at the use of his first name. Nicholson always used "Senator" in public but when they were alone he reverted to a familiarity Potterfield forbade with the rest of his staff. Unfortunately, he and his Chief of Staff shared too much history and he had given up trying to change his friend.

Potterfield had pulled Nicholson off the streets in Richmond almost forty-five years before. As a successful young lawyer, Potterfield had seen politics in his future and realized he needed someone who could work behind the scenes. Someone who could act as part bodyguard, part investigator, and part middleman. Nicholson had been a wise-talking street punk who had been picked up for numbers running. His mother had a friend, who had a sister, who knew Potterfield's aunt and the young lawyer had been talked into taking the case. He had gotten the kid off with probation, his fee set at one year's servitude to the lawyer.

The teenager had been a real problem at first, but had eventually adapted and become an asset to the practice. Potterfield had seen something of himself in the youth and eventually mentored his advancement through high school, and then a prominent university.

Nicholson was now an irreplaceable asset. He managed the campaigns, prepared background material, and ran the Senator's three offices. His degree was in Management but he was knowledgeable in technology and was surprisingly conversant in computers. Much of the wording for the *Potterfield Bill* had come from his Chief of Staff.

The association had been equally valuable to Nicholson. He owned an elegant townhouse in Alexandria and was seen as one of Washington's most eligible bachelors. His affluence surprised even Potterfield, given the paltry salary the Senator conferred on his staff. Potterfield knew better than to question his Chief of Staff too closely, however. Good help was hard to find and he knew everyone needed to keep a few secrets.

"Greystone did have something quite interesting that I want you to follow up on later. But what I need *most* is for you to explain this." Potterfield's tone was undeniably accusatory.

He spun the monitor around, hit a key, and let Nicholson read the message.

```
From: an6845@anon.trans.ua

To: richmondeagle@potterfield.senate.gov

Subject: Senator Lynch

Senator Potterfield,

Your ruin of Senator Lynch can no longer be toler-
ated. We have evidence of your complicity in his
death. You can no longer be allowed to represent
the people of Virginia. If you do not wish to have
further information on your activities released to
the public, you must resign in the next 60 days. We
will contact you again in the near future.

Citizens for Responsible Government
```

"What's this about, Nick? What information could they have? You said we buried everything about the Lynch affair."

"We did, David. We destroyed all the police reports. It all went away twenty years ago."

"Apparently not far enough away! You're the computer expert, who the hell is this 'Citizens for Responsible Government'?"

"It's from a remailer, David," Nicholson replied calmly. "There's no way of telling who sent it."

Nicholson's attitude was driving Potterfield crazy. "What do you mean there's no way of telling? I know everybody else that sends me shit on this damn computer. It's government issue!"

Nicholson closed his eyes and shook his head. A gesture that only made Potterfield madder.

"I know, David. But this came from a special system designed to give anonymity to individuals. You send it a mail message and a forwarding address. It strips off your return address and substitutes an ID, a kind of pseudonym, like this 'an6845'. Then it forwards the original message. If we reply, the remailer might send it on to the originator but we can't find out who he is."

"What the hell good is that?"

"Well it does have its uses," Nicholson continued as if he was lecturing to a class of high school students. "Unfortunately whistle blowing and blackmail are among them. Remember that sexual harassment suit against Senator Gillingham last year? It all got started after some anonymous emails."

"Can't you trace it? Can the FBI trace it? It ought to be illegal!"

"They're not illegal, although most countries have put a lot of pressure on the owners. Theoretically, you can get a warrant to determine the sender's identity, but that's pretty hard to do here. And you don't really want to get the authorities involved, do you?"

Potterfield was about to explode. He shook his head.

"Okay," Nicolson held up his hands in surrender. "I'll see what I can do. Most of the original remailer sites were shut down years ago, but new ones pop up all the time. See this 'ua' in the address? This remailer is in the Ukraine. I doubt they have a very active cyber-crime unit.

"If the remailer's not encrypted I should be able to trace the message. Give me a couple of days.

"This 'Citizens for Responsible Government' is likely just a front for some frustrated citizen. Who do *you* think might be behind this?"

"I don't have a goddamn idea," Potterfield spit back. "And how did they get my private mail address? I can't have this coming up again, Nick. Use your contacts and figure out who sent this. If all they have is hearsay we can probably ride it out. But if you missed anything else . . ."

"I *didn't* miss anything, David," Nicholson replied firmly. "I'll forward the message to my account and get started." He pulled the keyboard over and typed some commands. "And I'll delete your copy just to be safe. Anything else?"

"That seems to be enough don't you think? Just make this problem go away. For good."

He waved for Nicholson to leave and dropped his head in his hands. No one had ever threatened him directly in his forty years in office. Now someone was doing it in a goddamn electronic mail message.

Certainly there had been a few attacks on his reputation at election time, but the sources of the trouble had been easily identified and the innuendoes put to rest, so to speak. This was different. His attacker was unknown and had access to information no one should have.

He felt the fear of the threat as deeply as he had in '74 when he had brought charges against a white cop that beat one of his neighbors to death. "Stay out of this boy. It's none of your business," they had warned him. Then they beat him unconscious just to be sure he didn't miss the point.

But this wasn't another frustrated constituent. This was a threat to him and his dream. His afro was shorter and grayer than when he started in practice, but his mind was just as quick and his instincts just as sharp. He'd find a way to respond to this threat as he had the many others in his life.

After Potterfield had gotten the conviction, the cop had been gang raped then killed in a predominantly black prison.

* * *

Nicholson sat at his desk and reread the message. He couldn't imagine who could have sent it. It had to be from someone Internet-savvy, certainly not a typical government employee. They had to have knowledge of the remailer environment and the ability to find Potterfield's private account name. As well as having access to the Lynch history.

He had spent all of his adult life saving the Senator's butt. And he was good at that job. Over the past two decades he had been privy to more national secrets than he cared to remember. He had even played a role in a number of them. But lately he was feeling tired. The game held less passion; he was simply going through the motions.

It was ironic being on the defensive. It might be interesting for a change.

He turned to his desk and started typing.

CHAPTER 18

Georgetown University, Washington, D.C.
Wednesday, 2:45 p.m.

GEORGETOWN UNIVERSITY SITS on one hundred lush, green acres overlooking the Potomac River. Founded in 1789, it is the most well-known, and the most competitive, university in the District of Columbia. The campus has a quiet intensity about it, the students and professors going about the work of politics and government with a seriousness lacking at other institutions of higher learning.

The late afternoon breeze was cool and refreshing as Braxton sat back against a sprawling oak in Georgetown's quad. Around him stood four jewels of the campus: Dahlgren Chapel, Old North, Maguire Hall and finally, Healy Hall, the imposing Gothic stone centerpiece of the university. Taking in the serene dignity of the campus, he understood the awe it inspired even in this jaded city.

Before he had left police headquarters, Braxton had tried the number Fowler had given him. A pleasant female voice had answered and identified herself as Susan Goddard. He had explained that he worked for CERT/CC and was looking for some information on Ramal's research. She had agreed to meet him at three o'clock by the fountain in the quad. He was fifteen minutes early and he could easily keep the landmark in view from his position under the tree.

It had been a busy day. First the work of reviewing Ramal's files, the conversations with Fowler, the contact with Goddard and then a completely unproductive meeting with Ramal's advisor, Professor Eric Mendoza.

He had taken the opportunity to drop by Mendoza's office at

GW after a quick lunch. It had been immediately obvious that Cabot had alerted him of Braxton's presence. Mendoza spouted the same CYA party-line and claimed ignorance of details of Ramal's activities. He must have been one helluva advisor.

The lone positive note from the meeting was that Mendoza had mentioned that the FBI had *copied*, not removed, all of Ramal's server files. The original files would still be in the center's disk farm. Braxton had immediately called Williams and verified that Ramal's account had not been deleted. It hadn't taken much to persuade the SysOp to give him access privileges to the files. Everyone wanted to play cyber-sleuth.

He had done a quick inventory of the account and there still didn't seem to be any trail of Ramal's actions. What had led him to send the message? That lack of a record was confusing; Ramal had definitely sent the email just before the fatal explosion.

CERT/CC did, of course, receive a lot of crackpot messages and this could have been another. But Flanagan felt it was real. Braxton sensed that from his initial conversation and her recent request. Now Fowler was suggesting that the death may not have been an accident. Another coincidence? Braxton had been an engineer too long to overlook coincidences.

Then there was the money. He had never really thought much about getting paid before he was fired. A salary had always been there and he simply accepted it. He did his work, solved his problems, and reported to his management. He had had the freedom and expertise to work in areas he liked. The relationship between his work and the money that was deposited in his account every month seemed a remote, ethereal one.

The past two years had taught him the folly of that oversight, and he did not intend to ignore it again. There were still a number of avenues he could check out and as long as CERT/CC would . . .

"Mr. Braxton?"

He glanced up and saw a figure looking down at him. She, he could tell from the voice, was outlined in the glare of the afternoon sun. He checked his watch and saw that it was ten minutes past three.

"Miss Goddard?" he asked.

"Yes," the voice responded. "I waited for a while at the fountain then saw someone under the tree. I thought I'd give you a try. You looked a little old to be a student."

Braxton rose slowly and brushed himself off, her words amplifying the stiffness in his joints. "I'm sorry. I guess I was daydreaming and lost track of the time. Thank you for coming."

He could see her clearly now and liked what he saw. She was tall and slim, wearing stylish dark slacks and a purple knit sweater. Her blond hair was pulled back into a short ponytail that swung as she spoke. She had a very pretty face: oval with fine, delicate features, high cheekbones and clear blue eyes.

Rather than the mousy undergraduate he had envisioned, she was quite attractive, with an air of maturity he didn't remember in college coeds. She was smiling, obviously pleased at having caught him unawares, but was keeping her distance.

"I've talked to the police twice now," Goddard began. "I don't know what else I can tell you about the explosion."

"I'm actually more interested in the work Mr. Ramal was doing than in his . . . accident," Braxton explained. "He had sent us an email and we've been trying to get in touch with him ever since." Braxton glanced around at the milling students and thought that she might be more comfortable moving around. "Shall we take a walk?"

"Sure," she replied, and they started back across the quad toward Healy Hall. "I don't know that I can tell you much about Mohammed's work. Most of it was beyond me. What was in his email?"

"He said that he had found a problem with the Internet gateways on campus. He hadn't sent any other information and I wanted to discuss this with him. Did Mr. Ramal talk to you about what he was working on?"

"He had just started doing his thesis research with Prof. Mendoza. It was something to do with communication lines and traffic patterns I think he said. He was really into it. I could hardly pull him away for our project." She paused and considered her next question. "What would the message mean?"

"It could be nothing. But it could mean that someone had gained unauthorized access to some of the university's computers. That's what we're trying to figure out."

She stopped and turned to face him. "You mean some kind of hacker is breaking into our systems?"

Damn. CERT would have a meltdown if he was responsible for starting a rumor of a break-in at Georgetown. He had to redirect

Goddard. "Possibly, but we're really not sure and I haven't been able to find any record of Mr. Ramal's work. You were going to visit him that night?"

"Yes, we had a project in a multimedia course we were taking. He studied a lot at his apartment, so every once and awhile I'd go over there to work. He had lots of books and references."

"He had computer materials? Did he keep them in the apartment?"

She scowled at him. "Yes. Isn't that what I said?"

Quit trying to play detective. Just get to the point.

"Yes, you did. I'm sorry, but the police didn't find any computer books or disks in the apartment. Could he have taken them anywhere else?"

Goddard's ponytail swung provocatively as she shook her head. "I don't know where. Mohammed didn't like Prof. Mendoza all that much and he didn't get along with the other graduate students. He did most of his work at the library or at home. He had a stack of books and computer manuals right next to his desk. We were always going through them for ideas. What would have happened to them?" A sad expression appeared on her face. "Could his research have anything to do with his death?"

He was mad at himself for upsetting her. "I really don't know, Miss Goddard. I'm not a policeman. I'm just trying to find out if there's any information that would help explain his message."

"I understand, Mr. Braxton. But I'm afraid that's all I know. I do wish I could help more." She looked straight at him. "Mohammed was a good friend. I don't believe that he was a terrorist."

"I can see that. I'll talk with Detective Fowler and see if he can make any sense of this. If we find anything out I'll get back to you, okay?"

"Yes, I would like that." The smile finally reappeared. He liked that.

"If you think of anything else, please do give me a call." He handed her his card. "Thank you again, Miss Goddard. I am very sorry about your friend."

"Thank you." She glanced down at his card. "Oh, you're from Cambridge."

"Yes, why? Do you get up there at all?"

"Sometimes," she said hesitantly. "I have friends in Boston."

"Then perhaps we'll run into each other."

"Perhaps." She turned and walked back toward Maguire Hall.

Braxton watched as she joined a group of other students and disappeared into the building. Why was he so concerned about how she felt? She was attractive, very attractive actually, but she was just a student.

Of course she was a *graduate* student. How old was she? Twenty-four? No, she looked more mature than that. Twenty-six?

Enough! He really had been out of circulation for too long. There was no point in worrying about his social life now. The investigation had enough problems already.

He headed back through Healy Hall to 37th Street and flagged a cab for Reagan National. Resting in the back of the taxi, he replayed Goddard's words, searching for some hidden sign of encouragement.

It would be nice to see her again.

CHAPTER 19

JULIUS FLITTERMAN CALLED the Board to order at four o'clock sharp.

"I would first like to express my sorrow at the loss of a close colleague and good friend. Charles was an innovative founder and a diligent President, and I will miss his counsel greatly." He paused for the other members around the table to say their silent eulogies before continuing. "Unfortunately, we do not have the luxury to mourn his loss at this time. We have responsibilities to the employees and the shareholders to keep this business afloat. I want us to review the status of the situation, and then develop a plan for an orderly transition. Robert, what have you been able to find out from the police?"

Flitterman had discussed his approach with Greystone when the Senior Vice President had returned from the Hill. The Chairman would call on the Board members to provide their personal views of the catastrophe. He would then identify the areas needing greatest attention and make Board assignments to manage the issues in the short term. Decisions on the long term leadership of the company would wait until the aftershocks had subsided and operations were stable.

Greystone rose from his seat. "It appears that Charles was killed by Ted Lombard last night," he began, "for reasons that are unknown at this time. The State Police are continuing the investigation, and have asked to review all recent email and correspondence of both Charles and Lombard. Victor, can you please coordinate this and make sure that no sensitive documents are released?" The lawyer nodded, much calmer now that he knew he had control over at least the document access issues.

"Needless to say, everyone here is in a state of shock," Greystone continued. "We need to be sure that we get messages out to all the departments stating that the company is under strong leadership."

"Thank you, Robert." Flitterman nodded and Greystone took his seat. "Morale is critical. I'll work with Meredith to prepare a company-wide statement. I will ask that all of the senior managers meet with their staffs and see that the employees are comfortable with our plans.

"We must be understanding of the stress some may feel. Charles's secretary Clarice is taking it especially hard. I hope she can hold up. I'll need her assistance for the next few months."

Months! Greystone grabbed the table as the room spun around him. *Flitterman can't tie up the company that long. He can't possibly want to run the company himself.*

"If there is no objection, I will temporarily assume Charles' executive duties. I am not able to devote full time to the company, however, so I will need your support to manage an orderly transition. Victor will monitor the legal aspects of the case and prepare responses for the stockholders. We cannot let this tragedy compromise the company. Victor, be very careful of this thing with Lombard. If there is anything culpable as a result of the investigation, we must know immediately.

"Meredith, would you please reactivate the Audit Committee and work with Stanley on a complete analysis of our finances." Stanley Piccolo was Theater's Chief Financial Officer. "I want to be sure we are completely covered here.

"Finally, Robert, I would like you to take on full day-to-day operational responsibility. You are closer to the business than anyone." He focused his gaze on Greystone and added, "But the Board will retain ownership of strategic direction and partnerships. Is everyone clear on this?"

No one objected, and Flitterman completed the afternoon by assigning some specific reports due at the next meeting.

Greystone breathed a sigh of relief as he exited the room. The result wasn't everything he had hoped for, but he now had firm control of the operations of the company and some maneuvering room for his projects. But he still needed to get Board approval on the collaborations he had initiated. This would have to be his top priority.

He would be sure to schedule time on Flitterman's calendar later in the week.

* * *

Fowler rapped once on the door jamb and walked into Rodgers' office. His boss was sitting behind his desk talking with two business-suited men who were standing by the window. Fowler recognized them as the FBI agents who had been assigned to the Ramal killing.

He feared the worst.

"Sam," Rodgers said, "I believe you know Special Agent Brooks and Special Agent Salisbury?"

"Yes sir," Fowler gave the agents a perfunctory nod. It struck him that he had never seen just a *single* FBI agent. They always appeared in pairs. Their bosses probably didn't trust them out alone.

"We'd like to review the Ramal case," Rodgers continued. The pained look on his face didn't make the detective feel any more comfortable. "The FBI has suggested we turn it over to them and the department is inclined to agree. It appears to be terrorist-related and that's their territory. Any problem with closing it out from our end?"

This was just what he had feared. They were going to pull the case out from under him before he even had a chance. Maybe Rodgers was willing to give it away, but he wasn't going to go without a fight.

"Actually, yes, sir. It's only been a few days since the bombing. We're still getting the reports back from forensics and there are a number of loose ends that I'd like to investigate. It's possible that this was not an accident."

Salisbury and Brooks passed a knowing glance and remained silent. They had undoubtedly already told Rodgers what they thought of Fowler's theories.

"An interesting theory, Sam, but what evidence do we have? Any witnesses? Physical evidence? Papers? Anything?"

"I don't have anything hard yet, Captain. But there's a lot of crap that doesn't make sense. Books and files that should be in the apartment that aren't. Bomb paraphernalia in the wrong room. No suspicious history. All I need is a little more time to tie it together."

"So you believe, Detective Fowler," Brooks interrupted, "that there is a hidden conspiracy by unknown parties, not terrorists by the way, who blew up Ramal's apartment and planted some evidence but took other evidence away. Is there some motive for this heinous deed?"

Sarcasm dripped from the agent's voice. The bastard was almost laughing at him.

"That's enough, Special Agent Brooks," Rodgers barked. "Let's try to focus on the case. *Is* there anything else, Sam?"

"I think it has something to do with what he was working on at GW," Fowler replied. "A computer networking project." He felt the hole he was digging getting deeper. His anger was nearly out of control but he refused to give the agents the pleasure of seeing him blow up.

"Computer networking? Don't you think that is a little beyond our expertise?" Rodgers asked.

"Our Computer Crime Team studied Ramal's files thoroughly, Captain," Salisbury quickly replied to Rodgers. "We found nothing out of the ordinary."

Yeah, right, Fowler thought. The same experts who took two years to find out Aldrich Ames was a Soviet spy and left a Chinese mole at Los Alamos for a decade.

"How many open cases are you carrying at the moment, Detective?" Rodgers was delivering the coup-de-grace.

Fowler paused, took a deep breath and replied, "Eleven, Captain."

"I think we can safely let the FBI take this one off your plate, Sam. Close out your case file and leave it on my desk by the end of the day. The department appreciates all your work."

"Yes, sir."

"That's all, Sam."

Fowler turned on his heels and headed for the doorway. The smirks on the agents' faces were the last straw. He grabbed the door as he passed and slammed it shut with all the force he could muster. The door cracked against the frame and shook the privacy wall from the front of the building to the main corridor. The glass partitions chattered in their channels but stayed in one piece.

Fowler took their resilience as a sign of divine forgiveness.

The rest of the room had been prepared for the blowup. As soon as Fowler had gone in, they knew a confrontation was unavoidable. He was an old-time street cop who didn't like politics and hated the FBI. The combination in the Captain's office was incendiary.

Unfortunately, rookie Patrolman Thomas Moses hadn't seen the preliminaries and was just entering the squad room when Fowler struck. He lurched at the blast and drenched his freshly pressed uniform with a steaming cup of coffee.

Fowler made it back to his desk without further incident. For the rest of the afternoon, the corner was treated like a radioactive hot-zone by the rest of the cops.

He had been a D.C. cop for twenty-nine years. His father had been a cop; there were few better opportunities for black men in the District thirty years ago. Fowler had risen slowly, finally making Detective ten years ago. So far, his work in homicide at Investigative Services had been satisfying. His main complaint was that working out of headquarters put him farther away from the neighborhoods and closer to the bureaucrats at Police Headquarters and City Hall.

But he was nearly 50 and about ready to give retirement a try. The case load had increased and the bad guys were getting more dangerous. They had better weapons and better organization. He always felt like he was one step behind.

And what he really didn't need was the "help" from the FBI.

Couldn't Rodgers see how fishy this whole thing was? All Fibbies ever wanted to do was to stick their noses in your business, come up with a startling revelation, and grab your case. He doubted they'd even spend any more time on it.

He was pissed at Rodgers for putting up with their crap but knew the captain didn't have a choice. There wasn't any real proof that the terrorist story was false, but there were too many little things that were off. He had to get some proof.

There was this odd consultant. He thinks he knows more than God, but he might turn up something useful. If he finds anything, Fowler would throw it back in all their faces. But if his assistance ever got out, the detective would be lucky to keep his pension.

* * *

Braxton trudged up the last flight of stairs. He was sweaty, tired, and in a foul mood. The taxi had hit traffic on the way to National and they had inched along the GW Parkway for an hour. He had missed the 6:30 shuttle, had been forced to settle for a packed one at 7:30, and had spent the flight wedged between two patent attorneys recounting their day's conquests. At least the trip on the *T* had been uneventful. It was now 10:30 and he could think of nothing better than a hot shower before calling it a night.

He dropped his bag on the floor of the hall and fished in four different pockets before he found his keys. As he reached to turn the deadbolt, he froze.

It was already pulled back.

Options raced through his head: call out for help, rush downstairs, hope for surprise and storm in. There hadn't been much crime in this part of Cambridge for the past few years, but you always had to be careful. On the other hand, maybe he just forgot to set the lock when he left.

He cautiously pushed open the door a few inches and saw light coming from the room. Just as he was about to retreat to the manager's office he heard a familiar clicking coming from inside. Grabbing his bag, he tossed it into living room and went immediately to the study.

"Paul, what the hell are you doing here this time of night?"

Terrel was hunched over his MacBook. The floor of the study was littered with listings and an empty pizza box teetered on the edge of the desk. A heavy odor of garlic floated in the air.

Without bothering to look up, Terrel blurted out a "Hi man! How was the trip?"

"The trip was fine. Now what are *you doing* here?"

"I have to get my manual for the new quant routines finished by tomorrow. I knew you were out of town so I didn't think you'd mind if I used the place." He finally finished typing and turned to look at his neighbor. "You look beat, man. You need to get more rest." Terrel turned and went back to his typing.

Braxton shouldn't have been that surprised. He didn't mind Terrel using the hookup but he wished he would be a little more careful.

"Next time lock the door please. No use inviting trouble."

"Sure thing, Adam. I'll be done in a few minutes."

Braxton shook his head and smiled. "Don't stay too late, Paul. I'm gonna take a shower and pack it in. And please don't forget to lock up."

Terrel was still pounding away when Braxton fell into a deep sleep.

CHAPTER 20

Cambridge, Massachusetts
Thursday, 6:30 a.m.

THE CHARLES RIVER slices Greater Boston into two pieces: an upper half with Cambridge and its ivy-covered universities, high tech companies, and eclectic population; and Boston proper with its soaring skyline, gold-domed State House, and ethnic neighbor-hoods. The river is both a geographic and recreational focal point for the area. On its wandering course to the Massachusetts Bay, the river passes some of the State's most revered, and valuable property: Harvard University, Boston University, Northeastern University, the Massachusetts Institute of Technology, the Boston Museum of Science, and the Esplanade's Hatch Shell, site of the Boston Pop's renowned Fourth of July concerts. The river is also home to innumerable private, scholastic, and university crew teams whose pencil-like shells can be regularly seen on its surface from April through November.

Alongside the river run two of the area's busiest roads: Memorial Drive on the Cambridge side, and Storrow Drive on the Boston shore. Every morning tens of thousands of commuters use the roads to reach in-town offices. Running paths, squeezed between the heavily traveled routes and the river's edge as a contribution to healthy living, complete the urban transportation complex.

The paths especially, are truly a social catalyst. Dedicated joggers brave the worst of Boston's weather throughout the year to log their daily run. Completely egalitarian in nature, the paths accept execu-tives, students, and laborers alike, many of the participants forming friendships only consummated along the winding macadam trails.

Seven bridges cross the slow, lazy water in the short five and one-half miles between the river's elbow at Harvard Stadium in the west and the Charles River Dam in the east: Eliot Bridge at Route 2 and Mt. Auburn Hospital; the JFK Memorial Bridge on Boylston just outside of Harvard Square; the Western Avenue Bridge near Harvard Business School; the Mass Turnpike access at the River Street Bridge; the BU Bridge connecting Boston University to its Cambridge colleagues; the Harvard Bridge at Massachusetts Avenue, the primary route from the Back Bay to MIT and Harvard Square; and the Longfellow Bridge at the foot of Charles Street next to the Massachusetts General Hospital. The bridges connect the paths on each bank of the river like the rungs of a ladder and make a thankfully varied landscape for the thousands of runners that frequent the Charles' banks.

Braxton had returned from a run one summer morning and explained to his wife that there were 254 unique circuits possible starting at the JFK, looping around the river, and returning back to Boylston Street, never retracing a particular segment.

She had declared him an incurable nerd.

She had probably been right.

This morning, Braxton had risen early, put on his running suit, and headed out for the Charles. It was a bright, clear Boston spring day. The chill from the hostile New England winter had passed, and the humidity of Boston's summer had not yet laid its oppressive blanket over the city. The blossoms were just coming out on the dogwood trees planted along the Charles' banks, and gave a sweet smell to the air as Braxton ran the tour. It was a time of rebirth and awakening for the city; a time to put the solitude of a long cold winter into the past.

He chose a leisurely pace, one conducive to thoughtful intro-spection. Despite the difficulties of his trip to D.C., he felt more positive than he had in a long time.

The morning sun was warm on his face as he crossed the JFK Bridge to the Boston side of the river. It was still early and there were few other runners on the pathway. He turned at the Law School and headed east toward Boston.

As he jogged along the pathway his mind returned to the Ramal case. Could there be a connection between the student's death and the incident report? He wasn't so naive to believe that high technology couldn't raise dangerous passions. Companies like Amazon and Google continued to invest billions in e-commerce. His previous employer, Century Computer, had bet its future on the technology and pulled itself out of near bankruptcy. If there was a connection between Ramal's death and the CERT/CC message, they all were facing a very dangerous threat.

When he passed Harvard Business School, he decided to cut his run short and turned left to return to Cambridge over the Western Avenue Bridge. He needed to get back to his computer and finish the traffic analysis on the GW gateway. He didn't want to get melodramatic, but he felt an urgency that he couldn't shake. He would see what the program had caught, then decide his next steps.

Terrel was just leaving his apartment when Braxton reached his door. "Morning, Paul."

"Hey, Adam, how's it going?" The gangly programmer was dressed in jeans and a tie-dyed T-shirt. His hair was loose, a tangle of black curls. "Did you get my mail?"

"Yup. Looking forward to the trip. Thanks. Like to come in for a drink before you head out?"

"Sure."

Braxton knew that he and his friend shared a unique trait; they both took their morning caffeine cold. He retrieved two Cokes from the refrigerator and they collapsed on the living room sofa.

"You look a lot better than last night," Terrel finally offered. "The trip must have been a killer."

Braxton smiled. "An interesting choice of words, Paul. The guy I was looking for is dead."

Terrel's head snapped up. "Jesus, Adam. When? What happened?"

Braxton related his experiences at GW and his discussions with Detective Fowler. "I looked through all of Ramal's stuff but I couldn't find anything that looked like a monitor program. There wasn't a log either. He was a hell of an organizer but he sure didn't leave any tracks."

"Do you think he was really a terrorist?"

"I don't know. They found a bunch of flyers and some electronics for explosives, but I couldn't find any electronic files on terrorism or explosives. I checked his bookmark file and the links were all straight computer science. Nothing at all from any of the fringe sites. It just doesn't make sense."

Braxton felt his early morning bravado eroding away. Maybe he was reaching. Every time he went over the events, they just raised more questions. He had made little progress and there were no signs that this investigation was going anywhere.

"Look, there's got to be some explanation for his message," Terrel responded. "He must have been running a fairly sophisticated detector. I wonder why you couldn't find it?"

"Beats me," Braxton said. "The monitor I wrote before I left for D.C. did generate some interesting results. There were definitely messages coming out of the gateway that shouldn't be. But how did Ramal find it?"

"What about the time?"

Braxton looked at his watch. "It's about 7:45. That reminds me. I have to call Fowler this morning and send a note to Flanagan at the Center."

Terrel shook his head. "No, Adam. Not the time *now*. The time on Ramal's files. Can you track his activities by the time stamps?"

"Damn. Of course. The directory listings the FBI left didn't show the time stamps. I forgot all about them."

Braxton felt like an idiot. Computer systems routinely "stamp" or mark a file every time it is modified or created. This piece of information becomes a part of the hidden information in the header of the file. Unless it is specifically requested, it might not be printed in a directory listing. "GW gave me access to Ramal's network files. Let's see what he left us."

He rushed into the study. Terrel followed and pulled up one of the extra chairs. Braxton logged in and accessed Ramal's account at GW. He requested a directory listing with dates and times, and they watched as the lines filled the screen.

"When did you say Ramal died?" Terrel asked.

"Sunday," Braxton replied.

"Something's weird here, man."

"You're right." Braxton ran his finger down the screen. "The most recent date on these files is Friday. Ramal sent us that note just before he died. He would have had to update some of his files since then. Especially the analysis files. Someone deleted all of the most recent versions."

"Could the FBI have done it accidentally?"

"No. I'm sure they had the SysOps at GW do the dump. Someone wanted to erase any record of Ramal's recent work and the easiest way would be to simply delete everything after a certain date."

"And that would also be a lot less obvious than deleting all the data files or all the executables," Terrel added.

"Well, it sure fooled me." Braxton dropped his head into his hands and rubbed his forehead. He could feel the muscles clamping around his temples. "Somebody knows what they're doing."

"Can you recover the files?" Terrel asked hopefully.

"Not from the server. If we still had his laptop, maybe, but it's long gone." He turned back to the keyboard. "But let's see if we can piece together anything more."

*　*　*

On his way into the Capitol, Nicholson had finished working out his strategy. He had arrived in his office at 7:30 and by 8:00 had listed the critical steps he would take.

He had determined that the remailer used was of the *Pseudonymous* type. These systems were theoretically crackable since they supported replies. The *from* address was an artificial address on the remailer. An internal table on the system kept the correspondence, or map, between the generated address and the actual sender. When a reply was received, the remailer simply looked up the real address and forwarded the email.

All he had to do was break into the system, find the mapping table, and read it to find the original sender. Unfortunately there were two problems. First, the mapping tables were encrypted, in this case with a military–grade algorithm. Second, the messages didn't go through a single remailer, but multiple, operating in collaboration. Emails were passed from one to the next before reaching their destination. Each system had its own map table, compounding the tracking process.

He *might* be able to crack it eventually, but the time and effort would be prohibitive. He needed a different approach.

The messages could only be coming from someone familiar with the Lynch case. That meant the cops, the media, or someone close to the family. The police would never take so circuitous an approach, it was too close to entrapment, so that left reporters or the family. He needed to find someone that had access to personal information on the Lynches as well as to the public newspaper files.

The timing of the threat was also confusing. Why wait until now to come forward? Was the information just discovered? Why did the blackmailer choose this time to use his knowledge? Did it have to do with any of the Senator's current activities? There were too many possibilities.

He would put these questions aside for the moment. Most important was tracing the whereabouts of everyone connected with Senator Kenneth Lynch twenty years ago.

Normally Nicholson would simply order Potterfield's interns to do the leg work, but he needed to avoid any undue visibility. They could work on the follow up, after he had some specific individuals identified. Connections to the Lynch affair had to be kept completely invisible.

He left the Russell Building at 9:00 and walked down 2nd to the Library of Congress. After a little help from a friendly library matron, he was hard at work. Two hours later his eyes were teared and blood-shot, but he had the name of every reporter who had covered the scandal. Most were from the *Washington Post* and *Baltimore Sun*, but there had been a few from smaller Virginia and Maryland papers. None sounded familiar to Nicholson. He expected they all had either retired or found jobs on other papers over the ensuing years. At least neither Woodward nor Bernstein was on the list.

The same papers had also covered Lynch's funeral, despite the fact that Lynch had been "old news" at the time. He had left a wife and daughter. The photographs were faded but he could still make out the pain and anguish on their faces. The previous year's scandal had taken its toll on them as well.

Aside from the reporters, there were few mourners at the gravesite. Nicholson knew the hypocrisy of the Washington scene. No one ever wants to be associated with a fallen idol. It's too painful a reminder of one's own fallibility. That had all been factored into their plans.

Nicholson did recognize Senators Fitzgerald and Okima, longtime Lynch colleagues, and Gowling, the representative from Lynch's Virginia district. A couple of other faces were unfamiliar, so he made a copy of the article for later reference.

The computer index found no other citations for Lynch. The wife had simply disappeared. He would have to try another route to track her down.

Nicholson returned to his office and assigned the list of reporters to two new interns from the University of Virginia. He told them he needed backgrounds and current locations to verify their credentials for possible freelance work. They excitedly left his office, eager to help the wheels of Congress move more smoothly.

Pleased with the progress so far, at 11:45 Nicholson left to get some lunch.

CHAPTER 21

BRAXTON AND TERREL had spent over two hours analyzing Ramal's files and looking for any clues as to what he had been studying. The results were disappointing. Whoever had cleaned the account had been very effective.

They went back to Braxton's program and reviewed the data it had collected over the past two days. There had been a total of seventeen incidents reported by the detector. They occurred at all times of the day and under a range of traffic conditions on the gateway. In almost all ways they appeared to be random.

"So what have we got?" Braxton summarized. "All the incidents are correlated with an unmatched outbound message, and all only occur on one of the two gateways. A program inside that gateway is sending some kind of message to somebody. We don't know what the message is or who it is going to. That about sum it up?"

The scowl on his face said it all. He was tired and frustrated. The roller coaster ride of this investigation was going downhill and the rest of his life with it.

"Hey, come on man," Terrel coaxed. He put on his best supportive smile. "We're making some progress. You've verified Ramal's claim by identifying some kind of a rogue. Maybe it's a bug but maybe it's . . . a mole. We've isolated it to a single gateway. What's so special about that gateway? Is it the same as the other?" Terrel's unbridled enthusiasm could not be ignored.

"A mole, huh? You do have a vivid imagination. Okay, we'll look at the gateways." Braxton went back to the screen. "One is an old

Sun running UNIX. It probably became overloaded so they bought . . ." he tapped on a few more keys, " . . . a Century NetGate Model 2400."

"Which one is our target?"

Braxton hesitated as a chill ran through him. "The Century."

"Your old company, right? Can we get them to help?"

"I don't know. I suppose I could try." Further dealings with Century were not anything Braxton had ever wanted. "I'll give them a call sometime. First let's see what we can do with this data."

"I think you ought to call them, Adam. They might be able to help."

"I heard you, Paul." His voice got a little louder. "We don't know enough yet. This whole mole thing could just be a red herring. Century could be running some proprietary monitor and collecting their own statistics. I wouldn't put it past them to leave it undocumented."

"It can't be that hard to find out."

"I said I'd call them, okay? Just leave it!" And Braxton threw his notebook across the room, knocking a Sierra Club calendar off the wall.

"Sure, man. Right. Look, I think I'd better go." Terrel stood up and headed for the door.

"Paul! Please stop." Braxton's voice fell and he hung his head over the desk. "I'm sorry. I really feel under the gun on this contract. If I can't pull something off, I may never get another chance. And talking with Century is not real high on my favorites list. But I do need your help. Hang in a little longer?"

Terrel hesitated then said "Okay. Wallace won't miss me for a while longer." He walked over to the calendar and hung it back on the protruding nail. "But take it easy with my Christmas present."

"I promise."

They spent the rest of the morning going back over the original data and trying to discover any common aspects of the incidents. They weren't successful.

Terrel finally left about noon. Braxton fixed a quick lunch and went into the dining room to work out his next steps. After his blowup, he had better contact someone at Century and try to enlist their help or Terrel would leave him on a mountain top their next trip.

He would give his ex-boss a call and try to get some time with him in the next day or two.

He also owed both Fowler and Flanagan a status report. CERT/CC would be happy with an email, but Fowler would probably want a call. Two calls and then back to the PC.

The call to Century was short. He hadn't really expected to get through to his old manager directly. Florence Winters, secretary to Executive Vice President Warren Chamberlain, took the message that Braxton was consulting for CERT/CC and needed to speak with her boss on a network security matter. She promised to check with Chamberlain later in the day and get back to Braxton before five o'clock. Winters had always been helpful when he had worked at Century and her openness eased his anxiety.

The call to Fowler wasn't quite so simple. The police operator transferred Braxton to the detective's car phone. He could hear the sounds of traffic and police calls in the background.

"Fowler," the detective barked into the microphone.

"Detective Fowler, it's Adam Braxton. You said you wanted me to call."

"Yeah. What did you find out from Goddard?"

"Not a lot. She was sure that Ramal kept papers and manuals in the apartment. They should have been there. Whoever killed him must have taken them to hide what Ramal was doing."

"Anything else?" the detective said flatly.

"I got access to Ramal's files at George Washington. I went back over them and found that someone had deleted everything back two days. There's been a deliberate attempt to cover up what Ramal was doing. Can you get someone to check it out?"

The line went silent.

"Detective Fowler?" Braxton repeated.

"Look, Adam. I know you think all this missing stuff is significant, but it's not going to mean shit to the department. Maybe Ramal deleted the files himself. Maybe he threw out a lot of old books. It's still just circumstantial. I've got to have harder evidence."

"What do you need?"

"I need proof of a third party's actions against Ramal. Without it his death is still just an accident. Now can you help me or not?"

Braxton chose not to tell Fowler that he had confirmed Ramal's suspicions about the gateway. It would be too hard to explain the technical details to the detective and it might not have anything to do with Fowler's case.

"I don't know," he finally replied. "I've got a couple more people I need to talk to. If I don't have anything new after that I'll probably have to close the incident. I'll call you in a couple of days."

Braxton hung up the phone before Fowler could object. The detective was going to be no help at all. He just wanted Braxton to do all his goddamn work for him.

It was time to get back to the study and draft the update for Flanagan.

Half an hour later he had composed a short note on the status of his case and sent it off. It didn't say much. Just enough to keep her off his back until he had a chance to talk with Chamberlain.

He went back and reviewed the logs from his monitor program. They were as frustrating as ever. After another half hour he gave up.

He shut off the system in disgust and grabbed his coat. Maybe a walk around the Square would clear his mind.

*   *   *

Fowler squirmed behind his desk and tried to get his head into the morning's knifing in Rock Creek Park, but his mind kept coming back to Braxton and the Ramal case. The consultant had verified everything that Fowler had suspected, but there still wasn't enough to ask the Captain to reopen the case. He needed Braxton to find some kind of electronic smoking gun; a trail that the killers had left. It didn't look as if that was going to happen. Whoever pulled off the murder had been very careful. It was a professional job and that frustrated him even more. He didn't like pros operating in his city.

Fowler flipped open an ancient plastic and paper Rolodex and looked up the number of a friend who might be able to help.

"Forty-two twelve." A pleasant female voice repeated the extension number.

"I'd like to speak to Roger Slattery please."

"Just a minute."

Ten seconds later a voice came on the line.

"Slattery." The new voice was deep and resonant with a touch of a southern accent.

"Roger, Sam Fowler. How's it going?"

"Sam. Haven't heard from you in ages. Have they put you out to pasture yet?"

"Not yet. Still fighting the bad guys. How about you? Still getting paid for sitting around on your butt?"

"You betcha. This cushy government life is great. What's up Sam?"

Roger Slattery, or at least that was the name Fowler knew him by, was easily as old as Fowler, and even less likely to retire. He was the Central Intelligence Agency's resident expert in terrorists and terrorism. Fowler had met him on an assassination case a couple of years before and the two had discovered they shared a passion for hot Mexican food.

Normally a very reticent spook, Fowler had also found that Slattery became a little more talkative after a six pack of *Dos Equis*. He hadn't disclosed anything very specific, but it was clear he had seen his share of field work. Now apparently tied to a desk in Langley, he didn't seem to mind an occasional call from the detective.

"Did you happen to see something about a bomb explosion Sunday night?"

"Yeah. I did notice that. Some Arab student blew himself up. You involved?"

"It's mine." He didn't think it would hurt to stretch the truth a bit. "What little hard evidence I have points to a terrorist connection, but the rest of the picture doesn't fit."

"That little bee in your ear again? You want me to take a look for you?"

"I'd appreciate it. Unofficially, of course."

"Of course. You have anything I can look at?"

"I can fax a few things over. That okay?"

"Sure," and Slattery gave the detective a number.

"Thanks Roger, I owe you."

"Give me a few days and I'll get back to you. As for owing me, how about a Baja Combination sometime?"

"You're on. Soon as I get this case wrapped up."

Which could be real soon if he didn't come up with something fast. He opened one of the desk drawers, pulled his private copy of the Ramal file from under a pile of papers at the bottom, and headed for the fax machine.

* * *

The man scanned the log of intrusion alerts. Someone new was monitoring the gateway.

There had always been the chance, however slim, that someone would recognize the imbalance in the network statistics and realize the gateway was initiating messages. There had been a few over the years and all had been easily identified and neutralized. Including the latest from GW.

Now it was happening again. And much more aggressively.

Proof of the scanner's existence would cause a cyberspace witch hunt that would seriously reduce his flow of information. And he needed that information now more than ever.

Once he had identified the intruder, he would need to place another call to his friends.

CHAPTER 22

Fairfax, Virginia
Thursday, 6:00 p.m.

GREYSTONE REVIEWED THE latest competitive intelligence documents as his limousine cruised down the Dulles access road. He had heard that Hawthorne Systems was working on a new generation of command and control systems. They had heard rumors that they were hiring computer science grads from Berkeley, Carnegie Mellon, MIT and Stanford by the dozens, starting previously unheard-of salary wars. What he had in his hands validated the gossip and provided a solid foundation to the actions. He pulled a few pages from the sheath and replaced them in his briefcase, then folded the remainder and stuck them in his jacket pocket. No use making his colleague's job too easy.

The limousine suddenly swerved and the briefcase fell, spreading its contents over the carpet.

"What the hell are you doing, Enrico?" he cursed to his driver as he repacked the case.

"Sorry, *Señor* Greystone. That *loco* pickup driver cut me off. I had to turn to avoid an accident. You wouldn't want to have to stop and identify yourself would you?" The heavy Spanish accent was laced with poorly disguised sarcasm.

"Be careful, *mi amigo*. I keep you employed because of the benefits of our understanding. But I will not put up with any of your macho crap. I would hate to think of what might happen if certain agencies discovered your family was here illegally. They could be deported back to Cuba. You *will* take care of the records as usual?"

"Of course, *Señor*." Enrico Santana's bravado quickly vanished under Greystone's withering tone. "As always, the records will show we drove to the Capitol for an evening conference."

The chauffeur had a temper, but was not about to do anything that would disturb his client. When Santana had joined the limousine service, Greystone had done a background check. It had been easy enough to find that he and his mother had escaped from the Castro regime in 1990 to start a new life in the US. They had migrated to D.C. to live with relatives, but *Señora* Santana had taken ill and been unable to provide for her small family. Enrico had been their only source of support. Santana had worked mostly odd jobs for bare subsistence, but five months ago he had been accepted at the limousine service. He had thought it was a dream come true. Unfortunately, his first client had other plans. Santana had been indentured to the man ever since.

"Good. Now get us back on schedule for the District, and no more surprises."

* * *

Flanagan returned to her office at 6:30 tired and frustrated. She had been in an operations meeting all afternoon reviewing the status of her team's projects. The certification activity had become significantly more complicated, and time-consuming, than any of them had thought.

Valuable resources had to be spent contacting vendors, debugging network hookups, and arguing with lawyers. She was already pulling people off other projects to help, which caused their work to slip. She finally just collected all of the team's inputs and promised to work out a revised timetable based on the priorities as she understood them. Rydell and Candela would have to deal with the result.

She was packing her briefcase for the evening's work when she noticed new mail in her account. Checking her in folder, she saw a report from her consultant.

It was about time, she'd been waiting three days for him to get back to her.

She opened the message, expecting to only give it a cursory review before heading out. What she read was anything but ordinary.

From: braxton@cerberus.net

To: sFlanagan@cert.org

```
Subject: Status Report, Saracen Incident
```

After traveling to George Washington University on
Tuesday, I identified Saracen as Mohammed Ramal, a
graduate student in computer science researching
network traffic patterns. His message to CERT/CC
may have been a result of experiments performed on
GW gateways.

Mr. Ramal was killed in his apartment last Sunday,
just after his transmission, purportedly as a
result of an accident with explosives. It is
thought he may have been involved in some type of
terrorist activity.

I have contacted GW officials and District of Columbia
police to secure further information on Mr. Ramal.
Neither was of substantive assistance in clarifying
Ramal's activities relative to his message.

Based on Ramal's original note, I have been able to
independently confirm his report of anomalous
behavior in the gateways.

I will update you on further developments in a day
or two.

Regards,

Adam Braxton

Their contact was dead? He was a *terrorist*?

The consultant's report made her shudder. She couldn't believe that his death had anything to do with the Incident. It had to be a coincidence.

God, what will Rydell say?

She didn't have the time to worry about this now. It was only Thursday. The report didn't need immediate attention and Braxton said he'd get back to her in a few days. That was enough time to prepare her story for the staff meeting on Monday.

She moved the message into her actions folder and printed a hardcopy for filing with the other Incident papers.

Unfortunately, it didn't look as if the Incident was going to be the high visibility event she had hoped it would be. More like a small footnote on their monthly report. At least the consultant had been able to confirm the anomaly. Hopefully he'd resolve it without spending too much more of her budget.

Flanagan still had to work through the staffing plan, and she really needed to sweat off the stress with a trip to the gym. She left the Center offices at 6:45.

* * *

At exactly 7:00, the limousine pulled up at 739 Wilson Street. The side door of the car opened and Greystone emerged into the fading twilight. He took a deep breath; the clear, crisp air refreshed him as he mentally prepared for the meeting. Tonight would solidify his relationship with Akira Hajima, CEO of Takagawa Communications. The small pieces were coalescing into the bigger mosaic. A few more weeks and he would be able to reveal the masterpiece.

The blinking neon sign proclaimed "Mount Fuji Grill". Garish colors spilled onto the sidewalk as Greystone approached. It hardly seemed a fitting location to meet his contact, but the executive was used to surprises from the Japanese.

As soon as he walked in the door he was assaulted by pungent smells from the oriental dishes and irritating sing-song music played through the audio system. His disorientation was another reminder of how uncomfortable he always felt in Eastern surroundings. He also knew that this was exactly why Hajima had insisted on meeting here.

It had taken Greystone years to understand the Eastern philosophy behind Japanese business, and another decade to develop even the beginnings of a workable strategy for dealing with them. He had religiously studied Sun Tzu, Miyamoto Mushashi, and Gao Yuan. Logically, he understood the history and the cultural traits, but emotionally he wasn't prepared to adopt the life style and the teachings. Their feigned politeness and incessant bowing drove him crazy. He was a man who liked to get to the point and get on with business. Greystone didn't have to like someone to do business with them, and didn't care whether they knew it or not. Business was about mutual benefit, not companionship. The Japanese, on the other hand, had hundreds of years of ritual that they brought into all their dealings. To do business with them was to do it their way.

At least Hajima was a more modern samurai. He was of Greystone's generation with no direct memory of the war. The executive had been born in Japan, but had moved to the United States in the seventies with his father, a senior manager for Honda.

He had attended Stanford, eventually receiving degrees in both Electrical Engineering and Business, before returning to Japan to take up his career.

He was a clever, aggressive manager who was determined to make Japan, and his current employer, Takagawa Communications, a leader in battlefield telecommunication systems. Greystone had met Hajima at a conference and had singled him out as a key participant in his plan.

Over the years they had known each other, Greystone had sensed cracks in Hajima's rigid facade. He could still be the inscrutable Oriental when dealing with his bosses, the leaders of the powerful Takagawa Industries *keiretsu*, a huge business conglomerate, but when he was the senior manager, as he would be this evening, Greystone would find a more moderate personality.

Moderate in dogma, but certainly not in acumen. Hajima was the toughest negotiator Greystone had ever met. Their meetings left him completely exhausted. It was also not beyond Hajima to play psychological tricks; this location would only be the first.

He introduced himself to the tiny, exquisite hostess. She recognized his name immediately, bowed deeply, and asked if he would accompany her upstairs. Greystone nodded appropriately and followed her up the stairs.

The dark green silk kimono clung tightly to her body, accentuating her small breasts and slim waist. Her hips swayed gently ahead of him as she walked up the stairs. He couldn't keep his eyes off her. How much nicer it would be if she were his evening companion.

The decor changed abruptly as they reached the landing at the top of the stairs. Instead of the bright reds and yellows prominent downstairs, the second floor was lighted in soft blues. The atmosphere was one of quiet contemplation rather than noisy conversation. Greystone was sure that very few Washington *gaigin* ever saw this part of the restaurant.

He removed his shoes at the landing, placing them in cubby-holed shelves built into the side wall, and proceeded with the hostess down a long *tatami*-covered hall. On his left, male and female voices came from behind *shoji* screens hiding what Greystone guessed were small private dining areas. Between the doorways, original *ukiyo-e* woodcuts hung unprotected on the walls.

At the end of the hall the hostess opened a slightly larger screen

and again bowed. Greystone entered the room to find his business
partner and two colleagues sitting on the raised *tatami* floor behind a
richly lacquered low black table. The screen slid shut behind him as
he approached the table and he turned automatically to see if she
had entered. Just as quickly he realized his error; it was impolite for
him to divert his attention from his host. He looked back to see a
slight upturn at the corners of Hajima's mouth. Another point for
his colleague.

"*Hajima-san*," Greystone said as he bowed deliberately. "*Ohayo
gozaimas.*"

"Good evening to you, Robert."

An impeccably dressed man rose from behind the table. Akira
Hajima was Managing Director of Research for Takagawa
Communications, the telecommunications manufacturing arm of
Takagawa Industries. He was tall for a Japanese, almost six feet with
the body of a wrestler: thick neck, broad powerful shoulders, slim
waist and hips. Unmarried, he was completely dedicated to his
company. His dark eyes glowed with an intensity born from past
business battles; battles that had left their mark in the chiseled lines
on his otherwise smooth face.

Hajima bowed slightly, then motioned to his side. "I have asked
two of my colleagues to join us," he continued. "I hope you don't
mind. This is Mr. Mashitomi, and Mr. Kitari. They are researchers
from our Palo Alto facility. Being younger they have a much better
grasp of both your language and advanced technology." Hajima
smiled pleasantly and the three bowed again.

Greystone returned the bows. "Of course not, *Hajima-san*. I am
very pleased to meet your associates."

He could not help but smile at Hajima's justification. Fluency in
English was an obsession in Japan, and Hajima's English, or more
accurately American, was nearly perfect. He had no need of a
translator.

The irony was that through ignorance and stubbornness,
America had brought the world to its knees and forced business to
be conducted in its language. No country had ever before exerted
such an influence on world trade. Greystone hoped this would not
be his country's sole historical contribution.

Nor had Hajima any need for technical experts. He was well versed
in the technology of communications, perhaps better than Greystone,

and was not about to be led astray by the American manager. Most likely the associates were either bodyguards, a part of Hajima's normal entourage to protect him from the dangers of American life, or subordinates, brought to the meeting as a teaching opportunity. Either way, they would have little contribution to the affairs of the evening.

"Michiko is quite beautiful isn't she?" Hajima casually asked as they knelt at the table.

"Yes, very attractive," Greystone replied, angry he had let his attention waver from the evening's business.

"Perhaps if you wish to come another time, I could arrange to have her stay."

"I could not ask such a favor of you," Greystone said appropriately. He quickly tried to move onto a new subject. "This is truly a remarkable location, *Hajima-san*. Who would have thought of finding such a beautiful oasis in the center of our capital? I thank you for the opportunity to meet here."

"Think nothing of it. It is my way of thanking you for the opportunity you have presented to us."

"Oh no, the pleasure is ours to be working together with such a forward-thinking company. But, you must let me reciprocate at our next meeting. I shall pick an appropriate location in our Virginia countryside. I'm sure you will find it very pleasing."

"Thank you, Robert. It will be my pleasure." Hajima smiled openly and nodded to Mashitomi. The subordinate reached for a small ceramic flask sitting on the table, poured its steaming contents into four shallow cups, then offered the sake to each of the diners.

"*Compai*," Hajima said.

"*Compai*," Greystone replied.

CHAPTER 23

Washington, D.C.
Thursday, 7:15 p.m.

GREYSTONE FELT THE sting on the back of his throat as he swallowed the hot, thick liquid. He had to be careful. He had quickly learned that his business partner had an outrageous tolerance for alcohol. Undoubtedly another well-practiced negotiation tactic.

"It is good to see you again, Robert," Hajima continued. "I always enjoy dealing with someone that appreciates the subtlety of conversation."

Greystone accepted the compliment with a slight nod. "We have much to discuss my friend, but first I am anxious to know what delights you have planned for us."

"I am afraid you will be disappointed, Robert. This is a simple restaurant without the glamour of your fine establishments. But perhaps you will find it interesting no less."

Hajima understated the matter, of course. They began with a steaming bowl of *mizu* soup, rich in the taste and aroma of Japanese stock. Their palettes cleansed, young kimono-clad women placed trays of delicate vegetable *tempura* before them. Greystone carefully mixed his *watenabe* horseradish in his dipping bowl then feasted on the delicate apposition of the crisp fried batter around the soft, sweet vegetable centers.

So far the dinner had been very palatable.

As they were finishing the *tempura* a man whom Greystone assumed to be the chef appeared displaying a large, live shellfish.

"This is a langostino, Robert," Hajima explained.

"It looks like a lobster."

The Japanese smiled. "Yes, it does. But we are not blessed with lobster in Japan and must make do with this poor creature. Still, in my country it is considered quite a delicacy."

"I hope we do not eat it like this!" Greystone's face had a smile but there was an unmistakable seriousness in his tone.

"Of course not, my friend. The chef honors us by showing how fresh the animal is. He will now go into the kitchen and prepare it."

About ten minutes later the chef reappeared and placed a large platter in the center of the table. Lying on the dish was the creature much as it had appeared earlier. The Japanese immediately took up their chopsticks and began to poke at the head of the animal. Greystone withheld his shock when the langostino, obviously still alive, responded by moving its long, slender tentacles against the attacking probes.

Upon closer examination, he determined the method of preparation. The creature had been cut cleanly into thirds: a head, a middle, and a tail. The middle section of the shell, which apparently held most of the meat, had been emptied and the meat inside cut into small cubes. These pieces had then been meticulously piled back on the plate, between the head and tail, in a shape resembling the original body. The preparation had taken place so rapidly that the head of the creature had not yet succumbed to its demise.

"Robert," Hajima said, interrupting Greystone's observations, "as our guest, you must take the first bite. It is quite delicious." The trio halted their probing and watched as the *gaigin* contemplated the test.

Greystone resolutely positioned his chopsticks in his hand and reached toward the plate. He had recently come to enjoy sushi—in small doses—but raw sashimi was still more than his stomach could handle. A variety of condiments had been placed around the table and he recognized them as his savior. He bravely selected a piece of the langostino, dipped it into the most pungent sauce he could recognize, and placed it in his mouth. A few quick chews and he forced his throat to swallow the slimy meat.

"Excellent," he proclaimed, his stomach only slightly unsettled from the experience.

"*Hai!*" was the unanimous reply, and the Japanese enthusiastically attacked the remains of the unfortunate creature. Luckily they were distracted by their delight over the meal and paid little attention to the infrequent sampling by their guest.

The meal wound down and the table was thankfully cleared of all animal remains. Left in their place was a crystal decanter of Suntory scotch. Mashitomi poured drinks for the four.

"To good health and prosperous times," Hajima toasted.

Greystone noted the opening with relief. His knees, tucked under his body for the dinner, were screaming in pain. The dinner formalities over, he pushed himself back from the table and stretched his legs. It was time to get to work.

"And to a mutually beneficial relationship," Greystone replied after emptying his glass. But there was no movement from the Japanese to refill the glasses.

"Yes, our relationship," Hajima replied quietly. A somber countenance fell over his face. "We were quite concerned when we heard of the death of Mr. Keane, Robert. Reports in the press have suggested there is much instability in your company at this time."

The topic had hung over dinner like a Damocles sword. It had only been a matter of time before Hajima would broach it. The sensational nature of Keane's death must have sent tremors through Takagawa's executive suite, and Hajima would have borne the brunt of their wrath. Greystone had to assure his colleague that their activities would continue, and with enough assurances so Hajima could save face with his bosses. But he also knew he couldn't lie; many times before Hajima had proven his intelligence network was frighteningly efficient.

"You know better than to believe everything you read in our newspapers, Akira." He tried to produce a warm, friendly smile. "Management is in firm control. Julius Flitterman has taken Charles' position as President. He is a very capable man, as I'm sure you know. And he has named me to Chief Operating Officer. We are taking the transition very seriously and would do nothing to endanger our shareholder's investments. Or those of our partners."

"That is very comforting to hear. We are, of course, familiar with Mr. Flitterman. He has an exemplary reputation. You understand that Takagawa must evaluate the impact the adverse publicity surrounding Mr. Keane's death will have on our investment. My management is, as you say, rather conservative."

"I understand. Let me assure you that our plans remain on track. I discussed them with Julius only yesterday. While Charles' death was unfortunate, you must see that it opens the way for a more rapid achievement of all of our objectives. Charles and I differed on how best to move Theater forward. I am now in a position to see that nothing stands in our way. We will meet all of our commitments to Takagawa."

He had delivered the pledge with every ounce of his strength, never letting his eyes stray from Hajima's. Now all he could do was hold his breath and wait for the result. Would the sword fall or recede back into its scabbard?

After what seemed to be hours, Hajima slowly reached for his glass. "Then we shall toast to our coming success," Hajima replied.

Mashitomi again filled their glasses and shouts of "*Compai*" were exchanged. The complication had been successfully addressed. At least for the moment.

"Our progress so far seems quite good, my friend," Greystone finally said. "Our prototypes appear to meet all of the initial specifications."

"Yes," Hajima replied, his relaxed voice reflecting a return to comfortable territory. "Our laboratory has made significant progress. We have assigned many of our best researchers to the project. Still, we have much to learn in bringing such efforts to market. How I envy the drive of entrepreneurism in your country. Such dealings would be impossible in the bureaucratic processes of Japan. Perhaps we can learn some of these ways in our joint venture."

"Perhaps, *Hajima-san*. Perhaps." Greystone had no confidence in Hajima's desire to be entrepreneurial. He wanted access to the international arms market and partnering was the only way to do it. The field was complex: strewn with national tariffs, regulations and non-proliferation agreements. Too many possibilities of failure in the constantly shifting sands of policy and legislation. Hajima was betting Theater's, and Greystone's, political contacts could help Takagawa navigate that minefield.

Hajima's promise to his management was guaranteed success. The Japanese executive didn't care how the market share was achieved, as long as he was able to distance himself from the details. Greystone, on the other hand, needed Takagawa for their money and resources. He couldn't get any US firm to make a bet on the proposed changes in regulations. They were too busy trying to keep

Wall Street happy for the next quarter. So he and Hajima had formed the pact. For their mutual benefit. Both were taking huge risks, but the rewards for both men were even greater.

"Please tell us about your testimony at the Senate hearing," Hajima then asked. "Did the presentation go well?"

"Very well, my friend. I believe we are making progress in bringing the details of the Bill in line with our thinking." He decided not to bring up the private meeting with Potterfield. It was a valuable card to be played at another time.

"I am glad to hear this, Robert. We are impressed with your influence in these areas."

Greystone felt the dynamic of the meeting shift. It was time to execute his agenda. He pulled a sheath of papers from his pocket. "I have brought information on developments at Hawthorne Systems. They are investigating new technologies for encryption and key distribution. They may be of value to your engineers."

Hajima took the papers and quickly handed them to Kitari as if they were covered in poison. Hajima felt such matters were below his station. He would soon change his mind. "Yes, I'm sure we will find them interesting. Your contacts are quite extensive, Robert."

"As are yours, *Hajima-san*. It is only through sharing this information that we will be able to achieve our desired result is it not?" The Japanese bowed slightly in affirmation.

Having prepared the moment, Greystone steeled himself for his thrust. "It has come to my attention, my friend, that there may be some problem in achieving the required spatial resolution from the new GPS locators. Will this be a problem in the production units?" He had seen copies of the status reports only that morning. How convenient that Takagawa had recently upgraded their internal Internet infrastructure.

Hajima failed to completely shield his surprise. Taking a moment to calm himself, he turned to Kitari and spoke in curt, rapid Japanese. The exchange was brief and punctuated by numerous bows of deference by the subordinate.

"My associates assure me that the problem has been isolated and updates will be made to the chips within the month. There will be no compromise of either quality or schedule, Robert. I promise you."

Greystone nodded politely. "Of course. I knew it would be so."

The leak had caused Hajima to lose face this evening, whether or not he was even aware of the problem. He was a powerful man and would undoubtedly take out his anger on his subordinates. It would not be an easy night for Mashitomi and Kitari.

Greystone let the silence hang in the air for a few moments then picked up the decanter and filled the glasses. "To our mutual success then. *Compai!*"

"*Compai!*" returned the Takagawa team.

The glasses were emptied and returned to the table. Hajima rose first, quickly followed by Kitari then Mashitomi. Greystone slowly moved his legs. He hoped they would still be able to support him as he stood up. They complained with stabs of pain, but held and he joined the trio of Japanese as they made their way down the quiet hall.

When he took his shoes from the cabinet he noticed a piece of paper laying inside one of them. It was the restaurant's business card. Turning the card over he found "Michiko, 202-555-6952" in small, precise handwriting.

CHAPTER 24

Takagawa Communications, Crystal City, Virginia
Friday, 8:00 a.m.

CRYSTAL CITY, VIRGINIA is neither a city nor made of sparkling translucent glass. At best it is an aging urban neighborhood built around the metro stop of the same name. It lies southwest of the District of Columbia in Arlington County, Virginia, bordered on the east by the Potomac River, on the north by Interstate 395, and on the south by Reagan National Airport.

Takagawa Communications' US headquarters occupied the top five floors of a ten-story brick and glass office building in Crystal City. The building was one of the many corporate offices, urban apartments, hotels and shops populating the neighborhood. But this was only the visible part of the city. Crystal City was like the apocryphal iceberg, with an extensive network of concourses, restaurants and shopping malls below street level. Once considered the future of urban environments, it was now an example of a failed experiment, but still a dynamic component of the federal metropolis.

Today, Crystal City was best-known as the epicenter of the "beltway-bandits": a very popular, and frighteningly accurate, neologism for the cabal of Northern Virginia consulting and defense contractors that grazed inside the beltway—Interstate 495, D.C.'s circumferential highway—and fed exclusively at the government trough.

When forced to reduce internal headcount as part of never-ending, and typically misdirected, congressional budget-cutting strategies, the federal bureaucrats had simply taken their allotted monies and given it to third parties to get their work done. There was never a lack of commercial organizations immediately willing to provide the necessary services. Services that were carefully designed not to solve the presented problem, but simply to get the next, larger, follow-on contract.

The tenth-floor office of Takagawa Communication's CEO was starkly impersonal: bland white walls; a mass-produced desk covered with stacks of manila folders; mass-produced bookcases sagging from reference and business volumes; and a mass-produced sofa and chairs into which visitors and staff could sit uncomfortably. Two 18th-century woodcut prints and a meticulously-trimmed white pine bonsai provided the only reminders of the occupant's true home.

Akira Hajima stood at his window and gazed north across Interstate 395 to the target of his quest: the Pentagon, a massive, impenetrable fortress overflowing with the tax dollars of hard-working American citizens. Dollars that were only accessible to Takagawa by working with that bastard Greystone.

Hajima was tired; tired of the unending government regulations, tired of indolent employees and tired of this unprincipled country. He had been away from Japan for six years and felt the unrelenting weakening of his *ki*. He worked out nearly every day, studying aikido and judo under a *sensei* he had imported from Tokyo, but still the decline continued.

It was worse than old-age; at least that was something over which one had little control. This was something he could control; he had only to complete his assignment and return home. But completion had turned out to be much more difficult than his masters had imagined.

Takagawa was to be the leader of Japan's reemergence in the military intelligence stage. Part of a national program to restore his county's military capabilities, Takagawa had been chosen based on their proven expertise in electronic design and manufacturing. Expertise developed under Hajima's guidance.

He had directed the transformation of Takagawa Communications: hiring more engineers, investing heavily in training, and even sponsoring research at leading US universities to seed Takagawa innovations. These were the successes that led to Takagawa's selection.

Despite all these achievements, Hajima now sat despondent. His mission was stalled and he had a spy in his midst.

He had just finished the reprimand he had begun at the previous night's dinner. It was to have been an award of sorts for Mashitomi and Kitari; an opportunity for them to see in person how business in America was conducted. They were both fluent in English, of course, but had been under strict orders to appear dumb; they were there to observe not contribute.

The reality had been the heated exchange at dinner and a further humiliating dressing-down this morning. They had left Hajima's office questioning their continued employment at Takagawa.

In fact, the problem itself had been minor. Hajima's explanation had been accurate.

The exposure of the setback by his guest was, on the other hand, a disgrace to his subordinates, to himself, and to Takagawa. Personally, he had lost significant face to Greystone. Something that would take all of Hajima's skills to restore.

But that would have to wait. His immediate imperative was to locate the traitor.

*　*　*

"What have you got for me Nick?"

Potterfield stepping into his aide's office, closed the door behind him and pulled over his favorite chair.

Though much smaller than Potterfield's, Nicholson's office still reflected the polish and sophistication of its occupant. The desk and chairs were immaculate Louis XIV reproductions. Original pen and ink sketches depicting Richmond and the District decorated the walls. Loose paper was non-existent. A sleek flat panel monitor was the only concession to the modern, high-tech world.

The Chief of Staff had worked all night on the threat and seeing his boss first thing in the morning hadn't been on the top of his to-do list.

"I checked out the remailer system," he replied with a flat, tired tone. "It's a private remailer located outside Kiev. The site's run by a crusading engineer who's pretty well-known on the net. He manages it personally and so far has stayed within local laws.

"We can request to have mail to your account blocked, but we'd have to give a reason and it still wouldn't give us the identity of the originator. He routes replies through seven different sister servers. I tried to copy his internal files and directories but they're encrypted. Pretty well, too. I can't decode them. I doubt that even NSA could."

"That sounds like a big pile of nothing, Nick." Potterfield

slammed his hands on the baroque desk. "What do you suggest we do? Let this blackmailer make good on his threats and ruin us? I'm driving the most important legislation of my career and you're letting some goddamn Internet criminal do whatever he wants to us. Have you got any plan at all?"

Potterfield's mood hadn't improved since Wednesday. Nicholson sat back and let the anger blow past him. He had learned a long time ago to just let his mentor vent. The most important part of his job was keeping Potterfield's hair-trigger temper under control.

"Okay, David. Take it easy. It's only been two days. I don't think it's worth trying to crack the remailer electronically, so I'm going to try a little old-fashioned detective work. This guy has to be connected to Lynch; the message is too personal.

"This remailer handles replies. I want to keep up the dialog, keep the blackmailer talking. Every time he sends you a message, he's going to reveal a little more about himself. At the same time, I'm tracing the original Lynch paperwork. When these two tracks intersect, we'll find our man. Trust me."

"Of course I trust you, son," Potterfield said in most syrupy twang. "We're in this together, you and me."

* * *

The day had started dismally and gone downhill. The prior evening's forecast of sunny skies had been a typical Boston weather prediction. A slate gray sky had turned normally vivid scenery into a blur of monochrome shadings. Braxton had already turned on the headlights of his four-wheel-drive Jeep Grand Cherokee; the marginal visibility was making Boston driving even more dangerous than usual. It was not a good omen for his meeting.

Chamberlain's secretary had returned Braxton's call the previous afternoon and confirmed an appointment for ten o'clock the next morning. He extracted his car from the garage at nine-o'clock and headed out of town, picking up Route 2 at Mt. Auburn Hospital.

By nine-thirty, he still had ample time to get to Century's offices. Traffic was heavy going into the city but outbound was a breeze. The reverse commute from Cambridge had been one of his best decisions when he had started at Century.

It had been right after his Army discharge. With a bachelor's degree in computer science from Boston College and some very specialized experience in military systems, he had spread a wide net, hoping to find his dream job. From the handful of offers, one had stood out: Century Computer. Century was the recognized leader in network computing, a multi-billion dollar multi-national that almost single-handedly had driven the explosive growth of the Internet. An added bonus was its location: Boston, the original high-tech incubator.

As a graduate student, Braxton had read the history of the famous Route 128. 128 was Boston's inner circumferential highway. It ran from Braintree in the south to Gloucester in the north, encircling most of the area's business and population. In the nineteen-sixties it represented a kind of frontier border, separating the staid and polished Boston and its central suburbs from the wild, open territory beyond.

By the seventies, however, the action had moved from the plush legal and financial offices on Beacon Hill to hundreds of small companies forming along what was now called America's Technology Highway. Using ideas conceived in the laboratories of MIT and Harvard, entrepreneurs set up shop and created a new computer industry, one based on small machines called mini-computers. They built companies, and fortunes, not soon matched. Names such as Wang, Olson and DiCastro were legends to be spoken of reverently whenever business moguls gathered.

Like most dreams, however, this one had an end. By the nineties, the legends were gone and their companies were decimated. Route 128 had been defeated by newer ideas and more innovative technology from a desolate valley on the opposite end of the country. It was little compensation that the dreams and enthusiasm that had formed Route 128 were exactly the same ones, albeit in a different era and different culture, that created Silicon Valley in California.

One company had fared differently, however. Century Computer had started like many others, as yet another minicomputer company. But they had recognized the tsunami that would be the PC and, rather than fighting the approaching tidal wave, steered a totally different direction: to the fledgling technology called the Internet. They developed new products called routers and gateways; specialized in algorithms and local-area-networks. And as the Internet grew, so did they.

He had started as a team leader in Century's development organization; eight years later becoming its Director of Research. He was leading the company into new areas and designing new products. It had been a dream come true.

Then, with no warning, he had been called into his boss's office and laid off. An economic downturn, Chamberlain had said. The only downturn Braxton had seen was his own.

Over the coming weeks, his shock had turned to realization, the realization to anger, and the anger to despair. As he wandered the agencies and bureaus trying to revive his professional life, he lost contact with his personal one. He deserted his friends in fits of frustration over their inability to support his pain. When Megan, his wife of five years, left he had lapsed into serious depression, and had finally sought professional assistance.

The therapist had brought him back to life and together they had developed the possibility of a consulting career. He had reconnected with his old network, and was surprised by the positive response he received. Companies were looking for ways to fix failing projects and start up new ones. All without incurring the costs of employee recruitment, training and long-term benefits. Consultants were a perfect fit.

It had been a life-saving decision.

The Cherokee suddenly lurched and Braxton was thrown forward against his seat belt, nearly losing control of the vehicle. He clutched at the steering wheel instinctively and the half-car/half-truck stabilized. Glancing back in his rear view mirror, he saw the shadow of a large pothole left by the New England winter. A reminder from Mother Nature of the futility of man's so-called progress.

The jolt to the car's frame had been frightening, but everything felt in one piece and he again congratulated himself on the selection of the Jeep. The heavy four-wheel drive vehicle was hard to drive, uncomfortably stiff, and ate gas, but it could hold up to punishment. Not a minor consideration given the usual condition of Boston roads. He had purchased it four years before, principally for climbing trips to New Hampshire and emergency commuting during blizzards. Neither role had been particularly suitable for his Boxster. When his financial situation dictated reducing his expenses, he had taken the pragmatic approach and kept the Cherokee.

Paying significantly more attention to his driving, he crossed the iconic 128, now also known as Interstate 95, and moved west into the suburbs. As he sped over the Interstate, anxiety kicked in as if it were programmed into his internal GPS. The knots in his stomach always tightened the closer he came to Concord. It had been two years since he had traveled the familiar route, and he was now doubting his reasoning to see Chamberlain in person.

He felt like a prep school student called to the proctor's office after being caught cheating on an exam. Between the weather and his nerves he'd be lucky if he didn't end the day with an ulcer.

Braxton turned off the expressway at Sudbury Road and into the West Suburban Office Park. Century Computer owned three large brick structures in the Park. The buildings held the main corporate offices, as well as headquarters for three major business units. Century had been started out of one of the founder's homes in Concord, and they had pledged to keep corporate headquarters in the historic New England town, much to the pleasure of Concord's taxpayers. Sales offices were now scattered around the world, as were manufacturing plants, but the pulse of the company had always been in Concord, and always would be as long as the founders were in control.

Braxton saw the shining silver sign with the new Century logo, interlinked capital Cs, and pulled into the driveway leading to Building 2. As he had expected, there were spaces available in the visitor's area just to the right of the main entrance. He parked, grabbed a leather folio from the passenger seat, took a deep breath and started for the doors.

Time to confront his demons.

CHAPTER 25

Century Computer, Concord, Massachusetts
Friday, 10:00 a.m.

BRAXTON ENTERED THE building and was stunned at the transformation. Plexiglas and chrome had replaced the soft textures of fabric and polished wood he remembered. Where previously the exhibits had proclaimed Century's grand history in computing technology, they now hyped the company's successes in enabling the wonders of the cloud and social media. Century's transition to the twenty-first century had become complete.

He approached the young receptionist sitting behind a gleaming reception desk. She too was a recent addition.

"Adam Braxton for Warren Chamberlain, please."

She conferred with the terminal on the desk. "Yes, Mr. Braxton. We've been expecting you. Would you please sign in?" She handed him a red visitor's badge and pointed to a Visitor's Log on the end of the counter. "If you'll take a seat in the waiting area I'll call Florence to take you up. We have an Internet link there if you would like to check with your office."

Braxton turned and walked to the visitor's area next to the entrance doors. Three plush black leather sofas surrounded a large square glass and chrome table. A collection of business and computer magazines were neatly arranged along one edge. The scene fit well with the new look of the company.

A monitor and keyboard were strategically placed in the corner of the area, its screen inviting guests to log on and peruse the Internet. Braxton had no doubt that the marketing group used it to surreptitiously collect background data from Century's visitors.

He sat down opposite a rumpled, middle-aged man reading a hardcopy spreadsheet. The boxy briefcase at his side marked him as a manufacturer's representative, probably waiting to see one of the purchasing agents. Guessing professions was a well-practiced art Braxton had developed on numerous visits to other companies.

The unwritten rules of professional etiquette demanded that visitors completely ignore each other's presence. He had always assumed this was based on a paranoid fear of having secret business relationships revealed through casual conversation.

Apparently some things at Century hadn't changed, as an image of Florence Winters materialized in his head. Winters had been Warren Chamberlain's secretary for as long as anyone could remember. Some said she had been the first employee for the new company. As far as Braxton knew, Winters was a spinster whose whole life revolved around her duties for Chamberlain. Braxton had always gotten along fairly well with her, at least as well as had any of Chamberlain's direct reports.

The last time he had seen the executive secretary was in this same building two years ago. She had called him and asked if he could come up to meet with his boss, Warren Chamberlain, Founder and Executive Vice President of Engineering for Century Computer. It had been the beginning of a long nightmare from which he still hadn't completely awakened.

The sound of the elevator bell brought Braxton back to the present. He turned and saw Winters walking toward him. It was as if he had never left. Her silver hair was still pulled tight into a bun and she was wearing her standard uniform, a trim gray suit with high necked white blouse. Only a slight rounding of her shoulders revealed the inevitable passage of time. She had not been immune to the tensions of the past few years after all.

He stood up and met her by the reception desk. "Florence, it's good to see you again."

Her face opened into a wide smile, and she seemed genuinely pleased to see him.

"Adam, I was so happy to hear from you the other day. It's been such a long time." He extended his hand, but she surprised him with an unaffected hug. Then she signed the visitor's log and motioned for him to follow her. "Warren is waiting upstairs. Now tell me what you have been up to."

He gave her a brief, slightly embellished version of his last two years as they took the elevator up to the fourth floor. The doors opened onto the executive offices of Century Computer. Braxton had always known this area as "rug row". All of the other buildings were outfitted in standard, industrial strength nylon carpet and metal furnishings, but the senior executives lived in a world of plush broadloom and polished cherry.

Talking with Winters had let him momentarily forget his anxiety. Unfortunately, it came crashing back as she led him into Chamberlain's office. Little had changed: the same black-and-white prints of Boston hung on the walls; the same cherry desk piled with papers and folders sat with its back to the panoramic window; the same bland Scandinavian leather and teak furniture filled the unused corners of the space. As impersonal an office as Braxton had ever seen.

Memories pressed on him from all sides, so disorienting he was afraid he would collapse. He grabbed the back of a chair and steadied himself until the vertigo passed.

Chamberlain rose from behind the desk. Like his office, the EVP looked exactly the same as he had that day. Dark hair slicked back, contrasting sharply with the soft features of an almost pudgy face. A starched white shirt and red tie complemented the dark wool trousers pulled a bit too tightly around his waist.

He peered at Braxton through ever-present thick, gold rimmed glasses. Braxton had always thought he looked like someone that was desperately, albeit unsuccessfully, trying to be someone else.

"Adam, hello. I'm, uh, glad you could come." A thin smile crossed the executive's lips. "Let's sit down and talk about this problem of yours." He motioned to the small sitting area in the opposite end of the room. Chamberlain sat down on an uncomfortable-looking couch. Braxton took a matching chair on the other side of a glass-topped table.

"You said you are working for the CERT Coordination Center now?" Chamberlain began. The man was as abrupt as ever. His attention was always focused on the issue at hand, never letting the humanity of his colleagues get in the way. Early in his employ Braxton had learned not to take this impoliteness personally, merely accept it as his boss's way.

"Yes, as a network security consultant."

"Oh, a consultant." Braxton could feel the condescension in his voice. According to many executives, the old saw went: " . . . those who can't, consult."

"You mentioned some kind of report," Chamberlain continued. "What was it?"

"It was an email to the Center from George Washington University, Warren." He pulled a copy of the Saracen message from his folio and handed it to Chamberlain.

The executive took a moment to read the printout. "There's certainly not much detail here. Have you contacted this . . . Saracen?"

"I went down to D.C. earlier in the week, but unfortunately there was some kind of accident and he was killed. He didn't have much additional information in his files."

The calm in Chamberlain's face was suddenly replaced by a look of surprise. "He's dead? How?"

"A bomb. The police think he might have been some kind of terrorist and accidentally blew himself up."

Chamberlain looked down and appeared to be studying the message. When he replied, there was a chill in his tone. "How unfortunate. But what does this have to do with Century, Adam? Doesn't it mean the incident will be closed?"

Braxton felt his heart pounding. How could he approach Chamberlain with his suspicions? What would be his reaction? He seemed ready to write the incident off.

"Normally, I guess it would, but since I couldn't get any information from Mr. Ramal, that's this Saracen's real name, I started doing some investigating. I've been able to reproduce some of his results. It does appear that there are unusual transmissions from the gateway at GW. And it's a Century gateway, Warren. That's why I wanted to come and see you."

"You've been monitoring the gateway yourself?" Chamberlain was gripping the message so tightly his fingers were turning white.

"Yes, the Center gave me the appropriate access codes. I was hoping you might have a look at the monitor printouts and help me understand what might be causing the transmissions. They could just be from some internal software monitors that you have added to the system. If I could talk to some of your system designers, we can probably get this resolved right away."

Chamberlain paused and stared down at the printout. "That would be very difficult right now, Adam," he finally replied, bringing his eyes back to meet Braxton's. "The teams are working to finish a product release. If you give me the printouts, I can probably get an answer back to you in a day or so."

Braxton was shocked at Chamberlain's reticence. For all of his management faults, he was usually quite willing to delegate a detail like this to the experts. "I'm sure it would be easier if I could just speak with someone from the group, Warren. Is Terry Adams still around?"

Chamberlain handed the copy of the email back to Braxton. He slid forward on the couch and placed his hands in his lap, absent-mindedly playing with a large gold ring on his right hand. "Adam, please believe me that it is impossible right now. Everyone is very busy on a new release. Let me take the output and I'll make sure that we get you an answer."

What's the big deal? Why can't he have it checked out now?

Braxton felt Chamberlain's dark eyes pressing the point. He opened the folio, extracted a sheaf of listings and passed them across the table. Chamberlain skimmed the sheets then placed them neatly on the table top. "Have you shown this data to anyone else?"

"Not yet, Warren. I wanted to review it with you before anything went back to CERT."

Chamberlain's behavior was making him angry. And the EVP's face showed an emotion he couldn't quite decipher. Maybe he needed to push harder.

"But if you are unwilling to help," he added sharply, "I can request additional support from CERT. I was hoping that would not be necessary."

"Of course we will assist, Adam," Chamberlain replied quickly. His voice became sharp and cold. "I just wouldn't want anyone to be embarrassed by a premature disclosure. It could have a devastating effect on a career."

Braxton flushed. He should have expected Chamberlain to return the threat, but not with such wrath. *What the hell had just happened?*

Chamberlain rose from the couch. Another audience was over. "It was really good to see you again, Adam. I'll have these analyzed and send you the results. I'm sure we'll find that it's just some new feature that we've added."

He showed Braxton to the door. "Florence, can you please take Adam downstairs?" Chamberlain turned back to Braxton and offered his hand, "Adam, best of luck in your new venture. Be sure and call us again."

"I certainly will, Warren. You can count on it." He locked eyes with his ex-boss then turned and followed Winters to the elevator. For some reason, Chamberlain had wanted to play games over a simple request. *What was he so concerned about?*

Once downstairs he said good-bye to Winters, each of them making empty promises to keep in touch, and signed out. Before he left, he stopped and stood in the middle of the pretentious lobby, letting the demons of Century Computer have one more chance at him. None came. He knew he had finally put that nightmare to rest.

He also knew one other thing with certainty. Chamberlain had lied about not recognizing the anomaly. He knew more than he was saying.

Chamberlain had a "tell". Braxton didn't know whether anyone else had ever recognized it, but he had been in too many meetings with the executive to not have picked it up.

It was that damn rat. The gold ring on Chamberlain's right hand was his MIT class ring, better known as a "brass rat". It was Chamberlain's battle ribbon; a not so subtle reminder of his technical pedigree. Unlike other college rings with an oval bezel, the MIT ring's was square. And not inlaid with a colorful stone, but with an engraving of an *animal*: the American beaver, or "nature's engineer" as Chamberlain explained it.

He wore it at all times, when it served variously as proof of his technical chops when presented in an introductory handshake, as an attention-grabbing gavel at meetings by tapping on a table or glass, and probably as a pretty effective brass knuckle, if he had ever lost his famously frigid temperament.

But most importantly, the ring was his tell. When under stress, Chamberlain would use his right thumb to spin the ring on his finger. Then to spin it again, and again, and again.

Braxton had first noted the behavior in an important meeting with the DoD. When questioned as to the security of Century's newest enterprise router, Chamberlain had smiled, spun away, and assured the two-stars that the device met all of DoD's requirements.

As head of QA at the time, Braxton knew that they were only

halfway through the test suite, and the list of failures was growing daily. As did Chamberlain. The bugs were eventually fixed and six months later Century was the recipient of a ten million dollar router acquisition, but in Braxton's mind, Chamberlain had lied and risked the integrity of the whole company.

Braxton had spotted the tell a number of times after that, including the day Chamberlain had let him go. It had been another cold, rainy October day. He had just finished his staff review when Winters had brought him to Chamberlain's office and his boss had told him Century needed to cut back and his position was no longer required. The ring was spun throughout the sentencing.

Business *had* taken a down-turn and Braxton *had* been a part of a wider corporate layoff, so why the tell? He had always wondered what Chamberlain had not told him.

The meeting today had been very different. Chamberlain had seemed much less frightening, much less in control of Braxton's destiny. In fact, he had almost looked afraid.

Braxton looked out the glass wall and saw beams of sunlight cutting through the dark clouds. He calmly strode across the lobby, opened the door, and continued to his car.

He wasn't going to wait for Chamberlain; he had work to do.

CHAPTER 26

Cambridge, Massachusetts
Friday, 11:15 a.m.

Braxton savored his lightened mood on the drive back into Cambridge. A brisk wind from the Berkshires had driven the storm clouds out to sea allowing a bright yellow sun to revitalize the landscape. He felt exhausted yet strangely refreshed.

Why had Chamberlain seemed so uncomfortable?

He was sure the EVP felt just as awkward as he did as a result of their history, but Braxton had sensed something deeper than that. Chamberlain had always been a very private man. Even during the times when they were working closely together, Braxton had felt that he was holding something back. He was a brilliant computer scientist, often exhibiting flashes of insight that were out-of-place for a senior executive. As a manager he was less effective, but Braxton had accepted that as typical behavior for technologists with little interest, or training, in interpersonal skills.

Yet he had been sure Chamberlain would help him identify the anomaly. Incidents like this reflected negatively on the whole industry, and the sooner they were resolved the easier it would be to limit the negative publicity. There was too much at stake to ignore them.

The benign world of computing had been changed forever when the Morris Worm surfaced. The Worm had only infected computers manufactured by Sun Microsystems and Digital Equipment Corporation. The marketing staffs of these two hugely successful companies had been stretched to their limits to control the damage to their reputations, and their revenue streams.

There would be other incidents in the future, and other names such as De Guzman, Poulsen, Mitnick and Anonymous, that would be enshrined in the annals of computer history. Usually, the commercial impact of the incident greatly overshadowed the reality of the direct damage. Ultimately, the fallout of these incidents had affected all the vendors, as buyers' increased concerns over security slowed purchases and forced more extensive product testing.

As he entered Cambridge at Fresh Pond Circle, one particular aspect of the Worm kept coming back to him. Morris's rogue had been very specific, only affecting computers made by two vendors. What did this mean for his investigation?

* * *

Braxton stopped for a sandwich in the Square then returned to his apartment. There was something he was missing. All he had were disconnected pieces of a puzzle. Despite his relief after the morning's meeting, he wasn't doing very well at fitting the pieces together. Time to start again from the beginning; it was a technique that he had used numerous times before on difficult problems. It usually worked.

He went back to the study and grabbed a stack of listings and reports. Fifteen minutes later he had spread them over his expanded dining room table, completely covering its surface. He started jotting questions on yellow Post-It notes and sticking them on the documents. He would consider an issue, pick up a related pile of paper, and place it down on a different part of the table. Unfortunately, each new configuration seemed to lead to another dead-end.

About two o'clock he heard a knock on his door and a surprisingly sophisticated-looking Paul Terrel walked through the door. His hair was brushed smartly back, his short pony-tail hanging proudly over the collar of a trim, double-breasted business suit. Braxton almost didn't recognize him.

"Paul! Is that really you? I didn't know you even owned an outfit like that."

"Hey, come on, Adam. Give me a break. I had to present the results on the new quants to a tableful of VPs. I figured I'd better look the part or they might not even listen."

"How'd you do?"

A huge smile crossed his face and his eyes twinkled. "I nailed it!"

He yanked the knot of his tie loose, then glanced over to the stacks of papers on the table. "I smelled smoke and figured you must be hard at work. What are you trying to do, start a bonfire?"

"Still working on the CERT assignment." Braxton swept his hand over the table. "I was trying to lay out all the data; thought it might help me think through it better."

Terrel came over to the table and scanned Braxton's notes. "Looks like a whole lot more questions than answers. How'd the visit to Century go?"

Braxton shook his head and shrugged. "I actually got in to see my old boss, Warren Chamberlain. He's one of the Century founders and runs product development. But the bastard stonewalled me. He wouldn't even let me talk with any of his engineers. I gave him a copy of my notes and he said he'd get back to me. I don't know. But it sure felt like he was hiding something."

Terrel picked up one of the stacks and leafed through the printouts. "What's this?"

"That's the records of the transmissions. I was trying to figure out what might have caused them."

His neighbor smiled. "You don't like my mole theory? Couldn't some kind of virus or worm have gotten into the gateway?"

"I suppose it's possible, but I've worked on those systems and they're incredibly complex. And what would it do once it was there? The configuration maps are all public. Gateways don't have any files worth stealing."

"There must be some set of software functions the mole could use." Terrel flipped through another pile of listings. "How about any trapdoors?"

Getting no response, Terrel looked up and saw Braxton staring glassy-eyed out the window.

"Adam?"

Suddenly it all clicked. Trapdoors. The Internet Worm. Century. He didn't believe it was possible.

"What if the mole didn't have to break in? What if it was there already?" Braxton raced into the living room, ran his hand along one of the bookshelves, and picked out a small volume. Then he headed for the study.

"What do mean there already?" Terrel called out as he followed his friend's circuitous path.

Braxton dropped down at his PC. Terrel watched over his shoulder as he simultaneously typed commands and explained his discovery. "It started about five years ago while I was still at Century. My group had been investigating new algorithms for directing messages through networks. We decided to test our theoretical results by developing a new type of network gateway.

"A gateway, like a network router or bridge, is normally set up as a dedicated, black-box, system. Plug them in, connect the input and output communications lines, and let them do their thing: controlling and balancing the flow of messages through their ports. Gateways do handle management data streams, like the Simple Network Management Protocol, and sometimes they hold files that can be accessed across the net with *ftp*, but most aren't set up as general purpose systems. You can't just log on to them and run a program.

"This packaging is ideal for most users, but it made developing and debugging the new algorithms a real hell for the researchers. My team wrote a special suite of programs that would permit much faster and easier investigation of network problems. We could correct routing tables, modify algorithms, and examine messages all inside the gateway."

Terrel nodded in understanding. "You built a library of gateway software tools. I did the same thing when I wrote the quant program. I had specific routines for special calculations and unique user displays. I could add the ones I wanted and remove ones that didn't work. These systems are too complex to be built as single programs."

"Right. The tools made the researchers significantly more productive. When Century decided to make the prototype gateway into a product, the development engineers wanted access to our tools as well."

"It sounds like your work got Century up to speed fast."

"Yeah. They never would have been able to deliver their next generation network products without those capabilities." He paused, remembering the morning's trip. "My reward was a goddamn pink slip."

Braxton had stopped typing and sat back in his chair. He wasn't sure he wanted to take the next step.

"The tools were a boon during implementation and field

testing," Braxton finally continued, "but they couldn't be put into the production systems. Customers would freak if they knew we could manipulate the data they were pumping through the system. Engineering was supposed to remove the capabilities from shipping products." He looked up at Terrel and his face was grave. "What if they weren't deleted; if they were still waiting, dormant, in the systems?"

"Jesus." Terrel grabbed another chair and pulled it over to the desk. "Someone could get into the gateway and change the routing, or even the content, of messages. Could they generate new messages?"

"Sure," Braxton replied matter-of-factly. "We used that feature all the time to monitor the effectiveness of new algorithms. We'd have the router send regular statistical reports back to us for analysis."

"That could explain what we're seeing, but why send diagnostic messages? That's no big deal."

"What if they're not diagnostics? Our tools could query any part of the gateway, even the incoming messages."

"You mean they could be reading everybody's transmissions? Every email?" The look on Terrel's face was a combination of shock and horror.

"Absolutely. And if they liked what they read, they could copy it and send it on to someone else. Dammit, Paul, Century could be reading everything on the Net!"

Terrel raised his hands. "Whoa, slow down, Adam. What about encryption? Most email these days is encoded. I know Wallace's is. The gateway couldn't read that."

"Yeah, maybe." Braxton turned back to his desk and typed a search phrase into Google. He hoped he could find what he wanted. "You know all the rhetoric about it taking a computer a thousand years to crack a standard encryption?"

Terrel nodded. "Sure. That's the benchmark."

"So a thousand computers could do it in a year. And a million computers in less than a day."

"Okay, but who could commandeer a million computers, and get them to cooperate on a single problem?"

Braxton pointed to one of the screens. It showed a research report on the market for internet routers and gateways. The yearly shipments of these devices was over ten million units.

"Jesus," Terrel exclaimed. "There's that many routers in the world?"

"At least. Let's keep it simple. If we assume Century has a third of the market and the average lifespan of a router or gateway is six years, then their installed base is twice the yearly market. That's at least twenty million units in the field. More than enough to crack any commercial encryption technique. And they wouldn't have to crack all the messages; just the ones with the right metadata. Messages going from or to a specific target."

Terrel still wasn't convinced. "Okay, it's possible. But what about the analysis software? You said the developers were supposed to delete it. How would it get on these machines? It would never get past Century's QA group."

Braxton smiled and shook his head. "You're kidding, right? I was there. I know what goes on in these Quality Assurance groups. They're under intense pressure to complete the checklists. From their immediate managers all the way up the chain. Every extra day they take is a day the machines aren't available to sell. It's all about the money.

"And the damned software is so complex, they only have time to test what the machines are *supposed* to do. It's hard enough to test all the documented features of a computer product. No one can test for what could be present.

"Customers would never see the extra features. As long as the gateway does everything it's supposed to do, no one looks for it to do other things. It's a classic trapdoor. A hidden feature that only a few people know."

He paused, not wanting to voice the thought that had been screaming in his brain. "The routines could be found in a code-review, but all it takes is one manager somewhere along the chain to bury the discovery. Which is exactly what would happen if that manager is involved."

"Okay, but one step at a time." Terrel slouched back in his chair. "It's a great conspiracy theory but how do you prove it? Is there any way to tell if the routines are still there?"

"One way would be to look at the programs running on the system. The tools leave a distinct pattern in the map of processes on the computer. Like running Windows Task Manager. But I'd have to be back at GW to do that."

Braxton took a deep breath and tried to relax. His heart was racing. He had to calm down.

"There is another possibility. We implemented a special interface for remote testing of the software using a special port. It was like talking directly to the heart of the gateway."

"Great. Let's try it! Do you have any documentation?"

Braxton hesitated. "No. They didn't let me take very much when I left," he said with a frown. "But we can try this." He handed Terrel the book he had taken from his shelves.

Terrel sat up and read the cover of the book. "*A History of Concord Massachusetts*? What good is this?"

"Look up the date of incorporation of Concord."

Terrel gave him an odd stare, then flipped a few pages. "1635."

"That's it." Braxton logged onto his main account at CERT, then tried a telnet connection to the GW gateway, giving the specific port number. He should have gotten an invalid request response. Instead he saw:

```
Century Diagnostic Port

Password:
```

"Goddamn it! They didn't even change the log-in banner, the arrogant sons-of-bitches." Braxton's hands were clenched and his face glowed with a scarlet flush. "It was *my work*, Paul. And I'll bet someone is using it to pull data out of the gateway."

"Okay, but you still don't have any proof this is what Ramal found. You've got to find out what's going on inside the gateway. Do you have the password too?"

Terrel was right. They didn't have any *real* proof, as Detective Fowler would call it, that this had any bearing on the investigation. He had to get into the gateway. "I can try the ones we used before. Maybe they'll still work."

They spent the next hour trying to break the password. Braxton tried all the old diagnostic keys he could remember, then various common Century phrases and colloquialisms. He even resorted to a few cracking programs he had taken off the Internet. Nothing worked. Whoever had left the tools in the production release did it deliberately; they had changed the access passwords.

Terrel finally broke the silence. "Time for a break, Adam. It's hard enough to break a personal password, much less a corporate one. It could be anything. It's time to tell CERT. They need to know what you've found."

Braxton turned to face his friend. "But I don't know *what* I found. An old message on an output port? Who knows whether it does anything?"

He sat back in his chair and dropped his head in his hands. "Let me work on it some more. Maybe I'll get in. Or Century will get back to me with an explanation."

He thought back to Chamberlain's threat. "I can't afford to make a false accusation.

* * *

The man expanded the warning icon.

```
Warning:
Invalid login attempt; diagnostic port, GW-gate
```

Damn. He's discovered the port.

Reaching for the phone, he hoped there was still time.

CHAPTER 27

The Kennedy Center, Washington, D.C.
Friday, 9:00 p.m.

THE TOWERING CRYSTAL chandeliers of the Grand Foyer sent flashes of sparkling multi-colored light over the intermission crowd, reflecting off glamorous sequined gowns and shiny bald pates on the floor below. An opening night at The Kennedy Center was always a major social event, and tonight was no exception. The production company for "The King and I" revival had come directly from New York. It was an expansive and colorful production, very unlike the minimalist designs of the past season. The attendees were in good spirits, and were eager to begin the really important part of the evening: networking.

Potterfield made his way down the stairs from his balcony seat with his wife and entourage in tow. He had invited three recent additions to his staff to join him at the opening. The occasional favor was an important part of his position. It solidified staff morale and insured their continued allegiance.

Loyalty was the one thing that had been bothering him about Nicholson lately. He seemed to need Potterfield's favors and assistance less and less. Last week he had told the Senator that he had made separate reservations for the performance. How had he managed that?

"Have you seen Nick tonight, Mary Jane?" he asked his wife as they made their way to the lobby bar.

Mary Jane Potterfield was a stately, if plump, elderly black woman. Her gray hair was pulled back from her face revealing a broad forehead, prominent cheekbones, and piercing brown eyes.

About a head shorter than her husband, she carried herself with an aplomb suitable for the wife of one of Washington's most powerful men. She saw to his wants, ran their home like a general, and had become a prominent participant in the Washington social scene. It had been a difficult road from the streets of Richmond, and she had weathered many crises along the way, most caused by her husband's sometimes not so private indiscretions. But long ago they had decided that God had meant for them to travel this path together. Neither could imagine the trip alone.

"No, dear. But I'm sure he's here. He wouldn't miss the opportunity to dig up some dirt on someone." Potterfield glared at his wife. She held little respect for his Chief of Staff. For some reason, they had never gotten along. He had finally decided it was jealousy; he and Nick spent altogether too much time together.

Potterfield ordered a whiskey on the rocks and craned his neck to see over the crowd.

"Senator, I've been looking for you." Potterfield turned and saw Nicholson approaching. An elegant, ravishing woman was draped regally on his arm. She was tall and slim, her curvaceous body wrapped in a traditional African *dashiki*.

"Angelina, this is my famous employer, Senator David Potterfield and his lovely wife, Mary Jane. Senator, Mrs. Potterfield, this is Angelina Mowaru. Angelina is an attaché at the Rwandan Embassy."

"Senator, how very nice to meet you," Mowaru said with an inviting smile. "I have followed your activities with much interest. Your positions on increased aid to the developing countries of Africa are most progressive. I hope you will continue to pursue these policies."

"Why thank you, Miss Mowaru. I hope that my efforts have been of some small assistance to countries less fortunate than our own. How long have you been in Washington?"

"Only about three months now. But Nick has been showing me many of your lovely sites. He has been so very kind." She looked up at Nicholson and lightly squeezed his arm. He feigned embarrassment, but Potterfield noticed a satisfied smile cross his face.

"Unfortunately, I'm afraid I must speak with my Chief of Staff on some business matters," Potterfield abruptly interjected. "If you would excuse us for a moment, please."

"Come, my dear," Mary Jane offered as she put out her arm. "Let these men solve the problems of State by themselves. I would really like to get your impressions of the production. I'm on the Board of Directors for the Center, you know."

Potterfield, drink in hand, led Nicholson out the doors and onto the River Terrace. It was a brisk, clear Washington night. To their left, a procession of white and crimson lights floated across the Potomac over Francis Scott Key Bridge. To their right, Georgetown University and the National Cathedral warmed the black sky with an ethereal golden glow. There was no need to worry about anyone overhearing their conversation, the temperature on the terrace ensured they would be left alone.

"What have you found out about the email, Nick? We can't have this threat hanging over us any longer."

"I have some of the interns doing some research, I think . . ."

"You what! I said I wanted this taken care of quietly. Now you've got some loose-mouthed college brats doing your work for you?"

Nicholson raised his hands in defense. "David, calm down. They're simply checking out the locations of some reporters. We're getting closer every day to the identification. But we have to keep stringing the blackmailer along. If we lose contact we may never find out who he is. And he could reappear at any time."

"So I have to keep reading this crap?"

"Yes. If anything new comes in tell me immediately. We need every hint he may give us. You can hang on a little longer."

"Easy for you to say. But when you find out who got that information, make sure it gets buried for good this time. I don't want . . ."

"Senator Potterfield. What a surprise to find you here."

Potterfield's head spun toward the voice. Robert Greystone calmly appeared out of the darkness.

"How good to see you both again," Greystone said. "I hope I'm not interrupting anything?"

Potterfield exchanged glances with his aide. His anger quickly disappeared replaced by a broad smile. "Not at all. Just getting some fresh air, Mr. Greystone." He nodded at Nicholson. "You remember my Chief of Staff?"

"Yes. Mr. Nicholson, isn't it? Good to see you again."

"Mr. Greystone," Nicholson replied coldly.

"Have you and Barclay had an opportunity to follow-up on that matter we discussed in my office last week?" Potterfield said to the executive.

"No we haven't, Senator. Actually, I was hoping we might talk a little right now about how to proceed."

Potterfield looked over into the reception area. "An excellent idea, my boy. You must excuse me, however. I see my wife waving to me. Can't leave her waiting you know. But please speak with Barclay. He can be of enormous assistance in helping me to understand your position."

Potterfield turned and slowly walked back inside the Center. Once hidden by the crowd, he looked back to see the two men engrossed in animated conversation.

Good. At least something was going as planned. Hopefully, they can work out an agreement that will make us all very rich.

* * *

The two men stood uncomfortably in the bracing night air. When Potterfield had finally disappeared into the building Nicholson spoke. "Bob, what the hell are you doing? We can't be seen meeting out here together!"

Greystone smiled and threw his arm around the aide. "Of course we can, Nick. Your boss gave us the perfect alibi. We're discussing the new Bill. We should have thought of this earlier."

"It still makes me nervous."

"I must say you do look somewhat stressed. I hadn't heard anything from you in a week or so and wanted to check in. Is anything wrong?"

Nicholson considered hiding the blackmail threat but knew better than to keep anything from Greystone. Somehow he always found out.

"We received an anonymous email about the Lynch affair. It threatened to expose the Senator if he didn't resign. The original message came through an anonymous remailer. I'm trying to track down anyone that might still remember what happened."

Greystone's bonhomie immediately disappeared. "Christ. What next? Sorry I was so short with you. Need any help?"

"No, Bob," Nicholson said firmly. "I can take care of it. It'll just take a few more days. What's happening with the gateway intrusions?"

"I need to talk to you about that. The intrusions are getting more serious. We may have to take additional action."

"I don't like all this going on at the same time. Maybe we should . . ."

"There you are, Nick. Senator Potterfield said I would find you hiding out here." Mowaru came through the door and walked toward the pair.

As she approached, Greystone leaned over to Nicholson and whispered, "Manassas, Sunday noon."

Before Nicholson could respond, Mowaru had come up to his side. He wrapped his arm around her waist.

"Angelina. This is, ah, Robert Greystone. A very important industry constituent. Mr. Greystone, Angelina Mowaru from the Rwandan embassy."

"Mr. Greystone." Mowaru smiled and extended her hand.

Greystone paused and gave the attaché a prolonged look. Finally he took her hand.

"Miss Mowaru, how very nice to meet such a lovely addition to our city. Are you enjoying the evening?"

"Yes, Mr. Greystone, I am," she said, smiling up at Nicholson.

"I'm sure Mr. Nicholson is doing everything he can to keep you quite contented. I have a number of friends in Embassy Row myself. Perhaps we will meet again. I would certainly enjoy the pleasure of your company."

"Perhaps, Mr. Greystone. But who knows what the future will bring?" she replied with a chill that matched the night air.

The lights inside the Center dimmed, and the crowd in the lobby began making their way back to their seats.

"Well, it looks like it's time to return," Greystone said. "Very nice meeting you, Miss Mowaru. Mr. Nicholson. Until next time." Neither responded, and Greystone turned and went inside.

Nicholson waited until the executive had joined the crowd, then lead Mowaru back to their box. As they made their way down the aisle, she leaned over and whispered, "Nick, that man is quite strange. He makes me very uncomfortable."

"Yes, darling, I know. He does that to everyone. He always has."

* * *

Goddard dropped her Rollaboard onto the luggage rack and bounced down on the bed. Her hands were shaking. It was ridiculous to be so nervous.

The idea had popped into her head during the flight from Reagan National. There was something about the consultant that intrigued her. Unlike most of the people she had met who were involved in the investigation, he seemed genuinely interested in finding the truth, not in automatically labeling Mohammed a terrorist. She had to help him if she could.

And he was even quite pleasing to the eye.

She called room service, then stepped into the shower to wash off the travel grime. By the time she finished drying her hair, her dinner had arrived. Her butterflies wouldn't go away, so rather than ruining a perfectly good Caesar salad, she made the call.

"Adam Braxton," the voice said.

"Mr. Braxton, this is Susan Goddard, we met at Georgetown University the other day. I didn't wake you did I?" She hoped he wouldn't notice the tremor in her voice.

"Miss Goddard. This certainly is a surprise. And I am definitely awake; I was just working on a report to CERT."

"Ah, I've been thinking about Mohammed. About his work. I may have remembered some things he said about his project. If you're still looking into that message, I was wondering if we could talk."

"Certainly. I can come down to D.C. next week and we can set up some time."

His positive response made the next step significantly easier. *The worst he can do is refuse, right?*

"Actually, I'm here in Boston for an interview. If you're not busy, ah, perhaps we could get together for dinner tomorrow night?"

There was a pause on the phone and she held her breath. "Of course," she finally heard. "That sounds great. Should I pick you up at your hotel? Say about seven?"

"Can we make it earlier? About six? It's going to be a long day and I don't know how long I'll be able to last."

"Six is fine. Where are you staying?"

"I'm at the Parker House downtown." Not having planned anything else to say, she concluded with a short, "See you later then."

"Right. Six o'clock at the Parker House. 'Bye."

She set down the phone and released a nervous sigh. She had done it. No use in worrying about it any longer. Time to get back to her dinner.

CHAPTER 28

Century Computer, Concord, Massachusetts
Saturday, 8:00 a.m.

How did I ever let it go this far?

Chamberlain leaned back in his chair and let the warm morning sun streaming through his office windows bathe his beleaguered face. He had slept fitfully the night before, still disturbed by the meeting with his ex-employee. When the alarm had finally forced him out of bed, he elected to spend his Saturday in the office, hoping work would push the questions from his mind.

He had arrived at Century at 7:30 and prepared for his morning regimen: a cup of fresh coffee and a review of the daily papers. His coffee machine now sat ready on the ledge by the windows and the *Boston Globe* was spread across the top of his desk.

So why didn't he want to get started?

They had just been trying to do the right thing. To help each other out. What went so wrong?

He resolutely started on the paper.

The aura took form slowly, just below his sensory threshold. Halfway through the Metro section he recognized the warning signs but it was too late. Sweat formed at his temples and black shadows crept around his field of view, shutting off the light to his eyes like a closing camera lens.

The throbbing started at his eyes and spread up and back, encircling his head with a numbing ache. It was crushing his skull, making it impossible to think; he couldn't fight it.

He reached for the sumatriptan tablets in his top desk drawer. The migraines had come with increasing frequency over the past months. At this rate, by the end of the year he wouldn't be of much value to anyone. He hated the medication but there was no way to function without it.

Chamberlain popped a handful of pills in his mouth, and washed them down with now-tepid coffee. Staggering across the room, he collapsed on the couch and let the drug deaden the crippling pain.

He closed his eyes and tried to relax. As he lay there, his thoughts went back to the day, over forty years before, when they first had met.

* * *

He awoke at 5:00 a.m., pulled on a pair of jeans and an old sweatshirt with "Massachusetts Institute of Technology" squeezed on the front, and ran downstairs for a quick breakfast. Thankfully, their cook had remembered his schedule and had unpacked the delivery of cereal. The rest of the fraternity would certainly not get up before eight, and he knew a few who felt that arising before noon was an affront to the unwritten student credo.

He never really minded the quiet of the morning. As an only child, Warren Chamberlain was used to getting himself going. The solitude was comforting, it let him put his thoughts in order and plan the day ahead. He had always been an early riser, and the schedule set out for the crew team was one that he had fallen into with little complaint. The physical exertion of his chosen sport relaxed him for the mental challenges of the rest of the day. His schedule did put a helluva strain on his social calendar, but that had never been a particularly critical part of his life. He would worry about that after he graduated.

After the workout on the Charles he showered and dressed. This was going to be a good term, he decided as he jaywalked across Memorial Drive from the boat house to the campus. He had done well the previous term, receiving a 4.2 average, MIT based its grades on a 5.0 scale, more than enough to keep his scholarship. His family wasn't poor, his father owned his own insurance agency in Cincinnati, but tuition was unbelievable, over $2500 a year. He had heard about the "1700 Is Too Damn Much" student riots a few years before. What had they had to complain about?

Warren was taking the standard sophomore fare: math, physics, chemistry, and the requisite humanities course. He had also managed to get into a new computer class. He didn't know much about computers, but he'd heard this one would give him a pretty good introduction.

The catalog said "6.251—Digital Computer Programming Systems". Like all courses at MIT, the class was known simply by its number, pronounced "six two fifty-one". The six stood for the Electrical Engineering Department—Computer Science as a course of study hadn't been invented yet. No one ever figured out what the 251 stood for.

But then everything at the Massachusetts Institute of Technology was numbers. MIT was a numerologist's dream. Course 6.251 lectures were held in 10-250, that was "ten two fifty". Building number 10, second floor. The verbalization of punctuation was unnecessary. It was all a part of the mystique, the code that MIT students, and graduates, carried around to differentiate themselves from the uninitiated.

He walked east down Memorial Drive, then turned north into the verdant tree-lined Great Court—the academic quad at other universities—where students threw Frisbees, ate lunches and generally took a break from academic overload.

Around the Great Court lay the original MIT buildings. The granite-faced, neoclassical buildings, or more accurately interconnected structures, were placed on the sides of a gigantic square with the bottom side removed. The top of the square faced the Charles River and the two sides ran nearly down to Memorial Drive.

Straight ahead, at the square's top, was the imposing façade of Building 10, the centerpiece, and most-recognized symbol, of the Institute. Its Great Dome, housing the extensive Engineering Library, rose 150 feet into the sky, supported by ten Greek Ionic columns, representing the ten presidents of the university who preceded the move of "Boston Tech" across the river to Cambridge in 1916.

To Warren's left were Buildings 1, 3 and 5, to his right, 2, 4 and 6. The only consistency in the Institute's numbering system was that all buildings to the west of Building 10 had odd numbers; those to the east had even. It was a task to just find the locations of his classrooms.

He reached the top of the Court and walked through the entrance doors at 8:52. Climbing the single flight of stairs to the second floor, he entered Room 10-250, the main lecture hall in the center of the building. Warren had arrived early and found a middle seat in the eighth row. Less prepared students searched for dark corners in the upper rows to avoid being asked to contribute to the day's instruction.

The lecture hall reminded him of a theater. It was huge, twenty-five curving rows rising at a steep incline toward the back of the hall. From his central seat, he looked down on the still empty lecture floor. A large, battered metal table sat in the center of the "stage", undoubtedly government-issue from some long-forgotten research grant. It was littered with threaded rods and laboratory paraphernalia in preparation for a future chemistry experiment.

Behind the table on the front walls of the room were six enormous chalkboards that would hold the scenery of the day's performance. They were mounted three-abreast, covering the surface between the entrance doors and the opposite front corner of the room. The boards were stacked top to bottom, the upper one nearly reaching the vaulted ceiling. The upper boards had tracks on each side, and were counter-weighted, so that the professor—or more likely the unfortunate graduate-student-of-the-day—could pull them down over the lower boards at the start of class, fill them with notes, and then raise them out of the way to expose a new virgin area. This left all the notes visible during the lecture. A relief to those with less-than-perfect note-taking skills.

This morning, the scenery from the previous class was still there; Warren didn't understand it all but it appeared to be from an advanced calculus class. He could imagine the furious writing as the students attempted to recreate this outpouring of knowledge in their notebooks.

He watched as the rest of the class arrived. It was the beginning of a new term, and the students rambled into the classroom, looking for familiar faces, hoping that the genius from that killer subject last term was here to help them get through this one. Five noisy black students came in and sat toward the back. Chamberlain hoped they wouldn't disrupt the class too badly.

The last to arrive was a very preppy-looking scholar replete in a coat and tie. At first Warren had thought he was the professor, but he was dressed too well for even them. It was hard to believe the student came from the Institute. He located one of the last free seats along the side and was still getting settled when the instructor arrived.

"Good morning," the man began, "I'm Professor John Donovan and this is 6.251, Digital Computer Programming Systems." He lectured for a full fifty-five minutes, stopping just before the top of the hour. He spoke of compilers and assemblers, linkers and loaders - terms that were unfamiliar to most but would become a central part of their lives for the next four months.

The students had been quiet, almost reverent. For some this was their first introduction to computers. Others had some knowledge of the new type of machine. Those that finished the course would know more than most so-called experts in the field. 6.251 was a proving ground, an obstacle course for the future computer elite. It would be the most difficult course any of them had ever taken.

*   *   *

The culmination of 6.251 was the "term project". For other schools the effort expended would have been sufficient for a Senior Thesis, but for this class it was just half of the term's grade. What was so surprising was the zeal with which the students approached it. More than just a project, it was a rite of passage, a challenge to the manhood, or womanhood in a few isolated cases, of the students.

In later years the project would be more proscribed to limit the psychological damage, but for this term it was still completely student-designed. A simple approval from a teaching assistant and a team set out toward their goal.

Project teams were set up about a third of the way through the term. They normally consisted of two or three members. Most of the students in the class had already made their selections; they had friends, roommates, classmates from the same dormitory or fraternity in the class. Warren didn't know anyone else and simply hadn't had time to make any new friends. When the final team assignments were posted on the bulletin board outside 10-250, he tried to associate faces with the two names he saw printed with his.

As the other students filed off to discuss their plans, he noticed two classmates milling self-consciously around the board. Finally the one in the jacket and tie came up and introduced himself. "My name's Bob," he had said. "I'm from Harvard."

The other student, a gangly black with an impressively large afro, then joined them. "I'm Nick," he offered.

The team set about their effort with no small sense of trepidation. They had a distinctly unique range of styles and backgrounds, and their differences initially resulted in overt hostility. They were all confident of their individual abilities, Warren often thought the others arrogant, but soon they realized they were all in over their heads and would need to work together to get through the daunting assignment.

Each team's first job was to pick a name for themselves. It gave them a unique identity that served the purposes of both the instructors and the participants. After much heated debate, Warren suggested "The Cache". Its double meaning satisfied his sense of ambiguity. Webster's said a cache was "a hiding place for concealing and safeguarding valuables". In computer terminology, a cache was an intermediate storage area that, among other actions, mediated the flow of information from one part of a system to another. Unable to come up with anything better, the trio made their first decision.

Bob and Nick designed the project drawing on their particular interests. Warren was satisfied to just have a topic settled. The project was a natural language query system into a data base of financial records. Since data bases themselves were still a matter of academic research at that time, the team decided to design a new one for the project. This was typical of the 6.251 assignment. Having little insight into how difficult real problems were, the students simply picked a topic that sounded interesting and ended up inventing all the structures and algorithms that were needed.

Bob gathered the raw data. He collaborated with Warren on an appropriate data structure and on the programs to load and access the information.

Nick found he had a gift for programming. He designed and built the language interpreter, the program that would take user commands and convert them to the arcane instructions needed by the data base. Warren also worked with Nick to complete the necessary subroutines and operating system interfaces.

The effort went forward, albeit not without a number of fits and starts. The hours devoted grew longer as the deadline approached and all three students began missing other classes, social engagements, and sleep. They felt the exhilaration of success as a test run completed without error, and the frustration of failure when three days' work turned into nothing more than a stack of incomprehensible error messages.

The hours of effort were broken with discussions of thoughts and feelings that would have otherwise gone unsaid. They expressed their own goals and desires, their hopes for the future. They found common bonds in their intellect, their mental confidence—if not their personal—and their social perspective. The Cache finished their project on time, perhaps not in the grand form as they had originally planned, but enough to get them the grade they wanted.

It was the start of a complex journey that would take many more years to reveal its destination.

*   *   *

The drug finally took hold, masking the pain and giving Chamberlain the blessing of sleep. It was the most he could ask for. There were no easy answers to the questions he posed.

CHAPTER 29

Cambridge, Massachusetts
Saturday, 5:15 p.m.

BRAXTON HAD SPENT the day doing the chores and running the errands that had piled up from the previous week. He had badly needed a break from the investigation and had moved from one to-do list item to the next in mindless oblivion. Not coincidentally, it also had allowed him to avoid thinking about his upcoming appointment.

He couldn't procrastinate any longer, however, and now stared dejectedly into his bedroom closet. It had been a very long time since he had gone to dinner with an attractive female. In fact, it had been a long time since he had even thought much about the opposite sex. Ever since Megan had left, he had shunted those thoughts to the back of his mind. He had even taken the divorce lightly, too withdrawn in himself to really care, but he had felt the loss every day since.

At first he had blamed her. She just wouldn't understand. He now realized it had not been her at all. He had shut her off and driven her out of his life in the same way he had alienated all of his friends. Where was their compassion, he had cried. Couldn't they see how badly he had been treated? Why wouldn't they be depressed with him?

Megan had been unbelievably patient. She held him, talked to him, tried to get him to go for help. But he had rejected her at every corner. After a year, there had been nothing left to save. It wasn't that she had stopped caring for him. She simply knew there was nothing more she could do. He had to find his own way and that meant breaking all of his dependencies.

One afternoon he had come home from the unemployment office and she had told him it was time to go. She was in high-tech also, and had accepted an offer as Director of Marketing at a West Coast start-up. She was starting immediately. The next day she was gone.

They still spoke on the phone occasionally, and he received the obligatory birthday and holiday cards. He tried not to dwell on her memory, but there were times when her absence burned painfully in his heart.

Susan Goddard reminded him a lot of Megan. She was certainly appealing, and he sensed a wit and intelligence rare in a college coed, at least as far as he remembered. Her call had come as a complete surprise. He tried not to read too much into the invitation.

All of which brought him back to his closet. He only had a half-hour and he didn't have any more time to procrastinate. His blue blazer was clean, so he grabbed a pair of charcoal gray slacks and a button-down blue oxford. He threw on the jacket and headed out the door, hoping he didn't look too stodgy.

He met Terrel coming up the stairs as he was going down.

"Wow, Adam. You're all spruced up. Got a heavy date?"

"As a matter of fact, yes," he said proudly, only slightly stretching the truth. He flashed a broad smile. "Don't wait up for me."

"Cool. Before you go, I had a thought on the . . ."

Braxton checked his watch. He had to get going. "Sorry, Paul. I'm late already. I'll catch you tomorrow."

He waved over his shoulder and headed for Harvard Station.

* * *

The two men watched silently from their rented Taurus as Braxton left at 5:35. The lights along Brattle Street were on, their glow filtering through the heavy mist that had come in off the coast. Traffic moved methodically down the street toward the Square and the few pedestrians braving the weather were huddled under umbrellas.

It was perfect weather. People were generally depressed on days like this and not very perceptive. They didn't bother to notice new faces or out-of-the-ordinary events. It was enough for them to just get through the day. Harding was amazed how important these psychological effects had become to him. As he grew older, he had begun to focus much more on the subtleties of his profession. A necessity to compensate for the slow but inevitable diminishing of his physical skills. He had always been meticulously careful, you had to be in his business to stay alive, but bad weather gave him an extra edge. It was important to take advantage of every opportunity.

The discovery of his current colleague was a case in point. He had been in Houston on a contract. The target was a politician who had been a little too loose with some recent wealth he had received from local business concerns. The businessmen were worried that the man's actions would draw undesirable attention, and their warnings had gone unheeded. More reliable assurances had been deemed necessary.

The politician had hired a bodyguard and Harding was, of course, checking him out. The protector was young and undisciplined, hardly more than a thug, but he impressed Harding with his natural skills. He was about ten years younger than the professional and almost a foot shorter. Stocky and solid, he made a significant barrier but unfortunately was also quite obvious in a crowd.

His movements were smoother than Harding had expected. That meant he had had some physical training, probably boxing. He was reasonably thorough in securing perimeters and access, and was not afraid to use his considerable strength when it was required. Over this period of observation, Harding had actually developed a rudimentary respect for the man. It was unfortunate that he was going to fail so early in his career.

Harding had chosen a private, face-to-face hit. He entered the target's suite at 3:00 a.m., the generally accepted time of minimum human alertness. The bodyguard had incorrectly assumed the alarm system was sufficient and awoke to find his principal in a pool of blood on the bed and a 9mm Glock focused on his face. Harding had given him a choice: to come and work for him as an associate, or death.

His answer was meaningless, of course. What Harding had needed to see was his eyes, to watch his expression as he dealt with the dilemma.

Nathan had worked diligently over the ensuing ten years, often proving himself under fire, and the associate had become a trusted partner. Harding had been able to expand his business five-fold. Not a bad return on his investment.

At 6:15 Nathan spotted a familiar shape approaching the apartment. Among his other talents, he had a knack for faces and had noticed the elderly woman leaving the apartment earlier. The two men left their rental and made their way through the drizzle to the other side of the street. They were dressed in dark jackets and slacks and wore thin black cotton gloves. The crepe soles on their shoes were designed to provide secure footing even on wet, normally-slippery surfaces, another precaution for the day's forecast.

They timed their arrival to match that of the woman and followed her up the steps to the entrance. She unlocked the security door and thanked them when they held it for her as she fumbled to get inside with her umbrella and grocery cart. Tired and wet from the rain, she had no desire for small talk and struggled down the hall and around the corner. Harding was sure their faces would rapidly fade from her memory.

The men casually climbed the front stairs to the third floor and walked down the hall to apartment 3B. As Harding kept watch, Nathan produced two small metal wires from his pocket. It took him less than fifteen seconds to pick both the deadbolt and main locks. They entered the apartment, and Nathan relocked the door behind them.

They pulled out pocket flashlights and made a pass through the apartment together, each man making a mental map of the territory and noting possible emergency exits and concealment locations. Then they separated and prepared the cover. It was to be a bungled robbery. Harding took the kitchen and bedroom, Nathan the dining area and study. They left the living room untouched so as to not alarm the target when he entered. Being so sloppy was against Harding's nature but the result was all a part of the scene they needed to prepare. After fifteen minutes they completed the search, finding hardly anything worth stealing; only a few pieces of jewelry and a box Nathan had found buried on a hall closet shelf.

Harding was just as glad that this time they were to leave the computer shit alone. He had never been able to understand the damned things. Explosives were as high tech as he could handle. Their client had complained that they had been too "obvious" in D.C. Harding had pointedly replied that he wasn't a computer expert, and he had done exactly as they had agreed. If the gentleman persisted in complaining about their results, the relationship would be terminated and appropriate defensive actions would be taken.

That had ended the client's whining for the moment. It would not have been the first time that he had had to eliminate an unreasonable reference. It just wasn't good for business.

The target would enter the room, turn on the lights, and start to close the door. Nathan would perform the hit, while Harding secured the door. Then they would check the hall, and exit the building via the rear stairway. The trip to Logan Airport would be a breeze.

Nathan pulled two folding chairs into the corner behind the doorway and the two men settled in. They drew long cylindrical silencers from their pockets and carefully screwed the extensions onto their Glocks. Their motions were practiced and automatic.

Then they fell silent; the next minutes of quiet preparing them for the imminent rush.

CHAPTER 30

BRAXTON WAS ALREADY late, and fighting traffic was the last thing he had wanted to do. Boston's driving reputation was well earned. Driving and parking in the city was a hassle and frequently hazardous. Taking the *T* was a much better idea. He caught a train just as it was leaving Harvard Station, and fifteen minutes later he was emerging into the twilight at Park Street.

The clouds were heavy in the sky, but the sidewalks were dry. No rain yet. He cursed himself for not bringing an umbrella. He wasn't much of a well-prepared escort.

The Common was surprisingly busy; a mix of early-spring sight-seers and afternoon shoppers, the latter balancing bags and boxes as they headed home after raiding the stores at Downtown Crossing.

He turned up Tremont, took a right onto School Street, and entered the hotel.

Walking into the Parker House was like stepping back in time. Located on Beacon Hill between the Massachusetts State House and Boston's commercial district, it was one of the few grand old hotels left in the city. Heavy with oak and smelling of well-fed leather, it made him feel important just to be standing in the lobby. Perhaps it had lost a bit of its grandeur over the past one hundred and fifty years, but it was still a favorite of politicians, lobbyists, and business executives. He would have thought it a little pricy for a graduate student, but he was quickly discovering Susan Goddard was anything but typical.

He dropped into an overstuffed gold-brocade wingback chair

and settled in amidst the muted conversations of the gathered gentlemen and ladies. How could he be waiting here to take a Georgetown graduate student to dinner? He hoped he wouldn't make a fool out of himself.

The background chatter suddenly hushed and he followed the others' eyes toward the staircase from the floor above. Whatever he was expecting, it could not have done justice to the striking woman making her way down the stairs. Goddard was wearing a shimmering blue silk suit cut to highlight her broad shoulders, slim waist and shapely legs. She had rolled her blonde hair into a tight French Braid at the back of her head and added just a touch of makeup. A pair of three-inch heels completed the transformation.

Walking confidently over to Braxton, her long-legged strides reminded him more of a fashion model than a college student. Where had she achieved such grace?

"Mr. Braxton. It's very nice to see you again." Goddard smiled and extended her hand.

"Miss Goddard," he said as he accepted the gesture. Her skin was soft, but she returned the handshake with an experienced firmness. "Ah, you look really nice."

"Why thank you."

That was a stupid start. Get it together, Adam. "If you don't mind my saying so, you turned a number of heads just now."

A slight flush came to her cheeks and she seemed genuinely embarrassed. "I felt like dressing up a bit tonight. I hope you don't mind."

"Not at all. Although I'm afraid I'm a little under-dressed."

"I think you look just great." Her face brightened the whole room.

"Thanks. Do you like Italian food?"

"Absolutely."

"Good, then let's get going."

They took a taxi to the North End, Boston's version of Little Italy. A close knit, fiercely ethnic neighborhood, it was dotted with exceptional Italian restaurants. Mama Peirina's was a frequent tourist spot, but Braxton loved the food and the atmosphere.

It was early in the evening, so they had their choice of tables. Braxton selected one that looked out over North Square Park. The rain had started, and tourists rushed to their destinations waving their umbrellas and sidestepping the puddles.

They sat opposite each other beside a small candlelit sconce, surrounded by paintings depicting quaint Italian towns.

A young waitress with long dark hair, olive-colored skin and a thick Italian accent promptly appeared. They left their menus closed and ordered two glasses of Prosecco to start the evening.

"So what brings you to Boston?" Braxton asked as the waitress slinked back to the bar. "Did you say you had an interview?"

"Yes," Goddard replied. "I still have another year of grad school, but I'm looking for a summer internship at a TV station. Jobs at the networks in D.C. or New York are impossible. I thought I might have better luck up here."

"An interview on a Saturday"?

She gave him a sly grin. "They were very accommodating to my class schedule."

He wanted to ask why, but sensed an answer wouldn't be forthcoming. "How did it go?"

"Pretty well I think. I interviewed with the programming manager at WGBH. I want to learn more about the media production end. 'GBH does a lot of really good work in that area. They also collaborate with WNET in New York, so I would get back down there some as well."

"Are you from New York?"

"Oh no, I was born in Virginia but I've lived in a number of places on the East Coast. I like the excitement of big cities."

Her travels explained a lot. Goddard was clearly a very polished woman with extensive experiences. It would explain her ability to move so easily in a variety of environments. He felt a bit like a small-town yokel in comparison.

"It must be tough to move around like that," Braxton finally replied.

"It's not so bad. You get used to it. I never learned how to make many friends, though. I'm afraid I'm pretty much of a loner."

That was certainly a surprise. Why would she feel so isolated?

The waitress brought their glasses. Braxton raised his and toasted his lovely companion. "Cheers, Miss Goddard. To a successful visit."

"Thank you," she replied. "So far it's been very pleasant."

When she smiled, her eyes glowed with an excitement he couldn't resist. He expected that she was able to put anyone completely at ease; when she wanted.

"How did you get interested in TV?" he asked.

"It's not so much TV, but the whole area of news and information. It took me a long time to decide what I wanted to do. My undergraduate degree is in business but I just couldn't see spending the rest of my life behind a desk. I was interested in media and government, and got into a great program at Georgetown. I think I can play a role in bringing government and politics directly to the people. And I love being back in D.C., too."

He was taken by her openness and enthusiasm. Did he ever feel the same way about his work? Maybe a long time ago.

"Oh, I'm sorry," she said. "I'm just babbling."

"No, it's okay. I was just thinking how refreshing it is to talk to someone that really likes what they're doing. What's your major?"

"I'm in the Political Science Department, but my focus is on information and communications. I wanted to know more about the relationship between computers and the media so I started taking some computer science courses at GW. That's how I met Mohammed."

Braxton hadn't known how to broach her relationship with Ramal. Thankfully, she had provided the opening. He tried a small push. "How long had you known him?"

"We were in the same class last term. He helped me with some assignments. When we both signed up for Multimedia Systems, we decided to work on a project together. He was a really good guy."

She paused and he didn't know whether to continue. Her smile had changed into a sadder, more pensive look. Despite his initial jitters, he was enjoying her company very much. He hoped she felt the same way and didn't want to ruin it.

"Now tell me something about Mr. Adam Braxton," she asked, turning the conversation to a lighter subject.

"How about just Adam? Mr. Braxton sounds like a stuffy old man."

"Okay, Adam. And I'm Susan. Have you always worked with computers?"

"Pretty much. My dad was an engineering manager for GE. That was back in the days of vacuum tubes and relays. He got me started tinkering with equipment when I was just a kid. I spent a lot of time at his laboratory all through school."

"He must have been very proud of you."

"I think he was. When I got to BC I just naturally gravitated to computer science."

"You went to Boston College"?

"Yes. Another good Jesuit school like Georgetown." He grinned. "That almost makes us brother and sister."

"Well, maybe not *that* close. Is your dad still working?"

"No," he said flatly. His smile immediately disappeared. Why did she have to ask that? "He retired a number of years ago. How about your parents?"

"Oh, they've both passed away," she replied sadly.

They sat in an awkward silence, neither knowing how to continue the conversation.

Goddard finally broke the ice. "How long have you been a security consultant?"

The question felt like the stab of a knife. Why did she have to pry into that?

He couldn't just ignore her, so he paused, took a deep breath and replied.

"Consulting is still pretty new. I went into the Army after BC and learned a lot about networks and security. Then I spent a few years in network research and development. We were working on internetworking protocols and network interfaces; the hardware and software that glues computers together.

"When I decided to look for something new, a friend suggested consulting. To be honest, this is my first job for CERT. So far it has been quite an experience. And a pleasant one," he added with an awkward smile.

She acknowledged his attempt with a demur upturn at the corners of her mouth. "It must have been exciting helping to build the Internet. What made you decide to change?"

He felt a knot tightening in his gut. Why did she have to talk about Century?

"Uh, it really wasn't that glamorous. We were just another company trying to break into a new market. Competition was fierce and we were having some difficulties in other product areas. It was a tough time."

"That does sound bad. Is the company still around?"

The knots were getting tighter. Twisting up his backbone and squeezing his skull until he thought it would break. Beads of sweat appeared on his forehead.

"Yes, they're doing just fine. Selling all the products I designed before . . ."

"Did you get laid off?"

Why can't she just *drop* it? Can't she see how upsetting it is? He felt beads of sweat dripping down his temples.

"No, they fired me," he shot back.

"I'm sorry, it must have been really difficult."

"Look, I don't want your pity," Braxton suddenly yelled. He slapped the table, shaking the wine in their glasses. "I'm doing the best I can."

The room was struck mute by the outburst. Heads turned to locate the outburst, then, one by one, resumed their conversations.

Goddard waited until the unwanted attention had passed. "I'm sorry Mr. Braxton. I didn't mean to imply any pity." She straightened in her chair and drew back from the table. "Perhaps we should do this another time." Her voice was icy cold and distant.

Braxton dropped his head into his hands and slowly rubbed the side of his head. The blood pounded at his temples like hammers on an anvil. Slowly he willed the tension to pass. He had lost Megan by behaving like this. *God, please don't let it happen again.*

"No, Miss Goddard, I'm the one who needs to apologize." His voice was soft, almost pleading. "The last few years have been pretty hard for me. I thought things were getting better, but I guess I still haven't put the ghosts to rest." He managed a small smile. "I'd like to go ahead with dinner. I've really enjoyed the evening so far and we do still have some business to discuss. But if you want, I'll take you back to the hotel."

Goddard stared into her wine glass as she slowly turned it between her fingers. "I guess it won't hurt to stay. I want to help, and I did call you, after all."

"Thank you. I promise to keep the devils inside." *If I only knew how.*

He motioned for the waitress and they considered their menus. It provided a much-needed diversion from the previous conversation. Braxton ordered a Caesar salad for two and a small plate of antipasto. For their entrees, she selected a braised lamb and he picked the veal marsala. After a friendly debate, they settled on a bottle of Chianti Classico.

The ensuing small talk was forced, both of the diners uncomfortable with the situation Braxton had caused. Dinner finally arrived and they took the opportunity to focus on the meal and let the need for conversation subside.

It was 7:30 when they finished. The restaurant had filled with a lively Saturday night crowd whose cacophony provided a protective shield for further discussion.

"You mentioned on the phone that you remembered something about Mr. Ramal's, ah Mohammed's, work?" Braxton asked as their plates were being cleared.

He watched her brace for the painful remembrance. "I think so. He hadn't been making as much progress on our project as we needed. I asked him about it and he said he was tracking down some kind of network bug."

"Did he say 'bug' specifically?"

"I'm not sure. It could have been bug, or maybe he said virus. That makes a difference doesn't it?"

"Very much. A bug would be some kind of hardware or software error. They're usually accidental. A virus is intentional. It's a special kind of software program that can break into networks and systems."

"I remember reading about those ransom viruses, the ones that lock your computer until your pay the bad guys. All my classmates were worried about losing the data we had on our PCs."

"Those were definitely serious, but it was pretty easy to avoid being infected. I'm sure it bumped up sales of anti-virus software, though. The vendors made out like bandits. It would be a good case for one of your communications classes."

Braxton began to relax. The discussion was back on safe turf. He hoped his companion felt the same way.

"Mohammed had been working by himself for most of the week. I couldn't figure out what he was doing. He wasn't responding to my calls or email. I finally talked to him on Saturday and we agreed to get together at his apartment the next evening. That's when he mentioned the virus."

"Did Mohammed keep a log of his activities? A notebook of any kind?"

"He did have his research notebook. I know he put everything he did in it."

"Was it a real book or did he keep it electronically?"

"It was a regular lab notebook. His thesis advisor required he keep it in hard copy. It was usually right next to his PC."

Braxton couldn't remember seeing a notebook in the inventory.

It was another strange omission. "Was there anything else you can remember?"

"No, I'm sorry. I just wanted to get moving on our project. Mohammed seemed so preoccupied I wanted to see what he was doing. I had a new idea for the simulation and was thinking about it on my way over to his apartment. Then I saw the explosion. It was horrible." She started shivering and crossed her arms over her body, rubbing them as if to keep warm.

"The police came and I talked with that patrolman . . . and he said that Mohammed was dead. Why would someone do that?" Her eyes pleaded with him for an answer.

He reached over and placed his hand on top of hers. Her hand tensed and he feared she might pull away, but then it relaxed and she forced a weak smile.

"I don't know yet," he said. "But I'm going to find out."

He gave her hand a gentle squeeze.

"What about that Detective Fowler? Has he found anything?"

"Not really." Braxton shook his head. He realized he shouldn't go into too much detail. Fowler had gone out on a limb for him and he didn't want any blowback on the cop. "I think he believed you, but all the evidence goes the other way. I'm sorry."

Goddard took back her hand and placed it in her lap. He watched as her hope faded into acceptance and then sadness. He knew there was nothing he could say to bring back that smile tonight.

"It's been a long day for both of us," he said softly. "Why don't I take you back?"

They rode back to the Parker House in silence. The taxi made a tight turn and she leaned into him and her head fell to his shoulder. It remained there the rest of the trip.

Once in the lobby, they turned to face each other. In the light, he noticed a track of mascara down the side of her face.

"Thank you for the help, Susan. I really did enjoy the evening. I'm sorry we hit a rough spot." He waited for a word of encouragement that might mean he had not lost her completely. He couldn't bring himself to ask her directly.

She hesitated, then answered softly, "Me too, Adam. Call me when you get back down to D.C." Then she put her hands on his shoulders and reached up to kiss his cheek. She turned and headed for the staircase.

He stood in the lobby watching her disappear up the stairs. It had been a long time since a woman had affected him so deeply. No one, in fact, since Megan. He wasn't sure what to do about it.

The rain had stopped, but the temperature had dropped, nearly to freezing, and Braxton stuffed his hands in his jacket pockets as he walked back down Tremont. The street was now deserted, his only companions an occasional taxi loaded with evening party-goers.

He stopped briefly in front of the Old Granary Burial Ground, then hurried on to the station. Thankfully, the train came quickly and his chill passed in the dry heat of the subway car.

The scent of her perfume rising from his jacket only intensified his loneliness on the ride back to the Square.

CHAPTER 31

Cambridge, Massachusetts
Saturday, 9:00 p.m.

HARDING WAS THINKING about his son's last baseball game when he heard the snap of the deadbolt. The two men rose in unison and waited for Braxton to push the door open and turn on the lights. Instead, the door slammed back on its hinges and a huge figure stormed directly at them. Before Harding could react, he heard a shot from his right. The room instantly filled with debris and the target disappeared.

"Shit," he whispered. He fired two shots through the storm of paper in the direction of the careening body and dove left for the door. They had to block any exit and reduce exposure from the hall.

He didn't know who this intruder was but he would bet it wasn't their target.

* * *

Terrel had had the flash while he was watching the Red Wings demolish the Bruins. Of course the quant didn't converge. He had truncated the series too soon! He grabbed a stack of listings and rushed out the door. His friend wouldn't mind if he used the computer and he might even get a chance to see this new girlfriend. He really did hope that Adam would find a new lady. The guy deserved some good luck.

It was hard keeping the pile of papers balanced, so after he flipped the locks he just kicked the door open and headed for the study. He heard a strange spitting sound just before the sledgehammer hit him in his chest.

"Ughhh!" he cried as the impact spun him around and threw

him onto a nearby coffee table. The table collapsed with an ear-splitting crack sending a lamp and vase crashing to the hardwood floor, both shattering from the force.

"Shit," he heard from his right as he was falling. Then two spits and the floor next to him erupted into a shower of splinters.

There's someone else in the room! Someone shooting at me!

Cover. He had to find cover.

He felt Braxton's sofa next to him on his left. Without thinking further he jumped into the air and dove over the back of the couch.

Two more spits. He heard them bury into the furniture's deep padding just inches above his head. But they came from the opposite corner. Not back toward the door.

There were two of them! Why are they trying to kill me?

*   *   *

Harding rolled past the door, slamming it shut with his left arm as he passed. The light from the hall vanished and the room returned to familiar darkness. He came up in a shooter's crouch, listening for any evidence of the new target's location. What the hell had happened?

The room was silent, but there was no smell of death. The target was still alive. Who was this guy? What was he doing here? The contract was blown and the error would put a mark on his reputation. He'd probably end up owing one to his client. Dammit!

Concentrate! From his position by the door Harding had complete control of the room. He only had to wait for his quarry to make a mistake. He slowly scanned the Glock across the room.

There was motion straight ahead, then two shots from the corner to his right. Nathan again. They ended in useless thumps. The target was fast, but now he was pinned behind the sofa. Only a matter of time.

*   *   *

Terrel knew there were two of them: one at the front door, and another to his left. He didn't think they had moved but how would he know? The blood pounding in his ears would have drowned out any other sounds.

He considered going after one of them, but quickly rejected the stupid idea. They were armed and he was certainly no Chuck Norris. Soon they would be circling to close in on him. How could he get out?

The room was pitch black except for street glow coming through the dining room windows. The windows. There was a fire escape outside the kitchen window! He and Braxton had stored beer there in the winter. If he could make it to the kitchen, he could block the door and slide down the escape ladder.

His heart was beating so hard it made his whole body shake. Bile seared his throat as he rose to his hands and knees and edged along the back of the sofa.

He was nearly to the end when his hand came down on a large shard of glass. He muffled a yell then yanked the fragment from his hand, wincing from the pain. About to set the piece down, he had an idea.

He squatted into a runner's position. The door to the kitchen was on the right of the open dining area. The polished dining table reflected the light from the front windows and illuminated his path to safety.

Here goes. He shifted the fragment to his left hand and tossed it to the opposite corner of the room. When he heard the glass hit the wall, he pushed off and dashed toward the light. A bullet whistled behind him as he passed into the dining room.

He was going to make it! He knew it!

* * *

Harding heard the sound but did not react. He had expected a diversion. Nathan reacted as he knew he would, firing across the open area. Then, silhouetted in the glow from the windows, he saw a body racing toward the light.

"Always escape into the darkness," he recited silently, "never the light," as he squeezed off two shots.

Terrel had almost made it to the kitchen door when the two 9mm hollow point slugs buried themselves in his back. They mushroomed on entering his body and devastated his entire chest cavity. His chest jerked forward, the bullets adding to his already considerable forward momentum. He hit the window at the end of the open dining area, shattering the glass, and splintering the frame. His body fell through the gaping hole, tumbled down the three stories, and impacted with a soft crunch on the concrete below.

"What a goddamn night," Harding cursed as he motioned Nathan back to the door. "Clean up and let's get the hell outta' here."

He already heard yelling from the street below. Nathan pulled out his flashlight and checked the room to be sure they hadn't left any evidence.

Harding listened at the door, then cracked it open to view the hall. Seeing it empty, the pair quietly exited the apartment and headed for the back stairs. They heard a crowd of tenants forming in the front lobby as they reached the first floor. Still unobserved, they left the building by the rear door that Nathan had located earlier in the day.

They were just pulling away from the curb when the first patrol car arrived.

* * *

When Braxton turned up Brattle Street at 9:30, he saw flashing police lights in the distance. What could have happened? His neighborhood's crime record was low, certainly better than Central Square or North Cambridge. They hadn't had any serious violence in over two years. Hopefully it was just a small accident.

His anxiety worsened when he discovered the activity was outside his apartment building. Police were everywhere, talking with on-lookers and scribbling in little notebooks.

As he walked closer, he saw an ambulance near the front door. Braxton hoped it wasn't anyone he knew.

Another tenant, Charlie Milak, was speaking with a patrolman. Milak looked up, then pointed down the street toward him. The officer had finished speaking with his neighbor when Braxton reached the apartment entrance.

"Adam Braxton?" the cop asked.

"Yes, officer. What's happened here?"

"I'm afraid there's been an accident sir. You live in apartment 3B?"

"Yes I do."

"Does Paul Terrel have a key to your apartment?"

"Yes, he uses the computer in my apartment sometimes." He was getting a very bad feeling." What's happened? Has Paul been hurt?"

"We believe he may have entered your apartment and surprised some burglars, Mr. Braxton. He was shot."

"Shot?" He reached for the wall to steady himself. Who would want to burglarize his apartment? What was Terrel doing in there anyway?

"How is he?" Braxton asked automatically, but the answer was clear from the sober look on the patrolman's face.

"I'm afraid he's dead sir. After he was shot he fell from your window."

Braxton looked up and saw the shattered frame of his window. Below on the sidewalk a formless shape was covered with a blanket. He felt sick.

Paul is dead! Why?

* * *

It was eleven o'clock by the time the police left. Somehow he had managed to identify Terrel, give a statement as to his whereabouts, then assist the police as they searched his friend's apartment for his parent's address.

It had been unbearably painful going through his friend's belongings. It reminded him of cleaning out the apartment after Megan left. He had felt a part of his life wither away as he sorted through the bits of clothing and worn-out gifts. But she had been alive; he had only driven her away. Paul was gone for good. Was this his fault as well?

"Sorry about the noise, Adam. I'll be done here in a minute." Jerry Shepard, the building superintendent, was nailing a dirty sheet of plywood over Braxton's missing window. Shepard was an okay super; he was handy with tools, and friendly enough, although he did stick his nose into the tenant's personal affairs a little too often.

"Sure," was all Braxton could muster.

"It's awful about Paul. I know you two were really close."

"Thanks, Jerry. We'll all miss him."

"I can't believe somebody broke in here. Did he get much?"

Braxton shook his head. That's getting right to the point, Jerry. "Not much. Just a couple of old watches." And the engagement ring Megan had returned. "But it was 'they'. The cops think there were two of them. Mary Pritchard saw a couple of strangers in the building about 5:30."

"I'm sure they'll find who did it."

"I hope so, but the detective in charge didn't have many encouraging words. No one saw them leave and they didn't leave much behind."

Shepard finished the nailing and packed up his tools. "You're sure you don't want to stay in another apartment? 2B is empty. I could get you a cot or something."

"No, thanks. I'd rather be here than in some strange place. I'll be okay."

"Whatever. You take care of yourself now. I'll get that window replaced tomorrow."

Once the super had left, Braxton realized how exhausted he was. The dinner with Goddard had been draining enough; as he looked over the wreckage of the living room, a complete helplessness fell over him. It was a familiar feeling, but one he had thought he had put behind him months ago. He couldn't let it return.

He walked over to the small bar he had fashioned in a corner of his bookcases. Terrel had been a friend and a confidant. He had been too young to recognize his own mortality, but would listen intently whenever Braxton had discussed his. Terrel had been his closest, no his only, friend since the divorce. How had he let this happen?

He pulled one of Megan's crystal glasses from the shelf and filled it from his favorite bottle of Talisker single malt scotch.

"To you Paul," he whispered. Memories of Terrel flashed through his mind as he gulped a mouthful of the warm, biting liquid: camping trips in the White Mountains, late night discussions on work, fixing each other's PCs when they went haywire.

Why did they pick his apartment? What did they possibly think was worth stealing?

He couldn't shake the feeling that all this was his fault, despite the lack of any rationale for the guilt. It was just an accident, he argued, as he began to pace the room. The floor was still littered with the printouts from his friend's project. Running his hand along the sofa, he felt the grit of gunpowder on the fabric. His shoes crushed pieces of the broken vase. When he reached the end of the room, he rubbed his hands over the cracked plaster around the bullet holes.

What had Paul stumbled into? From the look of the room, he must have put up some kind of a fight.

Braxton's eyes were drawn to the bare plywood sheet where the window had been, where Terrel had fallen, perhaps trying to escape from the criminals who had invaded the apartment.

He threw the crystal glass at the window with all the strength he could find. It exploded on the wall, its fragments falling to the floor and disappearing in the other debris.

Someone will pay for this, he vowed. *Someone will pay.*

CHAPTER 32

Cambridge, Massachusetts
Sunday, 10:30 a.m.

THE RAIN HAD started at 1:00 a.m. and had continued throughout the night. The pelting of the drops on the plywood panel beat like a drum into the apartment and made sleep impossible. Braxton finally crawled out of bed at 6:30, took a quick shower, and fixed some breakfast. In the daylight, the disorder of his apartment looked much less ominous. He grabbed a handful of trash bags and began cleaning up the mess.

Thankfully there had been little blood spilled inside, and the ugly wooden board over his window hid the tragic scene on the sidewalk below. By mid-morning he had hauled three heavy bags of trash to the refuse drop. Then he rearranged the furniture in the living room, hoping the new configuration would keep the memories from returning too quickly. His superintendent called at 11:00 and said the new window couldn't be delivered until later the next week.

Running out of chores, he collapsed on the sofa, carefully avoiding the section with the bullet holes, and tried to think through what had happened. The only way he knew to deal with difficult situations was to work them out in his mind: analyze the situation, play through the options, and develop a strategy. His ex had believed he had hidden from problems that upset him and didn't recover until he had made everyone around him miserable. What had she wanted him to do, dump every little problem on her? He wasn't hiding; he just needed to work things out privately before he could discuss it with others. Why couldn't she have seen that?

The Cambridge cops had said the robbers were pros. They had hardly scratched Braxton's locks getting in. They also hadn't taken anything that was very valuable, although the cops felt this was due to Terrel's untimely entry.

But the timing was all off. Mrs. Pritchard had said she saw the two men enter the building around 6:20, just before she sat down to watch the evening news. Terrel wasn't killed until 7:45. What were they doing in his apartment for an hour and a half? Why didn't they take his valuable items: his computer and its peripherals? Nothing had been piled up or stuffed into bags; only a few pieces of jewelry were gone. It didn't make any sense.

He shook his head at how everything always came back to timing: his bad timing at Century, the contract with CERT, Ramal's death.

The thought caught him by surprise. What if the break-in hadn't been a robbery? What if they had been after *him* and Terrel had gotten in the way? Ramal had discovered the anomaly and he had been killed. Now Braxton was replicating the student's work. What had he stumbled into?

He had to get help. But who could he call? He walked over to the window and looked down. There were unfamiliar cars along the street. Could someone be watching? How would he know if they were? A chill of fear shook his body. He searched his wallet for the business card and grabbed his cell.

"Hello. Fowler residence." It was a resonant woman's voice.

"Detective Fowler please."

"Just a minute." He heard a muffled "Sam" in the background.

"Fowler." The voice sounded decidedly unfriendly.

"Detective Fowler? This is Adam Braxton."

"Braxton? It's the weekend. What the hell are you doing calling me on a Sunday?"

"I had to talk to someone. There was an accident last night. A friend of mine was killed in my apartment." He knew his voice was breaking up but he couldn't stop it.

"Jesus, what happened?"

Braxton related the events of the past evening. "I don't think they were thieves. I think they were after me."

"Take it easy, Braxton. You don't have any proof that they were waiting for you do you?"

"No."

"Have you had any other accidents? Anything that seemed suspicious?"

"No. I don't guess so."

"What did the police say?"

"They think it was just a blown robbery. I didn't tell them anything else."

"Okay. Look, you're in no immediate danger. Even if they were waiting for you, they're long gone now. They won't try anything else until this cools off. Be careful, but try to relax. Have you found out anything new about Ramal?"

Fowler's logic seemed sound. Braxton shook off his anxiety and lapsed back into the detached consultant. "Yes, I've verified Ramal's original claim. There is something strange going on in GW's gateways. I'm still trying to find out exactly what."

"Who have you talked to about this?"

"Just my friend Paul and my ex-boss at Century Computer. Oh, and I sent an update to the Center."

"Any of those electronic messages?"

"Yes, the one to the Center. But I'm sure they couldn't be involved." Except what if Braxton was right about the mole? CERT/CC wouldn't need to be involved.

"Right. Probably not. I'll see what I can find out about your break-in. I used to have a friend on the Boston PD. Call me back tomorrow . . . On second thought, are you coming back down here soon?"

"I didn't have any specific plans to. Do you think I should?"

"Yeah. It would be a good idea. As soon as you can. When can you get here?"

"I could get out tomorrow morning. We could meet for lunch."

"Good. I'll meet you at twelve next to the Washington Monument. I go there for lunch sometimes to get away from all the crap."

"See you tomorrow then, Detective. And thanks. I'm sorry I bothered you." He clicked off. Maybe he did overreact. Things were just happening faster than he was used to. He felt a little better and got up to fix some lunch.

* * *

Fowler went back into the kitchen. He lived in a small but comfortable single family in Silver Spring, Maryland, just over the border from D.C. The home was twenty years old and needed constant attention to keep it habitable. This weekend it was a leaky drain under the kitchen sink. Usually he was a wizard with hand tools, but plumbing drove him crazy. He barely fit inside the cabinet and had been barking his knuckles on the pipes or hitting his head on some nearby fixture all morning.

As he crawled back into the tiny space, he worried about the consultant. Braxton had been near panic when he called; he was lucky to have calmed him down. Unfortunately, the guy was probably right. Somebody was after him. The case had taken a bad turn and Braxton was in the middle, maybe because he had pushed the consultant too hard. He'd call Boston later and see what he could do to protect the civilian. It was the least he could do.

* * *

Goddard caught the 11:00 a.m. shuttle back to Washington. She had overslept her planned 8:30 departure from the hotel, and had had to rush to Logan to get out before noon. The combination of the interview at WGBH and the dinner with Braxton had worn her out.

She settled into her seat in the 727 and relaxed for the first time in three days. The consultant was certainly much more complex than she had imagined. First, he had nearly bitten her head off, then he was comforting her memories of Ramal. He seemed very bright and, well, human. Most of the men she had dated in the past few years were either pompous ego-maniacs, or insecure milquetoasts. She found herself drawn to the consultant's strange combination of strength and vulnerability.

He had experienced some rough times and obviously still felt the scars that had resulted. She remembered her pain when her father had died and the moments she had struck out at her friends. Who was she to judge him? He was trying to get his life back together. She had to respect him for that. For herself, and for Mohammed, she hoped his investigation would find some explanation.

She pulled out the Sunday *Globe* she had bought in the concourse and started to catch up on the news of the week. In the middle of the second page she saw an article titled "Cambridge

Resident Slain in Robbery Attempt". She almost skipped over it, but noticed a familiar name in the first paragraph.

```
    . . . The owner of the apartment, computer
consultant Adam Braxton, arrived only minutes after
the police were notified . . . A police spokeswoman
stated that it appeared the neighbor had entered
the apartment while a theft was in progress. There
was no apparent motive for the killing.
```

Someone was killed in Adam's apartment? What could have happened?

She read the article through three times, but it gave no additional information on Braxton. She spent the rest of the flight flipping through the pages of the *Globe*, much to the annoyance of her seat mate.

The instant the plane's wheels hit the runway at National, she pulled out her iPhone and dialed.

"Adam Braxton."

"Adam, it's Susan. Are you all right?" She tried not to sound too panicked.

"Yes, I'm fine. Where are you?"

"The tarmac at National. I just landed. I saw the report in the newspaper. It sounded awful. What happened?"

"It's pretty much as they described it. I went home after I dropped you off and found the police waiting for me. I've been trying to clean up the place ever since."

"Did you know the neighbor very well?"

"He was my best friend, Susan. It looks like we've both lost someone close." Braxton sounded very tired and depressed.

"Oh, Adam. I'm so sorry." Now she did feel awful. Why did she have to disturb him at a time like this? It had been so hard on her when Mohammed had been killed. Now this had happened to him. What an awful coincidence. *It was a coincidence wasn't it?*

"You don't think there's a connection do you?" she asked hesitantly.

"To tell you the truth, I worried about that all morning. I even thought the burglars could have been waiting for me. I called Detective Fowler but he didn't think there was any relationship. I'm still not so sure."

His answer sent a pang of dread through her. She couldn't stand to lose another friend. And she *was* beginning to think of him as a friend.

"Is there anything I can do to help? I feel like I'm involved in all this now."

"I did promise Fowler I'd come down tomorrow and talk the whole thing over with him. Would you like to join us?"

"Absolutely. I can even pick you up if you like."

"I would like that very much. I'll take the ten o'clock shuttle. It'll be less crowded than the earlier ones."

"I'll see you then. And Adam, please be careful."

"You bet. See you tomorrow."

She stared out the window and saw the plane was finally approaching the gate. Why did he have to appear in her life now? Braxton was awakening feelings that she had long suppressed. She couldn't get involved. It could ruin everything.

CHAPTER 33

Manassas, Virginia
Sunday, 12:00 p.m.

NICHOLSON PARKED HIS Lexus at the far end of the gravel parking lot, away from as many of the pickups and motorcycles as he could. The lot was only about half full at the Sunday lunch hour, but he didn't want to take any chances on getting dents or dings in his new car.

Why had Greystone chosen this place for his rendezvous? It reminded him too much of similar spots outside Richmond, and they weren't pleasant memories.

The building was little more than an overgrown Quonset hut. It had a corrugated steel roof and metal with timber walls. A huge sign across the swinging front doors declared:

Manassas Run
Country and Western Bar

The Run's primary attribute was that it was easy to get to. Just off Route 66 in Manassas, Virginia, it drew interstate truckers and local blue-collar Virginians alike. Occasionally, even a few white-collar bureaucrats came out looking for a good time. The Manassas Run management put up with their lack of country authenticity by overcharging them on the drinks and the other pleasures of the establishment. Nicholson knew he'd be pegged for this latter group.

He walked in and got the expected looks from the regulars gathered along the Formica bar on his right. He wondered whether it was the double-breasted suit or his skin color that caused more attention.

The Run was dark and smelled of stale beer and sweat. As he strode through the room, alcohol-soaked sawdust covered his polished wingtips. On his left was a small stage, thankfully now empty, where local groups came to perform on Friday and Saturday nights. Unfortunately, the audio system still blared twangy C&W through ancient scratchy loudspeakers.

The rest of the floor was covered with dirty wooden tables and chairs that looked as if they had been through one brawl too many. Civil War photographs and other memorabilia hung from the ugly metal walls, primarily to cover the dents and holes left from errant customers. He couldn't imagine what the honky-tonk would be like when it was packed with sweaty red-necks and their whores. He shook off the thought and carefully stepped through the mess to an empty booth along the back wall.

A buxom bleached-blonde in a short denim skirt and low cut calico blouse came over to take his order. She looked as if she didn't appreciate his taking up a whole booth by himself.

"I'll take a draft," he said. "I'm expecting someone in a few minutes. Bring one for him and then leave us alone."

"Whatever you want, sugar."

He gave her a long slow look as she swung back to the bar. She returned with the beers and dropped the check on the table. "Ten bucks."

Nicholson covered the check with a twenty. He hoped it would buy him some privacy. She palmed the money, gave him a smile, and left for a table of truckers in the far corner.

Greystone never ceased to surprise him. Like appearing at the Kennedy Center, or calling this outlandish meeting. It wasn't that he minded the clandestine encounters and the cloak and dagger procedures. He had been privy to Potterfield's back room dealing long enough to know where the real work was done and the important deals were made. It was just that sometimes his friend took things a little to the extreme. But as long as he delivered the results they needed, Nicholson could put up with it.

He picked up the beer and took a swallow. It was warm.

He was about to motion for the waitress when the din of the bar suddenly stilled. Looking up, he saw a man striding arrogantly across the floor. It was Greystone. He was dressed casually for a change, jeans and a black leather jacket. Nicholson had barely recognized him. The Chief of Staff waved his arm and Greystone made his way through the crowd to the booth.

"A little over-dressed aren't we, Nick?"

"I have a reception this afternoon. And a date with a very lovely lady."

"Miss Mowaru?"

"Leave it alone, Bob. What's so important to drag me out here?"

"Just a couple of things. This for me?"

"Yeah. I ordered it to give us some privacy. I'm afraid it's warm."

"Thanks. They always are." Greystone grabbed the beer and took a swallow. "By the way, what's happening with your blackmailer?"

"He's still there. I'm running background checks. It's got to be either a member of the family or some goddamn reporter trying to dredge up an old story. We'll find him."

"I'm sure you will. If you need any help . . ."

"I know. Look, my phantom emailer can't be the reason you wanted me all the way out here. What's up?"

"Right to business as always, Nick. Two things. First, I've put together the technical requirements for the Bill." He handed Nicholson a large envelope of papers. "They're consistent with NSA's analyses and give us the upper hand in getting product to market. Still think you can get the amendments through?"

"No problem. You've got the old man drooling. We can call in some favors and swing the vote. I've also got a few skeletons I can use if we have to. How is Takagawa working out?"

"Damn Japs have great engineers. They're ahead of schedule on the prototypes. We'll be ready."

Nicholson watched his partner; the glib smile, the overconfident tone. "What aren't you telling me?"

"You notice too much, Nick," Greystone admitted with a frown. "Hajima is a slippery guy. I can't help but think he has another agenda. I need to watch him, that's all."

"If you say so," Nicholson replied. His partner always thought he could handle anything. The play with Takagawa was risky; they'd known that from the beginning. But the reward could be staggering. He just hoped his partner wasn't in over his head.

"I still think killing Keane was a mistake," he added.

"It was necessary. And it makes the Board more amenable to our plan. Don't worry. I'll get what we need from Flitterman." He took another swallow of the beer and made a quick scan of the room.

"I've always admired your confidence. What's number two?"

"In a hurry to get somewhere, Nick?" Greystone's smirk only increased Nicholson's impatience.

"Jesus, Bob, get on with it. If you want to check out the merchandise do it on your own time."

"I was wondering if you had heard from Warren lately."

"Not for a couple of months. Last time was to get a review of their latest technology plans. I sent you a copy. Why?" Is this what Greystone wanted to talk about? What's he up to?

"I got a call from him yesterday. He's concerned about that CERT consultant working on the Ramal accident."

"Why not just get rid of him?"

"I tried but my contractors botched the job. They ended up killing his neighbor."

Nicholson stared across the table, then brought his hand to his forehead. And started rubbing. "Jesus, Bob. What's going on? Maybe you better get some new people. I can fix you up with some I know."

"Thanks anyway, Nick, maybe next time. It's nothing I can't handle; just a string of bad luck. CERT hasn't found anything and the consultant is still in the dark. He did talk to Warren though and that apparently spooked him."

Greystone paused and checked out a trio of local professionals congregating along the bar. When he turned back, his brow was furrowed and his voice thick with concern. "You don't think he'd do anything, well, inappropriate, do you?"

Nicholson stared back, trying to penetrate his colleague's carefully-crafted mask. He thought of Greystone as a friend, although not a close one, but had always wondered if the feeling was one-sided. Chamberlain was very insecure; he had expressed discomfort with some of their methods in the past. Nicholson had worried then that the engineer might become a liability. He hadn't heard anything lately, however, so there was no reason to alarm Greystone. He didn't want him going off the deep end.

"Warren? Certainly not, Bob," he said with all the bravado he could muster. "I'm a helluva lot more concerned about CERT and the damn consultant. We can't have them poking around in our network. Get those contractors to go do their job."

"Absolutely right, Nick." The smirk returned. "It was ridiculous to be concerned about Warren. And as for Braxton, I know how we can settle that very quickly."

"Great. Now as much as I love this place, I'm going back to the reception." He downed the beer and stood up. "Leaving?"

"No, you go ahead. I think I'll stay and admire the scenery for a while longer."

Nicholson shook his head and made his way back through the human stable. Greystone had been acting strange lately. There hadn't been any need to meet face-to-face. He could have sent the damn documents over the net.

Maybe all the pressure inside Theater was getting to him. He'd better keep a watch on his partner for both his and Chamberlain's sakes.

* * *

Greystone could have called Nicholson, but he had needed to see his partner's face. Some things just had to be done in person. His intuition had been correct; it had been clear in Nicholson's expression and hesitation. Chamberlain couldn't be trusted.

He had had to approach the subject carefully. Nicholson and Chamberlain had been close once and he didn't want to do anything that might alert either man. He was sure he hadn't aroused any suspicions; the plan could continue without modification.

A tall, dark-haired woman sitting alone in one of the corner booths caught his eye. He liked women with a sense of understatement. His next appointment wasn't until later that afternoon. He picked up his beer and walked toward the smiling face.

* * *

Fowler collapsed into his recliner and let out a tired sigh. Even a long, hot shower hadn't been able to relieve the relentless throbbing in his lower back.

It had taken him all day to fix the goddamn leak. And while he was gallantly toiling in the tiny cabinet space, his wife had reminded him she had to leave for a meeting at their church. She had said something about meatloaf in the refrigerator and disappeared, leaving him to fend for himself. Well, the cold Corona in his hand would have to do for now.

He had just settled into a repeat of *Law and Order* when the phone rang.

"Shit," he mumbled. "Let it go."

The noise stopped on the sixth ring as the answering machine picked up. All he heard was a dial tone; no message.

"Damn robo calls," he whispered.

Then it rang again. He let it go, same result.

The third time, he climbed across the sectional to the end table, pulling his back muscle again, and grabbed the phone. Someone was going to get hell.

"What?" he barked into the receiver.

"Good evening, Sam. Knew you were there. Having a bad day?"

"Roger? Sorry, it has been a bitch of a day. What's up?"

"I didn't want to disturb you at home but I thought it would be safer for both of us to talk tonight. That okay?"

"Yeah. Go ahead."

"First off, you didn't tell me your case had been given to our friends at the FBI."

"Must have slipped my mind. Did you find out anything?" *Get to the point, Roger.*

"That's what I figured, of course. I did some checking and came up blank. I can't find any evidence to tie your bombing to a terrorist group. I'm sure we don't have complete data on all the cells operating in the area, but we would have heard something through their communication channels. The Fibbies haven't found anything either but they're too dumb to know it."

"Always the politician, Roger. That must be why they keep you around. I'm not surprised. You just confirmed my intuition. Unfortunately, I don't have any other alternatives." It looked like another dead end. This wouldn't be of any help to him or to Braxton.

"Sorry I couldn't help more this time, Sam."

"That's okay. I appreciate the effort. By the way, have you heard anything about problems on the Internet? Strange messages appearing or anything like that?"

The phone went silent. When Slattery spoke again, his tone was sharp and formal. "Why do you ask, Sam?"

"The kid who blew himself up thought he found something funny in one of GW's computers. Somebody from the CERT Coordination Center been asking about it."

"CERT? What do you know about them?"

"Me, Roger? I'm just a dumb local cop. What do *I* know? That's what the guy told me."

"*What* guy, Sam? Who is he?" Slattery's voice ratcheted even higher.

"I don't remember his name. Why? Something going on I should know about?"

"Not at all, Sam. Just inquisitive. You know me."

"Yeah, I do, Roger." *Well enough to know you're not telling me everything.*

"Okay, guess I'd better get back to work."

"On Sunday night?"

"The government never sleeps, Sam."

"That's what I worry about. But thanks for checking on the terrorist angle. I owe you for that."

"Any time, Sam. Just give me a call."

Fowler hung up the phone and started worrying. He knew he had hit a raw nerve. What the hell had Braxton gotten into?

CHAPTER 34

Carnegie Mellon University, Pittsburgh, Pennsylvania
Monday, 8:45 a.m.

RYDELL FINISHED REVIEWING his prior week's Regent's presentation and prepared to bring the CERT/CC staff meeting to a close. Flanagan had been reasonably calm so far, but as the last agenda item approached, her anxiety level moved into the red zone. She couldn't afford another confrontation with her boss, but she had to report the news.

"All right," Rydell announced, "are there any short topics?"

"I believe Rachel owes us an update on that Saracen Incident," Candela volunteered.

Just like the little sycophant, she thought. Why couldn't someone have given her a little breathing room? She opened the already worn folder in front of her. "I have spoken with our contractor, and there has been a tragic turn in the investigation. Saracen was a computer science graduate student at George Washington University. I say 'was' because he died the night of the transmission."

Looks of surprise spread over the table.

"What happened?" Eisenkranz asked.

"The D.C. police believe that the student," she referred down to the papers, "a Mohammed Ramal, was constructing a bomb and it went off prematurely."

"An Arab? Constructing a bomb?" Candella exclaimed. "Are you telling us this incident was reported by a terrorist?"

"We don't know that for certain," Flanagan explained as flatly as she could. "That's just a theory."

"Theory or not, Rachel, that writes off the incident," Rydell continued as if he was checking off a shopping list. "Is there anything else?"

"Excuse me, Timothy," Flanagan interrupted, "but I think we need to look at this a little closer." She knew she was stepping dangerously close to the end of her corporate plank. "There may be some relationship between Saracen's death and his allegation. There were no computer documents found in his apartment despite the fact that he was working there the night he sent the message. And our consultant believes he has verified Ramal's claim of an anomaly on GW's systems. I think we need to keep the incident open a bit longer. At least until the authorities make a final determination."

"Rachel," Rydell began sternly, "we all sympathize with your desire to find some conspiracy in the Internet, but the District of Columbia's police department is much better trained to investigate murders than you and your consultant. Is it not possible that this Saracen was a terrorist, and that part of his plan was to damage the credibility of our communications systems by his allegation? We do not have the time to follow-up unsubstantiated claims and the beliefs of self-styled network experts. I think that is the sense of the room."

"Of course, Timothy," Flanagan replied, closing her folder. "I understand that we can only investigate verified, substantiated incidents. You can rest assured we will follow that policy to the letter."

"Good. I'm glad we have that resolved," Rydell said with obvious pleasure. "Edward, what else is there?"

As Candela went back to his notes, Flanagan thought through her next steps. Braxton *had* said he had verified the claim. Her investigation would continue with or without Rydell's knowledge. There was more to this than any of them knew and she was going to get to the bottom of it.

The problem was that she had lost contact with her consultant; she hadn't heard anything from him for four days.

* * *

Greystone heard a rapping and looked up from his papers to see Julius Flitterman standing in his office doorway.

"If it's not a bad time, Robert," Flitterman commented, "I thought we could spend a few minutes."

"Of course not, Julius. Please come in." Greystone motioned to the couch in the sitting area of his office. He had tried unsuccessfully to see the banker all the past week. Clarice had said his schedule was completely full. What little communication he had had with Flitterman had been limited to requests for operational reports. What was so important for him to make a personal visit?

"I'm afraid I haven't been as available to you as I should," the banker began after Greystone had joined him. "Between vetting documents with Victor, reviewing Meredith's audit results, and handling media and investor queries I have been completely occupied."

Greystone could see the strain taking its toll on the older man. His clothes weren't quite as crisp, his grey hair wasn't slicked back quite as neatly, and his voice was just a bit halting. The wrinkles on his pale face seemed darker and deeper than only a week before.

"I can only imagine how painful this must be for you," Greystone offered sympathetically. "I'm sure the worst is past." He hesitated, then asked, "Have the police finished their investigation yet?"

"Apparently not. They continue to ask for all kinds of documents and email. Victor is absolutely beside himself going through it all. It would be comical if it weren't for the ungodly amount of money we pay the man per hour."

"Have they found anything that would explain why Lombard would have done such a thing?"

"There did seem to be corroboration of the documents they found at Charles' cabin in our files. We discovered Lombard had a history of misuse of Theater property, and recently even copying of confidential documents. I also heard there were unusual deposits in Lombard's bank account, but the authorities have been unable to track them to a source. Unfortunately, it appears that Clarice was unwittingly the source of the leaks."

"I was afraid of that. I think we should not respond too harshly to her indiscretion, Julius. Clarice was devoted to Charles."

"I agree," Flitterman responded with an unusual sense of compassion. "She gave me her resignation, but I refused it. Clarice has been invaluable over the past week; I believe she knows more about what goes on in this company than anyone. With the exception of you, of course, Robert."

It sounded as if his efforts at disinformation had achieved their goal. Soon the whole affair would be put to rest and they could get on with business. With him in charge.

"How is the rest of the company taking the changes, Robert? I understand you held a teleconference with all the field offices?"

"Yes. I believe it was very effective. Charles' death was certainly a shock for everyone, but by reacting quickly we demonstrated that management was well-prepared to handle the emergency. We also prevented the spread of a number of dangerous rumors that would have impeded our recovery. I have spoken personally with all the area sales and manufacturing managers to be sure they can explain our plans to their staffs."

"I read your report on the discussions, Robert. Very well done. In fact, my main reason for stopping in today was to thank you for your efforts in managing the day-to-day operations. I know you and Charles did not always agree, but I always felt you had the best interests of the company in mind. I am convinced that we would not be able to weather this horrible event without your significant contributions.

"I also realize these new responsibilities have detracted from our making progress on your strategic initiatives. Please prepare a revised summary of your recommendations. I'd like to discuss them with you later in the week."

Flitterman then abruptly rose. "Thank you again, Robert. I'd prefer to stay and work through these items with you, but I must return to other duties."

"Of course, Julius," Greystone said taking the man's extended hand. "Thank you for taking the time to stop. And for your support. I will return to work on the initiatives immediately."

Well, the old man had been paying attention after all. The pieces were finally beginning to fall into place.

CHAPTER 35

The Mall, Washington, D.C.
Monday, 11:45 a.m.

BRAXTON HAD CAUGHT the 10:00 a.m. shuttle from Logan. Even at that late morning hour the plane had been filled, but he had managed to cajole a window seat from the gate agent. Still exhausted from lack of sleep the night before, he had wedged himself between the seat and the side of the airplane and dozed off.

Images of Terrel had filled his dreams. He had rushed to the apartment just in time to see his friend falling through the window. Reaching out, he had grabbed at his friend's shirt but was pulled through himself and fell helplessly toward the sidewalk. He had awakened in a sweat and found his hand clenched tightly around his seat belt, the plane in a steep dive toward Reagan National. Why were the shuttle pilots always such cowboys?

Goddard was to meet him outside the USAir terminal at 11:30, but there was no sign of her as he scanned the pickup area. Suddenly a shiny, midnight-blue BMW 320i sedan screeched to a halt in front of him.

"Good morning," said a familiar voice through the open window.

Braxton pulled open the passenger door and slid inside. As soon as he had closed the door, she accelerated down the ramp and onto the parkway.

"Nice car for a graduate student," he commented while struggling to get the seatbelt hooked.

"It's my only indulgence," she replied with a smile. She was dressed in jeans and a cream-colored V-neck sweater. Her ponytailed student alter-ego had returned. "And it's not that expensive to run."

"Right," he said, thinking back to his days as a student. He had hardly been able to keep his ten-year-old Volkswagen Beetle running.

It was a beautiful, clear day; the sky was a deep blue with just a few wispy clouds hovering at the horizon. Goddard had opened the windows and a warm breeze filled the car. It was almost enough to make Braxton forget about the case.

"I certainly didn't expect to see you again so soon," he said. "Thanks for coming with me."

"I feel like I'm a part of what happened too. I want whoever killed Mohammed to be punished. If I can do anything to help I will."

"And I thought you just wanted to see *me* again," he said with a smile.

She responded with a devilish grin. "Why would you ever think that?"

They crossed the Potomac into D.C. at Arlington Memorial Bridge and turned up 14th Street. Circling the Mall for a few minutes, they finally spotted someone pulling out in front of the Smithsonian. Goddard raced down Jefferson Drive and deftly pulled the BMW in the space.

"Nice work. For a girl," Braxton chided.

"Glad you liked it," she replied, hopping out of the car. She walked over to the curb then stood impatiently, arms crossed, as he fumbled to find the door release on the unfamiliar vehicle.

"Okay, I quit," he said, finally swinging out and closing the door behind him. "No more macho comments."

"That's more like it," she said patting him on the back. " I was about to call for a policeman."

"Let's hope it won't take too long to find ours," he replied, and offered his arm. She took it and they headed back toward the Washington Monument.

"I am so sorry about your friend. How are your neighbors taking it?"

"Everyone's pretty shaken. Cops were around all yesterday, and a lot of families were frantically installing new locks and security systems. It's scary. Paul's parents flew in from Detroit last night.

They came by for a few minutes and I showed them around his apartment. They're taking care of everything from now on. I can't help but feel somehow it was my fault he was killed."

"You can't think that way. It wasn't your fault." She drew him closer and stared up into his eyes. "And we're going to find whoever is behind this."

The Mall was filled with people: families in a rainbow of colors and clothing styles gawking at the monuments and museums, staring into cell phones, or even paper maps, navigating the geometric maze of paths to their next destination; business professionals and congressional staffers, in more conservative dress, lugging backpacks and briefcases, striding to their next meeting with the important work of government; and finally scantily-clad students, lying on towels spread on the grass, reading books or simply catching the first warm rays of spring.

As they approached the Monument, Braxton saw Fowler sitting on a bench along one of the pathways. His wrinkled tweed sport coat lay across the backrest and a *Washington Post* was spread out on the seat next to him.

"Found any good mysteries to solve, Detective?" Braxton asked as they approached the bench.

Fowler folded the newspaper and looked up at the pair. "I've got more than I need already, thanks. You didn't tell me you were bringing a friend, Braxton. Nice to see you again, Ms. Goddard. You two a couple now?"

"Just acquaintances, Detective." Goddard replied with a smile. "We have a mutual interest in your case."

"I see."

"Susan wants to get to the bottom of this as much as I do," Braxton explained. "I didn't think you'd mind." Fowler frowned but remained silent.

"An interesting location for a meeting, Detective," Goddard said. "Do you come here often?"

"Whenever I get fed up with the Department, Ms. Goddard. It gives me some perspective. The atmosphere on the Mall is pretty different from where I usually spend my time. So what have you two figured out?"

The pair sat on the bench, flanking Fowler, and Braxton began the explanation. "As I told you on the phone, I confirmed what

Ramal said in his message. There is strange activity on GW's gateway computer. Messages are being sent from the system that shouldn't be."

"What kind of messages?" Fowler asked. "Who are they being sent to?"

"All good questions, Detective. Ones that I don't have answers to yet. And it's complicated getting them unfortunately."

"We think it could be due to some kind of virus or worm," Goddard volunteered.

Braxton gave her a puzzled look. When had "we" start investigating the case? "That's one possibility," he quickly countered. "It also may be that someone has gained access to the software inside the gateway. If they did, they could reprogram it to send the messages."

"So how do you find out if that's what's happening?" Fowler asked.

"So far as I can tell, the messages are only generated from a gateway manufactured by Century Computer. I found a trapdoor, a way to break into the system. It was something that should have been removed before the computer was shipped. It could allow a program, call it a rogue, to get in."

Braxton struggled to make the explanation as simple as possible. He didn't know how much the old cop could follow.

"I used to work at Century so I called Warren Chamberlain, he's head of Engineering, to discuss what I found. I met with him on Friday."

"The day before your friend was killed, right?" Fowler asked.

"Yes." Braxton felt his stomach churn.

"You don't think Century could have anything to do with the break-in, do you Detective?" Goddard asked.

"No idea," Fowler answered. "Go on with your story."

Goddard had voiced the question Braxton had been too afraid to ask. He couldn't think about that now.

"Warren wasn't very helpful. He didn't believe anything could be wrong and wouldn't let me talk to any of the technical staff. You'd think he'd be more concerned if one of his products had been compromised. He said he'd get back to me but I don't know whether he will or not. Basically, I didn't find out a thing."

"So you still don't have any proof of this theory of yours?" Fowler pushed.

Braxton shook his head and scuffed his shoes in the dirt. "No. Not yet."

"Look," Fowler spoke directly to the consultant, "I need to tell you this case is now out of my hands. The FBI has taken over, but they're not going to do a damn thing with it. My advice for you is to just drop it. I don't know whether your friend's death is related or not. But there's no reason to take any chances. This is too dangerous for a couple of amateurs."

Braxton couldn't believe what Fowler was saying. How could he lead him on then tell him to stop?

"You look, Detective," he began angrily. "Maybe you don't have a case, but I do. I know there's *something* going on in those gateways and my job is to find out what it is. And whoever is behind it may have killed two people already. If you're not interested in helping me, then that's fine. We'll find someone else who will."

He stood up and looked over to Goddard. "Come on Susan, let's get out of Detective Fowler's way. He obviously has more important things to do."

"Whoa, slow down, Braxton." Fowler grabbed the consultant's coat tail and pulled him back to the bench. "Don't get all riled up. I didn't say I wouldn't help. You've just got to realize this is serious."

"We're very aware this is serious, Detective," Braxton said. "We've both had a friend killed."

"Can you help us?" Goddard asked.

"Maybe. I've been doing some checking. I called a friend in the CIA." Braxton and Goddard both raised their eyebrows. "No big deal, just a friend who owed me a favor. He couldn't find any terrorist connection with Ramal's death. Unexplained murder number one. The Cambridge police also don't have anything on your friend's murder. It looks like a simple burglary, but there are no prints, no forensics, and, according to you, no valuables taken. Very clean, very professional. But what were they doing in your apartment for over an hour?"

"They could have been waiting for me."

"We don't know that for sure. Nothing links the two murders. Except you. You've got to be careful. When do you expect to hear anything back from this computer guy?"

"Warren? He didn't really say. Maybe later this week."

"Okay, I'll see what more I can get down here. Where will you be?"

Braxton looked over to Goddard wondering what her plans were. "I'm not sure. I want to make a stop at GW and check on something. But I'll definitely be back in Boston mid-week."

"Call me when you get home." He glanced at Goddard and added, "And in the meantime, why don't the two of you spend some time together? Go sightseeing. See a movie. Maybe you can keep each other out of trouble."

"We appreciate your concern, Detective," she replied. "We'll try."

The couple stood and Braxton took Goddard's hand. "I'll talk to you in a couple days, Detective," he said.

"Yeah." They had started to walk away when Fowler's voice stopped them. "Ah, excuse me, Ms. Goddard. Something's been bothering me ever since I talked to you last week. We haven't met before have we?"

Goddard shook her head and laughed. "That's a terrible line, Detective. I was hoping you could do better."

"Hey, I didn't mean . . ." Fowler fumbled.

"I'm kidding. I don't think we've ever met, Detective. I haven't been in D.C. for a very long time."

"If you say so. Now get outa' here and let me read my paper in peace."

* * *

Fowler watched the couple stroll down the hill. *Crazy kids. What have they gotten into?*

There wasn't much he could do to help them, except be around if things got too hot. His contact in Boston had said that the Cambridge cops had squat on the break-in. It would become just another unsolved case of urban crime.

Maybe he could squeeze Slattery a little more. The spook had definitely been holding something back. If he could get any corroboration of this network problem he might be able to get the case reopened.

Fowler pulled out his cell phone and dialed.

"Forty-two twelve," said a distant mechanical voice. "No one is able to answer right now, would you like to leave a message?"

Damn. How could he get Slattery's attention without setting off any alarms? What did Braxton call that thing?

"Yes," he replied to the machine.

"Please leave your message after the tone."

"Roger. It's Sam. I've got some information on that rogue we were talking about. Give me a call."

That should do it.

CHAPTER 36

The Russell Building, Washington, D.C.
Monday, 12:30 p.m.

"Is the man in, Camille?" Nicholson asked. It had taken him all night and most of the morning to fix the problems his staff had created in the draft of the amendment. Why couldn't they have just left it the way he wrote it? He had to get the document to Potterfield before the caucus meeting.

"Yes, Nick. He came back from the White House a few minutes ago. I think he's expecting you."

"Thanks." He gave a perfunctory knock on the door and continued inside. His boss was sitting behind his disk staring into his PC. "David, I've prepared the amendment with the new technical requirements. We probably need to go over some of the highlights."

Potterfield turned to his aide and attacked. "Screw the amendment, Nick! Another of those goddamn threats came in over the weekend." Nicholson walked behind the desk and read the message over the Senator's shoulder.

```
From: an6845@anon.trans.ua

To: richmondeagle@potterfield.senate.gov

Subject: Senator Lynch

Senator Potterfield,

You continue to ignore our warnings. We know you
fabricated the evidence that discredited Senator
Lynch. We will release our proof to the media if
you do not announce your resignation immediately.
```

You have been warned.

Citizens for Responsible Government

"When do I get answers, Nick? We have to find out who this is and what they really have."

The investigation was going too slowly. Nicholson had expected that a solid lead would come out of the staffers' research. It hadn't happened that way. "We checked out all the reporters who covered the story. They have all either died or left the area. I don't believe any that are left are smart enough to pull this off. That just leaves the family."

"So where are they?"

"I'm still working on that. No one seems to know where they went after the suicide. The mother may be dead, or in a home somewhere."

"Your only suspect is a sixty-year-old woman? You're letting me down, Nick. Call the IRS. Or Social Security. They know where everybody is."

"We've got to be careful, David. I'm going to follow up with a friend of the family. It'll take me a few more days but I can't trust anyone else to do it."

"Just remember, the Bill is up for a vote this week. We can't have anything screwing that up."

"Understood, David, but I don't think you should worry about the Bill. I know you'll be able to get it through. As for the email, I'll send a reply this afternoon. We'll find this bastard." Somehow.

"I appreciate your confidence, Nick. I really do." Potterfield sat back in his chair and rubbed a very tired pair of eyes. Then he leaned forward with renewed energy. "Enough of this email crap. Show me the new amendment that's going to make us goddamn rich."

* * *

Nicholson leaned over his desk reviewing the latest email from "Citizens for Responsible Government". What a piece of crap! Who the hell were these people? And did they really have anything on his boss?

He shook his head to put such foolish questions aside. All that counted were facts and results. And he had always managed to discover ways to get the facts and create the results. Even if it sometimes required ascertaining just the right kind of motivation.

He would get the facts on this blackmailer and the results would follow. It hadn't been all that different when he had first met his future partners.

*   *   *

Potterfield had wanted Nick to go to the best school the Senator's influence could buy. His choice was a law degree from Yale, but Nick's grades weren't quite up to it. He did well in math and science, however, and his SAT scores caught the attention of a local recruiter from MIT. She needed to fill her minority quota and nearly swooned when she heard Nick's hard-times background. Nick convinced his mentor that MIT's Sloan business program would meet their needs, and six months later he was on his way to Boston.

Nick's experience in the law office had taught him how to work any system. It was easy to maneuver around the Institute's standard rules and regulations, especially for someone with "special circumstances". The rules were made for typical immature undergraduates who were happy to do whatever MIT told them. He, on the other hand, knew what he wanted and how he would get there. His college education was a time-consuming formality. He might learn some skills, although he really didn't need to go to a university to get them. They could be just as easily developed by reading and study. What he could get, however, were the contacts that would be the stepping stones to the positions, and the power, he desired.

He meticulously mapped out his four years. He took as few courses as possible, getting MIT dispensations as frequently as he dared. The subjects he did enroll in, he selected as much for the stature of the professor as the content of the material. One such addition was a class taught by a John Donovan. Nick heard that he was a rising star, and the course had a strong following both in Electrical Engineering and Management. You have to be open to new opportunities, he mused, as he talked the registrar into adding the class to his schedule.

Unfortunately, the course was much harder than he expected. Nothing he couldn't handle, but the work required significantly more time than he had planned, to the point that he had to drop one of his other classes. The term project was a particular time sink.

It was hell getting anything out of the other members of his project team. Nick was a couple of years older than most of his classmates and significantly more mature. He found he had to tone down his behavior to get some things done. Warren was a prime example. He was a quiet, introverted engineer; someone who let life lead him rather than the other way around. He was bright enough, worked hard, and could be counted on to do as Nick requested, as long as the request was prefaced with a "please".

Bob was another matter altogether. Arrogant and ill-mannered, he was the perfect example of a spoiled preppy. It was all Nick could do to keep from popping him in the face. Bob contributed very little to their project, except providing the money for the late night pizza and beer. He couldn't imagine why the Harvard student had even taken the class. But it was typical. Bob's worst problem was getting in over his head, and the rest of them always had to get him out.

Nick never took another class with either of the pair. The trio had their own goals and set out on independent paths to their futures. Nick graduated and went into the Graduate Management Program at the Sloan School. Warren became obsessed with computers and spent the rest of his time in the Electrical Engineering department absorbing as much as he could. Bob had apparently had enough of real work and finished his academic experience in reading and contemplation behind the ivy-covered walls of Harvard.

They never released the unusual bond that had been formed, however, and kept in touch in uniquely high-tech ways. Nick talked one of his professors into giving him an account on MULTICS, the next generation time-sharing system MIT was developing for GE. He quickly deciphered the system's internal operation and gave himself full system privileges. He created accounts for his friends, and they used their new-found power to solve problem sets, analyze economic models, and write elegant research papers.

Nick also discovered he could use his skills to make his life more comfortable. MIT had recently written a new computerized course scheduling system that ensured balanced student loads across the various recitation sections. With the old paper request system, early morning sections would be empty while afternoon ones were oversubscribed. It would take weeks to get new rooms allocated and the sections balanced. The new computer program automatically placed a student into a section based on the fit between his schedule and the overall distribution of other students in the class.

Unfortunately, this program wreaked havoc on Nick's carefully designed calendar. He routinely double booked classes, knowing he wouldn't attend many anyway, and set his schedule to accommodate other pressing matters, such as the Wellesley bus schedule. He and Warren had done some research, then made "improvements" to the scheduling algorithm. It was disgusting how inefficient the original had been. The new one worked much better.

Soon after the scheduler was corrected, Bob asked for some help. His parents had cut off his allowance for some trivial reason, and he needed to find a way to get some money. Someone had suggested that they could offer a custom scheduling "service" to other students. Nick thought it sounded like an interesting venture; he could use the extra cash as well. They made the appropriate modifications at Harvard and began an operation that provided all three ample spending money for the rest of their academic careers.

Warren had a tough junior year. His mother died just after Labor Day and he was having difficulty concentrating on his work. His grades slipped and he risked losing the scholarship that kept him at the Institute. They couldn't allow the short-sighted rules of the Financial Aid Office to cost MIT one of its finest scholars. Nick found the academic records data base and made the necessary corrections. Warren soon straightened himself out and graduated with honors the following year.

That was the way it had started, using their knowledge of computer systems to help each other out. Over the ensuing years, those skills had been immensely valuable to both Nicholson and his boss. The campaign against Lynch had been only one example. Potterfield didn't know about the occasional assists Nicholson received from his partners, and there was no reason to have him involved. Better that he attribute all those results to his exemplary Chief of Staff.

CHAPTER 37

George Washington University, Washington, D.C.
Monday, 2:00 p.m.

GODDARD DROVE BRAXTON back to George Washington University. He wanted to make one more request of Williams and didn't want any written, or electronic, record. They stopped at the computer center and spoke with the SysOp about the Century gateway. He was busy with a software upgrade to one of their new IBM servers but managed to print out a process map for *gwu-gate*. The whole visit only took ten minutes.

"It's probably good Williams was so busy," Braxton commented when they got back to the BMW. "He didn't have time to ask me why I wanted the map."

"What does it show?"

"A process map is a listing of the processes, or software programs, that are running on a machine. Besides just their names, this one gives each program's size, location in memory, and links to devices."

"Does the listing help?" Goddard asked.

"It's consistent with the maps I remember when we were developing the network software. There's definitely more going on than just routing."

"Can you tell what the programs are doing?"

"Not from this. There's not enough detail. It's just another piece of the puzzle."

"What do we need to do next?"

"Getting this was easier than I thought. I still have to figure out how to get through the trapdoor. Then I can really find out what this mole is up to."

"Mole? Is that what you're calling it?"

"Paul came up with the name. It's as good as any for now." His voice lost its excitement at the reference to his friend.

"Well," she continued rapidly, "while you were gone I got thinking about what Detective Fowler said."

"About being careful?"

"No." She playfully slapped his leg. "About sightseeing!"

"Sightseeing? I'm sorry Susan, but I've seen most all of D.C. already."

"I don't mean the District. A couple years ago I got sick of out-of-town friends always asking where to go and how to get there. So I wrote up a complete tour: *Susan Goddard's Guide to Historical Northern Virginia.* I think it's quite good. There's a copy in the glove compartment, but you get a personal showing."

"So you're kidnapping me?"

"Absolutely!"

Braxton happily succumbed to her enthusiasm, leaned back in the BMW's soft leather seat, and let his lovely chauffeur take over. It was irrelevant that he had seen most of the sights before. This time he was with a beautiful friend and he saw them anew through her eyes.

They headed south on Route 1 and stopped at Mount Vernon. Half an hour later he had learned more about George Washington and his home than he could ever remember. Then it was down through Lorton to see Gunston Hall, George Mason's elegant Georgian estate.

Next Goddard headed east for Washington's birthplace at Pope's Creek Plantation, and Stratford Hall, the birthplace of Richard Henry Lee and Francis Lee, the only brothers to sign the Declaration of Independence. Turning west, they drove through Fredericksburg for the James Monroe Museum and the home of Mary Washington.

The afternoon turned cool as Goddard roared passed the Fredericksburg and Spotsylvania County National Military Park on their way to Charlottesville. The BMW spun into Monticello just as a golden sun was setting behind the Appalachian Mountains. They found a bench on the stately grounds and watched as the bright orange and red sky dissolved into deepening blue.

The tour had been frenetic but it was a pleasant respite from the horrors of the past week. For Braxton, it also marked the transition of a tentative friendship into something a lot more personal. He hoped Goddard felt the same.

"You could become a tour guide if politics don't work out," he said as they waited for dinner at a rural Virginia inn outside Culpeper. "Where did you learn all that?"

"I told you I was born in Virginia. They taught us a lot of local history. I liked it and kept picking it up. Don't you know a lot about Boston?"

"Some, I guess, but nothing like this afternoon. You're a real expert."

"It was fun. Thanks for coming with me."

Her smile had been pulling at him all day. He wanted to tell her how he felt but was afraid of sounding foolish. "Thanks to you. You did all the work. All I had to do was sit back and enjoy the view."

They spent the next hour playfully arguing about their favorite part of the afternoon. A bottle of Cabernet Sauvignon helped to relax their nerves and release any lingering inhibitions.

"Do you have any brothers or sisters?" Braxton asked after they had finished dessert.

"No. I'm a spoiled only child. I thought you could tell."

"Not spoiled, just uniquely independent."

Goddard laughed at his euphemism. "How about you? Any siblings?"

"One brother. He's an art director at an agency in Miami. It's nice 'cause he lives close to our parents."

"An art director? That sounds pretty far from computers and engineering."

"Yeah, Megan said he must have gotten it from our mother." It came out before he could stop.

"Megan?"

"Uh, my ex-wife." Why had he mentioned her? No point in hiding it. He hoped he hadn't ruined the evening. "It was my fault, I was pretty impossible to live with."

"That's hard to imagine. Do you have any children?"

"No, we never took the time. We were always too busy with our careers. I got that from my father, too."

Goddard paused and those deep blue eyes looked far away. "It must be nice to have a family around," she said quietly. "Are you still close to your parents?"

"I think so. My father was very important to me when I was growing up. He had to retire a few years ago and it was tough on him. I try to get down and see them as much as I can."

"Couldn't he have stayed working?"

"No, it wasn't possible." He immediately knew his tone was too sharp.

"I'm sorry. I didn't mean to pry."

Braxton painfully remembered their conversation in Boston. Maybe he did owe her a better explanation.

"No, I'm sorry I was so short. My dad was a great engineer but not very good when it came to corporate politics. He got in a tough situation and was undermined by a subordinate. It destroyed his will to continue. The company shuffled him from staff job to staff job until he reached retirement age. It was awful to watch. Now he spends most of his time just sitting in a rocker."

"That's terrible. You feel so helpless when something happens to your parents. My mother died last year. She had been sick a long time but it still took a while to get over."

"I'm sorry." He took her small hand in his and squeezed it lightly. She looked back into his eyes and he felt a warm pleasure flow through him. It was like that first sip of his mother's hot chocolate after coming in from a biting winter's day. He never wanted that feeling to go away.

A stately grandfather clock chimed seven times and Goddard looked at her watch. "Oh, we'd better get going if we're going to get you back to National. What time is your flight?"

"I hadn't really thought about it. How late do they go?"

"I think there's one at eleven." She paused for just a moment. "If you need to leave."

As usual, he had hesitated until it was almost too late. He had left it to her to make the offer. "I'd rather stay with you. I am your prisoner after all."

She tipped her head and grinned. "Forgot about that."

He called for the bill and they headed back to the city, exchanging a few polite comments on the dinner and an occasional joke to hide their awkwardness. She left her hand resting on the shift knob, and he covered it, their fingers entwining over the soft leather.

Anticipation had taken control and there was nothing either of them could do to stop it.

* * *

"Susie, can you *please* get the door! I'm in the middle of something."

William Hastings, Democratic Senior Senator from Illinois, member of the loyal minority, and tonight, lonely single parent, was trying to struggle through the latest homeland security report. Normally a tumbler of 18-year J&B, a roaring fire in the study's fireplace, and his favorite over-stuffed easy chair would have made the work breeze by, but tonight's continuous buzz of telephones and doorbells had made concentration impossible.

Thank heavens this was the last night of Tracey's visit to her mother in Chicago. One week of dealing with his twin daughters, even with a part-time nanny, had been more than he could handle. Over the years, Hastings had stood his ground with the best in the Senate: Thurmond, Dole, McCain, even goddamn Trent Lott, but dealing with the thrashing hormones of two high school teenagers had taxed him to the limit. Only one more night.

"Package, Dad."

A petite waif with orange-streaked hair darted into the study, dropped a FedEx envelope on the corner of the weathered oak coffee table, and disappeared as quickly as she had come.

"Thanks, honey," Hasting said to the empty room.

Who would be sending him something at home? He hesitated touching it, the memory of anthrax-spiked letters was never far away, but then saw that it was from Karen, his aide that was working on the Potterfield backgrounder.

This must be the latest amendment. Another attempt by the Chairman to rescue the morally-flawed piece of legislation. Hastings saw no reason to believe the United States needed to support, much less become directly involved in, any foreign interventions. Too many American lives had already been lost.

Let our pompous, big-mouthed allies do their part for a change, dammit.

He dropped the package on the top of his reading stack and went back to the report.

* * *

Hastings dropped his head into his hands and pressed at the throbbing vessels in his temples. How did they get all this?

After he had opened the envelope, it had been clear it wasn't from Karen. The package consisted of twelve pages of computer printouts, detailing his wife's two decade-long battle with schizophrenia and mental illness: laboratory results that should have been confidential, police records that he thought had been sealed, physician notes from a supposedly private clinic. Records that painted a picture of violence, betrayal, and influence.

He paused for a moment, then got up, walked to the fireplace and tossed the package into the flames.

All he had tried to do was protect his family. What was so wrong with that?

The final typewritten page had said simply:

```
Pass the Freedom Bill. Or all this, and more, will
be public.

Do you really want to do this to your family?
```

* * *

Northern Virginia traffic had only been terrible not abominable, and, as a result, just before eleven o'clock Goddard pulled the BMW into a parking garage below a modern apartment building in Arlington. They got out and she led him to the elevator, pressing the button for the twelfth floor.

"How fast is this elevator?" Braxton asked as they stepped inside.

"It's pretty slow," she said turning to face him.

He took her face in his hands and slowly pulled her toward him. Their lips met with a tenderness neither had thought they possessed. As they kissed, the hunger inside them grew and they pulled closer in near desperation. They slowly separated and she buried her head in his chest as he encircled her with his arms.

She had been right; it took forever to get to twelve.

* * *

Goddard rolled over and stroked his long, muscled back. His breaths were slow and relaxed. He had been strong, yet gentle, and their release complete; the result of feelings long hidden. It was as if all the pain and anguish had been exorcised, if only for one short moment.

Now she was left with the aftermath of her impetuosity.

How could she have let this happen? What would she do if he ever found out?

CHAPTER 38

THE TROPICAL SUN was warm on his face. They had been swimming in a crystal clear lagoon then had lay on the beach to relax. Braxton rolled over onto his back and opened his eyes to gaze into the bright azure sky.

What he saw instead was a flat white ceiling. The morning Virginia sun streamed through the bedroom window and drew a band of yellow light across the top of the bed. It wasn't the Caribbean, but it was a much more humane method of awaking than his electronic alarm. He reached across the bed but his hand fell empty on the pillow. He hadn't even bothered to ask if she had to get up early. She must have had an early class.

He sat up and looked around. Goddard's bedroom was a small, neat space; or at least it had been before the pair had strewn their clothes all over the floor. White sheer curtains complemented pale green walls and a deep teal carpet. A green and blue flowered bedspread lay in a heap at the foot of the bed. The usual female appointments were arrayed on the top of a bureau next to an open closet door: perfume bottles, makeup, a small jewelry box, and a single family portrait of a proud mother and father holding their young daughter. On top of an end table next to the bed sat a lamp, a well-worn Baldacci paperback, and a gratefully quiet digital alarm clock. It read 7:48.

He felt more relaxed than he had in years. The incident was still an enigma; he didn't know where it would lead him. But last night he had rediscovered a part of himself that he thought had died. It was another step on his road back.

He didn't harbor any elaborate illusions about his new companion. She was a beautiful, young woman. Independent and mysterious in some ways, strangely vulnerable in others. He vainly hoped the encounter wasn't just an inquisitive fling with an older man, but he prepared himself for the worst.

As he lay in the bed recalling, as best he could, the events of the night before, he heard a soft tapping from another room. She must still be in the apartment, eating breakfast or reading the paper. He rolled over the edge of the bed, crawled under the bedspread in search of his underwear and slacks, and quickly pulled them on. The noise grew louder and sounded like the tapping of a keyboard. He peered around the bedroom doorway and saw her sitting at a small desk, typing intently on a laptop. Wrapped in a light blue silk robe, her hair fell softly on her shoulders. She looked radiant.

He stepped behind her, thick carpeting under his bare feet silencing his movement. Her typing had stopped and she sat transfixed, staring into the screen. He came closer and, without considering what he was doing, began reading the text.

```
From: richmondeagle@potterfield.senate.gov

To: an6845@anon.trans.ua

Subject: Re: Senator Lynch

We all mourned the tragic and untimely death of
Senator Lynch. I had nothing to do with this unfor-
tunate affair and will not address your accusations
through electronic mail. If you contact me person-
ally, I will guarantee your anonymity and answer
all of your questions.

I'm sure you realize the seriousness of threats
made against a member of Congress. If you continue
with this blackmail, or make public your unsubstan-
tiated claims, we will be forced to turn your com-
munications over to the FBI.

Senator David Potterfield
```

He suddenly realized that he had done something very wrong and very foolish. Trying to step away, he hit the coffee table; a pile of magazines fell noisily to the floor.

Goddard snapped her head around and saw him standing there. "What are you doing sneaking up on me like that? Get away from me!"

Her voice cut through him like a knife. He had never heard such hatred.

"I'm sorry," he pleaded. "I just came in to see what you were doing. I didn't mean to frighten you."

She stared back at him for what seemed like hours. He considered walking away; she was obviously in trouble and he didn't need any more problems. But he didn't want to walk away this time. That was how he had dealt with most things the past two years: don't get involved, don't commit to anything, and don't trust anyone. Maybe it was time to try another way.

He didn't know whether he could help or not; he only knew he had to try. He walked up to her and gently held her head against his side. Tears ran down his bare skin. Her arms encircled him and squeezed him tightly.

When she relaxed, he knelt down and kissed her hair. The smell of her perfume filled his head and made him shudder. "Let me help," he whispered. "Please talk to me."

The tears rolled down her cheeks, now leaving dark streaks on the cool blue silk. She looked up into his eyes. "They killed him," she cried softly. "They killed my father."

He gently lifted her off the chair, picked her up with a sweep of his arm, and carried her to the bedroom. Laying her tenderly on the bed, he sat next to her, stroking her head and letting her tears cleanse the pain. How long had she locked these emotions in her fragile shell?

She cried until the tears would no longer come, then reached over and drew his face to hers. Their lips touched once, then again. She pulled him next to her and they made love, no longer for personal release but for comfort and compassion.

* * *

He filled two glasses with orange juice and crawled back into the bed, piling his pillows next to the headboard and leaning back next to her.

"I woke up about six and couldn't get back to sleep," she explained after he had settled in. "You looked so peaceful I didn't want to bother you so I went into the living room." A smile returned to her face and her eyes regained some of the sparkle of the night before. She reached over and placed her hand on his arm. "I hadn't checked my email since yesterday morning."

"I am sorry about startling you. I wasn't trying to pry."

"I know you weren't." She took his hand in hers. "It's just that I had been hiding it for so long."

"What did the message have to do with your father?"

Her eyes drifted off to another place and another time. "It's a long story. My real name is Susan Lynch. My father was a U.S. Senator from Virginia. When I was eight, he ran for reelection. I can't remember much about the campaign, but I know it was very hard on him. People were saying awful things. The older kids at school would repeat them but I didn't understand. Why would anyone want to say bad things about Father?"

"He lost the election. After that, people just stopped talking to us. Even our friends didn't want anything to do with us."

She wiped a tear from her cheek and continued.

"Father took it very hard. He started drinking and arguing with Momma. They tried to hide it but I knew. I heard them at night after they put me to bed. I tried to be good but I didn't know what to do. After a few months he withdrew completely. He stayed in the house all the time. I thought it was my fault."

The story sounded all too familiar. He was afraid he knew the ending.

"One day about six months after the campaign we came back to the house and Father was gone. He didn't come home for dinner. That night Momma came into my room and told me that he had died. I didn't believe her and threw quite a fit apparently. We yelled at each other and got mad and cried a lot. She finally told me that he had killed himself."

She paused and stared out the window. He wanted to hold her, help her through the journey, but he didn't. She needed to remember in her own way.

"You don't have to . . ." he said.

"Yes. I do," she replied. "For us.

"I have a vivid memory of the funeral. Hardly anyone came. We had this big house in Fairfax. There had been lots of parties and Father would introduce me to all of his friends. I would stay up late and sneak down to watch the people come and go. But no one came to his funeral. I hated all of them for abandoning him. I still do.

"Momma was never the same. We sold the house and took her maiden name, Goddard. She sent me away to boarding school and bought a small house in Maryland. She couldn't stand to stay in Virginia.

"One of Father's real friends, a lawyer, handled all of the business for Momma. When I was fifteen we had to put her into a home. The doctors said she had a stroke but I think she just decided to give up. I tried to see her as often as I could but she never did recognize me after that."

She stopped, her head falling softly onto the comforter in his lap. He gently stroked her hair until she could continue.

"I'm so sorry," he said after a few minutes had passed. "It must have been very difficult growing up alone. It's hard enough when you have your parents around."

"I did okay," she whispered. "We had enough money from father's investments and the schools I went to were very good. I learned a lot, but never made very many friends. I've never trusted anyone after what happened to Father." She looked up at him. "I've never told this story to anyone, Adam."

Her eyes glistened from the tears, like pools of deep ocean water. All he wanted to do was take away the pain, if only for a moment.

"I went to the University of Maryland to be near Momma, then came here to Georgetown. I hadn't been able to decide what to do with my life. I just coasted from one degree to the next.

"Then last November Momma died. I had to take care of some paperwork and found a box of old letters and documents. There was a letter from Father that he had written to Momma the day he died."

She crawled over him and grabbed her robe. The silk billowed in the air as she moved over to the jewelry box. She pulled something out of the box, came back to the bed, and handed it to him. He looked back at her, testing the moment.

"It's all right," she said. "I want you to read it."

"Mrs. Maria Lynch" was written on the outside of a faded envelope. He carefully pulled out the single sheet of paper. The letter was written in longhand with strong, bold loops and even, straight lines.

Dearest Maria,

I can no longer bear seeing the pain in your eyes and having you endure the innuendo from our supposed friends. Please believe me when I say that none of the stories are true and that I would never betray your love or the trust the citizens of Virginia placed in me. I was naive and underestimated the forces behind the lies and, because of that alone, I have failed.

Go and make a new life for yourself and our Susan. Try to forgive me.

I shall always love you both,

Kenneth

She lay next to him, pulling the sheet up to her neck, lost in her thoughts. He couldn't imagine the pain she must have suffered. He was ashamed that he had felt his own problems so important. But the parallels in their lives were so unexpected. He lowered the letter to his lap and waited.

"I was shocked, of course. Momma had never shown me the letter or discussed it. All she ever spoke about was her hatred of the people of Virginia for deserting him, and for David Potterfield for spreading the lies."

"Potterfield? What did he have to do with what happened to your father?" Braxton knew that Potterfield was now the Senior Senator from Virginia. He was a powerful man on the Hill who enjoyed wielding that influence.

"He was Father's opponent for the Senate position. He won, of course."

"Was there any proof that Potterfield was involved?

"No," she replied reluctantly, "but who else had so much to gain? And from what I've read about him, he gets a lot of his work done behind the scenes."

"How does that email tie into this all?"

"After I read the letter, I had to do something to avenge Father. I decided to get all the information I could on Potterfield and tell him that someone knew what he did. I wasn't sure how to do it until Mohammed gave me the idea."

"Ramal was involved?"

"No, not directly. I never told him about Father. We were taking the multimedia course and Mohammed was always talking about networking. He was awfully shy but we just hit it off. One afternoon he mentioned the old remailers. It sounded like the ideal solution. I had Mohammed teach me all about email and Internet utilities. I got

Potterfield's private address from one of the Internet newsgroups, found a remailer, and started sending him messages."

Braxton gasped. "What did you think would happen? You didn't expect him to just confess did you?"

"I don't know what I expected. I just had to do something. I had to let him know that someone still remembered."

"Didn't you think it could be dangerous?"

"I didn't think they would be able to find me. Then Mohammed was killed. At first I was afraid someone had identified us, but since he hadn't really been involved and nothing else happened to me, I decided it was just a coincidence."

Coincidences. Too many coincidences.

"This morning I found the message from the remailer. That's what you saw on the screen. It scared me, I didn't think he would reply. I'm sorry I reacted so badly."

"No, I was wrong to be sneaking around like that." He reached over and hugged her.

"Will you help me? Help me find out who destroyed Father?"

This was not a tearful pleading; her voice was firm and resolute. She was looking for a commitment from him. Uncharacteristically, he answered without hesitating. "Of course. But what can I do?"

She looked over to the clock. It was 9:30.

"I almost forgot! You can start by getting dressed. We've got an appointment." She abruptly jumped out of bed, threw off her robe, and ran naked into the bathroom.

"We're going to see a lawyer," she called over the rush of the shower.

CHAPTER 39

Takagawa Communications, Crystal City, Virginia
Tuesday, 9:30 a.m.

HAJIMA CLOSED THE folder on his desk and dropped his head into his hands. He had completed his investigation and had failed.

Knowledge of the GPS resolution problem had been limited to a handful of employees. He had interviewed—interrogated might have been the more accurate description—all of them. Additional background checks had been performed by his security staff. He was now confident none would have exposed the fault.

He had ordered a complete trace of all related communications. They had been strictly limited to internal Takagawa systems; no external documents were ever produced. How had Greystone learned of the setback?

He was missing something. Or was he simply thinking too hard?

He dropped his hands, lightly wrapping his right fist in his left palm and placing them just above his waist, at the *hara*, the center of the body's *ki*. He sat back and closed his eyes. Next, he took a breath then held it. When he exhaled, his body had already begun the silent descent.

Meditation had helped him solve many problems over the years. Business, social, and moral obstacles had all succumbed. Perhaps this would be another example.

He let his thoughts flow freely, like ripples on a pond, passing through each other with ease. There were no prejudices, no assessments. Just stillness.

He arose from the state thirty minutes later calm and refreshed. He smiled.

For almost a year, Greystone had been providing Hajima with
confidential information on their competitors' efforts as well as
legislative drafts and proceedings related to the *Potterfield Bill*. Hajima
had assumed that the disclosures had been due to spies in the
associated organizations. A time-honored technique ably described
in *The Art of War*.

It had been his age that betrayed him. He had ignored what his
younger subordinates would have seen immediately.

Takagawa had been hacked. Greystone had a tap on the Internet.

Greystone and Theater were becoming more and more dependent
on Takagawa. Once the Bill passed, Takagawa would have control
over manufacturing of the devices. And their distribution around the
world.

But that was nothing compared to knowledge of the tap.

Now he knew he would return to Japan triumphant.

*   *   *

"Mistah Chairman, after due consideration on this item, ah move
we accept the amendment as proposed."

Potterfield smiled on hearing the rich southern drawl echo
through the chamber. Senator William Branchflower, Senior Senator
from Louisiana, was an anachronistic good ol' boy who had been a
fixture in Washington politics for forty years. Potterfield would be
surprised if Branchflower even knew what the Internet was; his
aides often commented that the Senator believed ball-point pens
were a communist plot. But Billy Joe had promised to move the
amendment, and he *never* reneged on a promise.

"Second," added Senator Farantino.

"The amendment to the Bill has been moved and seconded. Is
there any further discussion?" Potterfield had nursed the proposal
through preliminary debate all morning. He doubted any member of
the Committee, including himself, had any idea what it really said.
Nicholson had prepared a synopsis for him with citations back to
the specific sections. So far it had been enough to satisfy most of his
colleagues.

"Mr. Chairman, if I may?" came a voice from the end of the dais.
Right on time. Christine Rasmussen was a second term senator from
Georgia. She was a staunchly conservative Republican, backed by major
corporate interests in Atlanta, many in the military electronics business.

"The chair recognizes the Honorable Senator from Georgia."

"Mr. Chairman, members of the Committee. As you know, I have been uncertain as to my support of this Bill. While we Georgians surely want to assist emerging democracies, we also recognize a solemn obligation to never weaken our own national security.

"I am, therefore, very pleased to see the addition of this amendment. I personally want to thank the Chairman and his staff," she glanced to Potterfield, "for addressing the concerns of Georgia's citizens so completely. This amendment ensures that the Bill will foster the spread of democracy throughout the world, without endangering American lives and American safety."

Potterfield nodded in recognition of the compliment, then leaned back and relaxed as his colleague went through her well-rehearsed monologue. He wondered how supportive she would be if she knew that one of Potterfield's constituents would be garnering the lion's share of the business.

Despite her support of the amendment, in many ways Rasmussen was his most dangerous opponent. Young, well-spoken, and very attractive, she was an example of the new wave of anti-establishment Republicans. She deserved what she got.

He, on the other hand, was 75 and had been in Congress for nearly thirty years. The voters were looking for younger, more photogenic, representatives and Potterfield's aging, pock-marked countenance didn't hold up. It had taken all of his considerable resources to hold his seat in the last election. The party leaders had let him know it was his last campaign.

For now, however, he had his seat and his power. And much of that power came from the Chairmanship. Potterfield believed in hard work, and in the inherent fairness of reaping its rewards. Since taking over the Committee, he had sponsored a number of key pieces of conservative legislation. The final jewel in his legacy was to be the *Promoting Freedom and Democracy Bill.*

"The greatest impact of this amendment, however, will be its power to bring the benefits of democracy to all citizens of the world," Rasmussen continued, "rich and poor, black, white, Hispanic, and Oriental. "And democracy creates opportunity for everyone, including those here in the great United States. All will be enriched by a flood of creativity and potential."

"Blacks"? The "poor"? What the hell did this pampered socialite know about black poverty? Potterfield knew, however. He had known every day of his life.

David Potterfield had been born on the poor side of Richmond. His father had disappeared when he was three, leaving his mother and three brothers to fend for themselves. He was the first born, and was given responsibility for his siblings while their mother was working. She hadn't had much time to give to them, but she had taught them to have confidence in themselves and faith in God. Her simple faith had kept the family together through years of adversity. She had seen a spark in her Davey early, and sent him to the parish's parochial school. The Sisters took him under their wing, guiding him through the strange subjects, and filling in his social lapses. History and literature taught him of a world much wider than he had ever imagined. He began to see a life away from the rundown farms and dilapidated shanties that had been his family's only future.

Potterfield also discovered he had a gift for getting people to do things his way. Not by brawn, but by using his brain. Whether it was trading kitchen chores for a few stolen exams or taking credit from the Sisters for an accidental delivery of much-needed supplies, he grasped opportunity where he saw it. He cultivated this gift slowly, constantly testing its limits, but never reaching so far as to risk exposure. He didn't see this as manipulation; it was simply doing what the Sisters had taught: taking advantage of what God had given him. In four years, he became a power to be reckoned with in the school, demanding respect from black and white alike.

Unfortunately, during his senior year his mother became seriously ill. As the man of the house, it was his responsibility to support the family. After graduation he stayed at home, working as much as he could, to help his mother keep and maintain their home. He watched over and comforted her until she had died a year later. Her only request was that he stay and see his younger brothers through school.

The next four years tested his resolve more than any others, before or since. His brothers had a different view of life. They were lazy to a fault and could only see their way to dead end jobs and nights of drinking. What was the point of wasting time on useless education? Potterfield cajoled, threatened, and bribed his brothers through the ordeal. Before it was over, he was on a first name basis with teachers, politicians, and the police. These were contacts he would carefully cultivate over the next decade.

His brothers finally set out on their own lives and, at twenty-three, he was free to complete the plan he had laid out years before. A few telephone calls from the parish and he became the first in his family to attend college. Seven years later, he returned to Richmond with a law degree and a fire to use the system to help himself and his people. But there were no positions in the prominent Richmond law firms for blacks—we were Negroes then, he remembered—so he set out to make it on his own.

Potterfield could hardly be called charismatic. He was tall, over six feet, and gangly, with a coarse, weathered face. But he had a down-to-earth appeal that drew people to him. Opening a small storefront legal aid office in Richmond, he drew the disenfranchised from throughout the city. A few high-profile cases gained him fame, or at least notoriety, and the clients increased; as did his fees. Ten years later the small office had grown into a major law firm.

Looking for new challenges, he had been drawn to public service. Conservative, with a strong following in the black community, he was the ideal candidate for a Republican Party seeking new faces to meet the challenge of the mid-twentieth century southern electorate. They had embraced him in his initial campaign as State Representative.

Over the years it had been a mutually advantageous relationship; after eight years as State Representative, Potterfield had successfully run for US House of Representatives, then eight years later won a difficult campaign for Senator. Now Senior Senator and leading Party spokesman, he was one of the most powerful men in Washington.

At least for a while longer, the Rasmussen's of the country took their lead from him.

"And so, for all of these reasons, I wholeheartedly endorse and support this key amendment to our Bill."

"Thank you, Senator Rasmussen, for that insightful analysis," Potterfield quickly replied. "Are there any other comments on the amendment?"

His eyes scanned over the panel, slowly pausing at Senator Hastings, the senior Democrat on the Committee. His vote was critical, yet thus far, he had been uncharacteristically silent.

"Mr. Chairman?" Hastings finally asked.

"Yes, Senator Hastings. We would very much appreciate your capable evaluation at this juncture."

"Thank you, Mr. Chairman. I'm afraid I do not share the unbridled enthusiasm expressed by my colleague from Georgia. It is my belief that any involvement by the United States in foreign entanglements is a danger to the independence of both our country and that of our allies. The days of unbridled imperialism have long passed. And history shows that however well-intentioned so-called 'hands-off assistance' may be, American lives have consistently been put in jeopardy."

Hastings hesitated, as if struggling to find the right words for his thoughts. Beads of sweat appeared on Potterfield's brow. But he needn't have worried.

"I do, on the other hand, sympathize with some of my colleagues who feel an obligation to support, in some manner, emerging democracies. Much as countries like France supported our fledgling country over two centuries ago. Personally, I have decided that the present amendment, as brought forth by our Chairman, offers an acceptable balance. I will vote for the amendment as submitted."

Potterfield breathed a quiet sigh of relief and watched as the rest of the Committee silently weighed Hasting's decision. He didn't know what had changed the Senator's mind, but he felt the mood of the room decidedly shift in his direction.

Nick had been right after all.

Potterfield nodded regally and orchestrated further debate for about fifteen minutes. As the rhetoric drew to a close, he called the question.

"All those in favor signify by raising their hands . . . Those opposed . . . The ayes have it. The amendment passes eleven to five."

The climatic rap of his gavel resonated through the chamber.

CHAPTER 40

Richmond, Virginia
Tuesday, 11:40 a.m.

GODDARD HAD EXPLAINED that their appointment was with Wilson Lexington, the Lynch family lawyer. Lexington's office was on the outskirts of Richmond, and the pair were now speeding south on I-95 in Goddard's BMW to reach the capital of Virginia in time for a 12:00 noon appointment.

Braxton had begun the trip by reviewing the contents of a folder Goddard had given him as they left. It was a complete history on the last year in the life of Senator Kenneth Lynch.

By all accounts, Lynch had been a very effective and very popular Senator. Committed to representative government and to the people of Virginia, he had already served two terms in the senior chamber and enjoyed popular and media support. His victory had been a foregone conclusion. The nomination of the aggressive black lawyer, David Potterfield, had been a last minute gamble on the part of the Republicans. None of the party's regulars would touch the spot.

Then, only one month before the election, local Richmond papers began reporting on inquiries into Lynch's relationship with a questionable real estate developer, Thomas Coopersmith. Coopersmith had been buying up large tracts of government property, ostensibly for a new planned community. As the weeks went by, records of conversations and illicit payments appeared showing Lynch had profited handsomely from the dealings.

Surprisingly, the incumbent had not denied the accusations. In interviews, he dismissed the attacks as ludicrous and was quoted as saying that "the people of Virginia know me and what I stand for. They will draw the correct conclusion about the evidence."

But the evidence had continued to grow. Almost daily there were new revelations of secret letters and contracts. By the time her father had acknowledged the reality of the threat, it was too late. Potterfield had taken sixty percent of the vote.

"That's quite a story," he said when he had finished with the file. "Was there ever any follow-up on the Coopersmith affair after the election?"

"None that I could find. Once Potterfield took office, the story just disappeared. But the damage had already been done."

"How do you think Lexington can help?"

"He was Father's best friend and handled all of the family's legal business. He was also in the Virginia state legislature. I'm hoping he knows something about the accusations that will help us."

"Haven't you talked to him about this before?"

"No. I haven't seen Wilson in years and years. He manages the family trust, but we just never had any reason to meet in person. He would send me papers and I would sign them and send them back."

She hesitated and her knuckles turned white on the steering wheel. "For a long time I didn't want to discuss Father's death at all. I avoided dealing with anyone who was connected to it. Probably not my finest hour."

"Don't beat yourself up now. All that's in the past. Let's just hope he knows something about Coopersmith and how your father became involved."

She shot him an angry glance. "If he was ever involved, Adam."

Rather than parking in one of the high-rise garages in the center of Richmond, Goddard sped through the city, took an exit a few miles out of town and pulled to a stop in front of an ivy-covered ante-bellum mansion. Situated in a bucolic neighborhood south of the city, she explained this was the lawyer's office, a building that had been in Lexington's family for generations.

The old place was in remarkable shape, Braxton noted, as they walked up a pristine flagstone path from the street. Magnolia and dogwood trees, just opening their pale pink blossoms, spotted the expansive front lawn. Blue-violet clumps of wisteria hung from two large, sturdy oaks that framed the front of the house. They walked up the front steps toward the door and were suddenly surrounded by the sweet smell of jasmine. The vines encircled the pillars on the veranda, their delicate white flowers inviting the visitors ahead. He felt he was stepping back in time to a quieter, simpler life; before the complexity of computers, networks, and consultants made life a headlong rush of "progress".

Only a small brass plaque beside the door announcing "Howard, Lexington, and Morgan, Attorneys at Law", suggested that this was anything more than a peaceful private residence.

They opened the front door and entered a spacious foyer that served as the practice's waiting area. The interior of the home was just as elegant as the outside. Bright floral arrangements contrasted with dark wood and rich oil paintings. Closed doors filled the walls along each side of the foyer. In front of them, a regal staircase rose to an intermediate landing at the back of the room, then split continuing up to the right and left. A huge portrait of a distinguished-looking southern couple hung above the landing.

Open hallways looked down onto the foyer from each side of the second floor. A crystal chandelier suspended from the arched ceiling completed the anachronistic scene.

Braxton noticed a group of young people talking on the second floor. He guessed they were legal interns, probably from the University of Virginia. The only visible presence on the first floor was Mrs. Mary Ellen Burdick, according to another polished brass name plate sitting on her desk. She was a pleasant looking woman, about fifty years old. Light brown hair curled around her face revealing soft features under just a little too much makeup.

"Good afternoon," she said with a touch of a Southern drawl. "How may I help you?"

"We're here to see Mr. Lexington. My name is Susan Goddard."

Burdick obviously recognized the name. "Yes, Ms. Goddard. Mr. Lexington is waiting for you in his office. The second door on the left. You may go right in."

They thanked Burdick and followed an oriental runner along the left wall. The rooms on the first floor appeared to be for the partners; brass plaques hanging outside each office announced the room's occupant. They opened the door marked "Wilson Lexington, J.D.", and went in.

The office was straight out of some TV legal thriller. All wood and glass, polished to an optical shine. A few landscapes hung on the walls but the showpiece was a massive oak bookcase that took up the whole wall to their left. It was filled with legal volumes, each precisely placed just to the edge of their shelf, sitting in an order dictated by tiny gold embossing on the spines. Braxton couldn't imagine any profession having that many books of exactly the same size, or ever managing to keep such a collection so well organized. It looked more like wallpaper than a working library.

Then again, since the contents of all those volumes were now available on-line from Lexus-Nexus, he guessed no one needed to open the tomes anyway. Still, they must be hell to dust.

Lexington rose immediately from his desk in front of the shelves. He looked about sixty years old, tall and rail thin. He had his coat off, and his starched white shirt and bright red bow tie stood boldly against the muted tones of the room. Brown hair was combed back from his forehead and faded to gray as it reached his temples and ears, but he moved and spoke with the energy of a young man.

"Susan?" the man asked. "I wouldn't have recognized you. How long has it been?"

"Almost fifteen years, Wilson. You don't look a day older."

He took her hand in both of his and clasped it warmly. "I feel each new day, I assure you. But you look wonderful, such a grown woman. It's so good to see you again."

Goddard turned to Braxton. "This is Adam Braxton, Wilson. He's a friend that's helping me with some trouble."

"You're not ill I hope," Lexington said as he shook hands with the outsider.

"I'm a consultant, Mr. Lexington. So far as I can tell Susan is in excellent health." Memories of the previous night flashed into his mind. He glanced at Goddard, and saw her face flush with pink.

"Well, I'm certainly glad to hear that," Lexington replied innocently. He motioned to a tan leather sofa across from his desk and took a matching chair next to the window. "What are you up to these days, Susan? You're at Georgetown now as I remember."

"Yes. I'm studying political science. If you ever want to get back into politics give me a call."

Lexington tossed back his head and laughed. "I'm afraid that's not likely. But I doubt you came all the way down here to talk about my career. What can I do to help you?"

She pulled the letter from her purse and handed it to the lawyer. "I found this after Momma died."

"I was so sorry to hear of your mother's death. I hope you'll forgive me for not attending the funeral. I was out of the country."

He opened the envelope and looked down at the letter. Then he set the paper on his lap, shook his head, and leaned back in his chair.

"Your father was very distraught after the election. A number of us tried to help him but I'm afraid to no avail. I don't think there is any reason to bring this up again." He handed the paper back to Goddard.

"Wilson, I need to know what was going on," she said resolutely. "Please don't treat me like a child. Momma would never talk about it. She kept shrinking farther and farther away from reality. Please tell me what you know about this. Did Father really take those bribes?"

Lexington turned away and gazed out over the perfectly manicured lawn. When he returned, his eyes were washed with a far-away sadness. "Your father was one of my best friends, Susan. He helped me get started in politics and taught me the importance of public service. When the allegations surfaced, I let him down. I was too concerned with my own position and security. After his death I couldn't continue in the legislature. I came back to the firm and tried to put all those events into the past. I don't know that I want to dredge them up again. What good would it do?"

"Was it Potterfield? Was he the one behind the lies?"

Lexington sat mute.

"Dammit, Wilson," Goddard suddenly jumped from her chair. She locked eyes with the lawyer and clenched her hands into fists. "Talk to me! Potterfield destroyed Father's career and killed him, just as sure as if he had pulled the trigger. I am not going to let him get away with it. If you won't help me, I'll find someone else who will."

Braxton tried to retreat into the back of the sofa. He had learned too well about Goddard's temper. The delicate young woman could be a firebrand when those she loved were threatened or slighted. He hoped he would never be the object of that fury.

"Alright," Lexington finally replied softly. "You know, you're just as obstinate as your father. I'll tell you everything I know. But I don't think it will help very much." Lexington slumped in the chair as he began.

"It was early in March the year of the election. Your father wanted some legal advice, but didn't want to come to the firm directly. He said that he was being threatened to not run for reelection. An anonymous caller had said they would ruin him and his family. He tried to have the calls traced but never could. It was as if someone knew everything he was doing. He had tried to get the police to help but they never found anything. He thought it might be someone on his staff and had them all investigated. He was growing more and more paranoid.

"Then the records starting showing up. First it was bank deposits he couldn't explain. Big ones, tens of thousands of dollars. He began to receive faxes of documents showing contracts and real estate dealings. All related to a developer named Coopersmith. Your father said that none of them were real, but he couldn't prove it. He asked me whether he could be convicted if anyone took the records to court. I told him that it was all circumstantial evidence, but that a good prosecutor could probably make the case.

"The evidence was too accurate, too complete. People believe what they see on paper. He still refused to quit and the documents were slowly leaked to the press. Twenty years of loyal public service were destroyed in four weeks. I didn't know what to do."

"What happened to Coopersmith and the documents?" Braxton asked.

"After the election he disappeared. And the police couldn't follow the paper trail. Charges were never filed."

"No one thought that was suspicious?"

"No one thought at all. We all just wanted to put it in the past."

"But the public never forgot," Goddard said. Tears pooled in her eyes and her voice had an edge that made Braxton shiver. "Reporters hounded him everywhere he went. It became so bad that he couldn't stand to go outside our house. He would just sit in his chair and stare out in space. Momma and I tried to help him but he wouldn't respond. Then one day when we were out of the house he took his shotgun and . . ." She couldn't finish.

Braxton knew at least a little of how Lynch must have felt. The sense of loss, of repudiation of all that he had been. But he had been younger, more resilient. He had pulled himself out of the depths and started the climb back. For Kenneth Lynch it had been too far.

"Did Mr. Lynch ever tell you who he thought was responsible?" Braxton asked.

The lawyer hesitated. "There was one time. The threats had always come by telephone or fax. There was never a real person involved. But once, just before the election, someone approached him in the parking lot and told him to get out of the race or else. Kenneth said he was a big black man. Later, he told me he was sure it was someone named Nicholson, one of Potterfield's subordinates."

"Nicholson?" Goddard gasped. "He's Potterfield's Chief of Staff now. Did Father ever say he had any proof it was them?"

"No, Susan. It was just that one conversation. I don't think you can take it very seriously. Your father was in pretty bad shape by then. Please don't even think of accusing Senator Potterfield."

"I already have, Wilson."

CHAPTER 41

Richmond, Virginia
Tuesday, 12:30 p.m.

"NOTHING LIKE THE neighborhoods I was used to," Nicholson commented as he watched the flow of visitors to and from the law office. He had left the Capitol right after the Committee meeting and arrived in Richmond just after noon. The lawyer's name had been in some of the old newspaper clippings. It had been easy to find his current address. Nicholson was sure this was the link he needed.

Activity had slowed over the lunch hour, and he decided it was time to see what he could find out. As he crossed the street a young couple left the offices and returned to their car. Hopefully Lexington didn't have other clients waiting. He walked up the cobblestone path, opened the door, and confronted an elderly woman at the reception desk.

"Good afternoon, ma'am," he began. "My name is Nicholas Bedford. I'm from the Richmond Historical Society and would like to speak with Mr. Lexington."

"Do you have an appointment?" Burdick asked.

"No ma'am. But I will take only a moment of Mr. Lexington's time. It would be of such value to the Society."

Burdick hesitated, then picked up her phone. After a short conversation, she replied to the visitor. "Mr. Lexington can give you a few minutes. His office is on the left."

"Thank you so much, ma'am. You've been very kind." Nicholson gave a small bow for emphasis.

"Mr. Lexington, I'm Nicholas Bedford from the Historical Society," he said as he approached the lawyer's desk.

Lexington rose and took the man's hand. "Very good to meet you, Mr. Bedford. Please have a seat. Now, how can I help you?"

"As you may know, the Society has been presenting a series of exhibits on famous Virginians. We are collecting information on our next subject, and hoped that you might provide us with some additional background."

"I would be happy to assist if I can, sir, who is your subject?"

"Senator Kenneth Lynch."

Lexington's face turned pale. Nicholson had expected some trepidation on the part of the lawyer, but nothing quite so dramatic. "Is something wrong, Mr. Lexington? You were Mr. Lynch's lawyer?"

"Eh, yes. I'm sorry, Mr. Bedford. It's just that . . . well, it has been a long time and I'm surprised that the Society would consider Kenneth after all of the publicity."

Nicholson nodded, exhibiting all the sincerity he could muster. "I understand, sir. But we believe that the unfortunate incidents at the end of Mr. Lynch's career should not negate his exceptional contributions as a Senator. Don't you agree?"

"Of course." Lexington seemed to compose himself and continued. "What is it I can do for you?"

"We have been trying to gather some personal background and have been unable to locate any of Mr. Lynch's relatives. We were wondering if you could tell us where we might find his wife or daughter."

"His relatives? I'm afraid I can't help you there."

"You did handle Mr. Lynch's estate?"

"Yes, I did. You see his wife was quite distraught after the funeral. She liquidated the estate and moved to, ah," Lexington, glanced up to the ceiling, "New York I think it was. I heard she died a number of years ago."

"What about the daughter, Susan wasn't it?"

Lexington hesitated. *Why would he do that?*

"I haven't heard anything about the daughter since she and her mother left Virginia," Lexington replied.

"You don't have any forwarding address?"

"No. They haven't contacted me at all. I assumed they wanted to break all ties to their past."

Dammit. Another dead-end. He had to get a lead on the daughter.

"You wouldn't know anyone else I could contact?"

"No, I'm sorry." Lexington rose from his chair. "Now if you will excuse me, Mr. Bedford, I do have a lot of work to complete this afternoon. Is there anything else?"

"No. Thank you, Mr. Lexington," Nicholson stuttered.

The lawyer escorted his visitor to the door. "Good luck on your exhibit, Mr. Bedford," he added. "Good bye."

The door slammed behind him as Nicholson walked through.

Lexington's behavior confused him. Nicholson had been around lawyers long enough to know how they operated. Losing complete track of a wealthy client was not in their best interest. Could he have been hiding something? Lynch's name brought back unpleasant memories for lots of people, but the lawyer's reaction was too suspicious.

"Was Mr. Lexington able to help you, Mr. Bedford?" Burdick asked as he passed her desk.

"Eh, somewhat ma'am. Unfortunately he wasn't able to give me as much information on Senator Lynch as I had hoped."

"Senator Lynch? It's too bad you weren't here earlier then."

Nicholson stopped short and spun back to Burdick. "Earlier? Why is that?"

"Why, Susan was just here. Senator Lynch's daughter."

* * *

Lexington had given them everything he had and the couple left the lawyer to his own memories. Braxton insisted that Goddard wasn't up to driving and took the wheel of the BMW for the return trip to Arlington.

As they passed Fredericksburg, she pulled a sheet of paper out of her purse. It was a copy of Potterfield's latest email.

"I was wondering when you'd get back to that," Braxton said.

"I've got to do something about this bastard!" She was crumpling the paper in her hands.

"Hey, calm down. Read it back to me and let's see what it really says."

Goddard recited the lines of the message. "What do you think?"

"First of all, I doubt Potterfield wrote it. It was probably this Nicholson's doing from what Wilson said. He's younger and more likely to be familiar with the technology. Second, they're hedging.

He 'will' turn it over to the FBI. They haven't yet and probably won't. It sounds to me like they're fishing to see what else you have. They can't afford an investigation if there's any chance you do have real evidence."

"That's quite an analysis, mister consultant. Did it cost me much?"

"We'll talk about that later," he replied with a smile. "Let's tug on *his* line a bit. Maybe we can get *them* to reveal something."

They composed their reply on the rest of the way back to the apartment. When they arrived, Goddard typed it in and sent the message to the remailer.

"When are you going back to Boston?" she asked as she shut down her computer.

Braxton had been pacing the floor behind her, but now headed into the kitchen. It was small but well-appointed, with a granite counter top and gleaming stainless-steel appliances that looked almost new. This was clearly a woman who had the means to get what she wanted.

"I was supposed to go last night, but something important came up."

"I seem to remember that." Her smile sent a rush of pleasure through his body.

"I really need to get back tonight," he said with more conviction than he felt. "I've got a lot of work to catch up on."

"Okay, but you've got until ten. Can I talk you into dinner?"

"Only if you let me cook." He opened the refrigerator. It was surprisingly well stocked. "How about sesame beef and steamed vegetables?"

"You cook too?"

He shrugged his shoulders. "I've had a lot of practice lately."

"How could I resist?" She stretched out on the sofa and put her feet up. "Call me when it's ready."

* * *

The tall figure, dressed completely in black, stalked through the rear garden of the house. The last car had left hours ago. He was sure there would be no interruptions.

The sky was a dark gray, storm clouds sweeping across a thin crescent moon. The air felt damp and sticky. He needed to complete the search and be gone before the rain hit. Disregarding the hours of tender labor spent over the Siberian iris and yellow jonquils, he crushed the flora in the beds, crept to the back door, and pulled out a small plastic card. The SafeTAlarm security system he had identified earlier was a cinch to crack.

That bastard Lexington had lied to him. Now Nicholson was going to find the truth about Susan Lynch.

CHAPTER 42

Cambridge, Massachusetts
Wednesday, 11:00 a.m.

IT HAD BEEN midnight by the time he had gotten back to the apartment, and Braxton had simply thrown his dirty clothes in a pile in the corner of his bedroom and immediately fell asleep.

Eight hours later he was awake and refreshed, ready to attack the new day. He ran a three mile circuit, showered, and fixed a light breakfast of cereal and orange juice. The juice was a little tart, he hadn't been to the store in over a week, but he drank it anyway. A little acid never hurt anyone.

He browsed through the morning paper during his breakfast, paying closest attention to the business pages and the Celtic's scores. The mutual funds in his IRA were up but the Celtics had lost to the Pistons. Paul would have been happy, he thought sadly. He remembered to check his voicemails and found five hang-ups from the same number. It was eleven o'clock by the time he made it to the stack of mail he had picked up after his run.

There was nothing in the pile except bills, grocery store ads, and sweepstakes letters, so he headed into the study to check any new email. Two unread messages sat in his mail box. The first had been forwarded from his account at CERT/CC. It was from Flanagan, and she sounded irritated. Apparently she had been expecting another status report, and had been trying to reach him since Monday. He assumed the voicemails were from her. He composed a brief apology, added a promise of a detailed report by the end of the week, and sent it off. He didn't feel up to an explanation of the past five days just yet.

He brought up the second message and saw it had come from
Warren Chamberlain. But not from his account at Century, from a
personal one. The EVP had gotten back to him, and with a
response that posed more questions than it answered.

From: wec@usanet.com

To: braxton@online.std.com

Subject: Inquiry into Century gateways

Adam,

I need to speak with you about the gateways. There
is something terribly wrong. I have discovered some
new information.

We can't talk about this at the office. Please come
by my home Wednesday night at seven o'clock. I need
your help.

Regards,

Warren

Had Chamberlain discovered that the diagnostic library was still
on the gateways? If so, he probably wanted Braxton to help him
approach CERT/CC about the problem; he would still be
concerned about the effect a disclosure could have on Century.

If he could persuade Chamberlain to help him find who was
behind Ramal's and Terrel's deaths, he *might* be willing to try to keep
Century's name out of it.

There was no use in worrying about all this now. He would find
out soon enough. He typed a short acknowledgement and sent it
off.

If he was going out again, he had to tell Goddard. Before he had
left D.C., he had told her he would talk to her tonight. He tried her
cell but she didn't pick up—she was probably in class—so he just
hung up and reminded himself to try again before he left for the
meeting. She would want to know everything that was going on.

The day was already half gone and he needed some prep time for
the meeting with Chamberlain. He would go back over his notes
and prepare a summary of everything he had found on the mole. He
wanted to have all the evidence ready when he confronted the
executive.

* * *

Potterfield handed a copy of the message to his Chief of Staff. The Senator had been in a meeting with his press team when the email had arrived. He had abruptly cleared them out and called for Nicholson.

"They've implicated you now, Nick. I don't like this going on so long. I thought you said you could take care of it." Potterfield's left eye began an irregular winking. His tic was acting up again.

Nicholson reviewed the latest message:

```
From: an6845@anon.trans.ua

To: richmondeagle@potterfield.senate.gov

Subject: Senator Lynch

Senator Potterfield,

You are in no position to threaten. You and your
assistant, Mr. Nicholson, were responsible for the
Coopersmith documents. We will release our infor-
mation if you do not resign by this weekend. We
will not wait any longer.

Citizens for Responsible Government
```

"There's nothing new here, David. This is all public information and everybody knows I'm your Chief of Staff. They're guessing. I've already narrowed the possibilities significantly. As long as we keep them talking to us, they're not going to go to the media. I'll send another reply in a day or two. By then I'll have something solid to go on."

Potterfield scowled at his Chief of Staff. "I don't want *something*, Nick," he growled. "I want it closed. Have you located his family yet?"

Nicholson had hoped Potterfield would have forgotten that promise. He only needed a few more days. "I contacted Lynch's lawyer yesterday but he stonewalled me." Potterfield's jaw dropped. "Don't look at me like that, David. I didn't use my real name. I knew he was hiding something so I searched his files last night. There was nothing there. Not even old files on Lynch. Someone had cleaned them out.

"I did find out the mother is dead. That just leaves the daughter. I'm running another computer search for everyone in the surrounding states with her demographics. It'll take a while but we'll find her. I'm convinced she's our blackmailer." He decided against telling Potterfield that he had missed the daughter by minutes. It would only raise his blood pressure to know she had been so close.

"All right. At least you've made some progress. But be careful. We can't have some hick lawyer suspecting we're looking for the kid."

"Don't worry. He doesn't suspect anything." It was time to get his boss's mind on other matters. "When are you bringing the Bill up for a vote?"

"The Bill? Oh, this Friday. I'll force a vote before I let them adjourn for the weekend. That usually gets their attention. By the way, Hastings' change of heart was a bit surprising. You didn't have anything to do with that did you?"

Nicholson hesitated, then just smiled. "Some things are better not discussed, David. Let's just say the well-being of his family is very important to him."

"I expected something like that. Let's hope our luck holds for the Committee vote."

"Luck has nothing to do with it, David. It's just hard work."

"Luck always has something to do with it, Nick," Potterfield said with an uncharacteristic seriousness. "Never overestimate your ability to control people and events. Neither are rational." He shuffled some papers on his desk and set one on the top of the mess. "Are you still buddy-buddy with that Greystone?"

"We seem to be getting along all right. He needs the Bill."

"I know. I think it's time to put on some pressure. Set up a meeting for me next week. We'll see how much he needs us."

"I'll get it scheduled, David."

"Good. Now go find that bitch." He brusquely waved for his aide to leave.

CHAPTER 43

Carnegie Mellon University, Pittsburgh, Pennsylvania
Wednesday, 3:00 p.m.

WHAT THE HELL does he mean, he's "been busy"? Flanagan was reviewing the email from Braxton and it didn't help her mood. She'd been busy too, trying to keep those bastards off her back so she could get some work done. What do these damn consultants think she was paying them for? He'd better get that status report to her, and soon.

She was about to compose a testy reply when Candela stuck his head into her office.

"Rachel, I wanted to thank you for supporting the new research program this morning."

"Edward, ah, what a surprise." She fumbled with the keyboard and managed to get the screen cleared just as he walked over to her desk.

"Anything interesting going on?"

"No. Just the same old reports." What right does he have to come in here and spy over her shoulder? And what was she doing hiding a project from her boss? But that was all for another time. "Glad I could help with the program. Any research that helps security on the net will make our jobs a lot easier."

"We knew you'd look at it that way. Oh, just between us, I think you handled Timothy very well Monday. He needs to be reassured that we aren't getting into any questionable areas of investigation. It's just as well this Saracen thing turned out to be a dead end."

"Yes, Edward. We wouldn't want to waste our valuable time now would we?"

"Rachel, could you look at . . . oh, I'm sorry." A tall, ruddy-skinned man barged into the office then froze in his tracks on seeing Candela.

"You know Barry Lighthorse, don't you, Edward?" Flanagan said quickly.

"I believe so. Mr. Lighthorse." Candela turned to the intruder and Lighthorse nodded back.

"You will have to excuse me, Edward. Barry and I have a project review scheduled." She looked down at her watch for the effect. "But thank you for coming by. It's so good to see you expressing an interest in the operations side of our efforts."

"Of course, Rachel. Have a good meeting." Candela gave another brusque glance at Lighthorse and disappeared as quietly as he entered.

"I am sorry, Rachel, I didn't know he was in here with you. He is kinda odd isn't he?"

"Very. Be careful around him, Barry. His job is to find all the dirt he can and then use it to his own advantage. Sometimes I wonder who really does run this place, Timothy or Edward. Anyway, thanks for the interruption."

"We don't have a review scheduled do we? I just wanted to ask about the Linux schedule."

"No, that was just my little fiction. Let's get out of here, I need to talk to you about something as well."

They headed out of her office and into the operations area. Ops was a large, open area covering the rear half of the CERT/CC floor. Flanagan's office was on the left by the entrance doors. The rest of the room was a maze of five foot high partitions enclosing small working cubicles for the operations staff. The structure frustrated her; of all the members of her group, she was the one who couldn't see what was going on over the walls.

Across the expanse of cubicles was the computer room and operations center. All of the cubes had PCs or low-end work-stations, but the really powerful equipment was kept in the operations center for shared use. It wasn't the most convenient set-up, but it avoided a haves/have-nots stratification of the Ops team.

As they walked, Flanagan heard the light tapping of keyboards. She liked to wander through the cloth tunnels a few times every day to give her staff a chance to see "the boss" and ask any questions on their active projects.

Barry Lighthorse was her one concession to structure. His formal title was Manager of Operations. He ran the day-to-day details of the Ops group. Much of Flanagan's time was taken up with Rydell's meetings and pet projects. Lighthorse was the point of stability for the group. He was always on site, and always available for anyone. He was also one of Flanagan's few confidants.

"How is the Linux security evaluation going?" Flanagan asked as they walked through the area.

"That's what I came to tell you. We received the latest update from Red Hat yesterday. They've really enhanced the capabilities from the initial distributions. So far it has tested out perfectly. I think we may be able to certify it by the end of the week."

"That's a week ahead of schedule! Congratulations, Barry. I didn't think you'd be able to complete it that fast."

"Everyone has worked very hard and all the vendors have been really helpful. Can I hit petty cash for a little celebration when we finish?"

"Absolutely, but I'd also like to ask a favor."

"Sure, what is it?"

"Hold off on announcing the certification until next week. There's something I'd like you to look into and it would be easier if you could say you were still busy on the Linux study."

"Is it about the Saracen Incident?"

She was shocked he had guessed so quickly. She hadn't said anything to the team since Rydell's staff meeting on Monday. "Yes, but how did you guess?"

"Smoke signals, Rachel," he said with a broad smile. "That and a good ear to the rumor mill around the laser printers."

Lean and muscular, with dark swarthy skin and straight black hair, Lighthorse was a full-blooded Navajo from New Mexico. As a child, a tribal elder had chosen him to be an emissary to the white-man's world. He had been given special tutors and soon demonstrated remarkable intelligence. He had been accepted into New Mexico State University and blazed through their Computer Science Department in three years. He had taken a Masters from CMU before coming to work at CERT/CC.

The Native American led a strange split life. He was the Center's networking expert. He knew every network protocol that had ever been designed, and had made significant contributions to many of the newer ones. At home, however, he and his wife maintained their Navajo traditions. Their life style was austere and they made frequent trips back to their parents' reservation. He had once told Flanagan that the apparent contradiction was not that great, his Amerind pride and beliefs could be applied in a computer room as well as on the dusty plains of New Mexico. Having worked with Lighthorse for the past year, Flanagan wished some of the other staff at CERT/CC had the same moral code.

"I need someone to poke around in the GW gateway, Barry. My consultant says he's verified the report but he hasn't given me any details. I'd like you to try to replicate the findings."

"I'd be glad to, but I'll have to tell Rick and Christie."

Rick Spaulding and Christie Pratt were the two other team members assigned to the Linux certification. "I understand. But only them. Are they around?"

"Let's see." He peered over the partitions and searched the room. "Nope, neither one is in their offices. I would have sworn I saw Christie earlier."

"It's okay. You can talk to them. Just try to keep those smoke signals down. I don't want Timothy or Edward poking into this just yet."

"Understood, boss," he said with a serious smile.

She hoped she had done the right thing. It could certainly blow up in her face, but she wasn't going to lose the opportunity to show the bureaucrats how real computer security investigations worked.

* * *

Goddard had spent the day at Georgetown, attending her regular classes and trying to catch up on the assignments she had missed on Monday and Tuesday. Most of her friends had been glad to help, but it took all afternoon to track down her Cold War Policies professor. By the time she trudged up the stairs of her apartment building her legs throbbed, her neck muscles were knotted, and she had a killer headache. All she wanted was a long soaking bath and a good night's sleep.

As she reached her door at 5:50, she heard her apartment phone ringing. She was hoping to hear from Adam but she would have expected he would call her cell. She fumbled with the door locks, dropped her books and purse on the floor, and dashed toward the phone.

"Adam?"

"Eh, no. Susan? This is Wilson Lexington."

"Wilson. I'm sorry, I was expecting someone else." The disappointment was obvious in her tone.

"Your Mr. Braxton no doubt. I'm sorry to bother you, Susan, but there's something I think you need to know." His normally cool tone sounded forced and tired.

"What is it Wilson? You sound upset."

"Things here have been rather hectic. Right after you left, a gentleman came to visit me. He said he was from the Richmond Historical Society. He was looking for information on your father."

"On Father? What would they want?"

"That's what I wondered. He seemed particularly interested in the whereabouts of you and your mother. That's when I remembered our conversation. He was a black man, Susan. I think it was Barclay Nicholson."

"Nicholson! Wilson, what did you tell him?" Her hand started to shake and she grabbed the counter top to try to stop the tremor.

"I was suspicious and didn't tell him anything. I don't know whether he believed me or not. After he left I called the Historical Society. They don't have anyone researching your father. I became concerned that he might come back so I packed up all your files and took them to a friend's house. It was a good thing I did."

"Why?"

"I've been with the police all day. Someone broke into our offices last night and ransacked all of my files."

"Oh, Wilson. I'm so sorry we got you messed up in all this. Are you all right?"

"I'm fine, my dear. I am worried about you, however. Whatever you have started seems to be becoming increasingly violent. If Mr. Nicholson has traced you this far, he will certainly not stop. You must call the police and get some protection."

"Maybe you're right, Wilson. I'll call them right away."

"Please do, Susan, it would make me feel much better."

"Thank you, Wilson, for everything."

"You're very welcome. Your father was a dear friend. Please take care of yourself."

She clicked off the phone and slid helplessly down the wall to the floor. Her heart was pounding.

What could she do? The police certainly wouldn't help. She was the one blackmailing a Senator. Without any real evidence against either Potterfield or Nicholson they would simply throw her in jail. She needed more time and had to get some help.

What about Adam? If Nicholson had found out she had been at Lexington's perhaps he knew about him as well. He was as vulnerable as she, if not more so. And someone had already tried to kill him!

She ran to her purse to get her cell, kicked the door shut, and dialed. It rang and rang.

"Please Adam, please answer," she whispered.

It was only then that she noticed the voicemail message.

CHAPTER 44

Carlisle, Massachusetts
Wednesday, 6:50 p.m.

WARREN CHAMBERLAIN HAD never married. Not a great surprise since Braxton couldn't imagine how anyone could live with the self-possessed technocrat. But that had never stopped him from throwing the occasional party at his home in Carlisle. From carefully-crafted guest lists, to meticulous directions, to lavishly-catered menus, the events were classic Chamberlain.

Braxton and his wife had been invited to three such parties before he had been let go, so finding the home was not a problem.

He had tried to call Susan again before he left. She still hadn't answered, so he had left a message describing the email from Chamberlain and the planned meeting.

He had then picked up the Jeep, taken Route 2 out of Cambridge, turned north on I-95 and up Route 225 into Carlisle. By the time he arrived at Chamberlain's development, the sun had fallen behind the Berkshires and only a bright new moon, ably assisted by Braxton's xenon headlights, lit his way.

"Development" hardly described the neighborhood. This section of Carlisle was zoned for minimum four acre parcels, each plot holding a huge custom home. The owners were generally the Boston area's "old money", established physicians and financiers, although a few newcomers, mostly high tech executives like Chamberlain, had been admitted to the exclusive area. Braxton knew business at Century had been good but still had been surprised that the executive could have raised the cash.

Chamberlain was undoubtedly even wealthier now than when he

had built his castle. Century's entry into the network market had been nothing short of phenomenal. Six months after Braxton had been let go, they had introduced a completely new line of network systems encompassing servers, routers and gateways, exactly the products that Braxton had conceived and developed within the research group. Chamberlain had told him they were cutting the staff on the new products. Apparently he had been the only one they had needed to cut.

Industry analysts had given the products good reviews but had questioned Century's ability to achieve much share against the entrenched competition. Then Century had gotten lucky. Software bugs started appearing in their competitors' products. Network programs were notoriously complicated and some errors were to be expected. But these had been especially disastrous and had caused major failures at a number of universities and Fortune 100 companies. Surprisingly, the competitors had been unable to replicate the problems and had been on the defensive for over six months. By the time the problems had been corrected, Century had replaced many of the faulty systems with their own and had gained significant market momentum.

An odd thought suddenly took shape in his mind. Were the problems corrected, or had they just *disappeared*? What if they hadn't been bugs? What if they had been the result of sabotage? Could Century have been involved? They certainly had the most to gain. He wasn't sure what Chamberlain wanted to discuss, but he had a few new questions he was going to ask.

Braxton had been following Minuteman Lane for about a mile and a half when his lights shone on a perfectly square stone fence. Chamberlain's street number was chiseled on a flat slab of sandstone mortared into the other rocks. It was impossible to see the home from the road. Most of the houses, including Chamberlain's, were set far back in the large wooded plots. He turned the Jeep into the driveway and slowly drove up the macadam path. Aside from a few crickets, the woods were deathly silent.

He had gone about a quarter mile through the dense oaks, maples and pines when he saw the imposing contemporary around one last turn. The home was an amazing structure, all the more so because Chamberlain had drawn the plans and supervised its construction. Braxton remembered that every Monday morning for a year Chamberlain had subjected his staff to detailed presentations, complete with photographs, of the prior week's progress. The home was the executive's one true love.

It wasn't especially large but was of a striking design with a distinctive look of quality. On his right, floodlights bathed the front of the house showing few windows and sparse landscaping. This was the protected north side of the residence. It offered little opportunity for winter's winds to steal precious heat from the structure. The severe north facade was in stark contrast to the soaring glass walls and high clerestory windows of the southern exposure. Chamberlain had designed his home as a testament to passive solar technology.

In the front, only enough land had been cleared to place the house and the driveway. The closeness of the woods gave the place an eerie, foreboding feeling. The rear, on the other hand, was spacious, with a large lawn and extensive gardens. Also designed by Chamberlain with geometric precision.

The driveway continued past the front door, turning behind the house to a garage at the far end. Braxton pulled up and parked in front of one of the tall garage doors.

He approached the front door expecting Chamberlain to appear immediately, forewarned by some expensive electronic gadget. When no one greeted him after about a minute, he grabbed the heavy brass knocker on the door and rapped twice. The house echoed with the intrusive sound. He tried the knocker once again, but still getting no response he walked back to his car.

Chamberlain was an obsessively private individual who often barricaded himself in his rear office, oblivious to the rest of the world. Braxton retraced his steps, stepped around the rear corner of the garage and then jumped when an automatic flood lamp clicked on. But there was no reason for *him* to be nervous. It was Chamberlain's turn to give the answers this time.

The lamp bathed the expansive rear yard in bright light. Encircling the illuminated lawn and gardens, the woods formed a dark, impenetrable wall. He followed a path to the door of the study and knocked. There was a dim light inside the room but no movement. He knocked again, then tried the door. It swung open and he hesitantly entered.

Braxton had occasionally joined Chamberlain in the room when his ex-boss had wanted to discuss a piece of business away from the distractions of his dinner guests. It was large for an office, over 200 square feet he guessed, and appropriately appointed for the Executive Vice President. A single bookcase covered the back wall, original oils and lithographs decorating the other three. A large modern desk sat in the middle of the room and a small drafting table stood in an opposite corner.

The light was coming from a small table lamp on Chamberlain's desk. Across from the lamp, he made out the outline of a large LED monitor. He called out, thinking the owner might be in one of the other rooms.

Still getting no response, he walked farther into the room. As he approached the desk he saw that papers were scattered across the top. And the PC was on; a star field slowly spiraled into the screen. Chamberlain had to be around somewhere.

He thought he heard a low groan, like something from a cat or small dog. He headed for the door to the main hallway, keeping an eye on the floor for an errant tail.

Just past the desk he saw a shadow that made his skin ripple with fear. He inched toward it and discovered that the sounds were coming from the same location. On the floor was the body of Warren Chamberlain lying in a pool of blood.

CHAPTER 45

Carlisle, Massachusetts
Wednesday, 7:05 p.m.

CHAMBERLAIN WAS FACE up, wide eyes staring into the ceiling. Two small red holes stained his white shirt and a trickle of blood ran from the corner of his mouth.

Braxton saw Chamberlain's lips move slightly and he leaned down at the man's head.

"Warren," he whispered. "What happened? Can you tell me who did this?"

Chamberlain's eyes didn't move but he turned his head toward the voice. "Kaaaaa . . ."

Braxton somehow sensed that the executive's wounds were fatal. He should have run for help, but knew talking with Chamberlain would be the only way to find out what happened.

"Warren, it's Adam. Adam Braxton. How can I help you?"

Chamberlain seemed to be concentrating his strength one last time. A gurgling sound came from his throat. Braxton leaned down and turned his ear as close to his ex-boss's mouth as he dared. Chamberlain raised his head for one last effort.

"Use the cash," he hissed.

"What cash?" Braxton asked urgently. "Where is it?"

Chamberlain's eyes went dark and his head fell limply to the carpet.

Braxton stared at his nemesis as he lay still on the floor. For all of the anger and hate he had directed at Chamberlain and Century over the past two years, he could not help feeling sorry for the individual beside him. What had he done to deserve this?

Braxton pulled back from the body. What should he do now? He knew he shouldn't touch Chamberlain or anything else in the room for that matter. The police would go over the scene. They would want to talk to him. Maybe someone would finally believe what was happening.

As he turned to get up, a flash of light caught the corner of his eye. He turned back and saw it again. It was coming from the floor just under a credenza on the side wall. A reflection off something shiny. Still on his hands and knees, he climbed over Chamberlain's body and crept to the wall. Under the cabinet was what looked like a polished piece of pipe.

He crawled closer and saw it was the barrel of a gun. He reached out, then stopped. Don't disturb the evidence. But he was curious, so he grabbed a pencil from the desk, stuck it into the exposed barrel, and pulled the weapon across the floor to get a better look.

It was a small, shiny revolver. He recognized the model, a compact Ruger LCR 357. It was the same model he had purchased for Megan.

He had bought the gun over three years ago. There had been a spurt of news stories about crime in Cambridge and he had wanted Megan to have some protection when he was away. When he had brought it home, she defiantly announced she would have nothing to do with it. "Guns only bring tragedy," she had declared. They put it in a box and it had stayed untouched in their closet ever since.

He had forgotten all about it when Terrel had been killed. There was no doubt in his mind that the gun he was looking at was the murder weapon. And that it was his gun. Whoever had murdered Terrel had taken it. And now they had framed him with it.

Braxton felt an immediate, chilling fear. He tried to stand and almost fell over. His legs were shaking.

He could still call the police but how would he explain the gun? He knew exactly what they would think.

He backed away from the cabinet and tripped over Chamberlain's body, letting out a loud cry. He turned to get up, carefully avoiding any more contact with the body than necessary, and noticed something clutched in the executive's hand. He hesitated, then pried open Chamberlain's hand and found a small black USB stick. Chamberlain had been working on the computer when his assailants appeared. The last thing he had done was to grab the stick. Why? What if it contained something about the investigation? Braxton had to get that data.

There were no markings on the stick; nothing to suggest its contents. He was about to put it into the PC when he saw bursts of light in the hallway. Were the murderers still there?

He crept to the doorway and peeked around the corner. The flashes were coming through glass sidelights surrounding the front door. Continuing to the door, he squinted through the cut glass. Distorted shapes danced through the trees in front of the house silhouetted by pulsating red and blue lights. It was the police. They must have stopped at the foot of the driveway, and were spreading out around the house.

There was no way he was going to be able to explain this now. Things were happening too fast. He had to get away and think.

The shapes became larger. They were approaching the house.

What could he do?

He ran back to the study, grabbed the gun on the floor, and tucked it into his belt. No use in making it any easier for the cops. If he could only get to his car before they saw him.

He opened the outside door and peeked around the jamb. There was no movement on the lawn. He searched in his pocket for the keys, found them, then dashed for his car. His Jeep was at the back edge of the driveway, close to the house and nearly hidden from the front approach. He crawled inside as silently as he could, pulled his seat belt tight, and slid the key in the ignition.

This is it, he thought, as he turned the key and the engine came to life. Hoping it would give him a few extra seconds, he left his lights off and decided to rely on the moonlight from the cold, black sky.

He put the Cherokee into reverse and smashed his foot on the accelerator. It lurched up, then raced backward away from the house. He shifted again, jamming the lever into low and trusting the transmission could handle his abuse.

The Jeep jumped forward and he spun the wheel to the left, sliding the Cherokee off the asphalt and onto the back lawn. He thought he heard shouts, but they disappeared under the roar of his engine and the pounding of blood in his head.

His M+S tires slipped on the wet turf then dug in and the Jeep fish-tailed down the slight incline. It was all he could do to keep the vehicle under control. Mud and grass flew from under the wheels.

He headed for the left edge of the woods. The moon cast long shadows all along the tree line. Where was the damn path?

Braxton thought Chamberlain's parties had been incredibly boring, so he and Megan would frequently go for walks in the peaceful backyard. They had found the old cart trail on one of their escapes and had followed it through the woods. The trails were common in New England; they were originally used as primary transportation routes but more recently as recreation paths for off-road bikes or 4 by 4s. He didn't know where the trail led but it was better than staying around waiting to be arrested.

The car shook as he directed the Jeep over the rolling terrain. He heard popping noises and prayed the old engine wouldn't give out now. He swerved to avoid a lawn chair and his rear window exploded. They were shooting at him!

Suddenly he saw a dark hole in the tree line. The trail! He jammed the wheel to the left and the Jeep went into a power slide. The tires finally bit into the soil and the Cherokee dove into the blackness.

A searing pain cut through his left shoulder. He thought his arm must have been ripped off, but his left hand was still on the steering wheel. He managed a glance to his left and saw a bright red circle growing on his jacket sleeve.

As he looked left, the Jeep had veered in the same direction and struck a huge oak. The car bounced from the impact and was thrown back onto the path. He couldn't see a thing in the dense forest and finally yanked the light switch. Cones of light sliced into the darkness and illuminated a narrow path that wandered deeper into the woods.

The path was lined with an unyielding wall of trees. His right hand held the steering wheel so hard it was white but he couldn't feel his left. His body ached from the tension. The throbbing in his shoulder sapped whatever strength he had left. He couldn't keep up this pace much longer.

There were no sounds from the house far behind him; only random flashes of light reflecting from his rear view mirror. He didn't know whether they would try to follow him into the woods but he couldn't stop to find out. He pressed harder on the accelerator and concentrated on the winding trail.

The Jeep hit a fallen tree and he was thrown forward. His seat belt cut into his shoulder sending another spear of agony through his body. The vehicle climbed the obstacle and bounced back down, shocks bottoming out and sounding as if they would break through the frame. Braxton's head crashed into the roof and the world went momentarily black. He was on automatic now, relying on instinct and reflexes to pilot the Cherokee.

The trail turned to the right then immediately split. With no time to choose a direction he swung the wheel to the left. His right fender caught the tall pine at the split. The headlight blew out as the Cherokee bounced onto the new path and continued careening through the forest. If he lost the other light he wouldn't have a chance.

He negotiated two more forks in the next three minutes. He had no idea where he was or how far he had gone. There was still a lot of virgin land in Massachusetts and he felt as if he was driving through every mile of it.

The screams from the suspension were ungodly. The Jeep couldn't take much more abuse. He shot up another ridge and braced for the landing. The impact was more bone crushing than before. The frame shook unmercifully and the tires gave an unexpected screech. Braxton shoved the brake to the floor and prayed the car would stop.

He was sitting in the middle of a narrow, paved road. His left arm was numb and the pain in his shoulder screamed for attention. A chill cut through his body; taking away the feeling, and taking away some of the pain. Maybe he should stop and rest.

Ahead in the distance he saw points of light. They grew brighter. Someone was coming for him. Is this the way it would end?

The lights came closer. *Why now? After all he had been through.*

Light engulfed the vehicle.

The Jeep shook violently as a deafening roar filled the cabin.

Then the truck passed, its Doppler-shifted air horn still echoing in night air.

No, dammit! I won't let them get away with this.

Shaking his head to fight off the pain-induced lethargy, he tossed a mental coin and headed into the darkness to the right.

CHAPTER 46

SHORTLY AFTER THE Civil War, the citizens of New Hampshire's White Mountains realized that they could make more money attracting other people to look at their breathtaking forests and majestic peaks than by trying to chop and carve the beauty away. Thus began a period of growth and prosperity for the region.

At first it had been the affluent who had driven their motor cars up from Boston, or taken the railroad sleepers from New York, to populate new resorts: Glen House, Crawford House, Kearsarge House, and the Mount Washington Hotel. The retreats offered elegant accommodations, European cuisine, and thoughtful service, all nestled in the natural splendor of the Granite State. Guided tours provided informative, and safe, access to the Notches, the Flume, the Old Man of the Mountain, and Mt. Washington itself.

Over time, less wealthy travelers began to brave the journey north to walk the pristine trails and experience the magnificence of the terrain. Doctors, lawyers, teachers, and businessmen, came to set aside increasingly sedentary lives and be refreshed in the crisp air and physical challenges of the mountains. At first they stayed in private homes and public inns, but many later chose to make the region their second residence. By the early 1900s, small summer cottages and weather-beaten shacks rimmed ponds and lakes and lined ancient logging runs.

In the mid-twentieth century a new phenomenon shocked northern New Hampshire: alpine skiing. What had once been an exhausting necessity of life in the mountains was now a multimillion dollar recreation business. Investors rushed to the mountains with dreams of turning the barren hillsides into crowded ski slopes. Their money built roads and lodges, mundane rope tows and soaring gondolas. Towns appeared seemingly overnight, stressing rural facilities, and local planning boards, to their limit. Many of the old-timers rued the appearance of traffic jams and condominiums, but others reveled in the economic windfall.

Merritt was a small town five miles west of North Woodstock. Once a prosperous logging and trading center, it palled as the resort areas grew, and had gracefully aged to a hamlet of convenience stores and real estate agencies. In the winter it catered to the hordes of skiers coming "up north" from Boston and New York; its central location was convenient to both Loon and Cannon mountains. Now, in early spring, the 328 permanent inhabitants made repairs and tried to spruce up the town for summer vacationers. Summer would never be as busy, or profitable, as the winter season, but the clear air and flowered meadows still drew tired executives and their families to the area for rest and rejuvenation.

They started appearing in late April to reopen their cabins or to stake out the best territory in the managed campgrounds. The flow of tourists and vacationers continued through October, peaking along with the incomparable New England fall colors, and then subsided until the stone gray skies emptied their contents, covering the mountains and slopes with the white gold of New Hampshire.

Many of the visitors came to hike the tangled trails of the mountains. The very serious, or very foolish, went to Mt. Washington where the summer winds still averaged over 60 miles per hour, but for the recreational rock climber, magnificent views could be found just a few hours off Interstate 93.

Sitting at the foot of numerous scenic trails, Merritt was perfectly situated as a base for climbers. The town had cultivated its new role with a stock of boutiques specializing not in dresses or shoes but pitons, ropes, and maps. It was this concentration of fellow enthusiasts that had first drawn Paul Terrel to the area and had eventually resulted in the purchase of a small cabin three miles outside the town.

Braxton arrived in Merritt around 2:00 a.m., completely spent from the terror of the escape. He was soaked in sweat, but the pain in his shoulder seemed less intense. He didn't know whether that was a good sign or not.

The trip north had seemed so easy seven hours before.

The road behind Chamberlain's property had led to an intersection. A sign had said "Route 4 North, Chelmsford/Nashua", and he had known where he had to go. Going south back to Boston and Cambridge was insane, they would have been expecting him and the density of police would have made it impossible to hide. North was his best plan.

He took Route 4 up to Tyngsboro, then headed west on Rt. 113. He avoided the main roads such as Route 3 and Interstate 93; police alerts would have undoubtedly gone out and his Jeep was too damaged to be missed by even light scrutiny.

Braxton and Terrel had discovered numerous back routes while trying to detour around traffic jams to and from their climbing expeditions. He briefly considered going to MapQuest on his phone, then realized the cell was a homing beacon for the authorities. With surprising clarity he pulled to the side of the road and ripped the battery from the device, tossing it on the passenger seat.

Now having to rely solely on his hazy memory, he headed north on 122 at Pepperell, and cruised through a series of dark New Hampshire towns until he joined Route 3 just north of Franklin. The narrow two lane highway had been the only road to northern New Hampshire in the forties and fifties. In the sixties, however, Interstate 93 had been built, providing a faster, more comfortable route into the mountains. Tonight, Braxton knew he could cruise the smaller road and meet few obstacles.

Despite the lack of traffic, it had been difficult to progress very rapidly on the dark, winding roads with only one headlight. It had taken over twice as long as it should have, nearly seven hours including two stops for rest and relief, but he was nearly there.

He drove past Jamison's General Store and took the first turn to the left. The dirt road snaked rapidly into the mountains, switching back and forth as it negotiated the rocky terrain. After three miles he watched for the nearly invisible path that bore off to the right. He saw it just in time and continued slowly, even deeper into the dense woods. The path ran for about a mile ending in a small clearing cut from the virgin forest. In the middle of the open space stood his destination: Paul Terrel's small vacation cabin.

The Cherokee rolled up to the structure, stalling out when it struck the front porch. Braxton collapsed onto the steering wheel, ready to give himself to the pain and exhaustion.

No. He couldn't stop now. He had to get inside.

Braxton climbed out into a freezing New Hampshire night. The shock of the frigid air released what little adrenaline he had left, just enough to keep him going for a few more minutes.

The cabin was a reproduction log house, about forty feet long and twenty feet deep, with a covered porch that ran the length of the front. A rotting cloth hammock swung silently at the end to his left and a pair of rough wooden benches rested against the wall at his right. Two painted metal milk canisters sat on each side of the front door. Emerging from the canisters were stalks that would explode into colorful wildflowers in the coming weeks.

Aided by a still-burning headlight, Braxton staggered up to the door and kicked the left canister as hard as he could. Stems and dirt spilled over the porch surface. Shivering from the pain and cold, he stuck his hand in the soil, fished around in the mess for a few seconds, and retrieved the emergency key they left for forgetful climbers. He struggled in the shadows to put the rusty key into the lock. It finally clicked and he entered the cabin.

Slamming the door behind him, he went immediately to the first aid kit in the bathroom. At one of his rest stops he had wrapped his blood-soaked shirt around the hole in his shoulder; it seemed to have stopped the flow for the moment. He found a bottle of Tylenol, at least he still had the sense to know aspirin would probably restart the bleeding, and swallowed a handful of the white pills. Too tired to cope any longer, he stumbled into the bedroom, collapsed on one of the bottom bunks, and immediately lost consciousness.

CHAPTER 47

Capitol Hill, Washington, D.C.
Thursday, 11:45 a.m.

Gᴿᴇʏsᴛᴏɴᴇ ᴡᴀʟᴋᴇᴅ ɪɴᴛᴏ The Monocle on Capitol Hill at 11:45. He gave the maître d' his name and was quickly shown to a quiet corner table.

Nicholson had made a good selection. Just a few blocks away from the Capitol on D St., The Monocle had been a Washington favorite for over thirty-five years; a gathering place for legislators, military, lobbyists, and reporters. You could tell a lot about the latest deals on the Hill by watching who was hosting who at lunch. It was a notoriously difficult place to get a reservation, but somehow his colleague never had any problem.

The waiter brought him a glass of a popular New Zealand Chardonnay. He drew in the aroma and took a sip. The wine was cool with a tart fruity flavor, quite good, but he still missed the bite of a dry martini. Times change, however, and there was no use in calling undue attention.

Greystone noticed a number of city and state police uniforms at the next table. The House was debating a local law enforcement subsidy bill and it looked like the cops had come out in full dress. He'd have to ask Nicholson about the attractive civilian who was sitting with them. It never hurt to know an important staffer.

Publicly, they were here to discuss Theater's support of the *Potterfield Bill*. The real agenda was more critical than even the Bill, but there was no reason not to hold the conversation in a comfortable locale.

Nicholson arrived at 12:10, sat down, and immediately ordered a double Jack Daniels. "I'm sorry, Bob. I've been stuck in a damn subcommittee meeting all morning."

He was more agitated than Greystone had ever seen him. He had heavy bags under his eyes and a deep furrow down the middle of his forehead. The pressure from Potterfield must be tremendous. Greystone's news wasn't going to help.

"Then you haven't heard?" Greystone asked.

"Heard what?"

Greystone attempted a look of sadness. "Warren was killed last night."

"Killed!" Nicholson exclaimed a little too loudly. He glanced to each side hoping that he hadn't attracted too much attention, then continued in a lower tone. "What happened?"

"Apparently Braxton went off the deep end. He went to Warren's house last night and shot him. The police found him at the scene but he got away."

"Jesus. Warren's dead and we've got a lunatic consultant running all over the countryside. None of this would have happened if your people had done their job last week."

Leave it to Nicholson to immediately place blame. It was typical of these goddamn bureaucrats. "Let's not get into that now, Nick. We've got to find Braxton before the police do."

"Are we in any danger? Would this guy come after us?"

Greystone shook his head. "There's no way he could have connected us to Ramal. He's holed up somewhere. We just have to figure out where."

"What about Warren's papers? The cops must be all over his stuff. Would he have kept anything around that would point to us?"

Nicolson could hardly get the words out fast enough. His chest was heaving and he was flailing his hands over the table. Greystone had to get him calm before someone noticed. "Settle down, Nick. Don't go paranoid on me. Warren was too smart to leave any incriminating evidence around. He's always covered his tracks before."

"Yeah, I know." Nicholson dropped his arms and looked straight at his colleague. "Warren was a good friend, Bob. I want you to punish this guy. If you can't figure out how to do it, I will."

Jesus. Why did he always have to be the rational one? The one to fix their problems? It was bad enough that Nicholson was running all over Virginia trying to track down his phantom blackmailer. He couldn't let him start messing in the Braxton problem.

"Take it easy, Nick. I'm checking out all of his contacts. He doesn't have many friends left."

The waitress brought Nicholson his drink and he downed half of it in a single gulp.

"How is your search going?" Greystone asked, hoping to get Nicholson's mind off the consultant.

"I checked every goddamn newspaper story and computer file on Lynch I could find. Then I had Potterfield's interns run a check on every name. It's the first useful work they've done for us all year." Nicholson had learned to clean up his language in public, but when he was stressed, deep set behaviors reappeared. It was another bad sign. "Everybody turns out negative. I located Lynch's attorney yesterday and he told me the mother was dead. Said he hadn't seen the daughter for years, but his receptionist let slip she had just been there."

"Can we check his files?"

"Yeah, I did that. He had cleaned them out. I've been searching data banks and phone books ever since for the kid. It looks like she disappeared off the face of the earth."

Greystone dropped his head and tried to think of another approach. With Chamberlain gone, they didn't have the time to be working on two critical cases. They had to eliminate Nicholson's blackmailer and they had to find Braxton.

Nicholson finished his drink and waved for another. He finally noticed his colleague's silence. "I'm sorry, Bob. This thing's really got me on edge. Anything I can do about the damn consultant?"

Greystone slowly looked up. Maybe Nick could give him some ideas. "He could be anywhere, but the police report from Boston said he was wounded. That means he's got to find someone to help him."

"What about CERT? Would they give him any help?"

"I don't think so. The cops will be on their back after Chamberlain's death. And their head guy will throw a fit over the publicity. Anyway, I've put alarms on all of Braxton's computer accounts. If he tries to contact anyone we can track him."

"He could just be lying dead somewhere. Maybe we should just wait until they find the body."

"It's possible, but that bastard's luckier than any three people I know. I've got a feeling we'll hear from him again."

The waiter brought Nicholson's refill and they decided to go ahead and order. Greystone selected a light seafood casserole; Nicholson ordered a Monocle burger. The waiter returned and brought them both salads.

"Could Braxton have developed any contacts down here?" Nicholson asked. "You said he had spent a lot of time at GW."

"Braxton's primary contact was the detective-in-charge, Sam Fowler. Fowler gave him access to Ramal's files."

"The cop certainly wouldn't help him now. Isn't the Ramal case closed?"

"It looks that way. I hacked the District's record system and reviewed the case files. The FBI bought the terrorist story. It keeps up their funding. Fowler wasn't convinced but he was overruled. I checked his case log and he hadn't put much together.

"According to the log, Braxton talked to Robert Cabot, an assistant dean at Georgetown, and Eric Mendoza, Ramal's advisor." Greystone prided himself in his memory. He loved to recall minute details from reports or files he had reviewed. "Oh, and Ramal's girlfriend, a coed at Georgetown. Susan Goddard."

Nicholson dropped his fork into the Caesar salad. "Did you say Goddard? Susan Goddard?"

"Yes, Susan Goddard," Greystone shot back. What the hell was with Nicholson now? "I'm sure. Why?"

"Goddard was the wife's maiden name. How old was this girl?"

"Jesus Christ, Nick, I don't know. Mid to late twenties I guess. About the same as Ramal."

Nicholson slammed back his chair and stood up. "That's her, Bob. She's here in town! Georgetown, right? I'll get back to you this afternoon." Heads turned as the elegant black rushed through the crowded restaurant.

"Dammit!" Greystone exclaimed under his breath. Could we have put Lynch's daughter together with Braxton?

He called to the waiter. There was little point in trying to finish his lunch now; his stomach couldn't take it.

* * *

Braxton opened his eyes and his head immediately started to pound.

Pain pulsed through his shoulder and chills racked his body. As his mind slowly cleared, he remembered the events of the night before: the discovery of Chamberlain's body, the arrival of the police, the desperate race through the woods, and the exhausting escape to New Hampshire. It was hard for him to believe that it could have all happened.

His watch said it was 12:15. It was light outside so it must be noon. He wanted to get up but he felt so tired. His shoulder throbbed insistently, demanding attention. He rolled to the side of the bed and sat up, preparing for a trip to the bathroom. Instantly his vision blurred and he grabbed blindly for the bunk post. He fell back and closed his eyes.

At 3:00 he awoke again, sweat dripping from his head and chest. He carefully pulled himself up on the side of the bed and waited for his head to clear. Still shivering, he started the slow journey to the bathroom. Three steps from the bed he rested on the old cherry dresser Terrel had bought from an antique dealer in Lincoln. Two steps along the wall brought him to the bedroom door. He swung himself around the door frame into the main room. Inching along the dilapidated sofa they had picked up in a Concord flea market, he reached out for the large meeting table. It was too far and without support, he fell to the floor.

He rested on the tattered area rug then climbed up the end of the table and continued the trek. Using one of the chairs as a walker he hobbled to the bathroom doorway, then stepped over to the basin. Had he looked in the mirror, he would not have recognized the pale and drawn face staring back at him. The Tylenol was still open on the scratched Formica counter top. He swallowed another mouthful of pills and sat down on the commode, dizzy and out of breath.

His mind was adrift. He couldn't focus on anything. Thoughts seemed almost within reach, and then they dissolved into nothingness. He finally pulled himself up and walked the eight steps to the small kitchen in the front corner of the cabin. Sitting on the counter was a telephone.

The cops must have gotten his license plate number. They knew who he was. His picture would be on every news program in New England. He needed help, but who would help him now?

Braxton remembered his cell phone was in the car. And he remembered why it was not a good idea to use it. Even if he could.

Cell coverage was spotty at best in this part of New Hampshire; that was why Terrel had installed a land-line. Would his parents have thought of turning off the line? Only one way to tell.

He picked up the handset and felt a momentary flash of hope as the familiar tone reached his ear.

He picked up the phone and punched 411.

* * *

"Hello?" Goddard said, praying it would be Braxton. She hadn't heard anything from him since the message he had left on her answering machine the day before.

"Susan. It's . . . Adam."

"Adam! Where are you? I've been worried sick." The connection was awful. He sounded far away and barely intelligible.

"Warren . . . dead . . . shot."

"What? Adam, please speak up. I can hardly hear you. Who's been shot?" It wasn't the connection. Something was terribly wrong.

"Had . . . to . . . escape . . . police . . . please . . . help . . . me."

She was frightened. He was barely coherent. "Of course I'll help. Where are you?"

"Paul's . . . cabin . . . Merritt . . . New Hampshire."

"New Hampshire!" She grabbed a pencil and paper from the counter. "How do I get there?"

"Merritt . . . New Hampshire . . ."

"Adam! Please listen. I need directions. Tell me how to get to you."

"Left . . . at . . . Jamison's . . . three . . . miles . . . right . . . thank . . . you."

"Wait! Don't go! What is Jamison's? Where is the cabin?"

"Need . . . you." The line went dead.

What had happened at Chamberlain's? Why was Braxton in New Hampshire?

Maybe the detective would know. She pulled Fowler's card from her bag and dialed his number. The line was busy.

She couldn't wait any longer. To her surprise, the decision came easily. Her friend was in trouble and she was going to help. No second thoughts, no careful consideration. He needed her. That was enough.

She called for a cab then dashed into the bedroom. Yanking a duffel bag out her closet, she stuffed in some underwear and a change of comfortable clothes. From the bathroom she collected personal necessities. A shelf of medications caught her eye and she swept the array of pill bottles and first aid creams into her bag.

The cab pulled up as she ran out of the lobby. She tossed her bag in the back and followed it inside. It was still early enough in the afternoon that the traffic to Reagan National was light.

The driver stopped in front of the USAir terminal at 3:40. She hoped there was enough credit left on her Discover Card when she charged a ticket for the 4:00 shuttle to Boston.

*   *   *

As the cab pulled away from the curb in Arlington, a young black man stopped his bicycle on the opposite side of the street. He wore a scuffed black leather jacket, black jeans and neon designer sneakers. A worn denim backpack was slung over his shoulder.

He pulled a heavy chain from the pack and locked the 10-speed to the nearby lamp post. An iron bench sat empty a few yards away. The youth casually walked over, sat down, and dropped the backpack beside him.

A worn paperback next materialized from the pack. He opened the book and sat back. Every few minutes he would look up from his reading to the door of the apartment building across the street.

Then he would return to the novel.

CHAPTER 48

GODDARD LOOSENED HER seat belt and relaxed for the first time since Braxton's call. The plane had gotten off on time and she was hoping for a quiet and uneventful flight. Her seat mate, a Boston University professor, opened a laptop and began editing some kind of manuscript. Thankfully, he was too engaged in the effort for much small talk.

She pulled out the copy of the *Washington Post* that she had bought on the way to the gate and skimmed the headlines looking for anything that would help pass the time.

"Oh my God," she gasped as she read a small item on page five:

```
Computer Executive Found Murdered in Home

(Boston) Computer executive Warren Chamberlain was
found murdered in his suburban Carlisle, Massachu-
setts home last night. Chamberlain, Executive Vice
President for Century Computer, a leading computer
networking firm headquartered in Concord, Massachu-
setts, had been shot earlier that evening according
to police. Although no details were given, police
did say they had issued an arrest warrant for Adam
Braxton, a resident of Cambridge and former employee
of Century. Police would not speculate on a possible
motive, but did say the suspect could be wounded and
should be considered armed and dangerous. A spokes-
person confirmed that the suspect was seen fleeing
from Chamberlain's home in a dark red Jeep Grand
Cherokee.
```

An arrest warrant! Adam couldn't have murdered anyone. Why were they looking for him? And how had he been wounded?

She dropped the newspaper in her lap.

"Is anything wrong, Miss?" the professor asked.

"Ah, no. Thank you." She picked up the paper and buried her face as the tears came.

She arrived at Logan at 5:43 and bought copies of all the afternoon newspaper editions. The rental car representative was curt but helpful: she gave Goddard maps of the region, located Merritt, and provided general directions to New Hampshire. She was happy to have a backup in case Google maps or her cell phone died in the New Hampshire wilderness.

The only thing Goddard knew about New Hampshire was that every four years they held the first Presidential Primary and they had "Live Free or Die" on their license plates. She took an extra $300 from the ATM in the airport lobby.

By 6:30 she had made it through the Sumner tunnel and was fighting rush hour traffic up Interstate 93.

The congestion cleared when she passed I-95. The next part of the trip was straightforward: north on I-93 into New Hampshire and the mountains.

*   *   *

"Fowler," he growled into the phone. The detective had been enjoying a wonderfully greasy Italian sausage submarine sandwich and didn't appreciate the interruption. Patrolman Moses had brought everybody dinner from Santoro's down the street. The squad room smelled like a diner.

"Detective Fowler, this is Lieutenant Jacoby from the Cambridge, Massachusetts Police Department."

Fowler vaguely remembered the name. His friend in the Boston Police Department had given him Jacoby's name when Fowler had called about the Terrel case. "We spoke earlier this week about the Terrel murder, right?"

"That's correct, Detective. I was wondering if you had been in contact with Adam Braxton lately."

"I spoke to him a few days ago. What's up?" Why would Jacoby be calling him now?

"I'm afraid there has been another murder. The victim was a past associate of Braxton's and we'd like to ask him a few questions."

Alarms blared in the detective's head. The lieutenant was using all the standard euphemisms: "past associate", "ask a few questions". What the hell had Braxton gotten into now? "I thought he was in Cambridge, Lieutenant."

"We've tried to contact him at his apartment and he doesn't seem to be around."

"Who's the victim?" Fowler tried to sound calm and unemotional.

"A Warren Chamberlain, Detective. We believe he was Braxton's supervisor when Braxton worked at Century Computer. It appears Chamberlain had to let Braxton go a few years ago. Do you know whether he had any contact with Chamberlain recently?"

Damn. That's the guy Adam said he was waiting to hear from. "Not that I know of, Lieutenant. But then we didn't talk about much other than his current investigation."

"What investigation was that?"

"He told me he was a consultant looking into some kind of computer network foul up down here."

"Did that investigation have anything to do with Century Computer?"

"I don't think so. Braxton never mentioned them." He was being pulled in deeper and deeper. He had to stop the cop's interrogation. "How was this Chamberlain killed?"

"He was shot at his house last night. The local cops got a call about loud noises at the home and went to check it out. They just missed getting the murderer; he escaped through the woods in a Jeep Grand Cherokee."

"How did you get involved?"

"There was some information in Chamberlain's PC that referred to Braxton. We checked him out and found he owns a Cherokee. His prints were all over Chamberlain's house. If you know where he is, Detective, I would suggest you tell us."

Fowler did not like being threatened. "Look, Jacoby. I know the law and I know my job. If I knew where Braxton was I would tell you. Personally, I don't believe that this guy could kill anyone, but that's for the investigators to determine."

"All right, Detective, no offense. But if you hear from Braxton, you better tell him to get his ass in here. It's gonna get real rough for him otherwise."

Fowler didn't want to piss the cop off too much. He might need the contact later. "Don't worry, Lieutenant. If I find out anything you'll be the first to hear about it. Keep me up-to-date on how the case is going, okay?"

"Sure, Detective."

Could I have been wrong about Braxton? The consultant sounded legit, but could he really tell? Shit! And I got him involved with that woman.

He grabbed his cell and dialed Goddard's number. All he heard was her recorded greeting.

"Ms. Goddard. This is Sam Fowler. Call me as soon as you get home. It's urgent. It's about Adam Braxton."

* * *

"We're late, Enrico. Make up the time," Greystone ordered.

"Yes, sir," came the controlled reply.

Damn spic. He couldn't afford to be late for a meeting with Hajima. He would lose face. And he needed Hajima to keep up the effort on the project while he worked on Flitterman.

Greystone didn't have any misconceptions regarding Hajima's motivation. So far, he had been a stubborn but committed supporter of the plan. As long as it was still to his benefit.

Greystone was also supremely confident in his ability to get others to do what he wanted. It had always been that way.

* * *

At first, Bob hadn't understood what he was doing there. His advisor at Harvard had said it was a breakaway course that would give him a whole new way of looking at finance and economics. Classes outside the regular curriculum always looked good on a transcript, and he was able to fit it into his schedule without much trouble, so he had registered.

His trek from up river had been uneventful. He had taken the bus from Harvard Station and exited at the MIT stop. There across the street was 77 Massachusetts Avenue, an incredibly pretentious, Greek revival building adorned with the names of past scientific greats. Probably appropriate, he had thought as he crossed the street, since in his view, science was a course of study whose time had passed. The real forces of the world were economic and political, and no amount of technological tinkering was going to change that fact.

He walked up the granite steps, through the eight-foot-tall brass doors, and straight down a barren corridor until it became Building 10, apparently the spiritual center of the MIT campus. Stairs took him up to the lecture hall in room 250.

The bus had been late, and he had to take a seat at the end of the third row. He couldn't understand what all the fuss was about. All he saw was a classroom full of rather unkempt and ill-prepared adolescents. He was sure the student in front of him couldn't have showered in a week, and the coed—did MIT really have coeds, it was usually hard to tell—next to him was leisurely chewing on what looked like a day old sandwich and sipping a Coke. If this was where the action was, he would certainly be surprised.

As the weeks passed, his skepticism had been overcome as he sensed the power of the new tool. He was driven by the vision of access to enormous amounts of financial and business information. If he could harness that information for his own use, his power would be vast.

It hadn't been until the term project that he had discovered the instruments for his success.

Not knowing anyone else in the class, he had been at the mercy of a lottery for his teammates. His expectations had been low and, at least initially, well-founded.

Persuading his new friends to do his bidding had not been that difficult. Warren had been the easier. A few words of recognition and congratulations and he was set for the next assignment.

Nick had been harder. He was stubborn and moody. Bob finally found the right approach: simply offer assistance. Nothing drove his friend to work harder than a simple offer to help.

He had done his share of the work, of course: planning the project schedule, doling out the assignments, and writing the final presentation. Someone had to be in charge.

He found in his colleagues a willing and able resource for future endeavors. They planned and executed a small number of what could only be called pranks during their remaining college years. Primarily, he nurtured a pattern of behaviors that he would harvest years later.

After graduation the trio went their separate ways. They selected graduate schools, took jobs, and built careers. Computers became big business, and they were well prepared to capitalize on the opportunities.

They maintained contact primarily electronically, although there was an occasional reunion at a major trade show such as Comdex or NCC. The liquor would flow freely and they would reminisce and tell stories of the "good old days", although none of them would have ever really wanted to go back. The excitement was the future and they knew they would be a key part of it.

Bob understood that the business world was an irrational place. Good ideas don't get funded, and bad engineering makes millions, or even billions, of dollars. That Harvard dropout Gates being only one example. Technology is often used in unfair and inefficient ways. Sometimes an idea just needs a little push, or a piece of information needs to be disseminated a little more widely.

He monitored the markets looking for those opportunities. Then he would call his friends for help. They had the advantage of seeing the bigger picture. They knew where business and technology needed to go. He had persuaded them to lead rather than follow.

Warren had been reticent to assist in some of the projects. He liked to think he still had a conscience. Neither of his partners had any such delusions. But it had been Warren who had come to Bob to save his company when arthritic management had nearly brought it to its knees. They had reincarnated Century and made it into a leader in network computing, all of them sharing in the rewards of the success.

Bob had learned of the gateway's diagnostic port during one of Warren's product explanations. He had immediately grasped its potential to simplify their communications scanning. It had been increasingly difficult to crack into all the individual computer systems they had targeted. The scanner Nick had coded for placement into Century's gateways broadened their access to electronic sources without compromising security. It was a perfect solution. Until the past week, there had been no complaints from Warren.

If anything, Nick had become easier in the later years. He enjoyed the respect and prestige that wealth had brought him. And as Chief of Staff to a powerful Senator, he had access to information that could topple governments, or create industries.

Ever since the Lynch affair, he had been a willing participant in their projects.

*   *   *

The limousine lurched as Santana turned off Interstate 95 and onto a bumpy state highway. They were almost to the country farmhouse. It was time to focus on the meeting.

Nicholson and Chamberlain had been his hands, the manipulators and implementers of his plans. Now Chamberlain was gone, his liabilities finally exceeding his assets. But Hajima could fill the void, even though he was unaware of Greystone's other partner.

The pieces were falling into place. With Nicholson driving Potterfield and Greystone's pressure on Flitterman, Hajima would get everything he wants.

The only loose end was that damned consultant.

CHAPTER 49

Merritt, New Hampshire
Thursday, 9:00 p.m.

GODDARD MADE THE Lincoln exit on I-93 by 8:45 and headed west on Rt. 112 along the Lost River. The going was slow; she was having trouble following the directions from her cell phone while negotiating the narrow New Hampshire roads. Finding Jamison's had been easier than she had expected, but she missed the cabin's turn-off and had to double back to the town and try again.

It was 9:15 when she finally pulled up in the clearing. She would have thought it was the wrong place had the Jeep Grand Cherokee not been sitting in front of the cabin. The structure was pitch black; only her headlights illuminated the clearing.

She pointed the car at the front of the cabin and slid out. When she passed the Jeep she gasped.

What the hell had happened?

The rear windshield had been blown out, there was no front bumper and it looked like a Tyrannosaurus Rex had run its claws along the side.

She cautiously walked up the steps and knocked at the door. It creaked back slightly so she pushed more firmly. The door swung open.

"Adam?" she called softly. There was no answer.

She cautiously entered the lighted stripe beyond the door.

"Adam?" Soft moans came from a void to her left.

Her eyes accommodated to the darkness and the outlines of walls and furniture appeared. She moved to her left and found a doorway leading to a small room. The moans seemed to be emanating from a large pile of blankets on a bunk bed. She carefully pulled back the covers and found Braxton lying on his right side, curled in the fetal position, slowly rocking back and forth. The sheets were soaking wet and a large dark stain covered his exposed left shoulder.

"Adam? Adam, can you hear me?" she repeated as she gently shook him.

He responded with a louder groan. She felt his forehead. He was burning with fever despite the cold. It was even worse than she had feared.

What could she do? There had to be a doctor in Merritt. But then what would happen to him? There was no way to disguise his wound. They would find out and arrest him. What would he want me to do?

There was no time to debate this. She had to get him cleaned up and find a way to control the fever. The doctor could come later.

She found a working lamp in the front room then set off to make the cabin habitable. It was near freezing inside. She found electric heaters along the outside walls and turned them all on. Warm air rose immediately.

She ran out to the car, grabbed her bag, and locked up the rental. Old habits were hard to break; it was not likely anyone would be looking to steal it out here.

The kitchen yielded sponges, a pan, and running water. In the bathroom she found a clean set of towels and the cabin's first aid kit. She stripped Braxton, sponged him down, and tried to clean the two rough wounds in his shoulder. The bullet had passed completely through; she could see fresh red tissue and something shiny and white, she assumed it was bone, through the holes. His shoulder burned red from inflammation and a yellow puss oozed from the openings.

She cleaned the wound as best she could, smeared on antibiotic cream from the kit, and bandaged the shoulder with clean gauze. Luckily there were two bunk beds in the room. She made the other lower bunk with fresh linen discovered in a small closet and led her incoherent patient there. He managed to swallow some water, a couple more Tylenol, and two Erythromycin tablets she found among her inventory. He fell back to sleep immediately.

Satisfied she had done as much for her patient as possible, Goddard took an inventory of the cabin. On the left as she had entered was the dormitory bedroom. To her right was a small kitchen area that backed to the bathroom in the far corner. A worn sofa sat under the front windows. Bookcases, dressers, and cabinets were arbitrarily placed throughout the space. A large, hewn-wood trestle table and chairs occupied the center of the main room. It was a functional, if not comfortable, layout and undoubtedly just right for a group of young Boston bachelors.

Rustic living was not unfamiliar to Goddard. Her father had had a cabin in the hills of Virginia when she was a girl. They would go there every summer to get away from D.C. and fish and swim in the small lake down the road.

Her father had been a very organized man. He had made lists for everything and the cabin had been no exception. There had been a checklist for opening the cabin in the spring and one for closing it in the fall. Every year she had been given a new item on the lists as her responsibility. She had been so proud when he would "award" her the activity. It had been his way of recognizing her growth. She hoped she could remember some of those items now.

There were two more sets of clean bed linens in the closet. She was just about out of Tylenol and bandages. The cabinets in the kitchen held a limited stock of canned goods. The small refrigerator was empty and turned off. She plugged it in and it began a steady, if not quiet, drone. The water from the tap looked clear and the pressure was good. Nothing urgently broken.

She ached to sit down and rest, but there were still things that had to be done. Her movements were robotic, going from one task to the next without thinking. Checking him one more time, she stroked his forehead, kissed him gently, and left the cabin.

She hated to go, but they desperately needed more supplies. And she was less likely to be noticed tonight than during the day tomorrow. She reversed the directions back to Merritt and headed south. Five minutes down the road she found a twenty-four hour CVS that provided most of the critical items on her list, including an assortment of over-the-counter antibiotics. She hoped they would be enough.

She made it back to the cabin at 10:45. It was warm enough that she could finally take off her coat. She looked in on her patient and found he had kicked off all of his covers; his fever continued to rage. She redressed his wound, applied some of the medication she had purchased, and tried to make him more comfortable. He still didn't seem to realize she was there.

Pulling one of the chairs from the main room next to Braxton's bunk, she finally sat down and covered herself with a spare blanket. Time to think. What did she need to do next?

Two minutes later she was fast asleep.

* * *

Greystone slid his chair back from the table and downed the half inch of Drambuie remaining in his snifter. He felt satisfied and relaxed; quite ready to deal with the next phase of the evening.

His guest, on the other hand, looked considerably less comfortable. Hajima was squirming in his chair, apparently trying to find a position that would relieve the battle tearing at his insides. Greystone had insisted on a traditional Southern dinner: fried chicken, buttered grits, candied yams, and okra. Topped off with a huge piece of pecan pie ala mode. If that wouldn't give his Japanese colleague heartburn he didn't know what would.

"I'm so glad you were able to join me, Akira. I hope you enjoyed the meal." Hajima had come alone this time. He probably didn't want to expose his people to the toxic food.

"It was excellent, Robert. Your southern cuisine is truly . . . unique."

"Thank you. I asked you this evening both to share this lovely setting and to update you on the status of our project."

"Excellent, Robert." Looking exceedingly uncomfortable, Hajima tried crossing his legs. "I am anxious to learn of any progress. But may I first ask why the police have not closed the investigation on your President's death? My management is still quite concerned over this unexpected event."

What is he talking about? The frame-up was perfect. He must still be concerned about public opinion.

"The police have assured us there will be no additional publicity. They are satisfied that Lombard was responsible and acted alone. If there is any delay I'm sure it is just procedural."

"Of course, Robert, of course. It is just as I thought. But surely you understand how the delay in resolution puts our project at risk."

"I again can assure you, my friend, that Charles' untimely death does not in the least affect Theater's commitment to you and our partnership. You must believe that."

"I know *you* are committed, Robert. But we both know this has been a calculated gamble. I felt you could control the play of events at Theater. The unresolved murder of your top executive is hardly something that instills confidence in my management. What can I tell them? When can we sign the agreements that would form the joint venture?"

"Akira. These are delicate matters. As I'm sure you know, a critical amendment to the Bill was passed on Tuesday. An amendment that legislates the technology platform we have developed.

"I have also learned that tomorrow Senator Potterfield will pass the Bill out of committee. It will then be only a short time until it is signed. A matter of days. We will then be able to move forward aggressively.

"Julius and I speak frequently of the progress of our partnership. This is just as we had planned. Surely you do not want to withdraw now?"

Why should he have to appease Hajima as if he was a child? For all of his demands, the Japanese was in as deep as Greystone. If Hajima failed to deliver the venture he would go back to Japan in disgrace.

"I am not suggesting we stop our work. I only ask that you continue to educate your management on the benefits of our relationship. We have delivered on the feasibility studies, the design plans, and the technical prototypes. We needed only your assistance in the regulatory matters and a distribution channel. If you are not able to bring Mr. Flitterman to the table, there may be little I can do to hold off my management's impatience. Any further complications could be quite damaging. Do we understand each other, Robert?"

"Yes, Akira. We understand each other completely."

What a bastard! He's acting like this is his project. The venture was Greystone's concept. It was *his* work that resulted in the amendment. *His* company that will provide the distribution. Once the contracts are executed, we'll see how necessary his overpriced manufacturing capabilities really are.

"And there is one other small thing, Robert."

What now? thought Greystone.

"I will require access to your tap on the Internet."

Greystone's heart stopped. Hajima had to be bluffing. There was no way he could know anything.

"A tap?" he asked, hoping the catch in his voice wasn't too obvious. "What do you mean?"

Hajima sat calmly. He shook his head as if reprimanding a child.

"Oh, Robert. I really am disappointed. I thought we were getting along so well. Yet you had the arrogance to tap our internal communications and throw it into my face. Do you really think I wouldn't figure out how you got all that inside information?"

Hajima rose from the table. "We're done for this evening. Think over my request and decide whether you want to continue our *partnership.*

As he passed Greystone's chair, he turned and smiled. "Oh, and thank you so much for the dinner."

Greystone watched as the Japanese strode from the dining room to his waiting car.

He could feel the flush in his face and the sweat pooling at his collar.

Damn him! No one had ever suspected what they had created. Not for thirty years.

He slammed his fists on the table, not caring about its effect on the other diners. After the cracking of china and shattering of crystal had stopped, the room again grew quiet.

He had underestimated Hajima. And now his secret was compromised.

But he could still salvage this. *He* could control the flow of information. As long as Hajima received the data he wanted, he would be satisfied.

Greystone could still control the port. He didn't have to give Hajima the operating details. Just the results. He didn't even have to tell his friends.

It would still work out.

CHAPTER 50

Merritt, New Hampshire
Friday, 4:00 a.m.

GODDARD AWOKE DISORIENTED and in pain. Her mind quickly cleared, and realized the jabbing ache was from resting her neck on the hard edge of the captain's chair. She shook off the discomfort and took stock of her situation. The air in the small cabin was oppressive; it was so warm that both of them had tossed off all their blankets during the night. Braxton was thrashing naked on the bunk.

Lights glared in every room. This was not a good time to call attention to yourself.

She got up, stretched for a minute to unkink her muscles, and went to right the cabin. The heaters were first; she turned them down to sixty-five. Then she turned off most of the lights except for one in the kitchen and a small table lamp in the bedroom. She refilled the pan of water, cleaned Braxton's wound, and tucked him back under the covers. He seemed to be sleeping more comfortably.

There was no way she was going to go back to the chair for the rest of the night. She made up the other lower bunk, stripped to her underwear, and crawled in. She left the light on in case her patient woke up. It didn't disturb her sleep.

At 9:00 she again awakened, but this time more comfortably. Glancing to Braxton's bed, she saw he was still quiet. It didn't look as if he had stirred. She checked his forehead and his temperature was definitely down. His shoulder still glowed scarlet but the oozing had stopped. Maybe the worst was over. She tried not to think what would have happened if she hadn't come.

Her head throbbed and her muscles still ached from exhaustion, but there was no point in going back to bed. She had never been able to sleep late in the morning; Momma and Father had always been early risers and she had never been able to break their training. She picked up her clothes and tip-toed into the main room, closing the bedroom door behind her. In the light of day, she could see what a mess the cabin really was. The floor was littered with magazines and newspapers. Dust bunnies clung ferociously in uncountable nooks and crannies. There were cobwebs in most of the corners and an occasional spider ventured out to see the newest inhabitant of its lair. Stale dust covered every surface she could see, and probably most she couldn't.

The place was in critical need of a female touch.

First on the agenda was breakfast. She scrambled two eggs, toasted a couple of English muffins, and poured a glass of orange juice, all supplies she had purchased on her late night excursion. She was famished; it was her first real meal since lunch the day before at the Georgetown cafeteria. As she sat devouring the food, she scanned the papers from the day before. The news reports weren't good. Braxton had been identified as the prime suspect and alerts had gone out across New England. At least they didn't seem to know where he had gone.

The article reminded her of the Cherokee. It was sitting in plain view in front of the cabin. It was unlikely anyone would come by, but there was no use in taking the chance. She unsuccessfully searched Braxton's clothes for the keys, then went out and checked the vehicle. The keys were still in the ignition.

She turned the switch and was awarded with a weak groan for her effort. He must have left the car running when he arrived. She glanced at the dashboard and was relieved to see that the fuel gauge still floated above empty. It was just a dead battery.

After finding a pair of jumper cables stuffed under the back seats, she pulled up her rental, jumped the Cherokee, and parked it out of sight behind the cabin. So far, her father's training had done its job.

She left the rental in front. At least no one was after her.

When she came back in, she heard movement in the bedroom. Braxton was tossing in the bunk and seemed to be mumbling something. She tried to get him to take some juice. He seemed to recognize her, even attempting a small smile, then fell back asleep after a few sips. She decided to let him rest as long as he wanted.

The remainder of the morning was spent cleaning up and rearranging the contents of the cabin. The reading material seemed to be of two classes: male adolescent, epitomized by well-read copies of *Playboy*, and male sport, consisting of almost as worn copies of *Rock & Ice*. At least the sport pile was twice the height of the other. She considered throwing both piles out, but found a secluded corner in a closet and stacked them there instead.

Terrel's name was on many of the papers and mementos she found scattered around the cabin. It seemed to be his place, used freely by his friends as a secluded getaway. If Terrel really had been killed because of Braxton, she wondered how he would ever get over it.

She was washing her breakfast dishes when she heard a strange shuffling sound. She turned and saw her patient swaying precariously in the doorway to the bedroom.

"Aren't we domestic," he managed in a weak, thin voice.

"Yes, I am," she replied putting her hands on her hips. "And you are to go right back to bed. I haven't nursed you back from the dead to let you fall on your face." She rushed over to catch him before he collapsed.

"Okay, but I think you'd rather I get to the bathroom first."

She led him first to the small bathroom, then back to his bed. He seemed alert and anxious to talk, so she asked him what had happened. The story came out in a torrent of words and emotion.

He sketchily related the events since he left D.C.: receiving Chamberlain's email, traveling out to his home in Carlisle, finding the body, and taking the flash drive clutched in his hand. He described what he remembered of the escape through the woods. They both were amazed that he had made it to the cabin at all and managed the strength to call her. Without help, she was sure he would have died.

She asked a few more questions, and he tried to answer, but was too weak to continue.

"It's time for you to go back to sleep," she told him. "I'll go out and get today's papers. Maybe there will be some better news. You rest and we'll talk later."

He nodded obligingly, closed his eyes, and drifted off to sleep.

* * *

Flanagan was incensed. She had been in a meeting with Lighthorse on the gateway problem when she had gotten a call to report to Rydell's office immediately. It was urgent. Candela was already there when she arrived.

"It's bad enough that I had to listen to that incompetent FBI agent on the phone, but to have him imply that we might be involved was outrageous." Rydell was standing behind his desk ranting and pounding his fists together. Flanagan and Candela stood sheepishly in front of him hoping the tirade would rapidly pass.

"Why the FBI, Timothy?" Candela asked. "I thought it was a simple murder."

Flanagan raised her eyebrows at her colleague's insensitive characterization of Chamberlain's death.

"They've gotten it into their heads that there's some kind of Internet conspiracy going on. The fact that this Braxton was one of our consultants really set them off. We did terminate the contract didn't we, Rachel?"

It was clear there was only one acceptable answer to the question.

"Yes, we agreed to stop working on the incident, Timothy. I have been trying to get in touch with Braxton but I've not talked to him." At least her statement was technically true.

"Make sure there's a memo to that effect in my mailbox. Copy Lawrence and contracts. What about this computer company, Century? Do they have anything to do with the Incident?"

"Nothing I'm aware of," she replied. "Braxton never mentioned them. We do have some of their equipment on site but they're not tied to any investigations."

"Good, we'll stress that. Braxton's relationship with Century has nothing to do with the Center." Rydell recited it for their benefit.

"This FBI agent, Randolph," Rydell continued, "said that he would be coming around and questioning the staff. Edward, you are in charge of escorting him wherever he goes. I don't want him talking to anyone who hasn't been briefed. Rachel, you're in charge of the Ops staff. Tell them to keep their mouths shut. On second thought, Edward, get Walter and Lawrence out of the building until he is gone. They don't have anything important to do anyway."

"Is the FBI convinced Braxton really killed Chamberlain?" Flanagan asked.

"How the hell do I know?" Rydell barked. "I guess they are, but who cares? I will not allow any investigation to taint the reputation of this laboratory. We will convince them that we have no connection to this tragic event. Is that clear?"

Flanagan was tempted to snap a salute and yell "Yes, sir" but controlled the impulse. She nodded curtly instead. There was no reason she had to stand here and listen to him whine like a spoiled adolescent. She was sure he was much more concerned with saving his own precious reputation than he was in protecting CERT/CC. Still, she would have to be careful with her staff. Rydell would not tolerate anyone who wavered from the party line.

* * *

Officer Randy Collins had followed the out-of-state car when he saw it make the turn at Jamison's. It was still a little early for the tourists to descend on Woodstock, and he didn't recognize the flashy Camaro. When he saw it pull onto the narrow path, he decided it was time to check in.

"Jan?" he called over the radio.

"Dispatch," Janet Faraday responded. "What's up Randy?"

"I've been following a car with Mass plates over in Merritt. Number is seven eight five charlie david xray. It just pulled into the Terrel place. Didn't we hear something about him?"

"Hang on. I'll ask Weaver." Collins listened to static as the dispatcher checked with Lieutenant Mason Weaver. "Got it. Terrel was killed last week down in Cambridge. His parents called asking about getting someone to help them sell the cabin. Weaver says he gave them a couple of realtors' names."

"I guess it could be someone checking out the property. I'll go in and take a look. Run the plate, then try to find out who the parents called. See if they're expecting anybody. Collins out."

"Okay, Randy. Take it easy. Dispatch out."

CHAPTER 51

Merritt, New Hampshire
Friday, 2:30 p.m.

GODDARD RETURNED FROM the store with copies of the *Herald* and *Globe*, more canned goods and a few candy bars to stimulate Braxton's appetite.

She was sorting her purchases on the kitchen counter when she heard a noise out front. Going to the window, she looked out and gasped. Terror-struck, she saw a uniformed New Hampshire State Trooper getting out of his cruiser and approaching the cabin. He stopped at her car, looked inside, then continued to the porch.

Oh god! What can I do?

Braxton was still asleep in the bedroom; she had checked right after she had arrived back. She couldn't let the Trooper inside and see him. Rushing to the door, she stepped outside just as he was coming up the steps.

"Good afternoon, officer," she blurted out a little too loudly. "What can I do for you?"

"Officer Collins, ma'am. And you are?"

"Ah, Susan Goddard." Damn. She should have made up a name.

"What brings you up to New Hampshire, Ms. Goddard?" Collins stopped at the foot of the steps. He stood ramrod straight, his right hand resting by his handgun. "Is this your cabin?"

She was sure Collins knew it wasn't. What kind of a story could she use? The best lies are always based on the truth, she had heard somewhere. So it had to be something to do with Terrel and not Braxton.

"Oh, no. It belongs, belonged, to a friend of mine, Paul Terrel."

She tried her best to will tears to appear. "He died last week. I came up to get some things I'd left in the cabin and clean up for his parents."

"Are you from Boston?"

"Eh, no. I live in D.C." The Trooper gave her a puzzled look. "But I used to live in Boston. That's when we became friends. Paul let me use the cabin whenever I needed to get away from the city."

"I see." Collins' eyes wandered over the porch. She saw them stop at the pile of dirt by the door.

"I did that last night." Her voice was high and staccato. She hoped he wouldn't notice how nervous she was. "It was rather late when I got in and I stumbled against the pot. Guess I better clean it up," she said with a feigned smile. This wasn't going well. She had to get rid of him.

As Collins continued his silent search she saw a movement of curtains out of the corner of her eye. Braxton's face appeared through the shears.

"It was awful about Paul," she said stepping down off the deck. "Did you hear about it?"

"Yes, ma'am," Collins responded uncomfortably, having to follow her away from the door. "We heard he was killed."

Goddard continued walking over to her car. "He interrupted a burglary in a friend's apartment. It was so awful. He was a really wonderful person."

"Yes, ma'am. I'm sure he was. How long will you be staying?" They stopped halfway between the rental and the cruiser.

"Just a few days. Then I'll head back to D.C."

"Will you be all right out here by yourself?"

She managed a casual laugh. "Oh yes. I'm really a very independent woman. It's just a little sad being here without Paul. Is there anything else, officer?"

Collins paused and scanned the front of the cabin one more time. When he returned to Goddard, she felt like he could see into her every thought. "Not at this time, ma'am. If you need anything, be sure to give us a call. Afternoon." He touched the brim of his hat and walked back to the cruiser.

She watched as the cop got into his car. Please don't look around back, she prayed.

He pulled up to the house, turned around, and drove out the

path. When he had disappeared around a bend she ran back inside. Braxton was standing by the window wrapped in one of his blankets.

"What are you doing?" she cried. "He might have seen you!"

"I woke up and heard voices. What did he want?"

Goddard grabbed the wall to steady her shaking legs. "He wanted to know what I was doing here. I guess he was just checking up on the cabin since he knew Paul had died. I told him I was a friend and was here to pick up some of my things."

"Did he believe you?"

She nodded. "I think so, but he might come back. You have to be more careful and stay out of sight. And we are going to have to do something with the Jeep."

Braxton staggered slightly and she reached to steady him. "You've got to lie down. Would you like to stay in here for a while?"

"Yes. And I want to get some clothes on. I feel funny running around naked."

"I thought it was rather cute."

She walked him back to the bedroom and pulled the covers off his bunk while he rummaged in a bureau drawer for some clothes.

"Guess I've lost a little weight," he commented looking at the bagginess of his attire.

"You could say that." Actually he was frighteningly gaunt and yellow. Only his best friends would recognize him in this state. *Which may be a blessing, when we have to get out of here.*

She steered him back to the sofa and stood him against the wall while she smoothed out the sheets and positioned his pillows.

"Is that better?" she asked when he was finally settled.

"Much. I don't feel too bad."

"Well you look awful. Lie down there and rest." She threw one of the papers at him. "You look through that one. I'll check the *Herald.*"

She shuffled through the first few pages. "Adam, you won't believe what's here about you and Chamberlain! It says the police have found evidence in Chamberlain's house that you and he were secretly lovers. They believe you had been stalking him and then killed him because he threatened to go to the police. His secretary confirmed you went to see him two days before the murder."

Braxton let his head fall back on the pillow. "Whoever is behind all this certainly does a complete job. I bet all the evidence was electronic. In another week no one will believe me."

She couldn't help thinking of all the parallels. "Adam, you don't think . . ."

He looked up from the paper. "What?"

No. Don't make things any more complicated than they are. "Oh, nothing."

She continued to scan the article. "Here's some more. 'Police also confirmed that Braxton was the owner of a handgun matching the size of the bullets taken from Chamberlain's body. The gun has not as yet been recovered and may still be in Braxton's possession.' Do you have a gun?"

"Yes, didn't I tell you that?" The expression on her face told him he hadn't. "I knew it was mine as soon as I saw it on the floor. I didn't see how leaving it there would do me any good so I took it."

"How did it get there?"

"Whoever killed Paul must have taken it. I forgot all about it when I spoke to the police. Could they have planned all this that far ahead?"

"Where is the gun now?"

"It should be in the car somewhere." He tried to stand but hesitated when his head started spinning.

"Take it easy." She grabbed his shoulders and lowered him back to the sofa. "I'll go out and get it later. I don't think you need it right now. Remember, I'm your nurse and *I* say when you can get up. I've got to fix you something to eat." She tossed the paper onto the floor and walked into the kitchen area. "What does the other paper say?"

He read the first section. "It's about the same. The prose is a little less sensational but the message is the same. The *Globe's* got a better picture of me, though."

She glared back at him. "This isn't funny. What are we going to do?"

He turned and fixed his gaze on her. "We have to get back."

"Back where?"

"To D.C. I have to try to read Chamberlain's drive."

"Adam, you've barely got the strength to sit up. We'll stay a few days then see how you're doing."

"No. The police have already been here once. They're bound to come back. And I can rest all day tomorrow in the car."

"It's only a couple hours to Boston."

"We can't go to Boston. There is too much publicity. And we can't take a plane; it's too easy to track our credit cards. Do you mind driving all the way?"

"I guess not. Are you sure you want to go back now?"

"Yes, I have to get back and check those files. It's the only way to clear my name."

Unfortunately, she knew he was right. If they waited any longer they were sure to be recognized. "Okay. As long as you continue to improve. And that means doing everything I say. Deal?"

"Okay. I'm yours."

She poured a cup of hot soup and brought it over to him. "I just wish we didn't have to drive so far. How about flying from another city? We could fly under false names if we had enough cash."

"What did you say?" he asked quickly.

"I said we could fly out of another city."

"No, after that."

"Uh, we could use false names if we had the cash. Why?"

"That's what Chamberlain said, 'use the cash'."

"When?"

"When he was dying. He said 'use the cash'. It has something to do with the drive."

"Why would he say that? Use what cash? Did he want you to cash something? What does a disk have to do with cash?"

"I don't know. But I'm sure that's what he said. I've got to take a look at that disk."

"There's nothing you can do about it now. Lie back and get some rest."

He leaned back then bounced right up again.

"What is it now?"

"Fowler. We need to talk to him. He can tell us if they're looking in D.C."

"Now? It's Friday afternoon. He'll be on duty."

"Then we'll wait 'til later. But we have to speak with him."

"Okay. But later. Now you rest. Remember your promise?"

He gave her a sour look, but slid down on the sofa. She fluffed up his pillow, tucked the blankets around his neck, and headed for the door.

"What are you doing now," he called to her.

"If we're going back tomorrow, I've got to get you ready. Be back in a flash."

* * *

"Dispatch?" Collins called as he drove back to Merritt.

"Yes, Randy."

"Did you check out that car for me?"

"Of course. It's a rental. Checked out of Logan Thursday night to a Susan Goddard from Washington, D.C."

"That checks with what she told me. Said she was a friend of Terrel. See if you can find anything else on her. I'll go back tomorrow and take another look."

"Back so soon, huh? She must be cute."

"Come on, Jan. You know she couldn't compare to you. Collins out."

CHAPTER 52

The Russell Building, Washington, D.C.
Friday, 4:00 p.m.

NICHOLSON WAS HEADS down into a stack of folders piled on his normally spotless desk when Potterfield strutted into his aide's office like a puffed peacock.

"You missed all the excitement, Nick. The Bill passed fifteen to three."

Nicholson looked up and smiled at his boss's unusual show of emotion. "Congratulations, David. I knew you could pull it off."

"We're all going out for a drink. Care to join us?"

He shook his head. "Thanks, but I'm still trying to track down Goddard. I've followed her to a car rental agency at Logan. Then the trail dries up."

Potterfield's eyebrows furrowed. "When did she go to Boston? And why?"

"She charged a ticket on the four o'clock flight yesterday. I've had an investigator at her apartment since three, he must have just missed her. As to why, I don't know yet. It could just be for a weekend visit with some friends. She should be back in a day or so." There was no reason to involve Potterfield in the now Goddard *and* Braxton search. It would only make dealing with him all the harder.

"You're sure this is Lynch's daughter?"

"I'm positive. I've checked her records at Georgetown. She's the right age and I can't find any record of her before Lynch's death. She's hidden her past pretty well. That's why we couldn't find her."

"But a *woman*, Nick? And from Georgetown? How could she have figured out all the computer crap?"

Potterfield thought you had to be a genius to use computers. Maybe it was about time he retired. "She's been taking Computer Science classes at George Washington. She probably got someone to teach her the details."

"Yeah, that makes sense. You gonna wait until she comes back to town?"

"If necessary, but I'd rather locate her in Boston. It would be better to have an accident as far away from here as possible don't you think?"

"You're always looking out for us, Nick," Potterfield replied cheerily. "That's what I like about you." Potterfield's effuse mood was going to make Nicholson sick.

"Well then, if you're not going to join us, I'll leave you to finish." He headed for the door then stopped and turned around. "I'm taking the weekend off, Nick. Mary Jane and I need some time together. Can I assume you'll take care of things by Monday?"

"Yes, David. Next week things will be back to normal. Oh, I set up that meeting with Greystone you wanted for Wednesday. Camille put it on your calendar."

"Good. Now that we have the Bill on the way and this email thing resolved I can focus on squeezing Greystone dry. I do love this job, Nick."

"Yes, David. I know you do. Have a good weekend."

"You too, son."

Nicholson opened another folder and went back to his PC. He could wait until she appeared back at her apartment, but it would be better to locate her now. If he could find Goddard, she might lead him to Braxton. Then Greystone would owe him one.

He hacked into the TRW credit data base. His best chance was new credit card charges.

*   *   *

Goddard propped his head over the basin and squeezed in the rinse.

"What are you doing to me?" Braxton complained.

"If I'm going to be driving you all over New England tomorrow, I'm not taking any chances. We're going to take advantage of your new hungry look."

She had scoured the local store and brought back a collection of hair dyes and eclectic clothes. It took a whole bottle of black color rinse to hide the natural brown tone of his hair. She slicked it back and let it curl over the collar of his shirt.

Next came his beard. Braxton had one of those faces that showed a five o'clock shadow at one in the afternoon. His whiskers grew incredibly rapidly. She had noticed it that first morning in her apartment. After two days in the cabin he had a growth that would take most men weeks to develop. It wasn't quite enough for a full beard, but a little trimming produced an acceptable mustache and just the right amount of stubble.

She completed his transformation with a fitted vest, a lean pair of jeans, and cowboy boots.

"What do you think?" she asked, as he stood before the bathroom mirror.

"Unbelievable. I doubt my mother would recognize me." The result was startling; the upscale computer consultant had been turned into a gaunt, dark, artiste. "Is this another of your hidden talents? Disguising escaped felons?"

"But of course," she replied tossing her hair in the air and mimicking an Eastern European accent. "I am an expert in these ways. You will be quite at home in the liberal community of Georgetown."

"I should have known." He walked over and took her in his arms. "Thank you," he whispered, "for everything."

She held on to him as if to never let him go. When she finally pulled away, a single tear ran down her cheek.

"Back to the sofa for you," she ordered. "I've got to get us packed for the trip."

"First we call Fowler."

Goddard checked her watch. It was 6:45. "Okay, okay. He should have left work. You're such a nag."

"Will you call? Just in case someone is there?"

"Don't you think you're getting a little too paranoid?"

Braxton's eyebrows popped up. "Don't you think I have a reason?"

She retrieved her cell from her purse, found Fowler's number in her contact list and punched the call button. Nothing happened.

"Adam," she called. "My phone doesn't work."

"Sorry, forgot to mention that coverage is pretty bad out here." He pointed to the phone on the kitchen counter. "That's how I called you."

"We really are in the wilderness," she replied.

"Fowler," came a tired voice when the call connected.

"Detective, it's Susan Goddard."

"Goddard!" he exclaimed. "Where the hell are you? Are you okay?"

"I'm fine, Detective. Why?"

"Look. Braxton's in trouble. I'm worried he may have gone over the edge. Have you heard from him?"

Fowler's tone worried her. She put a finger up to her lips then pulled Braxton over to the phone. Maybe he was right. "What happened?"

"There was a murder in Boston. Warren Chamberlain from Century Computer. The police think your friend Braxton did it."

"*My* friend, Detective? I thought he was your friend, too. You were the one that kept pushing him into the investigation."

"Okay, *our* friend. To tell you the truth, I'm not sure about any of this. But there's a hell of a lot of evidence against him. And I don't want you to get any more involved."

She remembered what Braxton had said earlier. "All that evidence is electronic isn't it?"

"Electronic? What do you mean?"

"On the computer, email. Nothing written down."

"Well . . . Yeah. Most of it. But he was at the scene. And he ran."

"What would have happened if he didn't?"

The line went dead. Fowler returned after a few seconds. "This isn't a debate, Ms Goddard. Braxton is in lots of trouble. And I'm worried about you."

"I'm flattered, Detective. But you needn't be concerned. We're both fine."

"Both! Dammit, you're with Braxton? Where are you?"

"Outside Boston, Detective," Braxton interrupted. "I really want to thank you for your confidence."

"Uh, yeah. Look, I'm sorry. But what am I supposed to think?"

"How about that the same people who killed Mohammed Ramal and Paul Terrel, also killed Chamberlain and framed me," Braxton said. "Is it all that far-fetched?"

"I don't know. Tell me what happened."

Braxton again related the story of the night. He tried to remember everything for the detective.

"You really did get hit?"

"Yeah, caught me in the shoulder. I've had a great nurse, though."

"You're damn lucky. You've got to turn yourself in, Adam. The Massachusetts cops are sure to find you eventually. Just tell them what happened."

"Right, Sam. And what would happen then? Are they going to let me go? There isn't a bit of evidence in my favor. Without something to support my story I go to jail and they toss away the key. Any argument?"

Fowler's silence was answer enough.

"What's happening in D.C.? Are they looking for me there?"

"The Cambridge cops called once asking about you. Other than that I haven't heard anything. Why?"

"We're coming back to town day after tomorrow." Goddard was about to interrupt until Braxton shook his head at her. "I've got to see if Chamberlain's USB stick has anything useful on it."

"It's crazy. What if they pick you up on the way down?"

"We'll be careful. I have to take the chance."

"Maybe you do, but what about Ms. Goddard? Why get her messed up in this?"

"We're in this together, Detective," he said as he looked over to her. "It's more complicated than you think."

"Turn yourself in, Adam. For both your sakes."

"Sorry, Sam. Not yet."

"Okay. But we meet as soon as you get back. Monday morning. Same place as before. We can talk it through."

"We'll call you when we get in Sunday night. That's the best I can do. I'll explain then."

"You damn well better. Two days, Braxton. And be careful."

He handed the phone back to Goddard. "I thought you said we were leaving tomorrow?" she asked after dropping the handset in the cradle.

"We are."

"Don't you trust Fowler?"

"I don't know. But I sure don't trust any communication system. Especially the digital ones." He slid down on the cushions and flopped his head back. "Fowler's right you know. There isn't any reason you have to get tied up in my mess. It could be dangerous."

"I think there *is* a reason. Whatever is happening to us, we can work it out better together. Besides, it's clear you're lost without me." She leaned over and kissed him on the cheek. "Look what happened when I let you go off on your own."

Leaving Braxton to rest on the sofa, Goddard packed up the things they would need on the trip to D.C. and took them out to the rental car. Then she remembered that the Jeep was still parked out back. It was an all too obvious piece of evidence; she had to find a way to hide it. Searching the woods with her flashlight, she found a trail heading back from the house and drove the Cherokee as far into the dense forest as she dared. It was well out of sight from the clearing.

As she was getting out of the Jeep, her foot hit something under the seat. When she looked, she found Braxton's revolver. Gingerly lifting it off the floor with her thumb and index finger, she dropped it on the seat.

Should she leave it? It's caused nothing but misery so far.

It's evidence. I should hide it.

But what if there's trouble?

She finally grabbed the handle of the weapon, awkwardly pointed it away from her body, and walked back through the woods to the cabin.

* * *

They settled into their bunks for the night. The moon lit the cabin's interior with a soft, intimate glow. Only an occasional call from the crickets and bull frogs broke the stillness of the night.

"Susan, I feel chilled," he called.

She jumped out of bed and hurried over to his bunk. An impish grin immediately alleviated any concerns on his well-being. "Oh you do, do you? And what might warm you up?"

"If you lay down here for a minute I might get warmer." He patted the side of the bed.

"Well, as long as it's for therapeutic value only. Nurses should never get too involved with their patients you know," she said with a crooked smile.

"I completely agree," he replied as he pulled down the blanket.

She unbuttoned the heavy flannel nightshirt she had purchased in Jamison's and let it slide off her shoulders to the floor. Standing naked in the moonlight, she watched the desire grow in his eyes. Then she crawled under the covers and felt his warmth against her cool skin. She had missed him so and had prayed he would still want her.

"Are you sure you're all right?" she asked as she stroked the bandage on his shoulder.

"I've never wanted anyone more," he replied softly. They made love gently and slowly, relishing in each other's touch. They made it last as long as they could, finally ending in a rush of emotion that spent them both completely.

After he had fallen asleep she carefully left the bed for her own. Romantic as it was, the narrow bunks were much too small for a comfortable night's sleep and they'd need all their strength for the upcoming trip.

How peaceful and safe the world seemed tonight. The rustic cabin, the clear star-lit sky, the crisp, clean air. It might as well be another world. Would they ever see any of it again?

She looked over at him, finally resting quietly after his ordeal. Whatever happened next, she had found something more important than all the pain of her past.

She would not let them take that away from her.

CHAPTER 53

Merritt, New Hampshire
Saturday, 6:00 a.m.

THEY STARTED OUT at the break of dawn. Goddard had already packed the car and had only to load her wounded passenger into the back seat.

Braxton looked a little better. He had gotten a good night's sleep—they playfully discussed the reason behind that—and a pink tinge had returned to his cheeks. Now he looked like an only partially underfed Bohemian.

"Don't you ever get anything normal?" he asked when he saw the arrest-me-red Chevy Camaro. "No wonder that New Hampshire cop followed you."

"Don't complain. I was going to get another BMW, but thought it might be a little too obvious. Anyway, it's comfortable and has lots of power. It might come in handy."

Goddard was to drive the rental car to D.C., then she would get out to work on her to-do list and he would take the car and find a place to stay outside the city. He was adamant that they should stay separated. They needed to be able to keep making progress in case either were caught. The plan agreed to, they locked the cabin, each wondering if they would ever see it again, and headed for Merritt.

Outside Lincoln they picked up I-93. Then south through Concord and Manchester, and into Massachusetts at Lawrence. They followed 93 down to I-95 and took the circumferential south, the old Route 128, America's Technology Highway.

The computer companies were long gone, but 128 now shown bright with the gleam of bio-technology. All born in the research laboratories of Boston and Cambridge. So many fortunes to be made and lost. So many secrets to be protected and exposed. It didn't seem like the area had changed that much after all.

In Canton, 95 split off to the south. The Interstate ran west through Connecticut and New York then down to Baltimore and D.C. They kept with the flow of the traffic, Goddard struggling to stay within five miles per hour of the posted limit. She stopped every couple of hours to stretch her legs and walk off the fatigue of highway monotony.

It was a good day for driving. The roads were dry and clear, and the metropolitan traffic on a Saturday morning was light. They did hit construction on the New Jersey Turnpike, but the work teams were small and the State Troopers paid little attention to the frustrated faces of motorists backed up along miles of seemingly available pavement.

The sun shone brightly all the way down the coast. By the time they reached Maryland, they had even turned on the air conditioning. Goddard had intended to drive the whole way, but finally yielded to Braxton's whining and let him take the final leg from Baltimore.

"Adam?" she asked once they had passed through the Fort McHenry Tunnel under Baltimore Harbor.

"Yes?"

"Yesterday you said Chamberlain's killer was very thorough. He planted evidence, lured you to the scene, called the police."

"Right. It's like he knew everything I was doing."

"You know, that's exactly what Wilson said about Nicholson."

"Nicholson? You don't think he could be involved?"

"You're the one who doesn't believe in coincidences. What do you think?"

Braxton took a moment to respond. "What would be the connection? They could be about the same age, but Warren never had anything to do with politics. He was a hard core technologist."

"A very rich technologist. You said you thought Century's turnaround could have been as a result of sabotage of their competition. That sounds a lot like Nicholson's specialty. Could Chamberlain have done all that by himself?"

"Warren was really bright, but I must admit, I don't see him masterminding a play like that."

"They were in it together. All the murders, all the suspicion."
She was sure this was the answer.

"Hey, slow down. Why would Nicholson want to kill his
partner? He's the aide to a Senator for god's sake. Extortion and
murder may not be his style anymore."

"Oh yes they are." It was time to tell Braxton the rest of what
she knew. "I didn't tell you. Nicholson visited Wilson just after we
were there. He was asking about me. Wilson didn't tell him anything
but that night someone broke into Wilson's office."

"Then they know who you are!" The pain in his shoulder
suddenly ratcheted up.

"No. It's all right. Wilson had taken the files. But Nicholson is
getting closer. And he won't stop."

"We still don't have any proof of a connection. If you're right,
there has to be something in their backgrounds. We can focus on
that. You need to do some more research," he patted his breast
pocket, "and I have to read this damn drive."

They crossed into Virginia at 4:30. Braxton took the George
Washington Parkway along the Potomac then dropped Goddard off
at the Rosslyn Metro station.

"Where are you going?" she asked as she pulled her bag from
the back seat.

"I'm not sure. Somewhere out of the District, maybe Fairfax.
Where should I meet you for dinner?"

"How about Auberge on M Street? About eight?"

"Okay, I'll find it. When you get in, check on your email to see if
Nicholson has sent anything back yet. Maybe he'll have left us
something we can use. Oh, I almost forgot." He pulled the USB
stick out of his pocket and handed it to her. "Get a directory listing
of this. Print out anything that looks interesting. There's got to be
something on here that will help us."

He pulled her over and gave her a kiss. "Don't worry, we'll get
back at them."

She touched his cheek for a moment, then slid out and walked to
the escalator, disappearing underground to the trains. She didn't
look back so he wouldn't see the tears welling in her eyes.

* * *

"Dispatch."

"Hi, Jan. It's Randy. I'm out at the Terrel place."

"Oh. How's your girlfriend?"

"Gone. The place is locked up tight."

"Too bad. I know you wanted to see her again."

"Give me a break, Jan. Guess she didn't want to stay with the memories any longer than necessary."

"Don't blame her on that. See you later, Randy. Dispatch out."

"Collins out."

*　*　*

"Good morning, Clarice. Is Julius in?"

"Oh, good morning, Mr. Greystone. Yes, he's waiting for you." Montonet gave him a quick smile, then buried her head behind her monitor. She had kept to herself even more than usual the past weeks; hiding from the rumors about her and Lombard that still whirled through the office.

She must be quite lonely, the executive thought as he passed her and entered Keane's old office.

Flitterman was on the phone when he came through the door, but waved his Senior Vice President to a small conference table on one side of the room. Other than the table and a massive President's desk, the room was barren. Keane had covered the walls with photographs and paintings, and had placed corporate memorabilia everywhere else, but all of those mementos were gone. On the desk, Flitterman had placed only a plain desk set and a small folding frame with family pictures. Greystone hoped the sparse furnishings pointed to the temporary nature of the assignment.

This morning's meeting was crucial to Greystone's plan. He had to get Flitterman to agree to the alliance. Hajima had made it clear he wouldn't wait any longer. And without Takagawa's engineering, the plan was worthless.

"Robert, good to see you again," Flitterman said as he took up a chair across the table.

"And good to see you, Julius. I must say you look more relaxed when we met last week."

"Thank you. I do feel like we have passed a critical point, Robert. Charles' death was a great loss for all of us, but we must not forget our responsibility to the other employees and to our stock-holders. We must keep Theater viable through this transition."

Despite his feigned compliment, Flitterman looked no better and possibly worse. There was a weary sadness in his expression. His eyelids drooped, and heavy purple sacs hung below his eyes.

The banker can't be used to this level of effort. He probably hasn't worked on a Saturday in twenty years. All the more reason to let go of some of the reins.

"I absolutely agree. You know I will be happy to do whatever I can for the company."

"Thank you, Robert. We all appreciate that very much. Now, what have you brought for me?"

Greystone handed Flitterman a folder of papers. "As you requested, I've put together a briefing on my proposal. First," Greystone pulled a document from his stack, "is this analysis of the new Senate Bill. The *Promoting Freedom and Democracy Bill* they call it. It cleared the Senate Foreign Relations Committee yesterday. We have been working with Senator Potterfield and his staff for several months now, and I believe the results are clear.

"The new technical specifications are based on the proposals we submitted. This Bill puts us in an ideal position to be first to market with a new class of command-and-control communications systems. A class that is guaranteed to be approved for export to countries fighting insurgencies and terrorists. I have also developed some projections of the market potential on the last sheet. You can see what this would do for Theater."

Flitterman thumbed through the pages of his copy. "Yes, they are very promising, Robert. What is your analysis of the Bill, however? Will there be major changes as it goes through the full Senate?"

"We do not expect any. Senator Potterfield is a powerful force on the Hill. He's able to get his way most of the time."

"Still, it would not be prudent to commit to this strategy until we see the final version. Why not wait the next few weeks?"

"There are two problems with waiting, Julius. First, we give the competition time to react and set up their own partnerships. Some of the companies with whom we are in discussions may interpret our delay as a lack of commitment. They too may be afraid of being left out and might seek out other agreements. Second, this is an ideal way to show Wall Street that we have not given up, that we are an innovative and aggressive company in this new market. It would strengthen our credibility significantly."

"*If* the partnerships are effective in creating the new product line and the State Department approves the exports," Flitterman added. "That is my concern with the *Potterfield Bill*. I have seen too many examples of last minute legislative changes that have had significant, and often unforeseen, effects."

Damn. He was so close. Why didn't this banker see the potential? He couldn't let Flitterman off the hook. "I would be happy to set up a meeting between you and the Senator, Julius. Perhaps that would alleviate your concerns."

Flitterman paused and contemplated the suggestion. "No, Robert. That is your territory. I'll review these documents tonight. If you feel this is the right strategy then we should stop arguing and proceed."

Greystone tried to remain calm. Soon they would all see how perfect the plan was. It would, without question, succeed, and he would be recognized as the genius behind it. "Thank you, Julius. I will work out the operational details over the next few days."

"Just one thing, Robert. I don't want to begin implementation for a week or so. We need all the publicity around Lombard to die down. The State Police are still continuing their investigation."

"Why? I thought they had all the evidence they needed?" Hajima was right! There was a problem with the investigation. How had he found out?

"I don't know the details, but I spoke with Agent Jefferson and he said there were some discrepancies in times and some unexplained evidence at Charles' estate. We can't have any more adverse publicity. No, we have to wait until this clears. For now, you watch the Bill. And pray nothing happens with it."

"Yes, of course, Julius. I'll monitor it carefully." He couldn't hold Hajima off indefinitely. He needed another deadline to keep Flitterman in line. "Let's get together later next week and review the status," Greystone suggested.

"Fine, Robert. Thank you again for coming in."

That should be enough to keep Hajima off his back. Now he could devote more attention to the other problems.

His mind shifted to Braxton and Goddard as he left the office. The damn consultant was still loose and now he was tied into the Lynch affair. If that went public, Potterfield would be history and the Bill would die. He couldn't afford to have Nicholson running loose.

"Good bye, Mr. Greystone," Montonet said interrupting his concentration.

He stopped and looked over to the secretary. "Clarice," he replied walking back toward her desk. "How is Julius treating you? Well, I hope?"

*   *   *

The young black man had been on duty since seven that morning. He had read every book from his small apartment, and his bladder was about to explode from the coffee he had consumed. There had been a few strange looks over the past few days, but he had moved among four different surveillance points and had changed his outfit at least twice a shift.

His partner wouldn't be back for two more hours. The twelve hour schedule he had created was a killer, but it saved him a lot of money. He hoped the target would show up on his shift. The ten grand bonus would be real handy.

He was about to head for the bathroom in the McDonalds down the street when he saw a woman walking up from the Metro station. He pulled the tattered picture from his pocket, made sure he had the image fixed in his head, then jaywalked across the street. Turning at the curb, he walked toward her. They passed as she reached the entrance to the building.

"If it ain't the bitch," he whispered.

CHAPTER 54

GODDARD ARRIVED AT Auberge first, took their table and ordered a bottle of Merlot. She was on her second glass when Braxton appeared fifteen minutes later, out of breath and looking like he'd run a marathon.

"Adam, are you okay?" she pleaded as he sat down.

He huffed for a minute before responding. "Yes, I'm fine. But parking in this city is worse than Boston. I finally found a space five blocks away. I didn't want to be late so I ran the rest of the way."

She wanted to jump across the table and strangle him. "Do you realize how stupid that was? You've been shot, for heaven's sake." After her heart quit pounding she shook her head. "I really can't leave you alone, can I?"

"Nice to see you again, too," he replied and gave her a peck on her cheek.

She flashed her most irritated scowl, then filled his glass with the deep red wine.

"To our health," she said lifting her glass. "It looks like you could still use some."

"Okay, point taken." He clicked her glass with his. "Forgive me?"

"I'm thinking about it. How is your shoulder?"

"Not too bad." He rotated his arm and only winced once. "It's still sore but at least I can move it."

"Did you find a place to stay?"

"More or less. I rented a room at an old motel in Vienna. It's pretty small but the place is isolated and I can come and go without any hassle. And it's not very far from the Metro in case we need to dump the car. It'll do for now."

She squinted at him across the table. He was wearing a blue sports coat, snappy striped blue oxford shirt and Docker trousers. "Where did you get the new outfit?"

"I'm so glad you noticed," he said with a grin. "I stopped at Wal-Mart and picked up a few things. Those wool shirts you bought in New Hampshire were getting a little scratchy."

"It looks like you did just fine. Maybe I can let you out on your own."

A pencil-thin waitress wearing a blonde butch haircut, black lipstick and a black sheath dress appeared at the table and recited a long list of nightly specials with a well-practiced indifference. They looked at each other blankly. Finally, Goddard spoke and ordered a filet mignon for two.

"Thanks," Braxton said as the waitress left. "I wasn't up to making any more decisions tonight."

"That's what I figured."

"Did you have any messages?"

"Nothing on the telephone or email. I did get a package from Wilson. It was some background on Nicholson." She reached into her purse, pulled out a sheath of papers, and handed then to Braxton. "He's been with Potterfield for over thirty years. They must be really close."

Braxton reviewed the documents. "Hey. Nicholson went to MIT. So did Chamberlain."

"Are you sure that's where he went?"

"Absolutely, he wouldn't let anyone forget it. Chamberlain could have known Nicholson from school. Can you check the library tomorrow and get some more detail? Attendance dates, previous employers? Maybe we'll find more that ties them together."

"Sure. Georgetown's got a great library. I'll go over first thing in the morning."

"What about Chamberlain's flash drive?" Braxton asked as he handed the papers back.

"Unfortunately, it wasn't very helpful." She reached back into her purse and set the drive on the table. "There was only one file and it was nearly ten megabytes. I tried to print some of it out but all I got was gibberish."

He picked up the drive and stuck it in his shirt pocket. "What was the name of the file?"

"Journal dot pee gee pee."

"A journal! Warren must have kept a history of everything he did. That would be just like him. It could explain why he was killed."

"And why he wanted you to have it. But I couldn't read any of it."

"It was encrypted. That's what the PGP means. He didn't even trust his own systems."

"What's PGP?" Goddard asked.

"PGP stands for Pretty Good Privacy. It is the name of a set of programs that perform encryption and decryption. PGP is based on a technology called public key encryption. It was developed in the nineteen-nineties by three academic researchers. It was so good the NSA tried to get the algorithm declared secret because they couldn't break it. There were a lot of legal battles, but eventually so much documentation was made public, NSA just gave up.

"PGP is used for email, files, databases, all kinds of information. If used correctly, and I'm sure Warren did, it would take years to crack the encoded text. That's what you saw when you tried to print out the file."

Braxton had obviously recovered from his run. His eyes were twinkling and his cheeks were flushed with pink. He was really cute.

"Thanks for the lecture, professor," she said with a smile. "But does that mean we can't read it?"

"Without some help, probably not. But I'm sure Warren tried to give me a clue to the passkey. I've got some routines in my account in Boston that we can use. I'll get them tomorrow."

"How can you do that?"

"I was thinking I'd go back to GW and use their systems. I can route through Ramal's account to access my Cambridge files and the archive at CERT."

"What if someone is monitoring the accounts?"

"I'll be hiding behind the GW computers. I can cover my tracks pretty well."

"I hope so. Just be careful."

Their dinners arrived and they turned their attention to the skillfully-prepared meal. The conversation drifted off into more mundane topics, both of them badly needing a few moments away from the tension of the past days. As they were finishing their entrees Braxton noticed that his companion kept looking past him toward the door.

"Is something wrong?"

"I don't know," she replied. Her voice dropped to a whisper. "There's a man at one of the tables in the front. He keeps looking over this way."

"He's probably just flirting with the very attractive lady sitting across from me."

"Adam, I'm serious." She gave him a very hurt look.

"I'm sorry. But there's no way anyone could know we're here. And if it was the police they would have arrested me by now."

"I'm not worried about the police. I think it's Barclay Nicholson."

Braxton started to turn around but thought better of it. "Are you sure?"

"I think so." She pulled out the papers Lexington had sent her and found the photograph. "It's him, Adam. How did he find us?"

"If he was able to discover who you are, he could have been watching your apartment. Let me see the photo again."

She handed it over. "I'm so sorry," she pleaded. "I didn't think anyone was following me."

"It's all right. There's no way you could have known. Besides, he could have tracked the rental and identified me. We don't know how he found us and it doesn't matter. We just have to find a way out of here that he won't notice."

He motioned for the waitress and asked for their check. As he turned to pay, he looked across the room. A stocky, well-dressed black man was busily eating a plate of pasta at a corner table. He was a little bit older than the picture in the photograph, but it was clearly Nicholson.

The waitress took the bills and Braxton turned back to his companion. "You need to go to the ladies' room."

"What?"

"Go on. It's in the back to the right. I'll meet you there in a few minutes. Then we'll find another way out."

"Okay, but don't be long or I'll be back to get you." She stood and headed for the rear of the restaurant.

He considered leaving without her to draw Nicholson away. But he couldn't be sure the aide would follow him. Goddard was his most likely target.

Braxton waited three minutes then followed her to the back. The man in the corner didn't move. He went down a narrow hallway and knocked on the door marked "Madame". Goddard emerged looking as frightened as he had ever seen her.

"Now where are we going?" she asked.

"The servers come down this hall when they deliver food. The kitchen has to be this way. And there's got to be a delivery door there we can use to get out."

He took her hand and they followed the hallway around the corner. In front of them was a pair of swinging doors.

They pushed through the doors into the kitchen. The room was filled with huge stainless steel tables and rows of cooking paraphernalia. An immense gas stove filled the left wall where four white-hatted chefs attended to the preparations. The smell of garlic and frying oil permeated an atmosphere already heavy with heat and humidity. Braxton felt a wisp of cool air brush past him and headed for its origin. Next to a gigantic built-in refrigerator was an open exit door, the cooler night air providing some relief to the employees stuck in the sweltering heat.

Ignoring the startled looks of the kitchen staff, they shoved their way through the aisle and escaped into the fresh air behind the restaurant.

* * *

Antonio, the head chef, was appalled. Sure that the impolite diners had chosen to leave his establishment without paying, he yelled something in Italian at them, then left a skillet of simmering osso buco to his younger brother and stormed into the main dining room.

The black man in the corner didn't understand French, but he observed the commotion and gesturing between the chef and the maître d' attentively. He threw a pile of bills on the table and ran out the front.

CHAPTER 55

Bʀᴀxᴛᴏɴ Qᴜɪᴄᴋʟʏ ʟᴏᴏᴋᴇᴅ around. They were in an alley along-side the restaurant. It was littered with trash cans and empty produce boxes, the waste products of the businesses that lined the narrow access way. Light streaming from the restaurant's kitchen provided the main illumination. To his right, the alley opened back onto M Street. On his left, the pavement sloped down to an area behind the buildings. The deserted passage was no place to be if Nicholson came to look for them.

"This way," he whispered, grabbing Goddard's hand and running down the incline.

The alley ended at a foot path that paralleled M Street and ran along the old Chesapeake and Ohio Canal. The C&O Canal was the last intact example of the great canals of the nineteenth century. Originally George Washington's dream to connect the Potomac to the West, the C&O had only gotten as far as Cumberland, Maryland before it lost its economic advantage to the railroad. Established as a National Monument in 1961, the canal and its banks were now frequented primarily by jogging enthusiasts during the day and strolling lovers at night.

A rusty pipe guard rail was all that separated the foot path from a six foot fall into the early spring mud. Braxton and Goddard took a right at the end of the alley trying to put as much distance between them and the restaurant as possible. The spill-over glow from M Street provided enough light for their flight down the old brick way.

They couldn't stay on the path. They were too conspicuous by themselves and the alleys and building corners left too many places for an attacker to hide.

"Let's get back to M," he said between breaths. "We can lose him in the crowds, then circle back to the car." He started to pull her up the next alley.

She resisted his lead. "Not this way. It's too dark. Wisconsin is only a little way farther, it's more public."

He took her suggestion and they continued down the foot path. They were about a hundred yards from the cross street when a tall shadow stepped into their path. His hands were in his pockets and he slowly walked toward them.

Goddard pulled them to a stop. "It's Nicholson!"

"You can't be sure. It's too dark."

"It's him. I just know. We've got to turn around." Her voice was near panic. She spun around and headed up the alley they had just passed. Braxton had no choice but to follow. They saw the traffic of M Street only fifty yards ahead.

Beams of light suddenly shot out from the gloom. They shielded their eyes and saw a huge truck rolling down the alley toward them. There was no room on either side for them to squeeze past. Braxton was not about to second guess the delivery van and pulled Goddard back toward the canal path.

He hoped Nicholson had seen them enter the alley and had gone back up to M to cut them off. If he had, they could go back toward the restaurant, then cross the canal farther down. He would never be able to follow them that far.

They had nearly reached the foot of the alley when the truck's lights disappeared. They kept running as their eyes adjusted to the darkness.

The trash can rolled directly in their path. Braxton managed to side-step it, but it struck Goddard's right foot and she went down hard on her knees. She grabbed for Braxton and pulled him after her, both ending sprawled on the rough brick surface. Goddard's legs were bleeding, and Braxton's jacket and trousers were ripped. Both were gasping for breath and partially dazed from the fall.

The can continued down the slope, clattering all the way to the railing.

"Mr. Braxton and Ms. Goddard," a deep resonant voice said

from out of the shadows. "Or should I say Lynch? How nice to finally meet you. I have been looking for you for weeks."

Nicholson calmly stepped in front of the pair. He was wearing a long grey coat that billowed in the light breeze. As they started to get up, he pulled a huge-looking automatic pistol from one of the coat's pockets. His face was relaxed; his expression one of a man used to being in control.

Braxton stood up first, then helped his companion. "Are you okay?" he whispered.

"Fine." She said bravely. "So far."

Goddard's hands were bloody and she was shaking badly. Braxton put his arm around her and she clung tightly to his side.

"What now, Mr. Nicholson?" Braxton asked. "Another accident on the streets of Georgetown?"

"Unfortunately yes, Mr. Braxton. Crime is getting so out of hand in the District. It will be just another senseless murder."

"You're the murderer!" Goddard cried, pointing a bloody finger in his direction. "You killed my father!"

"As I remember he did that to himself, Ms. Lynch." Nicholson's face was impassive.

The words sliced at her heart. "But *you* destroyed him. You and all the lies."

"He was a politician," Nicholson replied, as if that was a satisfactory explanation. "He understood the game. But apparently not well enough. He simply wouldn't listen to reason."

"Someone will stop you." The words spit from Goddard's mouth.

"Perhaps the 'Citizens for Responsible Government'? I commend you on the use of the remailer. It had the Senator quite upset. Did you think of that yourself or did the consultant here help you?"

"Mohammed helped me you bastard! Why did you have to kill him?"

"That Arab helped you? What a strange coincidence. I really had nothing to do with him. He simply stumbled onto something he should have left alone. It was his own fault. Not unlike your bringing up old memories, Ms. Lynch. Some things should just be left alone."

"How did you find us?" Braxton asked.

"Quite accidentally. I recognized Ms. Lynch's new name when

we were looking for you. I had her followed. Finding you with her is an added bonus. It makes things so much easier."

"I suppose you killed Paul Terrel as well?" Braxton asked.

"Not personally. But I'm sure you've guessed we were after you. I promise I won't make the same mistake they did."

"You won't get away with killing us." Goddard said.

"Of course I will." Nicholson's voice was cold and emotionless. "I'd probably even get an award if I stayed around to take the credit. You're so hypocritical, Ms. Goddard. You're both wanted criminals. Mr. Braxton killed one of my friends. He will pay dearly for that."

Braxton and Goddard exchanged confused glances.

"Killed your friend?" Braxton said. "I didn't kill Warren, if that's who you mean. I was set up. Didn't you do it?"

"I don't have time for these games, Braxton. It won't change anything." He straightened his arm and pointed the pistol at Braxton's head.

Goddard pulled herself even closer and buried her head into his chest. The pinch he felt from his shirt pocket gave him an idea. It was a long shot but it was all he had. He only needed one moment of distraction.

"I would think you would want to know what we have learned first. Warren's journal was very enlightening."

Nicholson's hold on the pistol relaxed. "Journal? What are you talking about?"

"Oh, you didn't know that your partner Chamberlain had kept a computer journal of your exploits? It tells all about Senator Lynch and Senator Potterfield, all about the trapdoor in Century's gateways. I designed that access point. Did you think I wouldn't be able to recognize it?"

Nicholson hesitated. His smile disappeared. "You're bluffing. Warren would never leave a journal."

"He gave it to me just before he died. It goes all the way back to MIT. I know all about the cash too."

Nicholson's eyes opened wide in surprise. Then Braxton heard the roar of an engine behind him and suddenly the alley was again ablaze in light from the truck's head lamps. Nicholson cried out and raised his arm to block the blinding glare.

Braxton saw the opening and reacted. One thing he had not told Goddard was that he had entered Boston College on a football scholarship; he prayed all that practice had not been in vain. He lunged at Nicholson like a linebacker, carefully leading with his right shoulder, lifting and driving him across the path. The surprised aide tried to keep his balance but couldn't stop the younger man's fanatical momentum.

Nicholson's back hit the top rail of the guard fence and cracked like a shattered baseball bat. His gun, caught between the two hurtling bodies, exploded with a flash.

Braxton jumped back and saw Nicholson slide down the railing to the ground. Red liquid oozed from a dark hole in the raincoat.

Goddard muffled a scream and ran across the path.

"My God!" she cried as she saw the body. "Is he dead?"

Braxton reached down and placed his index finger on Nicholson's neck. "I think so," he replied.

"Are you all right?"

Braxton looked down at himself, almost expecting to see a hole in *his* jacket. He was so pumped full of adrenaline he doubted he would have felt the pain.

He patted his chest, shook his arms and replied with a quiet, "I guess."

She threw her arms around him and squeezed so tight he thought he would break. After they both stopped shaking, he slowly pushed her arms away and stared down at Nicholson.

Now he really had murdered someone. It was self-defense but no one was ever going to believe them now. The police would know he was in D.C. and focus the search even tighter.

Worst of all he had involved Goddard.

"What are you doing?" she whispered as Braxton knelt down next to the body.

She turned her head and saw the truck driver getting out of his cab to see what had happened. "We've got to get out of here!"

"I need to find something first." He searched Nicholson's pockets and stuffed what he found in his jacket.

Glancing at the gun at Nicholson's side, he shook his head. Better to leave it. Megan had been right. Guns do only bring tragedy.

"Now we run." He grabbed her hand and they raced down the path to Wisconsin, eventually disappearing into the evening crowds on M Street.

CHAPTER 56

Georgetown, Washington, D.C.
Saturday, 10:00 p.m.

"T HIS IS INSANE, Adam. You can't go in there."

They were parked along Forsythe Street in Georgetown. It was only five blocks from where they had encountered Nicholson, but felt like a world away. Forsythe was a quiet neighborhood of million dollar brownstones. The inhabitants were embassy staffers and upper level government employees who traded smaller homes than their Virginia and Maryland colleagues for proximity to the city center. The properties were well kept and exclusive, Rock Creek Park separating them from the urban dangers of the rest of the District.

They had picked up the rental, driven to Forsythe and spent the last half hour sitting in the car watching the house at number 2376. There had been no visible activity. When another car drove by they had either ducked out of sight or assumed an amorous embrace. So far no one had bothered them.

"Nobody's going to come," Braxton said emphatically. "I took Nicholson's wallet and keys. They haven't had time to identify him. I'm going in and look around. He must have some kind of records; something that will link him to Chamberlain or your father."

"If you're going, I'm coming too."

"No you're not. You're going to stay here and keep a lookout. I'll stay a half an hour. If anybody comes around, honk your horn and leave. I'll get out and meet you on Wisconsin. Please, Susan, we've got to get some evidence or we'll be running the rest of our lives."

"All right, but take care of yourself." Then she added, "I love you."

"I love you too. See you in an hour." He kissed her hard on the lips and jumped out of the car.

The row houses were close to the street; it only took him fifteen seconds to cross the street and dash up the five steps to get to the door. There were four keys on Nicholson's key ring: one was imprinted with the distinctive Mercedes logo, two more were easily recognized government issue, the last was a heavy duty Schlage. He ducked into the shadows of the entry way and tried the Schlage. It turned easily and he went inside.

Street light filtered through the transom above the door and fell on a deeply carpeted hallway. Braxton groped along the side wall, found a light switch, and flipped it on. Above him a crystal chandelier filled the foyer with sparkling light; ahead and to his right a staircase spiraled up to the next floor.

A large room opened to his left. He gave it a quick look and verified that there was little of interest. It was a formal living room, appointed with expensive leather furniture and varied *objets d'art*. It had the warmth of a professional decorator. Braxton doubted that Nicholson spent much time there.

He moved deeper into the home going through an oak-paneled gathering room and entering the dining area in the back of the first floor. Arched windows looked out upon a small but well-manicured back yard and garden. He poked his head in the kitchen, then gave up on the first floor and started up the stairs.

Braxton didn't expect any trouble, he actually believed most of what he had told Goddard, but his heart was racing and his hands shook as he climbed the stairs. From murderer to cat burglar in one night. He was doing really well.

A carillon of electronic tones froze him on the landing. At first he thought he had tripped some kind of alarm, but the regular rhythm exposed them as telephones. There had to be at least five of them, chiming from all over the house.

After three rings, he heard Nicholson's disembodied voice coming from an answering machine up the stairs. The pretentious greeting ended and the machine waited for a response. None came. A final click from the device and Braxton's heart started beating again. He continued climbing to the second floor.

To his left a set of French doors led to a large room above the living room. A single door faced him on the side wall and another was to his right. A new flight of stairs curled around the stairwell to the third floor.

The double doors opened onto Nicholson's play room. There was no other way to describe it. One whole wall was covered with electronic devices and controls: two complete stereo systems, various electronic games, multiple brands of DVD players, all clustered around a huge six-foot projection screen. Hanging from the ceiling was a triple beam professional video projector. A matched set of sofa and five chairs were splayed in an arc through the middle of the room.

Bookshelves filled the wall behind the furniture. He scanned the titles and came away impressed but disappointed; Nicholson had a diverse collection of popular fiction, historical and political titles, and biographies of statesmen and sports figures. Good references, but nothing that would shed light on his clandestine activities. He pulled a few of the books to check on their authenticity then decided to move on. If Nicholson had wanted to really hide something in these volumes it would take him all night to find it.

He had to find an office.

The middle door led to a bathroom. It was clean, functional, and distinctly masculine. Another door connected to a large rear bedroom that appeared to be for guests. It was neat and sterile, without any personal touches. He checked the closet and bureau drawers, they were empty, then left by a second door that led back to the landing.

One more floor to go, he thought, as he started up the stairs. The third story felt much closer and confining. Darkness enclosed him as he passed the ceiling of the open stairwell. He found a light switch at the top of the stairs and looked down the quiet corridor. Recessed flood lights washed the side wall with soft ovals of light, each beam highlighting a delicate pen-and-ink of the Virginia countryside. Five doors lined the corridor: three along the side and one at each end.

He started at the front. It was a small sitting room that connected to Nicholson's bedroom. The master suite was the only area of the house that looked as if it was ever used. Clothes were hung on a few handy chairs and the bedspread was thrown casually back over the bed. Aside from one hardback novel and a copy of the *Wall Street Journal*, there was nothing of interest in the suite.

Two more doors led to a bathroom and linen closet.

All that was left was the door at the back end of the hall. He tentatively pulled it open. There was no question that he had finally found what he had been searching for. A small bedroom had been converted to a computerized information center. It looked like a TV control room. Lined up on a long modern desk were two large flat panel monitors with a keyboard and mouse, a high-speed HP laser printer and Fujitsu scanner. A professional CD burner/duplicator sat on top of a cluttered media cabinet. More wires and cables came from communication hookup boxes on the wall. Nicholson had indulged himself in nothing but the best.

Bookshelves next to the window contained the latest Internet publications, computer science references, and indices on data repositories. Folders and other documents were stacked in piles on the floor.

He checked the stacks and found a wealth of business and financial information on military suppliers. There were Dun and Bradstreet summaries, 10K filings, and Dow Jones reports. Nicholson had been doing some heavy background work, undoubtedly in support of Potterfield's Bill, but it all looked like public information.

Braxton hit a key on the keyboard and the monitors woke up, filling every corner of the room with light. A pulsing password window appeared. He considered guessing, but given what he knew about Nicholson that would be a waste of time; time he didn't have. Lugging the whole deskside unit was possible, but that would be a last choice. Better to finish his search first.

Running out of other options, he finally tried the closet. He pulled back the double doors expecting to find a space full of old clothes and forgotten shoe boxes. Instead he faced six three-drawer government filing cabinets. The back of the closet had been cut out and extended to make room for the massive units.

Nicholson was obviously "old-school": he still believed in paper. Braxton had hoped to find a well-marked set of CDs with all the incriminating evidence. A quick grab and he would have been done. This was going to be substantially more complicated.

The six cabinets were organized into pairs. The first two were marked "Systems", the second two "Senate", and the third set

"Other". Within each pair, the drawers were labeled with alphabetic ranges. Nicholson apparently wasn't concerned about security in his own home; the cabinets were unlocked.

Braxton started with the "Systems" section. After checking two or three drawers he determined they contained background on computer procedures and networking, including a complete set of Internet RFCs, reference documents and specifications. Good data for a computer jock, but nothing that would implicate Nicholson in the recent events.

The second two cabinets were equally disappointing. They contained copies of old Senate Bills, legislative history, and policy and procedure manuals.

He apprehensively opened the top drawer in the last set of cabinets. It was crammed with folders each with a name on the small label at its top. He pulled one at random and shuffled through the contents. The file was filled with computer printouts of telephone logs, credit card bills, and what looked like private investigator reports. It was a personal history of a Wilmont Brankowitz. Braxton didn't recognize the name, but from what he could read, Mr. Brankowitz was another Senate aide who had rather unique sexual preferences. He would certainly not appreciate any of the information being made public.

Braxton stuffed the file back in the drawer and slammed it shut. He reached for the drawer labeled "K-M".

CHAPTER 57

Georgetown, Washington, D.C.
Saturday, 10:15 p.m.

Had Braxton been more observant when he entered the town-house, he would have noticed the small panel on the wall opposite the light switch in the foyer. As he had opened the door, the red LED began to blink. Thirty seconds later, a coded message was sent over Nicholson's telephone line to Capitol Security Services in Rockville, Maryland.

Jerry Cooper, a three year veteran of Capitol, saw the alert on his terminal and checked the client's record. The owner, a Barclay Nicholson, had been a real pain-in-the-ass recently, complaining to Capitol of numerous false alarms that had resulted in substantial charges from the District Police.

Cooper checked the alarm code and determined that it was due to a normal entry from the front door. He figured Nicholson had probably just forgotten to reset the alarm. He waited a few minutes to give the owner time to remember, then gave him a call. When the call went unanswered, Cooper decided he had better forward the alarm.

Dispatcher Liza Benedict took the call from Capitol at 10:38. She checked the log and verified the cars on duty in the area. Fortunately for Braxton, it was another busy night in the Second District. There was an accident on Key Bridge, and two teams had just been dispatched to M Street to check on a reported assault. It took three minutes for the dispatcher to get through to Patrolman Roger Loudon.

Loudon checked with the officer-in-charge after getting the call.

The assault turned out to be a murder and they would need all the patrolmen they could get to control the scene. His superior told him to investigate the alarm and then get back to the murder scene as soon as possible.

Ten minutes later Loudon turned onto Forsythe Street. The street was deserted, not unexpected for that hour, except for a lone Chevrolet Camaro parked across from his destination. The driver was a pretty young blonde. He was about to call for wants and warrants when she beeped her horn twice, waved good-bye to a friend in the townhouse, and pulled away.

Canceling the request, he had enough things to worry about already, he reported his position and got out to check the house. There didn't seem to be any evidence of a forced entry, which was consistent with the security company's report. He walked up the front stairs and noticed that the front door was ajar. Not normal behavior for a resident of D.C. Putting the flashlight in his left hand, Loudon drew his revolver, and pushed open the door.

* * *

As Braxton pulled the folder labeled Kenneth Lynch, he heard a car horn. At first it didn't register, but then he remembered his instructions to Goddard. Folder in hand, he went down the hall to the sitting room and looked out through the curtains to the street below. The rental car was gone and there was a police cruiser stopped in front of the house.

"Dammit," he whispered.

He went back to the hallway and listened for some sign of the police. He didn't hear anything. Walking as softly as possible he stepped down the deeply carpeted stairs and peered into the open staircase. He didn't see any movement and decided to sneak out the back door while the cops were still searching the front yard.

As he continued down the stairs, a beam of light flashed across the floor on the first floor. He froze. Someone was swinging a flashlight and searching the rooms. The light hit the stairs and a figure started moving up to the second floor.

He was trapped. He'd never get past the policeman on the next floor and he was sure to work his way upstairs. Where could he hide? The rooms on the third floor had all been spacious and neat. They offered little in the way of cover.

Images of capture and detention flashed into his mind; cameras and lawyers and sensational publicity. He would be convicted before he set foot in a courtroom.

He would not cower in a corner and wait to be discovered. There had to be another way.

Sneaking back to Nicholson's office Braxton looked out the window. The moon lit the grass and garden in the rear yard. Directly below the window, only one story down, was a small roof that jutted out from the rough stone wall of the townhouse. Braxton guessed it covered the rear entrance to the building. It would be a simple jump from the roof to the yard below. If he could just climb the ten feet between the window and the roof, he could get away while the cop was still searching the house.

He folded the Lynch file in half and stuck it in his coat pocket. As quietly as he could, he opened the window and felt the face of the wall. The stones of the facade were rough and large, nearly one foot square. They were square struck, the deep set mortar providing ample room for solid foot and finger holds. He and Terrel had climbed rock faces a lot tougher than this.

The sound of a squeaking door came from the floor below. It was time to get going.

Braxton lowered himself out the window, grabbing onto the sill and searching for a foot hold. His toes found a solid edge and he shifted his weight from his arms to his legs. He moved off to the left, clearing the sill and avoiding the second floor window directly below him.

He slowly moved down the wall one block at a time. At first, adrenaline masked the pain in his shoulder; it reasserted itself as he continued the descent. He was badly out of shape and the effort was exhausting him. His shoulder screamed whenever he stretched to get a new foothold.

He had to stop halfway down to get his breath. His heart pounded; his breathing rapid and shallow. Sweat started to dampen his hands. All bad signs. Time was running out.

He was opposite the window in the back guest room when a light flashed out of the dark interior. The surprise broke his concentration. He muffled a scream as his shoulder gave out and he lost his footing. His feet scrambling on the wall to get a hold, he hung by the fingertips of his right hand as the beam of light scanned across the back yard. His toes finally found a wide ridge and he clung to the wall in desperation. The light turned back into the room.

He counted to one hundred to give the cop time to move out of the room, then restarted his descent. All he could hear was the rush of blood through his head and the pounding in his chest. His legs were trembling from the buildup of lactic acid. He made one more course of block before his strength left him completely. His fingers slipped and he slid down the remaining four feet of the wall.

The roof struck him while he was still trying to remember all of the techniques for breaking falls. He pulled into a crouch and rolled. The slope directed him down, over the side of the entryway and into one of the flower beds.

He hit the ground hard, nearly losing consciousness, but fought to keep control. Looking up, he was in clear view of the back of the house. He scrambled on his hands and knees back behind the structure.

The fall had taken its toll; his trousers were ripped open, and his knees and shins were scraped and bloody. The pounding in his head had lessened but there was a sharp pain over his right eye. He wiped the sweat from his face with his arm and saw a red streak on the sleeve. Still, nothing seemed to be broken, and he hadn't heard any reaction from the house.

He waited another three minutes, then crawled along the side fence to the back of the property. The bushes were thicker and higher the farther he went. The fence suddenly stopped and just as abruptly the ground turned into sharp, painful gravel. It was an access road that tracked between two streets of houses. The end of the block was down to the right.

He tried to brush himself off, gave up, and awkwardly jogged down the path.

*   *   *

Patrolman Loudon finished his search of the house at 11:20. When he found the open window in the rear office he looked down with his flashlight and saw dark stains on the stone and back roof. He called in a probable burglary and went downstairs to check out the rear yard.

*   *   *

Braxton saw the Camaro on the corner of Forsythe and Wisconsin.

He crept up from behind and tried to get a look at the driver. Seeing Goddard, he breathed a sigh of relief.

He knocked on the window and she nearly jumped through the roof. Her mouth moved rapidly and silently, he was just as glad he couldn't hear her, then she reached over and unlocked the door.

"What happened to you!" she cried as he climbed in the car. "I've been waiting for half an hour. I thought the police had found you." She gasped as she looked at his appearance. "You look awful."

"That seems to be a common occurrence." He patted the folder in his sport coat. "I think I found something interesting, but right now, let's just get out of here."

"Where to? My place?"

"No. Not after Nicholson found us. We don't know who else knows about us. We'll have to go to the motel."

"I get the greatest offers from you," she said as she pulled away from the curb. "What did you find?"

"We may finally have some proof. Nicholson had two cabinets full of personal dossiers. I took the one on your father." He opened the folder and turned on the small map light. "Unbelievable," he said a few minutes later.

"What does it say?"

"According to these documents, Nicholson and Potterfield had tried everything they knew to get something they could hold over your father. When all the investigations turned up empty they created a fictitious kickback scheme. There are copies of private correspondence and records of payoffs to bank employees and real estate lawyers. They did one helluva job."

"Then we have enough to clear my father!" Goddard nearly took her hands off the wheel to hug him. "Where can we take this?"

"We can't. That's the problem. Nicholson was right. No one will believe anything we have. They'd just say we made it up."

Braxton's mind was racing. They now knew what had happened but no hard evidence that could directly tie Nicholson to the actions.

"The police are looking for me, and you're now an accomplice. We need some kind of corroboration for this file. Unless we can make a direct connection between Nicholson and the deaths of Ramal and Chamberlain, we'll still be fugitives."

"Then what can we do?"

"We have to break the encryption of Chamberlain's journal."

CHAPTER 58

Vienna, Virginia
Sunday, 7:15 a.m.

GODDARD KNEW THERE was no use in trying to sleep any longer. She rubbed the haze out of her eyes and turned to her right. Her partner-in-crime lay on the far side of the bed. A fear that he might have died in the night shot through her, but the slow swell of the blanket betrayed Braxton's peaceful state. He had fallen immediately asleep when they had returned from the adventures of the night before.

How could he sleep like that? It's just like a man.

She, on the other hand, had been a jangle of nerves. Exhaustion had finally overcome her three hours into a Troy Donahue cinema extravaganza being shown on channel 53, but she still had tossed in the small double bed most of the night.

She carefully slipped out of bed, showered, and was finishing getting dressed when a movement from the bed caught her eye. An arm emerged from under the covers followed by a mass of dark, greasy hair.

"What time is it?" Braxton mumbled.

"It's time for you to get up. It's 7:40. I'm taking the car."

He stretched and sat up against the rough plywood headboard. "Where are you off to this early?"

"I've got some research to do, remember? I want to get to the library before all the study cubes are taken. It'll be a lot more private." She pulled her hair to the back of her head and tied it neatly in place with a deep blue elastic scrunchy. "Anything else you want me to do?"

"We ought to call Fowler sometime, but I don't want to do it from here. I'll call him later. How are we doing on cash? I'm pretty low after the clothes and the room."

She walked over to the dresser and checked her purse. "I'm down to about thirty dollars. We probably could use some more. I'll go up into Maryland and use my bank card." Goddard closed the purse, threw the strap over her shoulder, and turned for the door.

"That sounds okay. Just be careful. Before you go, I've been thinking . . ."

She jerked her head back to face him. "What now, Adam? I've got to go."

"Hey, don't jump on me. I thought we were in this together?"

She sighed and recognized the return of the fear and anger that had driven her for much too long. "I'm sorry. I'm just so scared. Mostly for you. We've got to get some evidence on Potterfield."

"We'll get it. All I need is my password and decryption software. You'll see." He managed a smile. "I am a hot shot consultant after all."

This time Braxton's enthusiasm couldn't break her concern. "But you can't stay at GW. They'll eventually trace the connection."

He nodded. "That's the problem. I can't just sit there trying to decrypt the drive. It could take hours." Suddenly his smile turned into a devilish grin. "Now if I had a good laptop, I could come back here and ..."

Goddard's mouth dropped open. "You want me to buy you a computer?"

"Can your credit line handle it? It would make it a lot easier to work on the drive and to talk with Flanagan at CERT."

"I think I can do it." She picked up her bag and shook her head. "You are not a cheap date, Adam Braxton." She had managed a weak smile but it had disappeared by the time she reached the door. "Please be careful. I want to see you back here this afternoon."

"Guaranteed," he replied with another grin. "Good luck on your search."

As she was closing the door she heard a yell from the bed, "Oh, and we might need a printer too."

* * *

He lay in the bed another half hour watching the Sunday morning news programs. Nicholson's death was a top story, but there was no report on a break-in at his townhouse. The incident was being described as a fatal mugging. Braxton's name was never mentioned.

His own condition could not be described quite so positively. He felt like he had been rolled in a wet sandbox. Dirt and caked sweat encased his body. The cuts on his arms and legs were red with inflammation and a purple bruise on his forehead was tender to his touch. He had also torn some of the freshly healed tissue on his shoulder. It was time to get cleaned up.

He showered, trimmed his beard, and smeared antibiotic ointment on the wounds. Breakfast was a handful of aspirin. The preparations didn't take the pain away completely but they were the best he could do at the moment.

He grabbed a pair of jeans, an oxford shirt and a rugby pullover from the sacks on the floor. His trip to Wal-Mart the day before had been limited to the basic necessities: underwear, toiletries, and a couple of changes of clothes. Not a lot, but enough to get through the next few days. And who knew what would happen after that?

Still worried about his financial state, he checked his wallet and found a lone twenty dollar bill. More than enough to get to GW and back.

He walked to the Vienna Metro station, picking up a couple of donuts and a cup of coffee on the way, and took the train to Rosslyn. Back up on the street, he found a pay phone in a convenience store and dialed Fowler's home. The detective's wife answered and gave the phone to her husband.

"Fowler," said the sleepy voice.

"Good morning, Detective. It's Adam."

"Braxton? Where are you? I thought you were driving in today?"

"There was a change in plans. We got in last night. I need you to check on something."

"Hey, slow down. You need *me* to do something? I need you to tell me what the hell's going on. What else are you involved in?"

Braxton didn't have time to dance around his problems with the detective. "Did you hear about the Nicholson murder last night?"

"Yeah. Senator Potterfield's aide. Jesus, you didn't have anything to do with that did you?"

"I'm afraid I did. He tried to kill us."

"And the break-in at Nicholson's home?"

"That was me too. That's what I need you to look at."

"Why would Nicholson want to kill you? What would the aide to a Senator have to do with your network problem?"

"Everything. Nicholson and Chamberlain were working together. They were using Century computers and the Internet to gather blackmail information. Ramal accidentally discovered their network mole and they killed him. They've been after me ever since."

"Look, Adam. You've got to give this up. It's gone way too far. I can't follow all this conspiracy stuff. Tell me where you are and we'll talk. Anywhere you want."

Braxton could tell the detective didn't believe a word of what he was saying. He would've hung up but he needed Fowler's help one last time. "Can't do it, Sam. I've got Chamberlain's journal. It's encoded on a thumb drive. If I can read it, it may explain everything."

"Great, Adam. Why not give it to me? I've got friends that know how to do that sort of thing."

"I can handle it, Sam. Thanks anyway. But I do need you to check out something. I found cabinets full of blackmail material in Nicholson's townhouse. You've got to go over there and get them. They'll show what Nicholson and Potterfield were up to."

"Potterfield? So he's involved in this too?"

"Yes . . . we think so." The detective was confusing him. It was so clear last night.

No, they *were* right. He would have to make the detective understand!

"We? What about Goddard, Adam? Is she okay?"

"Yes, dammit! She's fine. *She* believes me. Why the hell can't you!" He was screaming into the phone.

"Calm down. Let's all talk, Adam. The three of us."

"Tomorrow, Sam. We'll talk tomorrow. Noon, the same place as before. But you've got to get the files at Nicholson's. Okay?"

"Sure. I'll check that out today. But Adam, where can I . . ."

Braxton hung up before Fowler could finish. He walked back to the Metro station and down to the trains. GW was a straight shot on the Orange Line.

* * *

What a colossal screw up! Greystone had received Nicholson's email at seven the night before and had immediately tried to stop him, but he had been gone by the time Greystone had called. The executive had waited until midnight to hear a result, then had gone to bed and struggled to sleep, dogged by a premonition of disaster.

The CNN news report at eight that morning had confirmed his fears. His initial shock was quickly replaced by a blinding fury at his flamboyant colleague. Nicholson had gone after Braxton and Goddard alone and gotten himself killed in the process.

Stupidity! How could he have jeopardized their plans with such an attempt?

Nicholson always thought he could take care of everything himself: he had to plant the leaks on Lynch, he had to track down his anonymous blackmailer. If it hadn't been for Greystone, he never would have identified Goddard in the first place.

"Unknown assailants" the CNN report had said. Unknown bullshit. Braxton and Goddard had killed Nicholson. He was sure of it. Now another of his partners was dead and they were loose in D.C.

First Chamberlain and now Nicholson. What could he do to control the damage?

Greystone stalked the hallway between his living room and kitchen. A once expensive dark green Bokara lay on the floor, now rendered nearly worthless by a furrow worn down its middle from its owner's obsessive behavior.

He had to get rid of Braxton and Goddard and stop the publicity. Nicholson's death would only make matters worse. Hajima and Flitterman were both worried that he didn't have control of the *Potterfield Bill*. If there were any more disclosures, Hajima will pull out and Flitterman will certainly terminate the alliance plan.

He had to see Potterfield.

Greystone didn't know how the old war-horse would react to the death of his aide. If he could get the Senator alone he might be able to head off an intemperate response.

He stopped at an ornate Louis XIV writing desk and called Potterfield's home. After a long and only marginally intelligible conversation with the Senator's heavily accented housekeeper, he determined that the Senator had rushed to his office earlier that morning after being contacted by the police. She didn't know when the Senator would return.

Greystone slammed the receiver down. Another obstacle thrown in his path. He considered calling Potterfield's office but knew he would never get past his secretary. The situation required a face-to-face encounter.

He grabbed the phone and dialed Santana.

CHAPTER 59

George Washington University, Washington, D.C.
Sunday, 8:45 a.m.

Braxton arrived at GW and immediately went to the basement of Science and Engineering Hall. Instead of taking a right at the bottom of the stairs, however, he turned left into the Computer Information Resource Center. Past the doors, the narrow basement corridor opened in a wider hallway, decorated with the latest information on user procedures, student helplines, and campus freeware.

Along both sides of the hall were classroom-sized "Student Laboratories". Large windows between the hall and the rooms gave Braxton a clear view of the interior of each lab. They were filled with long tables and personal computers, arranged to accommodate both personal use and group instruction. In his college days, these would have been called "terminal rooms"; simple time-sharing terminals had now been replaced by much more powerful personal workstations. The Resource Center provided convenient computer access for those students who didn't have their own equipment; a category that fit Braxton to a tee.

This early in the morning, the rooms were nearly deserted; one lone student in a lab to Braxton's left was typing furiously into a word processing program. He paid no attention to the arrival of the gaunt, bearded newcomer.

He was too old to look like a student, so had picked clothes appropriate for a post-doctoral researcher. Even at his advanced age, he figured he could pass a cursory examination. If anyone started asking questions, he would just have to get out as fast as he could.

Avoiding the other student, Braxton went into the first lab on the right, selected a station that afforded a clear view of the entrance to the Resource Center, and went to work.

* * *

Goddard settled in at Lauinger Library at the corner of 37th and Prospect Streets NW. Lauinger had the best collections of commercial and federal government references on the Georgetown campus. A quick session at the catalog PC yielded Dun and Bradstreet summaries and a corporate backgrounder on Century. She found short entries for Chamberlain and Nicholson in Who's Who and followed the bibliographic references deeper into the stacks.

Chamberlain had published frequently early in his career but there was little in the last few years. The citations provided at least some leads. Nicholson was a bigger problem. The notes she had received from Lexington were better than anything she had been able to find so far.

By eleven o'clock she had exhausted her sources and herself. She gathered the printouts and copies and headed back to the car. On the way, she remembered that the Library of Congress had a major section on law and politics. Maybe they would have something on Nicholson. Without thinking any further, she drove back M Street toward the Capitol.

What she had forgotten was that it was Sunday and the Library of Congress was closed, facts that she only remembered after climbing the daunting steps to the Great Hall at First and Independence Avenue. Embarrassed at her stupidity, she trudged halfway down and sat, tired and dejected, at one of the benches on the LoC terrace.

The sun was high in the sky and rapidly warming the cool morning air. There was no reason to go back now. Braxton had said he wouldn't return until mid-afternoon and she was not going to stay in that hovel of a room alone.

She had decided to do her shopping in Maryland; putting as many miles as possible between the stores and their location in Vienna. The malls didn't open until at least noon, however, so she decided a short walk might clear her mind.

She headed down to First Street and turned right. The site of the

Capitol in the distance brought back many memories. When she had been a child she had felt something special, a certain pride, when she walked through the city. Perhaps it was the reverence with which her father had held the seat of government. Unfortunately, the limestone columns and carved facades looked grayer than in those early days, perhaps a result of the new breed of politicians inhabiting the halls.

Pedestrian traffic had picked up. Tourists had begun to arrive for an afternoon of sightseeing and gawking. First was lined with tour buses, their sleek silver sides reflecting the bright midday sun. Their licenses were a sampling of the republic: New Jersey, Maine, Ohio, and Florida. The city still held a fascination for at least some of the country's citizens.

The encounter with Nicholson gnawed at her mind. She had had no idea that anyone had been following her. How would she know if she was being followed? She glanced behind and looked at the faces on the street. There was a couple about ten feet away and a young man a few paces behind them. They looked normal. A man and a woman were across the street watching as three children ran up and down the sidewalk. She didn't recognize any of them, but how would she?

She crossed First Street and began walking faster. Her heart was racing. She tried to shake off the growing anxiety, but it wouldn't go away. Stopping to try to calm herself, she glanced at the silvered window of one of the buses and saw the reflection of a face behind her. He was a young white man, with curly blonde hair and wearing a dark jacket.

Had she seen him before? Was he the man she had noticed earlier? She didn't remember! *Why hadn't I looked more carefully?*

Goddard was frozen at the window. The face smiled then continued down the street. She spun around and pressed herself against the cold metal side of the bus, her book bag clutched at her chest. She had to escape. Where could she be safe?

She started running down First. Panic had taken over.

A man in a Redskin's sweatshirt smiled at her. She turned to see if he would follow and tripped over an unexpected curb. The pavement tore her jeans and reopened the cuts on her hands. She quickly got up and kept going, ignorant of the concerned looks on the faces around her.

Goddard didn't know what to do. She stopped at a crosswalk and saw a crowd of people gathered in front of a large imposing building.

She could hide in the crowd! She rushed up to the group and inched her way inside their perimeter as they walked up a set of stairs.

"Isn't it just marvelous, Nancy?" she heard in a faint Western twang. "You don't see buildings like this in Ada."

Goddard kept her head down as they approached a uniformed guard at the building's entrance. Out of the corner of her eye she saw him smile politely and nod as they passed.

The group filed through a metal detector, then gathered in an enormous open space; an area suddenly very familiar to Goddard. Her heart ached as she stared at the circle of eighteen Corinthian columns rising majestically to a dome with a glazed oculus in the ceiling: the Russell Building rotunda. She remembered when her father had first brought her here. She had been so proud.

A black panel on a side wall drew her gaze. Against a sea of white letters, one line leapt out at her:

```
Virginia David Potterfield SR 421
```

* * *

"Where the hell have you been?" Greystone cursed as he slid into the back of the limousine. "I've been waiting two goddamn hours."

"I'm sorry, *Señor* Greystone," Santana pleaded. "But it is Sunday. My day off. And this is my daughter Maria's birthday. We were all at the zoo."

"I don't care if you were at the damn White House! When I call, I expect you *now*. Not when you friggin' feel like it. You do this again and you'll be visiting your little daughter in Havana, if they ever let you out of Leavenworth."

"Please, *Señor* Greystone, I . . ."

"Shut up and drive, Santana. Get me to the Senate Office Building without getting us both killed and I may forget about your unfortunate error in judgement."

CHAPTER 60

The Russell Building, Washington, D.C.
Sunday, 11:30 a.m.

GODDARD WALKED THROUGH the office door and up to the stern-faced matron sitting behind the desk. The secretary was too busy filling out a stack of forms to notice her approach. "I'd like to see Senator Potterfield, please."

Camille Johnson looked up with a start. "What are you doing here?" she asked. "The offices are closed."

"I have important business with the Senator."

"I told you the office is closed. The Senator's Chief of Staff was killed last night. We have a lot of work to do. If you will excuse me . . ." She turned away and went back to her paperwork.

"I have some information about Mr. Nicholson for the Senator. I think he would want to hear it."

Johnson considered the request for a moment, then reached for the telephone. "And what is your name?"

"Susan Lynch."

A flash of recognition and surprise crossed the secretary's face. She spoke quietly into the handset.

Goddard heard a soft "Of course, sir" and the secretary replaced the phone.

"You may go right in, Ms. Lynch," she said, her eyes still showing disbelief.

Goddard took a deep breath and walked toward the door. What was she doing here? For all her planning and scheming, she was completely unprepared to meet her father's killer in person. What would she feel when she finally confronted him? What should she say?

It was too late to go back now. She shook off the fear and pulled open the heavy oak door.

Potterfield sat calmly behind his imposing desk and watched as she entered the room. His hands were clasped together, resting comfortably on the polished glass desktop. He looked even older than she had expected, withered and weary from a life of lies and deceit. Still, the setting gave him an aura of power that she could not ignore. As she moved closer, she felt his eyes bore into her looking for some weakness, some secret he could use to soften her resolve.

"Ms. Lynch," he began quietly. "I've been wondering when you might come to visit. You have grown to be a very lovely woman. Your father would be proud."

She had wanted to stay calm and cool, to face him rationally, but the reality of seeing him at last was too overwhelming. His condescending tone finally broke her control.

"You bastard!" she yelled. "Don't you dare talk about my father. You killed him. You and that damn assistant of yours. I won't let you get away with that!" She had kept moving forward, narrowing the gap between them, and was now directly in front of Potterfield's desk, her face only inches from the aging Senator's.

"I don't have any idea what you are talking about, young lady," he replied, completely ignoring her outburst. "Your father committed suicide. There wasn't anything any of us could do to alleviate his suffering."

"You were the cause of his suffering and now I can prove it."

"Oh yes, that alleged information you mentioned in your email messages. It was you wasn't it? I'm afraid you will need a lot more proof than that, my dear girl. By the way, who is supporting you in this fruitless quest?"

"Proof, you want proof? How about this file your friend Nicholson kept. Rather sloppy of him don't you think?" She pulled a handful of papers out of her bag and threw them on the desk.

Potterfield hesitated, not wanting to break eye contact with his accuser but desperate to see the evidence. He finally glanced down at the top sheet, quickly scanned the remaining papers, and raised his eyes back to his visitor.

"An interesting story, Ms. Lynch. But surely you don't think anyone will believe it. It will be written off as a fiction by a distraught family member."

"Oh it's true, Senator. And everyone will believe it. Along with all the other records of ruined careers, bribes, and back-room dealings. We've got you and I wanted to be the first one to tell you."

Potterfield's calm demeanor finally cracked. "Others? Where did you get this? From Nick? You killed him!" He reached for the phone.

Goddard didn't care what happened any more. She had to see him punished. If she was caught, she would confess. She had acted alone.

"You can do that if you want to Senator, but then you would have to explain that report. It's only a copy of course. The original is safe."

Potterfield slowly replaced the receiver and pushed himself up from the desk. While his voice was as steady as before, Goddard saw his face betray an unusual sadness.

"What do you want?"

"I want you to resign, today."

A smile appeared on Potterfield's craggy face. "No, Ms. Lynch. I will not satisfy your childish need for retribution. You will find that the world is a much more complex place than you can imagine. It is run on power and favors. And you will soon see what power a Senator can wield in this city. If I were you, I would try to get away while I could. You might yet be able to live a normal life."

"I'm not like you, Senator. I won't look the other way. I'll be in the front row when they convict you. You and all of your friends, Nicholson, Chamberlain. All of them."

Potterfield's brow wrinkled even more than usual. "Chamberlain? I don't know anyone named Chamberlain, Ms. Lynch. I suggest you check your evidence more carefully. Perhaps you have me confused with someone else."

She couldn't put up with Potterfield's posturing any longer. She wanted to grab his pompous face and slam it into his pompous desk again and again; until he felt all the pain that her father had. But she knew where that would lead. And she wouldn't be able to help Braxton from a D.C. jail cell.

But his days of lying and blustering were over. She would see to it.

"There's no confusion, damn you. I have the proof and I'll use it. For my father. It's all on Chamberlain's drive. You can go to hell!"

She spun on her heels and rushed out of the office, nearly knocking down a well-dressed gentleman in the outer office, promising herself that she would not break down in front of her father's murderer.

There was a women's restroom just down the hall. She nearly made it.

* * *

When Greystone had arrived at the Russell Building, he had been amazed at the level of activity in Potterfield's suite. Young aides scurried in and out of the offices balancing stacks of books and piles of legislative folders. The Senator must have called in his whole staff when he had heard the news.

As he approached Johnson's desk, a very attractive blond suddenly rushed out of the Senator's inner office, sweeping past him and leaving in her place a warm fragrance of expensive perfume. He stared openly at her as she pushed out the door and began to run down the hall.

Must be tough working for a Senator.

"I wonder what the Senator said to her?" Greystone said.

"I wouldn't know," Johnson replied coolly. "The office is closed sir. You will have to come back at a later time."

"Mr. Robert Greystone to see Senator Potterfield."

"The Senator is not seeing anyone today," Johnson repeated.

"He will see me. Call him, and tell him it's about the messages."

"I'm sorry, Mr. Greystone. Perhaps I could set up another appointment next week?"

Johnson's aloof, efficient drone only added to Greystone's rising level of frustration. He spoke again, this time without any suggestion of temperance. "I need to see the Senator *now*. It is quite important. Just tell him I'm here."

She picked up the phone and punched a button. Greystone couldn't hear what she was saying, but he doubted it was anything complimentary. After a few moments she turned back to him.

"Senator Potterfield is unable to meet with you right now. He has some personal arrangements to make for Mr. Nicholson."

Greystone was not about to be put off by this government service secretary. His career was in the balance and all Potterfield wanted to do was stew about his aide. He strode past a protesting

Johnson and threw open the door to Potterfield's office. The Senator sat behind his desk staring out the window.

"Senator, we need to talk," Greystone began loudly.

Potterfield turned and glared at the executive. "What do you think you're doing, son?"

"Senator, I'm sorry." Johnson raced into the room behind Greystone. "I told him you were indisposed. Should I call security?"

"This is about your message from the Ukraine, Potterfield," Greystone quickly added.

Potterfield's face went white. "Ah, no. That's all right, Camille. I'll hear what Mr. Greystone has to say. That will be all."

"If you're sure, Senator." Potterfield nodded and Johnson withdrew to the front office. She closed the door quietly behind her.

Greystone walked forward and pulled a chair directly in front of the Senator's desk. He sat down and stared straight into the statesman's face.

Potterfield looked exhausted. The crow's feet around his eyes and mouth had become dark caverns. His skin had an ashen pall calling even greater attention to the alcohol-induced flush of his nose and cheeks.

Greystone had been right about coming. There was little time before the man would finally crack under the strain.

"Are you all right, Senator? You look a little pale," Greystone began.

"My aide's death was quite a shock, Mr. Greystone. We had been friends a very long time. I thought of him as the son I never had."

"Yes, I know you did, Senator. Such a senseless tragedy."

"Yes, a tragedy. But what brings you here on a Sunday? Something about some messages?"

Greystone had had all the small talk he could stand. He rose from the chair, placed both hands on Potterfield's desk, and leaned over the legislator. "I don't have time to spar with you, you old bastard. Nick and I worked together. I know all about your remailer. I know all about Lynch. I know all about every dirty deed you have pulled for the last thirty-five years."

Potterfield's bloodshot eyes were bulging out of their sockets. "How could you know all that?"

"Where do you think Nick got his information? Do you really

think he did it all himself? Where do you think all the technical details for your Bill came from?"

"You worked together on the Bill?"

"Worked on it?" Greystone laughed in Potterfield's face. "I conceived it, you anachronistic relic. Nick and I wrote it. We stole the technical data from NIST and added our own spin. You were just the pawn we needed to get it passed."

"You're lying. Nick would never do that."

"No, I'm not. And you know it. The charade is over. The only question is what do we do now? We have business we need to attend to."

"What do you want?" Potterfield said. He held his head in his heavy, callused hands and sunk lower into his chair.

"I want you to do your damn job. Get our Bill passed. The deal still goes. If you get that Bill through, you can retire successful and rich. If you don't, I'll see that your grimy history appears on the front page of the *Post* for a month. You'll spend the rest of life in prison, without any Congressional pension."

Potterfield looked up at the executive. Greystone thought he saw a flicker of resolve behind the defeated visage but put the impossibility aside. He was a beaten man.

"Susan Lynch was just here."

Now it was Greystone's face that flashed into shock. He remembered the attractive blonde in the outer office. She had been so close!

"Here? When? What did she want?"

"Just before you came. You didn't recognize her, I see."

Potterfield's voice became stronger and his eyes met Greystone's with surprising vitality. "Too bad. We might have been able to stop her together. She said she had papers from Nick. All of his private files. I don't know how she got them."

"She and a man named Adam Braxton killed Nick and broke into his house."

"She kept saying 'we'. She must have meant this Braxton."

"Did Nick keep his records at home?"

"I don't know. Do you? It appears I didn't know as much about him as I thought I did. What do we do about her? Nick thought he could stop her. If she really has all this we're *both* in a lot of trouble. I assure you I won't go down alone."

Greystone was shocked by the change in Potterfield. At first he was completely defeated, now he's threatening. "I'll take care of Lynch and Braxton. You just do your part with the Bill. In a couple of days things will be back to normal."

"Except Nick is gone."

"Just do your senatorial thing, Potterfield. Everything else will be taken care of. Think of me as your surrogate aide." Greystone had done what he had come for. He turned and headed for the door.

"Greystone," Potterfield called. "Who is Chamberlain?"

The executive froze. "What did you say?"

"Lynch also said she had some kind of computer thing from someone named Chamberlain. She said it had more evidence. What was she talking about?"

"I have no idea, Senator." He continued out the door. "Just worry about your own responsibilities."

My God. What has Warren done now?

CHAPTER 61

Silver Spring, Maryland
Sunday, 2:00 p.m.

"FOWLER," HE BARKED into the phone.

The detective's wife had gone to a church social and left him alone for what he had hoped was a peaceful afternoon with a new Richard Castle mystery. He had just settled onto his favorite sofa when his Sunday was interrupted by another telephone call. He was not happy.

"Hey, Sam. How're you doing?"

It took a few seconds to recognize the gravelly voice. "Roger? Is that you?" He had hoped it was Braxton calling back. The consultant seemed to have lost all reason and Fowler needed to bring him in. Slattery, on the other hand, was just being a nuisance. "What the hell are you doing calling me on Sunday?"

"That's no way to greet an old friend, Sam. Especially after that nasty message you left me."

What message? Oh, yeah. Braxton's imaginary rogue. That had been almost a week ago. "So what took you so long?"

"I've been busy. And it sounds like you have too. I thought you were going to drop the Ramal thing."

"I did drop it," Fowler countered. "What do you care?"

"Well, your friend Braxton didn't drop it. You're pushing into things you don't understand, Sam. Stay away."

Dammit, Slattery could be a real pain-in-the-ass. "Don't give me that spook shit, Roger. But you're right; I don't know what's going on. Why don't you tell me?"

"It doesn't work that way, my friend."

"Then why call me?"

"Cause you're always a wealth of information. Like who's Susan Goddard?"

Goddard! How did the Agency find out about her? I have to keep her out this. "Uh, she was a friend of Ramal's. A student at Georgetown. Why?"

"Oh, nothing much. Her name keeps coming up with Braxton's. You don't know why she would have visited Senator Potterfield's office today do you?"

Jesus. Potterfield again. "No, Roger, I don't. Hey, what's really going on?"

"Can't say, Sam. But it might help if you tell me where Braxton is."

"Don't know that either, *my friend.*"

"Too bad. Maybe we could help him."

How could the CIA help Braxton? Maybe Braxton had been right after all. And now the CIA, and likely their friends in Maryland, have him in their sights. "What did he find, Roger? Something you lost?"

Slattery went silent. When he responded, his voice had lost its bravado. "Last time, Sam. Stay out. This is a national security issue. Way above me. They've been on it for a long time."

They? This was wider than the CIA. Maybe there *was* a problem on the Internet. Braxton had been telling the truth. But Fowler didn't believe Slattery's denials for a minute. "They need help, Roger. We ought to do something."

"Look, Sam. Sometimes folks get in over their heads. That's when they need to leave it to the professionals. And you *really* don't want to be in the middle of this."

"But Braxton and Goddard are?"

"That was their call, right? You had nothing to do with it. It's all under control."

This is going nowhere. Time to poke the bear one more time. "So there really is a rogue?"

Another few seconds of silence. "Have a good day, Sam."

And the line went dead.

Fowler stared at the silent phone as if it could somehow still reveal the answers he wanted.

Christ. Braxton and Goddard were in deeper than even they knew.

His friend Slattery certainly didn't have all the answers yet. He wouldn't have called otherwise. "Under control" bullshit. The spook was waiting for Braxton to crack the case for them. Unfortunately, neither he nor Goddard was likely to live long enough to get any of the credit.

They needed help more than ever. And he was their only conduit to the outside. But could he afford to get any more involved?

He grabbed the phone and punched in another number.

"Who's this? . . . Jefferson? This is Fowler, CID. Get a unit over to the Nicholson break-in. I want the place sealed tight until I get there. Do it *now*!"

*   *   *

Nicholson's death had hit Potterfield hard. Apart from Mary Jane, Nick had been his best friend. The only one, in fact, with whom he could share his most private feelings about life and career. He looked upon their years together as a partnership, a time of mutual respect and reward.

Now, after all he had given the poor street kid: a decent home, the best education, a powerful position, he finds out the bastard had been holding out on him. Nick played him for a sucker. Using him, and others too it appeared. Maybe it was good that asshole Greystone had burst in. The time to mourn Nick was over.

Greystone can go ahead and take care of Lynch. And Chamberlain too, whoever the hell he is. Greystone hadn't expected him to know that name. A little research will make the connection. The executive could turn into a more valuable asset than he had thought.

"Camille," he called into the intercom. "Get my PR staff in here! Then call legal. I want them here in fifteen minutes. Then call transportation and get my limo ready. We're all going on a little expedition."

*   *   *

The meeting had left Greystone both energized and confused. He again paced the Bokara and reviewed the morning. The Senator was a more complicated man than he had thought. He would have to be careful not to underestimate him.

Things *were* finally getting back on track. Potterfield would push the Bill through. That would get Hajima to consummate the deal.

Soon Greystone would be running Theater and have a Senator in his pocket to boot. It was a good start.

But first, he had to make arrangements for Braxton and Goddard. He called Harding's contact line, got the expected greeting, and left a message. The call initiated a sequence of message drops that would culminate in a prearranged face-to-face meeting the next day. Unless Harding was out of the country, in which case Greystone would receive a return call in a few hours. That message would give an alternative time that would delay the meeting for days. He cursed the contractor for his ridiculous procedure. Perhaps it was time to cultivate some additional resources.

Now, how was he going to find them? They'll never go back to her apartment. That's how Nick had located them. Who would they contact?

Fowler! The old detective was their only choice. Greystone had suspected Braxton was getting inside information from somewhere. It must have been from the detective. He couldn't tap the cop's phone—the FBI might already have—but he could do them all one better.

He went to his desk and opened his laptop. The on-line telephone directory quickly gave him Fowler's home number. He reasoned they were more likely to call there than into District headquarters. The computer dialed the number and he got lucky, Fowler's answering machine picked up. He hung up and went to work writing a special script for his communication program. Fifteen minutes later he was ready.

His system dialed Fowler's number. When the recorded announcement started, the program redirected the audio to the digitizer on his multimedia card. Fowler's greeting was now record-ed on Greystone's disk. The script linked this audio file to the computerized announcement on one of Greystone's spare telephone lines. When anyone called that number they would get Fowler's greeting.

So far, the job had been easy. For the next step, Greystone went back to his TAP documentation. He programmed the call-forward number sequences into another script, added the sequence for caller recognition, and had the system dial Verizon's secure access line. The program did everything else.

As he relaxed back in his chair, he noticed a blinking icon in the corner of his screen. He had been so focused on the Fowler effort he had missed its urgent call. Clicking the icon open, the log report scrolled onto the screen:

```
Warning:

Unauthorized access; saracen@rdvax.gw.edu
```

The alert had been in place for weeks and he had forgotten to remove it after the accident. His adversary was indeed clever to have picked this avenue to reconnect. The accesses appeared to be from a local connection.

Braxton couldn't be allowed to get away this time. At least now he wouldn't have to rely on Harding. Without another alternative, Greystone reached for the phone.

CHAPTER 62

BY NOON THE laboratories had been filled, students milling in the hallway waiting to catch a seat should any of the current squatters complete their assignments. Conversations had ranged from discussions of weekend escapades to complaints of grading curves used by the Comp Sci professors. So far, no one had bothered the slightly older colleague working intensely in the corner.

Braxton transferred the last files from his CERT/CC and personal cloud directories to Ramal's account at GW. By the time anyone tried to trace the alarms he was sure he had set off, he would be long gone. Who would be looking for a break-in on Sunday morning?

He stuck a flash drive he had found lying on a table into the PC and copied the files he needed. Then he started to run the decryption codes. Failure messages scrolled off the top of the screen faster than he could follow. This was a waste of time. He didn't have enough data on Chamberlain or Nicholson to attempt to guess their key phrases. As he watched the last attempts report their results, a movement in the hall caught his eye.

Two men had entered the main corridor and were peering into the labs. Braxton instantly hunched over his workstation, trying to hide his face the best he could, but still watching as the intruders took visual note of the users, then turned back into the hallway.

They were dressed in neatly pressed suits, not an uncommon attire for the streets of D.C., but flashing beacons in the midst of the jeans and sweatshirts of the Resource Center. The taller man wore a trim blue suit that emphasized his broad shoulders and long legs. The shorter man had on a light gray and was similarly well proportioned. They could have been computer salesmen except that this was Sunday and none of the salesmen Braxton knew wore dark glasses and crepe-soled shoes. They had to be FBI.

Passing the labs, the pair marched solemnly to the end of the hall and disappeared into a room marked "SEAS Library". Braxton guessed he had only a few minutes to pack up and get out of the building. He sent the decryption log to the printer and signed off the system. Then he added the log to a stack of other listings and stuffed them all into a notebook an earlier student had left behind. The flash drive was already safely in his pocket.

He breathed a sigh of relief and headed for the door. When he was halfway across the room he heard the clank of a metal door. He looked up and saw the two agents coming down the hall directly toward him. There was no way he could force his way past them in his current state. He fought off the terrified voice that was screaming for him to run and walked as calmly as possible toward the exit.

When he reached the lab's door, he glanced around the suite of rooms to gauge his position. Looking in the direction of the stairway, he saw another blue suit standing at the base of the stairs. He was still trying to decide what to do when he ran directly into the taller agent.

"Excuse me," the man said. "In a hurry to get somewhere?"

Braxton looked up only to see the reflection of his own face in the agent's mirrored lenses. He had come too far to be bullied now. "Yes, I have a seminar to give in five minutes."

"On Sunday?"

"Of course," he responded with fear-induced bravado. "It never conflicts with another class. Why? Who are you?"

"Special Agent Brooks, from the FBI. And you are?"

"Uh, Professor Wilson Lexington. May I go now?" Braxton tried to move forward but the agent stopped him with his hand.

"This will just take a moment. Have you been on these systems long?"

"Just a few minutes."

"Did you see anyone unusual while you were here? Anyone that looked like he didn't belong?"

Braxton and the man were blocking the door to the hallway. A couple of students had left their PCs and were waiting to get past them. "I have been busy, ah, sir, and did not notice anyone else. You are the only one I see that doesn't belong." He heard a positive reaction from the students behind him and raised his voice. "I would like to get to my class if I may." He tried to push between the agent and door frame.

"I said in a minute," the agent replied as he narrowed the gap through which Braxton was trying to escape. "What is it you were doing with the computer?"

Jesus, what an asshole. Braxton was tempted to say something about having on-line sex but thought better of it. He needed a plausible cover story fast. The students behind him were getting impatient and one gave him a shove.

"I am studying the etymology of early Christian chants," he began. "They have a very unique vocabulary and pattern of rhyme. I use the computer to correlate and categorize the various ethnic varieties of chant and relate them to religious events of the period."

The agent stared back in silence. Braxton stood his ground and waited, cold sweat streaming down his side under his shirt. Strangely, his only thoughts were of Goddard. What would happen to her if he were caught? Would he ever see her again?

"I think we'd better . . ."

One of the students suddenly pushed between the two older men. "Hey Professor, you're teaching a course on chants? I got this cool CD of Gregorian chants for Christmas. Is that the kinda stuff you're working on?"

Braxton immediately turned to the youth. "Why yes. Gregorian chants are an eclectic variation of standard Christian chants. They actually evolved from some of the early folk songs of the Arthurian era." He reached out and pulled the student forward through the crowd. "There was, of course, a significant Druid influence . . ."

The taller agent shook his head and nodded to his colleague at the end of the corridor. Braxton and the student continued unchallenged through the entrance and up the stairs. By the time they had passed the last ring of agents outside the building, Braxton had given the student an ornately fabricated lecture in chant-ology. The new acolyte pledged to sign up for the course the next semester.

*   *   *

Braxton arrived back at the motel at 3:30. After the confrontation at GW, he had collapsed of exhaustion in his Metro seat and slept all the way to Vienna. A shower and change of clothes improved his state, at least his pulse had returned to normal, and he had regained enough presence of mind to begin to worry about Goddard. There was no reason to be concerned, he tried to convince himself; it was still early and Fairfax County traffic was heavy, even on a Sunday afternoon.

To pass the time while he waited, he made some notes on a pad of paper he found by their telephone:

Chamberlain

Nicholson

What connected these men? What would cause two well-educated professionals, extremely successful by anyone's standards, to engage in deceit and murder? Money? Power? What had they been up to?

He added a few more lines to the list:

Potterfield

Lynch

Goddard

computer

router

gateway

Century

Concord

message

cash

He'd need to add birthdays, spouses, pets and anything else relevant from Goddard's notes, but somewhere in these words lay the key to Chamberlain's disk, and his and Goddard's future as well. Would he be smart enough to figure out where?

There was a knock on the door and Braxton leapt up, praying it was Goddard. He checked the security fisheye, let out a sigh, and opened the door for his accomplice.

She marched right past him, two large shopping bags hanging from her arms.

"Your computer is in the car," Goddard announced, dropping the bags on the floor. "I'm exhausted and going to take a shower."

She slammed the bathroom door behind her. The click of the lock echoed through the motel room.

Braxton considered trying to talk to her about it, but decided this was probably not the time. She'd come out when she was ready and they could discuss things then.

And he could use the time to work on Chamberlain's file.

He pulled the four cardboard boxes from the rental and piled them on the bed. Then he went back out and moved the car out of sight behind the motel. He didn't know who might be looking for them but there was no sense in taking any chances.

Back inside, he spread the equipment cartons on the bed. As he extracted the various components, he tossed the abundant packing material into a pile in the corner of the room.

The trash did little to damage the ambiance of the place. The motel was a shabby remnant of the early days of interstate travel, a weathered strip of dirty windows and peeling doors in a less than successful neighborhood of Fairfax County. He couldn't understand how the structure was still standing in the face of the inflated metropolitan D.C. property values. Convenient to the Metro terminus, yet unassuming and set in the shadows of a large stand of oak trees, it was frequented primarily by truckers and other travelers of the night.

The room was small; the double bed, dresser, sofa, chair and coffee table nearly filling the available space. An even smaller bath led off through a door along the back wall. A tiny LED TV sat on the dresser. At least the motel offered cable and Wi-Fi—he had watched CNN while waiting for Goddard—although the anchors' faces did have a decidedly greenish cast. A heavy scent of deodorant permeated the room no matter how much he had tried to air it out. He didn't want to think of what odors it was covering.

For once, setting up the PC had been easy. The laptop had been preloaded with all the right software. All he had to do was turn it on. The printer had a USB cable and worked the first time. He copied Chamberlain's original file to the computer, then the files he had downloaded at GW.

It was time to get to work.

CHAPTER 63

Vienna, Virginia
Sunday, 4:00 p.m.

THERE WAS A sound from the bathroom and he looked up to see Goddard coming through the door. She was wrapped in one of the thin terrycloth towels that passed as linens from the motel management. It barely covered her breasts and hips, and dangled suggestively as she walked over to the dresser. He couldn't help but wonder if it had been carefully draped that way by his companion.

Looking at her now, he realized he cared deeply for the young woman standing before him. Unfortunately their current situation was hardly conducive to a lasting relationship. He wasn't sure if either of them would ever feel safe again.

"Get some clothes on," he ordered with a smile. "We've got work to do and I can't concentrate with you flagging around like that."

"Like this?" she said feigning an innocent smile and striking a very distracting pose. "Okay, I'll go find a sack to put on."

Goddard grabbed some items from the bags on the floor, and disappeared back into the bathroom. She seemed in a much better mood so he wrote her earlier behavior off to fatigue and a long day. When she returned a few minutes later, she was wearing a loose calico blouse and a pleasingly snug pair of designer blue jeans.

She would have been just as appealing in the potato sack.

"Any progress?" she finally asked, crawling onto the bed next to him.

He leaned over and gave her a kiss on the cheek. "Not much. There's still a lot of questions. How about you?"

"I got some information, mostly on Chamberlain. It's in my purse. Nothing that would tie him to Nicholson though."

"We've got to find the connections. I think Nicholson really believed I killed Chamberlain. If he didn't kill Warren who did?"

"Maybe someone else is involved. Did Chamberlain have any close friends?"

"Not that I remember. He was a real loner. What about Potterfield? Could he be behind all this?"

"I don't think he knows about Chamberlain and the mole." Her voice was oddly flat and her smile had vanished.

"Why not? He doesn't seem the computer type, but he certainly was involved with Nicholson from the look of those files."

She avoided his look and straightened the papers on the bed. "I went to see him today."

"You went to see him!" Braxton nearly dropped the computer on the floor. He grabbed her shoulders and turned her to face him. "Why? He could have had you arrested! What happened?"

She pushed him away and glared back defiantly. "Nothing. I didn't stay long."

"Why did you go?"

"I don't know. I was walking around after the library and found myself at the Senate Office Building. I had to go in."

"What did he say when he saw you?"

"Oh, he denied everything, of course. I got upset and just ran out. I'm sorry. Okay? You don't have to get mad."

She fought to keep her composure but tears welled in her eyes. He now understood what had caused her emotional entrance.

"I'm not mad," he said with a sense of relief. "But you could have been caught; he could have called the police. We don't know who is out there looking for us." He reached out again, this time she didn't resist, and pulled her closer. "Promise me you won't do anything like that again."

"I promise." She wiped her eyes on his shirt and straightened up. "There, I'm fine. Now tell me about your day. Did you call Fowler?"

"Yes, this morning. He gave me a lot of grief about Nicholson. I agreed we'd meet with him tomorrow."

"Is he going to get Nicholson's files?"

"I think so, but our credibility is running out. He's gone way out on a limb for us. We've got to get him some proof."

"Did you make any progress on Chamberlain's file?"

"Not a lot. The good news is that we know what encoding program he used. Chamberlain would have had access to all kinds of technology. He could have used nearly any encryption program. Luckily he used PGP. I downloaded some PGP programs from the Internet that can do the decoding."

"I still don't understand why Chamberlain would use something so easily available."

"The strength of PGP is that it is so available. And so secure. It was the best when Chamberlain chose it and he had no reason to change.

"I also figured out that he used a symmetric cipher. That means we only need a single passphrase or keyword. Unfortunately that phrase could be anything."

"So how do we find the keyword?"

"What we can't do is break it by brute force, trying all the keys. It's essentially impossible to crack. At least for us. That's why the government tried to stop anyone from using it."

Goddard looked dejected. "You mean we can't read Chamberlain's journal?"

"I didn't say that. We just need to figure out what passphrase he used. I made a few simple guesses at GW but they didn't work. I didn't figure it would be that easy."

"How do we find the right one? What would Chamberlain have used?"

"The safest keyphrase is a string of random letters, no one can guess it. But most people use something that is easier to remember: a date, the current month, the name of their sister's dog. What do you use for your password at Georgetown?"

"We have to change it every semester. I use the name of the season and the year, like spring-oh-one."

Braxton smiled and shook his finger at her. "Seasons are really popular. It would take a security expert about two minutes to break into your account. One of the files I copied from CERT was a keyword list that was taken from one of the cracker newsgroups. It should help get us started. But Chamberlain would know enough to pick something more complex. We need to add words that were important to Chamberlain. That's where you come in. Let's look at what you got from the library."

Goddard reached into her purse and pulled out a small stack of papers. "Like I said, it isn't much. Will it help?"

He took the papers and scanned them quickly. There were copies of biographies and a few recent magazine articles on Century Computer and the *Potterfield Bill*. She had also taken some handwritten notes from smaller articles. "Everything helps. These are a great start. Besides the keywords, I also wanted to see if there was anything that might explain the connection between them."

Goddard pulled a few pages from the stack. "I did find that they were at MIT at the same time. That doesn't mean they knew each other though. Chamberlain was an engineer and Nicholson was a business major. The only other common element was Century's support of Potterfield's Bill."

"Do you think we can guess the right keyphrase from any of this?"

"I'm certainly going to try. But there's something else. Warren wanted me to have the drive. He must have realized his life was in danger. Remember I told you he tried to tell me something just before he died? I'm sure that had something to do with the keyphrase."

"Did you try it today?"

"I tried 'cash' and it didn't work. But that's too simple. He would have complicated it; added some more words, duplicated it, changed case on some of the letters. We should be able to find the right one eventually. That's what those programs I downloaded do. It's just going to take some time."

"Great! So let's go back to GW and try it out."

Braxton hesitated. "Ah, there's just one problem. The FBI came to the Center this afternoon."

"Adam!" Goddard's eyes popped wide.

"It's okay." He raised his hands in mock defense. "I got out before they recognized me, but they'll undoubtedly put a watch on the terminals and Ramal's account. I don't think I can go back there."

"Then how do we decode the file?"

He pulled the GW memory stick from his pocket. "With this and our new computer, we're going to find the answer."

"Then let's get started," she said.

"One thing first. This is for you." He handed her Chamberlain's original drive. "Put it somewhere safe. Just in case."

"In case of what?"

"I don't know. Just in case. Okay?"

"Fine." She grabbed the drive from his hand, reached inside her blouse and stuck it inside her bra. "Safe enough?"

He gave up trying to argue with her and ignored the question.

Setting the keyword list on the bed beside the laptop he began pecking away at the keys. "I'm entering the word list we talked about. The programs I downloaded will take the words and combine them in different ways to form a key phrase. Like 'chamberlainpotterfield' or 'nicholsonchamberlaincash'. It will try all the combinations and permutations, backwards and forwards. I can vary the case of the letters and do substitutions like replacing 'a' with the at sign as well. The program will send each generated keyphrase to the PGP program. The right phrase will decode his journal."

"How long will it take before we know?"

"It only takes a few milliseconds for each phrase. That may not seem very long but there are a lot of combinations. Let's hope we get lucky."

They watched the screen in anticipation as it displayed each attempt. Each result was a frustrating rejection. Goddard made some coffee after about 10 minutes.

At five-thirty Braxton stood up and stretched. Goddard was on the sofa reading the background on Chamberlain and Potterfield.

"Do you have to watch the screen?" she asked.

"No. The program will announce when it's successful. I'm just anxious. But it's giving me a killer headache."

He walked over to the sofa, dropped down and put his feet up on the rickety coffee table. "Maybe I'll join you. When's dinner?"

Goddard looked over, flashed a withering scowl and threw the papers at him.

"Guess that means I call out, huh?" he replied.

*   *   *

Braxton had gone out for pizza and when he returned he saw that Goddard had straightened up the mess of boxes, papers and shopping bags and set out drinks. The room wasn't home, but at least it was now livable.

"Any luck yet?" he asked as he set the box on the coffee table.

"Nothing but silence," she replied. "What did you get?"

"One meat-eaters delight and one veggie. Thought I'd cover all bases."

"Hope you like the veggie," she countered.

They sat and picked absently at the slices.

"We're not going to find it, are we?" she said, verbalizing what they both had been thinking. Depression was filling the room. She knew they couldn't go on this way much longer.

Braxton glanced over to the laptop which Goddard had set on the adjoining chair. "The key length is up to fifty characters," he said. "I can't believe Chamberlain would have used a phrase that long. We don't have the right words." His voice reflected his weariness and dejection.

"It was just our first shot," she said. "Let's think about what we need to do next."

"I think what we need is a good night's sleep," Braxton replied. "I'm beat. Let's go back over your notes tonight, update our word list, and give the program another shot. We can see what happened in the morning before we meet Detective Fowler."

Goddard nodded and they went back to the pizza. After a few minutes of silence, which felt like hours, she said, "How about we check the news? See what they have to say about Nicholson. Maybe we'll hear something helpful." *And break the dark mood of this place.*

They sat back on the sofa and snuggled together, the talking heads reciting the news of the day in the background. He drew her to him and softly kissed her cheek.

He really was handsome, despite his ridiculous disguise. She realized how much better she felt just having him next to her. Together they would find the proof they needed.

Nicholson's murder was still a top story. Aides to Senators didn't get killed every day, even in the crime-ridden District of Columbia.

The police concluded Nicholson had tried to fight off an attempted robbery; a conclusion that was supported by the powder burns on his raincoat and Nicholson's missing wallet. It was believed the subsequent break-in at his house had been thwarted by the quick action of the police. There were cries for increased police presence, complaints about drug abuse, and requests for increased congressional funding of D.C. law enforcement.

No one mentioned the incident at the restaurant.

They acted like a pair of teenagers in their parent's basement, awkwardly hugging and stealing a kiss while the reality of their lives was played out on the TV screen. Goddard didn't know whether to laugh or cry. In the middle of one particularly extended kiss, they heard a familiar name.

"In related news," the male anchor said, "this afternoon Senator David Potterfield, the Senior Senator from Virginia, spoke to reporters outside his slain aide's townhouse."

Braxton broke the embrace in time to see Potterfield coming out of Nicholson's home. "Dammit, what is he doing there?"

" . . . I have recently discovered that my long-time friend and Chief of Staff, Barclay Nicholson, has been involved in the theft of confidential legislative documents. We do not know why he took the documents or if they were passed to any outside individuals. I am personally saddened by this disclosure and truly hope that we will find some explanation for his actions. Barclay was a dedicated and hardworking servant of the people."

"Senator," an invisible voice said. "Is this theft connected to Mr. Nicholson's death?"

Potterfield looked aside briefly then replied. "The police have no reason to suspect that Barclay's death was anything but an unfortunate accident. I'm sorry, but I will have no further comment on this situation until the investigation has been completed." The Senator then marched past the reporters followed by a gaggle of well-dressed staffers. Behind them, Braxton saw uniformed guards taking cardboard boxes out of the townhouse and loading them into vans.

"It's Nicholson's files. They're taking them away! Where the hell is Fowler?"

He jumped up from the sofa.

"What are you doing?" Goddard yelled at him.

"Calling Fowler. He screwed up!"

Braxton walked over to the dresser, picked up the handset from the room's land line and punched the buttons. After three rings he heard the familiar Fowler family greeting. Where was he?

"Dammit, Sam, it's Adam. What happened? I just saw Potterfield on TV. He took our evidence. Call me at . . ." He stopped, realizing that even giving out his number over the telephone was probably a bad idea. "Never mind, we can talk tomorrow. I want to know what happened."

Goddard watched as he slammed the handset back in the cradle. Her face was drawn and tired from the day's trials.

"How could Potterfield have found out about the files?" Braxton asked as he paced in front of the sofa.

"Adam," she whispered.

"I guess the police could have contacted him. But I'm surprised they acted so quickly. Why didn't Fowler stop them?"

"Adam!" she demanded. "Listen to me."

She sighed and dropped her head. "I told Potterfield."

Braxton's head snapped to face her. "You what?"

"Today, when I went to see him. He was so pompous, so sure of himself. I couldn't stand it. I didn't think he could do something like this. I'm so sorry." She collapsed in his lap, sobbing.

He held her tightly and softly stroked her hair. If only he could absorb all the pain she held inside her. "It's all right. We're not to blame. It's their fault."

She looked up into his eyes, tears streaming down her face. "That's it isn't it? Potterfield has won."

"Not yet," Braxton said, his voice prickling with hate. "Not yet."

CHAPTER 64

The Mall, Washington, D.C.
Monday, 11:30 a.m.

DELICATE PINK AND white blossoms burst from the cherry trees along the Tidal Basin. In 1912, the Japanese people had given 3000 seedlings to their new friends across the Pacific. The two countries' political tides may have ebbed and flowed over the ensuing years, but every spring the gift brought a flash of promise and rejuvenation to the staid nation's capital. Not to mention a horde of visiting tourists.

The Basin was filled with sightseers admiring the colors and taking in the warm noontime sun. A breeze stirred the air and brought the blossom's light, sweet aroma to two overworked bureaucrats taking a break on the bench just off the main path. The white limestone of the Jefferson Monument glistened behind them. Their eyes lazily scanned the grounds taking in the peaceful beauty.

"Here is the address where you will find them," Greystone said as he laid a folded newspaper down on the seat between them.

"Them? There's more than just Braxton?" Harding asked.

"Yes. He's with a woman, Susan Goddard. Her picture's in the envelope. Make it look like he killed her."

"This gets tougher every minute, Greystone. Braxton was already armed. He's going to be expecting trouble after that stupid attempt by your friend. Did you have anything to do with that?"

Greystone shook his head. "An unfortunate decision on the part of my ex-colleague. I was unable to stop him."

Harding casually picked up the paper and opened the envelope hidden inside. He turned and stared coldly into his client's eyes. "The girl will cost you another hundred grand."

"Look, Harding, if you hadn't messed up in Cambridge we wouldn't be here at all. I'm not paying for Braxton again and I'm not paying for Goddard. If you ever want to get another contract you'd better get this done and get it done right. I have more information on you than you'll ever know."

Harding turned to his employer and gave him a stare that froze even the ruthless executive. "You look, *Mister* Greystone. This is a business deal and we go by my rules. If you don't want me, that's fine; get somebody else." Harding rolled up the paper and pointed it at Greystone's head. "But don't ever threaten me again. All that computer crap won't do you a goddamn bit of good if you're not around to give it to anybody. One hundred for the girl, period. Braxton's already been settled. Make up your mind."

Greystone knew Harding wasn't kidding. He had pushed the assassin about as far as he dared. But he wasn't going to let some well-dressed street thug intimidate him either. He couldn't afford to have Braxton and Goddard on the loose and he couldn't afford to have anything to do with their deaths. Going along with the current plan was the best he had. "All right, one hundred for Goddard. But no screw-ups and it looks like Braxton kills her."

"Agreed. We'll take care of it tonight." Harding started to get up.

"One more thing." Greystone drew his briefcase up to his lap, opened it, and pulled out a square black case. Harding quickly dropped back down onto the bench and reached across his chest into his jacket.

"Take it easy," Greystone said raising a hand in defense. "It's only a laptop computer. You do know what that is?" Harding threw him an icy glare but relaxed as the executive continued. "Braxton stole a memory stick from Chamberlain's house. It contains information that I need. Before you kill him, make sure he gives it to you. I don't care what you do; just get it."

Damn that Chamberlain. Why did I ever get involved with him in the first place? It was so like that self-absorbed weakling to leave incriminating evidence lying around. "You know how to operate one of these?"

"Sure," Harding replied.

Greystone wasn't so confident. "I'll show you what to do."

He flipped up the screen on the computer and it blinked on. He had spent all night getting the programming and the laptop ready.

"When you get the stick, just put it in here. The computer will check that he's given you the right drive. If it doesn't come back with Chamberlain's name, it's not the right one. Can you follow that?"

"Yeah, I follow. We'll get the damn stick." Harding took the laptop and folded it up. "What's on it?" he asked nonchalantly.

"Some old records, ancient history. Don't worry about the contents of the disk, Harding. Just get it. And don't screw up again."

Greystone stood up and walked off toward the Jefferson Monument.

*   *   *

Harding gingerly clutched the laptop like a first-time father holding his newborn baby. It had taken all of his control to keep from strangling the executive on the spot. The arrogance of some of his clients never ceased to amaze him. They hired him to do jobs they didn't have the guts to do, then treated him like they were doing him a favor. Maybe he didn't know how to work this damn thing, but he was sure Nathan did.

There might be an extra reward in this transaction after all. Despite his client's clumsy attempt to minimize the importance of the drive's data, his tone and body language suggested it was of significant value.

He'd talk to a few of his contacts after he retrieved the disk. The information might be valuable in the future and it would serve the prissy bastard right for threatening him.

*   *   *

As Harding walked back to his car, a young couple strolled hand-in-hand along the path leading toward the Washington Monument.

"There he is," Goddard said. "On the bench to the left."

They continued toward the black man sitting quietly on a slat wood bench. He appeared to be deep in thought while nervously gnawing on a small toothpick.

"Detective Fowler?" Braxton asked as they came around the bench.

The detective raised his head and Braxton saw an expression that was hardly compassionate. He suddenly wondered if he had done the right thing in calling for the meeting.

"Jesus, what happened?" Fowler asked. "I hardly recognized you."

"That was the idea, Detective."

"It's about time you surfaced."

"Good to see you too, Sam. You remember Ms. Goddard?"

"Sure, of course. I still can't figure why you look so familiar."

"Perhaps if I use my real name, Detective," she said. "It's Lynch. Susan Lynch."

"Lynch? You're Senator Lynch's daughter! It's been nearly twenty years since I saw you last. You were just a kid."

Goddard smiled at the detective's surprise. "And now I remember you too, Detective. You came to the house and gave us the news of Father's death. We were all a little younger then."

"Yeah, I guess you're right. I found his . . . your father that morning. Sergeant Brady and I went to your home. I'm very sorry Ms. Lynch, er, Goddard."

"Thank you, Detective. Either is fine. Momma and I changed our names to avoid all the publicity after Father's death. You were very kind to us throughout the ordeal. I never thought I'd be meeting you again under these circumstances."

"I need to know exactly what 'these circumstances' are, Ms. Goddard. Things have gotten a little crazy over the past few days." He turned to Braxton. "Are you sure you've figured all this out?"

"Yes, we're positive," Braxton replied. "Chamberlain and Nicholson are behind the Internet rogue and all the murders."

"But why get Goddard mixed up in all this?"

"We found we were both investigating crimes," Goddard explained. "I've discovered who was responsible for my father's death, Detective."

Fowler shook his head. His voice softened to almost a whisper. "Ms. Goddard. I'm sorry, but your father killed himself. There was never any doubt of that."

"I know. But someone drove him to it." Her hands squeezed into tight white fists. "Someone that spread the lies and destroyed his life! It was that damn Potterfield and his aide Nicholson."

Goddard's shoulders began to tremble. Braxton moved over to her and gently wrapped his arm around her waist. He led her over to the bench.

"Dammit, Adam. What is this all about?" His demeanor turned back to the hardened cop. "You can't go around accusing senators of murder."

"I can if it's true, Sam." Braxton gave a brief synopsis of their investigations and the connections they had unearthed between his network infiltration and Senator Lynch's death. He described finding Chamberlain, his escape to New Hampshire, and their fatal encounter with Nicholson.

Fowler continued chewing on his toothpick as the story unfolded. Braxton couldn't read a single emotion on the detective's impassive face. "That's quite a story. Do you have any proof to back it up?"

"It was all in Nicholson's house on Saturday. What happened to you? What happened to Nicholson's papers? I saw Potterfield gloating all over the goddamn TV last night. I thought you were going to secure them?"

"I tried. By the time I got there, Potterfield had arrived with a truckload of lawyers and the Secret Service. He claimed the papers had national security implications. They gathered them up and carted them away. There wasn't anything we could do."

"Doesn't that show you that we were telling the truth? That the evidence was there?" Goddard pleaded.

"All it shows is that Nicholson had some papers in his house. Not all that surprising for a Senator's aide. Yeah, Potterfield's story is a little unusual. But we'll never see those documents again. I doubt anyone will. Look, I would have called you if I had known where you were."

"I called *you* when I saw the report on the six o'clock news."

"You called? I was home all evening."

Braxton squinted his eyes and shook his head. "Whatever you say, Detective. It doesn't matter now. Every time we get close to something they stop us." Braxton slammed his fist down on the hard seat. "Dammit. That was our only proof."

"We've still got Chamberlain's file," Goddard said.

"Yes, but I haven't been able to decipher it. And we still don't know if it will implicate Potterfield in your father's death," Braxton said to Goddard.

Fowler pulled the worn toothpick from his mouth, snapped it between his fingers, and tossed it onto the grass. "Look, Braxton. Quit feeling so sorry for yourself. You don't have the time. Boston's still looking for you and the D.C. cops aren't far behind. And it sounds like somebody's connected you too, Ms. Goddard. You've got to find a way to clear your names. Could the stuff in this file explain Chamberlain's death?"

"I don't know. Maybe."

"Okay then. What can we do to crack the file?"

Braxton wrinkled his forehead as he looked back at the detective. "Whose side are you on? First it sounds like you don't believe us and now you're trying to help."

"Let's say I've had a change of heart. But the only thing that's going to save your ass is proof. What I feel isn't worth horsepiss. If the only proof you've got is on that disk then you've got to break it. How far are you?"

"Basically nowhere. We tried guessing Chamberlain's password all night and most of this morning. It could be anything, a family pet, his favorite toy, the day he graduated from college. There are too many possibilities."

"Do you need a computer? There's some at headquarters that I could probably use."

Braxton just sat silently with his head in his hands. There had to be a way to get the keyphrase. And it had something to do with what Chamberlain had said.

"I already bought him a brand new one," Goddard said glaring over to her companion. "A Lenovo with an i7 processor, sixteen gigabytes of memory, six megabytes of cache and a terabyte of disk. You'd think he . . ."

Braxton's head jerked up. "What did you say?"

"I said I bought you a computer."

"No. You said 'cache'. That's what Chamberlain said. Not 'cash' like money but a computer 'cache'." He jumped to his feet and grabbed for Goddard. "We've got to go. It makes all the sense in the world."

"Wait a minute!" Fowler grabbed Braxton's arm and pulled him back. "Where are you going and what are you going to do?"

"We're going back to the motel to break the code. See what you can find about Nicholson's history. There's a connection to Chamberlain somewhere. Maybe at MIT. I'll call you tonight. I promise."

Braxton broke Fowler's grasp and pulled Goddard down the path, leaving Fowler sitting on the bench with a very confused expression on his face.

CHAPTER 65

Vienna, Virginia
Monday, 1:00 p.m.

GODDARD HAD WANTED to leave the car at the Mall in case it was being followed, but Braxton had refused to take the time to ride the Metro. They hadn't gotten caught yet and he wasn't about to delay any more.

"We've got to get back," he had said on the way to the motel. "I'm an idiot. Chamberlain didn't mean cash as in money, he meant cache as in storehouse, or computer cache. It's a perfect word for his journal. I just hope it's enough to break the code."

As soon as they had arrived he added the new keyword to his password file and started the test program. They both watched anxiously as the results scrolled by on the screen. Ten minutes of breathless silence later there was still no breakthrough.

"Well, it's nothing really simple," he said. "Can you take over the vigil? I've got to make a pit stop."

He had just gotten comfortable when he heard Goddard scream.

"Adam! Adam! What do I do?"

He rushed out of the bathroom, pulling up his pants as he came in. "What's the matter?"

"It stopped!" She struggled to get out the words over her excitement. "What do we do?"

He reached over her and typed in a few commands. Hundreds of short lines scrolled on the screen.

"It looks like you got it," he said and kissed her on the top of the head. "These are the key phrases the program tried." He paused and pointed to the last line. "What do you think?"

The line read:

```
JournalOfTheCache
```

"Is that it?" she asked.

"I hope so. Let's look at the plaintext."

He entered another command and the screen filled with text. It was Chamberlain's journal.

The document went for 580 pages. The first half hour they huddled next to each other on the sofa trying to read it together on the small laptop, but they fought so much over when to flip each screen-full of text that Goddard finally gave up and printed out individual sections.

Now they sat at each end of the couch, reviewing year after year of frightening activities.

They were mesmerized by Chamberlain's discourse. It was a history of The Cache, a trio of men who had used every capability at their disposal to destroy their enemies and further their own selfish goals.

The identities of two of the students were clear, even from the author's first name only references: Warren, the introverted MIT engineer, and Nick, the older, street-wise power-broker-to-be. The third member was not so easy, however: a mysterious Harvard student named Bob who had gone on to become an important executive in the electronics industry. For some reason, Chamberlain had never revealed their full names or even the companies they had worked for.

Chamberlain described their introduction at MIT, the project for the 6.251 course, the small hacks while they were students. He traced their job movements and their occasional reunions.

Tens of pages were spent on key incidents: the infiltration of the Phone Phreaks, technical stock manipulation, insider trading in the mid-80s, and the rebirth of Century Computer, based significantly, as Braxton had guessed, on sabotage of competitors' systems.

The deeds of the Lynch affair were described in painful detail: Potterfield's obsession for the seat; Nicholson's manipulation of the police and the press; the satisfaction of the final result. Goddard sat silently, finally reading proof of these agonizing events.

The most recent entries had to do with the *Potterfield Bill* and public/private sector collusion in the military contractor industry. It was to be their most profitable endeavor, opening the doors for massive deployment of sensitive, but intentionally-compromised, command-and-control equipment in war zones around the world.

"Amazing," Goddard finally said at 3:15. She dropped the manuscript on the bed along with six densely written pages of notes.

"It is quite a story. It would make a great novel. Did you notice a change in Chamberlain's tone the past few years?"

"Yes. He started out so positive and enthusiastic. He really thought they were going to change the world for the better."

"The enthusiasm of youth," Braxton explained.

"Or the *naiveté*," Goddard added. "He sounded so tired and resigned toward the end. The Cache had taken on a life of its own and he couldn't control what was happening."

"Now that I think about it, he didn't seem well when I saw him that time in his office."

"He knew they were going too far. Nicolson didn't kill him. This Bob must have sensed he was becoming a threat. He had Chamberlain killed and put the blame on you."

"All the lives he ruined, the people he used."

"Like you," she whispered and gently stroked his back. "But now we have the proof. You can stop running and I can clear my father's name. And we can implicate Potterfield as well."

Braxton slowly shook his head. "It's not that easy. This is a startling document, but we have no corroboration. We can cross-reference it to some historical facts, but there's no additional proof. I'm a prime suspect in two murders, and you're the disgruntled daughter of a suicide victim who tried to blackmail a U.S. Senator." She glared at him. "I'm sorry but it's true. The financial transactions would surely be buried. Chamberlain said so in the journal. And it's not a crime to make money. The police would say we wrote up this little piece of fiction as a way to justify our crimes."

"Then we just have to get the evidence to back it up. The third member of the Cache is the key. There must be a way to identify this Bob."

"Unfortunately Warren didn't leave us much to go on. The electronics industry is pretty big."

Goddard's mouth twisted into a grimace. "All we have to do is find the names of everyone that took classes at MIT when Chamberlain and Nicholson were there. I wonder if the records even exist."

"Probably not on any computer we can get to."

"Then we'll find another way."

"The trapdoor!" Braxton suddenly leapt from the sofa and ran to the laptop on the bed. He started typing furiously.

"What are you doing?" Goddard cried.

"Maybe Chamberlain used 'cache' as a password more than once. We're going to track Bob through the Internet."

* * *

"Flanagan." It was 4:00. Rachel Flanagan wedged the phone between her ear and her shoulder and continued typing her monthly report.

"Ms. Flanagan, it's Adam Braxton. I need to talk to you about the Saracen Incident."

She nearly dropped the phone on the floor. The FBI had spent all afternoon Friday at the Center grilling every employee on what he or she knew about the consultant. She had spent two hours with them, trying to calmly answer their inane questions.

When did she speak with him last? *A few days ago.*

Why did she request him? *He was recommended by the personnel office.*

How did he sound the last time they spoke? *Normal.*

It hadn't been a pleasant experience.

One of the agents had said that Braxton might call but she never expected to hear from him again.

She took a moment to compose herself before she responded in her most concerned voice. "Adam, are you all right? We've heard all kinds of awful things about you."

She scribbled something on a sheet of paper and frantically waved it over her head, hoping that one of her staff would notice.

"Don't get all excited, Ms. Flanagan. I don't intend to stay on the line long enough for you to get it traced. I sent you an email a little while ago. Have you seen it?"

"Uh, not yet, Adam. What is it about?" She finally caught Barry Lighthorse's eye. He got up from his desk and walked toward her office. His movements seemed in slow motion compared to the racing of Flanagan's heart.

"There's a security trapdoor in Internet gateways made by Century Computer. The people behind it have run rampant through the Internet for years. They killed Ramal to keep him quiet and they have framed me."

Lighthorse finally made it to her office. She shoved the note into his face and pointed to his desk.

"I don't care who you tell. Just check it out. The instructions are in the message. Reply to the email when you have verified the trapdoor and I'll give you more information." The line went dead.

Flanagan replaced the receiver and stared at the notes she had made. She looked up and saw that Lighthorse was still on the phone.

"Rick, get me the network log!" she yelled across the room to Spaulding.

Braxton's email had arrived fifteen minutes earlier. It had been sent from his local CERT account.

Flanagan forwarded the message from the public input queue to her private account. As she scanned the message on her screen, the local FBI agent-in-charge returned Lighthorse's hurried message. She told him that Braxton had called but had only denied his guilt before hanging up. He thanked her politely but curtly and said he did not think further follow-up would be necessary. The simple explanation seemed to satisfy him.

She printed the email and laid it down in front of her. The message contained explicit instructions on how to unlock the trapdoor and how to test the security hole. If what he claimed was true, especially the murders, this was dangerous information for Braxton and for her.

It would be easy to simply give the message to the FBI. Why had she lied about what he had said?

Knowing the answer only too well, she turned to her terminal and typed the first commands.

*   *   *

"That was quite a performance Senator. I didn't know you had it in you."

Greystone sat back in the plush wingback chair and tried to appear relaxed. When he had returned to his office after the meeting with Harding, he had found a message from Potterfield's office, asking him to come to the Russell Building as soon as he returned. It had sounded more like an order than a request.

Intrigued by Potterfield's openness with the message, he had decided not to argue with the old coot over the phone and had agreed to the demand. Santana drove him into the District and he had been shown into Potterfield's office at 4:30.

"You'll find I still have quite a bit in me, son," Potterfield replied from a matching chair in his sitting area. "But I do admit I underestimated you. I spent most of last night going over Nick's files. Now I understand how he always seemed to be able to get those special jobs done."

Potterfield looked tired but content. He was wearing a freshly pressed blue suit with a pale red pinstripe. In a starched shirt and red cravat, he appeared ready for another round with the TV interviewers.

"Nick was very effective, Senator. A little headstrong and independent at times, but a good man. I'll miss him."

"As will I, Mr. Greystone. I hold you responsible for his death, by the way. You should have been more careful with this Braxton."

Greystone felt the blood rushing to his face. He wasn't sure he could keep from blowing up at the damned civil servant, or if he even cared if he did. "Now look, Senator . . ."

"All right, Greystone, take it easy." Potterfield raised his hands in a mock defense. "I didn't invite you here for a fight."

The executive cringed visibly at the representation. "I didn't realize it was an invitation, Senator."

"Don't get so testy, son. If we're going to be working together, we may as well learn how to get along. Now that I've got all the documents I want Braxton taken care of. And that damned Lynch girl as well."

"As do I, Senator. I arranged for that this morning. It was why I couldn't join you until now. It will all be over tonight."

"You found them already? Where are they?"

"The less you know the better, Senator. You can trust me."

"Of course, son. Of course. Nick said the same thing to me. Then I found out about his damn library. You're sure there is no tie back to us?"

"Absolutely not. We are all professionals here, Senator. And speaking of that, why the urgent call? It would be best if we did not meet so openly."

"I can handle that. The reason I called you is that I'm moving up the vote in the Senate. It's tomorrow."

Tomorrow? Greystone's eyebrows unconsciously jumped. Why would he rush the vote? He was running scared and would blow the whole affair. *Damn you Potterfield.*

"I can see you're surprised. No, I haven't lost my mind. I have found over the years that even Senators feel empathy, especially to one of their own. They will attempt to lighten their hearts by giving me their most precious possession. Their votes. I would like to have you available in case I need some technical background, however. With Nick gone, you'll have to do. Be in the chamber at 10:00 a.m. I'll make all the arrangements."

With that, Potterfield slowly pushed himself out of the chair and turned to go back to his desk.

Technical background, bullshit. Potterfield just wanted him there so he could gloat over the passage. If that's what it took, Greystone would be there all right. But they weren't finished yet.

"One more thing, Senator."

Potterfield came to a halting stop and turned back to the sitting area. "Yes?"

"Nick's files. Where are they?"

"I have them. They're quite safe."

"I'm sure that's how Nick felt as well, but I'm still concerned. We are in this together, remember? Let me take them. I have a significantly more secure environment for them."

Potterfield broke into a wide smile. His white teeth shown like a snarling tiger's.

"More secure than the federal government, Mr. Greystone? I doubt it. I think I'll just keep them for a while longer." The smile instantly disappeared. "Good-bye, Mr. Greystone. I will see you in the morning."

CHAPTER 66

FLANAGAN STOOD IN the shower stall letting the hot, surging water pound her neck and back. She still couldn't understand why Candela had been so combative. He was a little creep with a chip on his shoulder, but his reaction to her request had been well beyond his normal obstinacy. She had met him late that afternoon on her way to Rydell's office.

"Edward, have you seen Timothy?"

Candela looked her up and down with the familiar leer he used for all the women at CERT. "Not today. He's at that Internet security conference in Los Alamos."

"Oh, I thought he'd be back by now."

"What's the problem? Timothy left me in charge."

She wasn't sure whether to mention it to him, but decided she may as well. He would hear about it from Rydell anyway. "I think I've found a security hole in one of the Internet gateways. I'm going to assign a couple of my people to check it out and I wanted Timothy to be aware of it."

Candela's face changed to a look of concern. "Perhaps we should discuss this in private." He put his arm around her waist and pushed her toward his office. She escaped from the claw, but followed him in. They sat down around his small conference table.

He wrinkled his nose and began the inquisition. "This wouldn't have anything to do with that consultant Braxton would it?"

It was a strange first reaction, but then she was used to the paranoia of administrators. She had already decided not to reveal the source of her discovery. "Nothing with Braxton, but it is consistent with the incident at GW. It looks like the alert we received was correct."

"I'm not quite so convinced, Rachel. I'm concerned that we could get negative publicity from any work you were to do now. We can't afford to have any further connection to the consultant. I'd like you to put off any investigation until I can discuss this with Timothy."

"Edward, I don't see what this could have to do with Braxton. We've found a security hole. I can't just ignore it." Her voice was rising and she realized she was losing her temper. His attitude didn't make any sense.

Candela stood up and confronted his Deputy Director. "Ms. Flanagan, in Dr. Rydell's absence I am in charge here. The Internet will not collapse while we think this over. You are not to proceed without my okay. Are we clear on that?"

"Yes, Edward. Your *orders* are perfectly clear. You can be sure I'll take this up with the Management Committee as soon as possible." She had abruptly risen and marched out of his office. She hadn't stopped until she had reached her car.

The hot shower was helping her to relax but wasn't making her confrontation with Candela any less frustrating. Who the hell was he to tell her what to do? If that was the way Rydell wanted to run CERT that was fine, but she wouldn't be a part of it. And she'd make a helluva noise when she left.

Quitting wasn't going to fix the gateway danger, however. If Braxton was right and the security hole was intentional, if it was being used to subvert the Internet, she was going to find out about it.

She stepped out of the shower, toweled herself off, and immediately went to the phone. It was only 6:15. Most of her staff would still be on campus.

"Barry Lighthorse. How may I help you?"

"Barry. It's Rachel."

"Hi," Lighthorse's voice instantly lost its formality. "Are you still here?"

"No. I'm at home. I have another favor to ask."

"Something new on the Incident?"

Damn. How does he do that? "More smoke signals, Barry?"

"No. Terry and Phil saw you leave Candela's office. We figured it was something about Saracen. Everything okay?"

"Let's just say I've got a project to discuss with you. Can you meet me in the Ops Room about eight?"

"Tonight?"

"Yes. It's important."

"Sure. I'll be there." There was no hesitation. "Anything you want me to bring?"

"Nope. Just yourself. But let's keep this between us for now?"

"Okay, Rachel. If you say so."

"And Barry?"

"Yes?"

"Have some dinner. We might need to stay late."

She made two more calls before hanging up the phone. The results were all the same; the young professionals had heard something was up and accepted the invitation eagerly. She knew they would love the idea of being involved in a cloak-and-dagger activity. Ever since an unknown SysOp at Berkeley named Cliff Stoll had become a computer legend for tracking down the German Chaos Club, it was every computer jock's dream.

She slipped into a clean pair of jeans and pulled on a snow white V-neck pullover. May as well be comfortable. Breaking the gateway rogue was going to be complicated and tedious. They would all need to be at their best.

She left the house at 7:00, leaving just enough time to pick up a case of Coke and two dozen donuts before meeting her staff.

*   *   *

Flanagan arrived in the Operations Room at 7:50. It was hardly the stuff of techno-thrillers. CERT's budget had certainly increased under Rydell, but the Director was not one to lavish funds on fancy trappings, even electronic ones. The Room was large, about twenty feet square, buried in the middle of the building. The only window overlooked the artificial landscape of the adjacent computer room. The walls were stark white; they were completely covered in porcelain white-board. Magnetic trays with erasers and markers had been randomly stuck on its surface.

The boards were eternally covered with scribblings; the room provided an ideal environment for brain-storming and training. Whenever she came into the room, she felt like an archeologist entering a cavern of undiscovered cave drawings. It was a personal challenge to decipher the graffiti. Tonight's sketches looked like a comparison of network protocol stacks.

Along the wall under the window was a curved Formica table top, the closest CERT came to a command center. On the counter were the front ends of four top-of-the-line quad-processor workstations. They were loaded with the latest in graphics and video technology. A large television monitor hung from the ceiling above the workstations. The staff technicians had rigged a quick and dirty video patch panel that enabled any of the four screens to be displayed on the monitor. This made for easy viewing by other operators or observers sitting in the back of the room.

Behind the workstation console was a large oval conference table. It was used for impromptu meetings or discussions over listings and results. Apart from a few dark brown coffee stains, tonight it was clear. Barry Lighthorse and Christie Pratt were already sitting at the table when Flanagan entered. She dropped the donuts and a pile of papers on the table, pulled over a chair, and waited for the last member of her conspiratorial team to appear.

Pratt was tiny, only about five foot two with short curly hair, a pixie-like face, and dark impenetrable eyes. She was a very private person, keeping to herself and seldom joining in CERT/CC group activities. Frighteningly intelligent, she was also terribly introverted, a stark contrast to her boss, the only other female on the operations team. Pratt was satisfied to play a role behind the scenes, quietly working out a subtle software correction, or developing a new network certification procedure. For months after Flanagan had arrived at CERT/CC, she hadn't even known Pratt worked there. She had finally noticed that all of her hot-shot male troubleshooters would eventually disappear to an out of the way corner cubical when they were stuck on a problem. They would invariably return with a solution.

Rick Spaulding arrived at 8:10. Spaulding was one of the Center's old-timers. He had been with the organization since its formation and was their computer virus expert. A graduate student and systems manager at CMU when the Worm had struck, he had played a key role in directing critical information around the net during the attack. Intrigued by the character of rogue programs, he had focused his ongoing studies in this area. After he finished his degree, he had jumped at the chance to join CERT/CC. Over the ensuing years he had worked with all of the well-known computer viruses, and was a consultant to many of the commercial anti-virus vendors. This wasn't exactly a virus problem, but Spaulding's background would be valuable nevertheless.

"Okay, boss. Why all the secrecy?" Lighthorse finally asked after Spaulding had sat down.

"You remember the email from GW?" Flanagan began. "The one about the network anomaly?"

They all nodded.

"Saracen was right. A rogue program has infiltrated the net. Specifically, gateways made by Century Computer. It apparently monitors traffic and selectively intercepts messages."

"What do you mean 'intercepts'?" Spaulding asked with an incredulous look on his face.

"I'm not sure, it may copy the message and forward it to another system on the net."

"You mean someone can read every message on the Internet?" Lighthorse asked.

"Not everyone, but at least the ones that go through Century gateways," Flanagan replied. "Whoever has set this up can take whatever they want from the net."

"Encrypted messages are safe aren't they?" Pratt asked.

Flanagan hesitated, then decided she may as well go all the way. "We think so, but there are millions of Century routers in the world. It is possible they are cooperating."

"Jesus!" Spaulding exclaimed. "People believe in the security of the net, Rachael. This is a national security issue. How did the rogue get in the gateways, anyway?"

"We believe it was intentionally placed by someone inside Century." She realized the slip too late; it was already out of her mouth.

It didn't take long for Spaulding to react. "That'll make it even harder to find. No offense Rachel, but how did *you* find it? And who's 'we'?"

"Let's call it another anonymous tip."

"It's that consultant Braxton isn't it?" Spaulding said.

"I said it's anonymous," Flanagan said with an uncharacteristic edge.

Lighthorse jumped in to break the confrontation. "What do you want us to do? Try to find a way to deactivate it?"

"Not yet," Flanagan replied. "First, I want to find the bastard that's responsible. I want to track the messages back to him."

"Saracen must have discovered the statistics on the rogue messages," Pratt calmly explained. "It would have put the counters off. Is that why he was killed?"

The implication of the question left everyone silent. Flanagan suddenly realized what she had gotten them all into. Going against Candela was one thing. She could take the heat on that. But putting her staff into jeopardy was something else entirely. Had she gone too far this time?

"We don't know that. Look, maybe this is too serious for us. We can contact the FBI and let their folks handle it. I don't want anyone to get hurt."

Her team silently glanced at each other around the table. It was fifteen seconds before anyone said anything.

"Hell no," Spaulding said. "The FBI wouldn't know what to do if we did tell them. And I'm not about to miss out on this one. I'm in, Rachel."

"Me too," Lighthorse said.

All eyes turned to Pratt. Her head was bowed as if she was praying. Then it tilted up and Flanagan saw a mischievous twinkle in her eyes.

"Shit, yes," she said loudly.

No one had ever heard Pratt raise her voice, much less curse; it was the perfect tension breaker.

The team exchanged high-fives while Flanagan passed out Braxton's detailed instructions for accessing the Century diagnostic port.

"Here's what I have so far. This gets us into the diagnostic port. I'm hoping that you three can use what you find there to figure out what the rogue does and then determine the destination for the messages. Easy, huh?"

"Sure, Rachel," Spaulding said sarcastically. "No sweat. Do you have anything at *all* on the command set for the port?"

"The last page. It's some notes on general capabilities and command formats. No guarantees, but it should be roughly correct. Work out an approach yourselves and see what you can come up with. We'll get back together at 9:00. I'm going to try to get more background."

She picked up her notebook and left the Ops Room.

When Flanagan got back to her office she dropped into her chair and put her head down on the desk. There wasn't any way for her to get additional information on the rogue; she simply used the excuse to leave her team alone. She had learned a long time ago that it was better to set a direction and then get out of the way. Her continued presence would only inhibit their thinking.

But would they be able to do it? How could she expect them to crack a rogue that had been hiding in the Internet for years? And one with insider access and knowledge as well?

But she did expect it. They were the best. If they can't defeat it, they all had better start looking for new jobs.

CHAPTER 67

Carnegie Mellon University, Pittsburgh, Pennsylvania
Monday, 9:00 p.m.

Flanagan wasted the next half hour reading the latest Internet Monthly Report from the IETF. A few minutes to nine she walked back to the Ops Room. Her team was sitting exactly the way they had been when she had left almost an hour before.

"Okay, where are we?" she asked as she walked to the front of the room.

The engineers looked at each other sheepishly, none wanting to go first.

"Braxton didn't give us enough data," Lighthorse began. "We can't figure out what capabilities are really present."

"The gateway is just too complicated," Spaulding added. His hands fidgeted nervously on the desk top. "There's no way to determine where the rogue is or what it's doing."

Pratt sat silently staring at some papers in front of her.

This was not a good start. But she wasn't going to let them off the hook this quickly. She started walking around the table. "What about a memory map and process list? Can't you figure out something from that?"

"There over two hundred processes in that system," Spaulding replied. "We can't check out every one of them."

"Nobody said this was going to be easy. What are we supposed to do? Just forget about it and hope nobody else finds it?" Flanagan's voice was growing louder by the minute. She kept walking, then stopped behind Pratt. "Christie, what do you think?"

Pratt looked up from a well-worn notebook. "I'm not sure,

Rachel. The data from the diagnostic port is pretty sketchy. It could take a long time to figure out how to really use it. There is a pattern in the process allocations that might help, but . . ."

"There's no way to correlate those processes with the rogue," Spaulding interrupted. "We don't even know if the rogue is connected to any of them. It could be modifying the table to hide itself."

"I know, but if we map the processes to memory usage . . ."

"You can't do it. I've tried." Spaulding slapped his palms on the table and leaned over toward Pratt. "You think you know more about rogue behavior than I do?"

"Hey, slow down, Rick." Lighthorse turned to his colleague. "Just 'cause you can't find it doesn't mean it's not there."

"I didn't say it's not there," Spaulding shot back. "I said we can't locate it the way Christie wants."

"Enough!" Flanagan yelled. The team snapped their heads toward her and slowly sat back in their seats. "We're not getting anywhere this way. Maybe the approach is wrong. If we can't break it from the inside out what can we do?"

"We could try to track it," Pratt said hesitantly.

"Like a black box," Lighthorse added. "We monitor the outbound connections and follow the copy."

"Rick?" Flanagan asked.

"It might work."

"Okay," Flanagan said. "Take ten minutes and walk it off. Get some fresh air and come back with some ideas. I'll check in later."

* * *

She waited until 9:45. When she entered the Ops Room, the three were crowded in front of a complex diagram on the left white board. Spaulding was arguing, Pratt was silently staring at the diagram, and Lighthorse was drawing sweeping arrows on the wall. She couldn't tell if he was planning an assault or diagramming communications lines. She backed silently into the hall.

They asked her to join them at 10:05.

"I think we've got a plan," Pratt began from her position at the table. "We still don't know what's going on inside the gateway, the rogue is just too well disguised. But we think we can track the messages it's creating. It's probably scanning incoming messages in a background process, selecting the ones it wants, then sending another message, maybe just a copy of the original, to another location. If we can track those messages, we should be able to locate the recipient. He's our target."

"Can we pick out the rogue messages from the normal gateway traffic?" Flanagan asked.

"We think so," Lighthorse said. "Rick thinks we can isolate them by checking the message timing. But it means we need to seed the rogue."

"Seed it?" Flanagan asked.

"Christie's going to make up some sample messages," Spaulding answered. "Mostly gibberish, but with lots of phrases that might fit a pattern matcher: stock symbols, numbers, and technical terms. We'll send them through the gateway and see if they generate any unexpected traffic."

"If they do, Barry will track them with the Sniffer," Pratt explained.

"Braxton's program might help in that," Lighthorse said. "I think I can get it to report back to us from the downstream gateways. It'll make the tracking go a little faster."

"It's unlikely we'll get the source in one hop," Flanagan said. "Our experience says crackers take as indirect a routing as they can."

Pratt picked up the enthusiasm. "We'll just take it one step at a time, Rachel. We may have to repeat the injection a number of times, but we'll get there. How about it?"

Flanagan was impressed. The initial frustration had disappeared and they were finally acting as a team.

She would have loved to get her hands dirty in the experiment, but that was not how this was going to work. "How long will it take?" she asked, still playing the administrator.

Lighthorse hesitated and looked across the table to his colleagues. All he saw were raised eyebrows and shaking heads. "We're not sure. It'll depend on how many hops we have to follow."

"But you can do it?"

Lighthorse took one more glance around the table. This time he saw nods. "Yes."

"Then do it," Flanagan said. "Call me if you need anything." It was 10:18.

The three took up positions at the workstations. Flanagan couldn't resist and pulled up a chair behind them, keeping her eye on the monitor hanging overhead. Spaulding had connected it to the video from his workstation. It was his job to monitor the path of the messages. He called up a map of the Internet's eastern seaboard connections. The screen flashed and a labyrinth of lines and dots appeared, each one a possible path for the message they would track.

Pratt constructed the bait, a message made up of hopefully appealing phrases: a confusion of stock symbols, technology terms and names of Internet bigwigs. She sent the email into the gateway at GW.

Lighthorse monitored the gateway using its standard management protocol, SNMP. It could only give him statistics on overall activity, not particular messages, but it would be sufficient to tell him if an internally generated message had been sent.

Spaulding loaded their message identification program, the Sniffer, into the gateways connected to *gw-gate*'s six outgoing communication links and Pratt injected her first message. They waited for three minutes before Lighthorse reported. "Nothing unusual."

Everyone tried to hide their disappointment.

"Here goes message two," Pratt said as she hit the key.

Flanagan could sense the tension growing in the room. It was one thing to put the plan together; it was another to make it work. Would Pratt be able to generate a message interesting enough for the rogue? They had no idea what type of information it was looking for.

Spaulding fidgeted in his chair and it let out a squeak. Flanagan threw him a withering glance.

"Sorry, nothing," Lighthorse finally said.

Pratt's third message was a combination of high tech industry symbols and business data she had extracted from a D&B on-line database. She sent it off.

Only the eerie buzz from the workstation's fans broke the silence as they waited for the result.

Suddenly Lighthorse let out a war cry. "Message count anomaly."

Immediately Spaulding followed. "Positive return. *SURA-gate*, a gateway into the Southeastern University Research Association subnet." He highlighted the link and the *SURA-gate* node on the workstation map. The path glowed bright red. They had their first hop.

Each step took them about fifteen minutes to set up. As the minutes passed, the red line slowly zigzagged across the monitor above their heads. The line took long leaps across the screen then jumped back before it pushed out again. The rogue was not going to make it easy.

By 11:30 they had gone as far as they could. Her team was exhausted. Flanagan could see it in their faces and the way they hunched uncomfortably over the workstations. The message had traveled through seven gateways on its way to its destination. Hardly a direct route considering the target was only fifteen miles from where they had started.

They identified the last drop from InterNIC's site database. The answer confused them; they had expected a secret government agency or foreign company. Reality was much less glamorous.

Flanagan copied the address into her notebook and thanked the team for their efforts. They erased the diagrams from the boards and shut down the systems. Flanagan collected the piles of paper containing their notes. She wasn't about to leave any evidence behind.

"What now?" Lighthorse asked as they filed from the room.

There was now no question that someone had introduced a very dangerous rogue into the Internet infrastructure. It monitored communications and tapped confidential transmissions. Flanagan had to get back in contact with Braxton and see if he could supply the missing pieces of the puzzle.

"Now I try to find our consultant," Flanagan replied.

She flipped the light switch and the room turned black.

CHAPTER 68

"Do you think CERT has found anything?" Goddard was sitting on the floor of the room polishing her nails. It was the third time she had done them since he had returned from making the call to CERT/CC.

"Susan. I just checked at midnight. It's only been a half hour. I can't just stay connected and wait. Someone's liable to be monitoring the account."

"They must have *some* answers. Try again."

"Okay."

Braxton had been alternately entering through his CERT/CC, Cambridge, and GW accounts to throw off any authorities. He logged in and checked his CERT/CC mail account.

"I've got mail from Rachel!"

"What is it?" She jumped up and looked over his shoulder:

```
From: sFlanagan@cert.org

To: braxton@cerberus.net

Subj: Century Rogue

Adam,

We could not disable the rogue, but did track the
receiver to a company in Reston, Virginia named
Theater Electronics. I hope this is of some help.

I cannot keep this unreported. How would you like
me to proceed?

Regards,

R.
```

"My God! It's him."

"Him who? You know who did it?"

"Greystone. Robert Greystone. He's an executive at Theater here in D.C."

"He's Bob? Do you know him?"

"I should. He was the one that got me interested in computers."

"What?"

Braxton's reply was interrupted by a loud knock on the door.

"Who could that be?" Goddard asked.

A deep voice came through the door. "Adam Braxton. It's Detective Fowler. Open up, we need to talk."

They exchanged questioning looks, then Goddard hopped off the bed and headed for the door. "Hang on, Detective," she yelled.

"Susan, wait up. Make sure it's . . ." Braxton said as she turned the knob.

The door flew back, slamming into Goddard's side, and knocking her to the floor. Two men rushed into the room and kicked the door shut behind them. Automatic pistols with long canister-like silencers on their barrels appeared from under their coats and were quickly trained on the occupants.

The shorter man immediately turned to Goddard. She started to get up, but he struck her across the face with the frightening weapon. She fell back against the wall and slowly slid down to the floor, a stream of blood flowing from the corner of her mouth.

"Susan!" Braxton called out.

The taller man turned to him. "Shut up and listen, Braxton," he said. "Our job is to get a certain computer drive from you. You two be quiet and cooperate and we get out. Where is it?"

Braxton tried to fight off his fear and think. He had never stared into the barrel of a gun before; it paralyzed him. The race through the woods in Massachusetts didn't even compare. Then he looked into the eyes of the weapon's owner and was even more afraid. This wasn't a simple robbery. "Look, we don't know anything about a drive. You've got the wrong couple."

Harding stepped up to him and thrust the extended barrel of his gun into Braxton's left shoulder. The searing pain of the gunshot wound instantly returned and he doubled up on the bed. The intruder then slapped the side of Braxton's head with the automatic. Blood spurted around his ear and he rolled onto his back.

"There really is no use in continuing a charade, Braxton. You and Ms. Goddard here are quite famous now." Harding grabbed Braxton's collar and yanked the consultant up to his face. His eyes were cold and unfeeling. "We can make this easy or hard. Where is the drive? You wouldn't want anything unpleasant to happen to her would you?"

Harding nodded to his partner and Braxton heard a dull spit come from the corner of the room. Goddard screamed as a bullet splintered the molding next to her leg. She was trying to keep her composure, but he could tell she was hanging on the edge. Whatever was eventually coming, he couldn't stand to see them torture her.

"That's enough for now, Ms. Goddard," Harding said. "Although I doubt anyone around here would do anything about your screams. It's probably standard evening fare." He pointed the weapon toward the computer lying next to Braxton. Nathan walked over and searched it for a flash drive. He shook his head.

Harding glanced around the room and noticed a nylon bag by the dresser. "Check out that bag."

Nathan slid past Goddard, picked up the bag, and shook the contents out on the end of the bed: cables, a spare battery, a pile of installation disks and a couple of USB drives. He slipped a similar bag off his shoulder and opened a laptop. Braxton watched as he stabbed the first drive into the laptop and stared at the screen. What was he doing?

A look of frustration crossed his face and he pulled the drive out, replacing it with the second.

"No match," he said. "It's not here."

"Well, Mr. Braxton," Harding said. "It looks like we start again. Where is the drive?"

Braxton's head was ringing. He couldn't hear out of his left ear and his head and shoulder pounded with pain at every heartbeat. He rose up to try to say something and the man struck him again in the shoulder. He cried out and fell to the floor.

"You bastards!" Goddard jumped up and ran toward the bed. Nathan tried to grab her as she passed but she knocked his arm away and dove to the spot where Braxton lay. "Why are you doing this?" she cried. "Don't hurt him anymore. It's in the bathroom behind the medicine cabinet. Just leave us alone!" She reached down and cradled him in her arms.

Braxton felt the world slipping away, just like in New Hampshire, except this time he knew he wasn't going to wake up. He reached out to grab her. If this was to be the end, at least she would be close. She took his hand and held it tightly.

Harding nodded and Nathan grabbed the laptop, went into the small bathroom, and set it on the sink. A dirty shower stall filled the end of the tiny room. The chipped porcelain sink was wedged in the front corner; a commode sat between the two. There was just enough room for one person to squeeze along the right hand wall. A tarnished mirror covered the small medicine cabinet just above the sink.

Nathan swung the door shut to get some more room and leaned over the basin. Running his hand around the sides of the cabinet, he felt the corner of a small plastic object. Pulling a small knife from his belt, he pried the object loose. It was another drive. He pushed it into the machine.

*   *   *

Upon recognizing a new drive, Greystone's program searched all the files on the device for a PGP extension. Greystone knew this was Chamberlain's referred method of encryption and not one that would likely be used by Braxton or Goddard. The program rapidly found *journal.pgp*.

The program then used Chamberlain's public key, the one he made known to his colleagues, to check the file's author block, or signature. This would verify that the file had indeed been written by Chamberlain. The file passed the test.

As the verification name "Chamberlain" was being written to the laptop's screen, the program sent a special signal to the computer's parallel interface. The interface was internally wired to a small Radio Shack relay and then to a tiny Belgium initiator.

The initiator was pressed into a half-pound of C-4 plastic explosive that Greystone had meticulously molded around the other components in the laptop's case.

Three milliseconds after the program sent the signal to the interface, the initiator detonated. The detonation wave traveled through the compound, initiating a complex exothermic reaction that vaporized the laptop and sent an unearthly scream through the still Virginia night.

CHAPTER 69

A CALM STILLNESS washed over him. Braxton felt the world slowly slip past in a kaleidoscope of soft colors. It was quiet and peaceful.

Then bursts of light shattered the tranquility. They burned through his eyelids, interrupting the serenity of his travels. He tried to ignore them, shut them out, by closing his eyes tightly, but they were too insistent.

He forced a look and saw strange faces above him. Two men and a woman, hovering over him, shining small flashlights in his eyes, poking at his body. Why were they doing this? Why would they disturb him so?

Slowly, voices joined with the images.

"Pulse is 50, BP 130 over 65. Pupils are responsive." It was a thin male voice.

"This one looks okay for now. He'll hold out 'til the ambulance gets here." A female voice. But deep and harsh, not like Susan's. "Let's get back to the woman."

The images disappeared and he was alone again. He tried to go back to the other place, but somehow realized that he couldn't return; it was time to move on.

Pain racked his body as he tried to push himself up. He looked down to his legs and found he was nearly buried: pieces of furniture, plaster sections of wall and ceiling, the remains of clothes and belongings.

The last thing he remembered was Susan telling the intruders the location of the drive. She had held him close and taken away some of the pain. He had closed his eyes.

Then there had been an explosion. He had apparently survived, but where was Susan? She had been next to him on the floor.

He dug through the rubble, sat up, and surveyed the room. All the walls had been blasted out; he could see the courtyard in front of him and the interior of adjacent rooms on his sides. The bathroom was a dark abyss.

There was no sign of Susan, no other bodies at all. Hadn't there been others with them?

He looked toward the courtyard and saw that the paramedics— he had determined their identity by now—were huddled over a stretcher in the parking lot. He climbed out of the room and staggered over to the group. They were working on Susan.

"How is she?" he asked the female as she ran past him toward the ambulance.

"She's unconscious," the paramedic replied without looking around. She yanked a case out of the side of the vehicle and turned around. "Who are . . . Jesus, you were inside! Go sit down."

"Will she be okay?"

"We don't know. We're trying to get her stabilized. What's her name?"

"Susan. Susan Goddard. She's a student at Georgetown. You've got to help her."

"Any allergies? Medical conditions?"

"I . . . , I don't know."

"Okay. We're doing everything we can. Who are you?"

"Eh, Adam."

"Okay, Adam. Go sit down over there on the grass. We'll get back to you as soon as we can." She pointed to a grassy area at the end of where the building used to stand.

She left him and rushed back to her colleagues.

He didn't see any sign of either assailant. They couldn't have escaped the blast. They must be buried in the rubble.

He suddenly felt very dizzy and searched for a place to sit. There was a small bench behind the ambulance and he managed to struggle over to it. He dropped his head into his hands and tried to stop the world from spinning.

As his head cleared, he heard the wail of sirens. He peered around the back of the truck and saw two police squad cars skid into the parking lot. Four patrolmen jumped out, went toward the crowd that had gathered around the scene, and began herding the on-lookers away from the demolished unit.

With crowd control begun, one of them, Braxton guessed the officer in charge, went over to the paramedics. They spoke for a minute or two, then the woman paramedic pointed to where Braxton had been found. She glanced around, trying to find her lost patient. Finally shrugging her shoulders at the officer, she returned her attention to the patient at his feet. The officer said something into a microphone at his shoulder, and headed into the remains of the room.

There was nothing more he could do here. He hated to leave Susan, but the police would question him and it wouldn't take long before he was identified.

The paramedics could help her more than he could.

What he had to do was find who had done this to them: Robert Greystone.

Braxton slipped back around the ambulance, squatted behind a large elm in the woods behind the motel, and watched as the search played out.

* * *

The police gave up at 3:00 a.m. After the last cop had left, he limped out to the street. He had two missions: determine Susan's condition, and find Robert Greystone.

Susan had been certain the cops would have CERT's phone lines monitored, so she had made him take the car and call Flanagan from a pay phone. He had finally found one at an all-night Fast-Freddie's convenience store a mile away. After the call he had decided to split the distance. The Camaro was parked a half-mile away behind a Readi-Clean dry cleaners. It only took him a few minutes to get there.

He went back to the Fast-Freddie's, borrowed a real paper phonebook and started dialing. Three calls later he found her.

"Fairfax Hospital."

"This is Adam Goddard. My sister Susan was brought in earlier tonight. Could you please tell me her condition?"

"You're Ms. Goddard's brother?"

"Uh, yes, and I'm calling from Boston. Could you please help me?"

"Well, I guess so ... Oh, I'm sorry. Your sister is in critical condition. She's in intensive care."

"How is she? Is she conscious?"

"I really don't have that information, sir. Would you like to speak with one of the nurses?"

"Yes. Please."

A few seconds later a new voice came on the line. "ICU. Nurse Wald."

"This is Adam Goddard. I'm trying to get some information on my sister, Susan Goddard."

"Goddard. Yes. I'm afraid she is in critical condition, Mr. Goddard."

"Has she regained consciousness?"

"No. I'm sorry. You may want to come to see her as soon as you can, sir."

My God. She can't die! "How is she doing? Is there anything more you can tell me?"

"She is critical, Mr. Goddard. That's all I can say. There are some police here. Perhaps you'd like to speak with one of them?"

"No! Thank you." He quickly hung up.

She was critical but still alive. How could he have let this happen to her? Fowler had been right. He should never have gotten her so involved.

He returned to the phone book to find Greystone. This job was easier, the executive was listed at the top of a page. His destination determined, Braxton ripped the page out the book, stuffed it in his pants' pocket, and went back to the counter. He bought two extra-large bottles of Coke, a shriveled hot dog, and a Fairfax County street map. It was going to be a long night.

Greystone lived on Cutter's Lane in McLean, Virginia. The house was on a dead-end, set back from the road in a wooded section of the exclusive community. He stopped the car along the side of the cul-de-sac and peered down the driveway. The house was a vague outline at the end of the winding asphalt path. Only a single lantern shining at the front door broke the ominous darkness of the property. Braxton shrugged off the fear and tried to relax. All he could do now was wait.

A bright light flashed across his eyes and he jerked up, hitting his head on the frame of the door. At first he thought he was back in the motel room, buried under the debris of the explosion, but quickly realized he was outside Greystone's home. The pain came from muscles cramped from his unnatural position in the front seat.

He had been awakened by the morning sun's reflection off a long stretch limousine that had just turned into Greystone's driveway.

Braxton rolled his shoulders to loosen the knots from the uncomfortable night and checked his watch. It was 7:30. He had slept through the night! He feared the executive could have already left, but the appearance of the limo suggested otherwise. He waited impatiently, rapping his fingers on the top of the wheel, hoping to get a glimpse of the car's passenger as it left the development.

Through the sparse spring foliage of the trees he saw a figure leave the house and get into the car. From the swagger he knew it was Greystone. He waited until the limo had turned off the cul-de-sac, then started the car and took a careful position behind his quarry.

They headed out the Dulles Access Highway to Reston and Theater headquarters. Braxton considered trying to get inside and take Greystone there, but realized he would never get past the security guards in his disheveled condition. As he debated his next step, the executive emerged and climbed back into the limo. When it pulled onto the highway, Braxton was right behind.

The limo went east on the Access Highway, passing the Beltway, and joining I-66 toward the city. They crossed the Roosevelt Bridge and carefully navigated through D.C.'s morning congestion. Braxton had managed to keep a couple of cars between himself and the limo while they were on the expressways, but the morning traffic made such subtlety impossible. He finally gave up the effort at covert surveillance and just tried to stay as close as he could.

At 9:05 the driver dropped Greystone off in front of the Capitol steps and drove the long white vehicle to the waiting area off D Street by Columbus Circle. Braxton double parked in front of Union Station and bought a copy of the morning's *Post* at a kiosk. The "Today in Congress" section showed that Potterfield was bringing his *Promoting Freedom and Democracy Bill* before the full Senate. Greystone must be attending.

It was only 9:15. There was no telling how long Greystone would stay, but he wouldn't have come all this way for only a few minutes.

Time for some special errands.

Braxton jumped back in the car and headed out of the city on Rt. 50. Stopping at a small strip mall, he found another payphone and called the hospital. Susan was still unconscious and they couldn't, or wouldn't, give him any more information. The day nurse was pleasant but kept putting him on hold. He finally decided he wasn't going to get any help and abruptly hung up.

Next, he went into the K-Mart for a few supplies.

Then he was ready to return to D.C.

CHAPTER 70

Capitol Hill, Washington, D.C.
Tuesday, 10:30 a.m.

BRAXTON DROVE INTO the limousine parking area. His hands were shaking, an unfortunate result of the abundance of caffeine he had put into his body over the past twelve hours. As he readied himself for the imminent confrontation, he realized even this affliction would work to his advantage.

The chauffeurs were gathered around one limo's hood, playing cards and biding their time before being called back to duty by their self-important masters. He drove slowly past them, wondering which would be his target, then continued down the next row, locating Greystone's limousine at the end of the row.

He pulled out onto 2nd Street, and found a space down about a block. He was as ready as he would ever be. There hadn't been much he had needed for the disguise; his clothes were still ragged and torn from the explosion. K-Mart had supplied a long wool women's coat that he had turned inside out, and a very unfashionable purple felt hat he pulled low over his forehead. A pair of scuffed sneakers replaced his leather brogans. They better fit his disguise and would come in handy if anything went wrong.

His other purchases were stuffed into a worn nylon backpack sitting on the seat next to him. The pack had stood up admirably to his accelerated aging process: he had driven over it four times in the mall parking lot. He finally reached into the glove compartment, pulled out his revolver that Susan had retrieved from the Cherokee, and dropped it into the bag.

Braxton shuffled slowly down 2nd Street keeping his head down, and occasionally checking on the location of the drivers. The efforts to hide his face were quite unnecessary; citizens on the street did their best to avoid his path and his look. It was clear they wanted nothing to do with the shoddy, homeless man walking the streets of their capital. Braxton went his way alone and unbothered.

The vagrant made his way into the parking lot, stopping on the passenger side of a long white limousine. He pulled a piece of crumpled newspaper from the trash basket next to the car, and meticulously smoothed it out on the windshield of the limousine. His motions were slow and careful, as if this was a ritual he performed at only the most holy times. After the paper had been flattened, he folded it twice and set it back down on the hood of the vehicle. Then he leaned over the car as far as he could, cleared his throat with a loud cough, and spit a large dollop of saliva in the middle of the windshield. Taking the carefully folded newspaper, he spread the slimy liquid over the glass.

He rubbed the windshield for about a minute, then repeated the rite. This time one of the drivers noticed him.

"Hey 'Rico," a short, balding man said, "who's that messin' with yo' car?"

"Shit," a taller, black-haired driver replied. "Stinkin' tramp's screwin' with my limo. My boss'll have my ass if anything happens. Be right back." Santana threw his cards on the hood and headed for the end of the aisle.

"Need any help, 'Rico?" a burly black chauffeur called to him.

"Nah. I can handle some crappy little bozo."

Santana walked about halfway to the car and yelled. "Get the shit away from my car, man!"

Braxton ignored the order and continued carefully smearing his spittle over the windshield.

Santana ran to the limo, grabbed the tramp, and shoved him back along the polished doors. "I said get the hell outta here, stupid."

"I clean your car real pretty," Braxton slurred.

"The hell you'll touch this car. Look what you did to my windshield! How am I gonna get this crap off?" Santana grabbed the newspaper and tried to remove the slimy fluid.

"I got good stuff to clean. I'll clean it up good." Braxton reached into his backpack.

"Go to hell you bastard. Just get the . . ." Santana stopped abruptly when he felt the barrel of the revolver in his stomach. He looked down at the weapon and into the cold eyes of the tramp.

"Just keep your mouth shut," Braxton ordered. "We're going to take a little ride and you're driving. I've got no beef with you but I've already killed two people this week and you're next if you mess with me. Get into the car, this side!" He motioned for the driver to open the passenger's front door.

The chauffeur took another look at the hate in Braxton's eyes, then mouthed a silent prayer, opened the door, and slid across the seat to a position behind the wheel. Braxton followed him in and told him to start driving.

*　*　*

"What happened to 'Rico?" the balding chauffeur asked as he watched the limousine leave the parking area.

"He musta had to get the damn car washed," the big black man replied. "Stinkin' bums are a pain in the ass."

*　*　*

They circled the Mall and drove down South Capitol Street. Braxton had a rough plan in mind but was completely lacking in the details. He had no experience in coercing people with guns, but he wasn't going to let anything get in the way of stopping Greystone. He would just have to rely on his instincts.

As they approached the waterfront, Braxton saw what he had been searching for. He motioned with the revolver and Santana turned at K Street, eventually stopping in front of the burned-out shell of a warehouse. The relic was a reminder of more prosperous commercial times in the District, before law and politics became the economic imperatives. Braxton pulled Santana out of the car and shoved him through a battered, charred doorway.

"Hey, man," Santana pleaded. "I don't know nothin'. I got kids, a family. Don't kill me."

"Do as you're told and you'll have a great story to tell. Take off your clothes."

"Please, *Señor*. I don't do no funny stuff."

"Oh, Jesus. I just want your uniform. Now *strip!*"

Santana stripped to his briefs and handed Braxton the clothes.

"Face down on the ground," Braxton ordered.

"It's dirty down here, man. What I've got to do that for? I won't try anything."

"The *ground*." Braxton yelled. He punctuated the order by poking the chauffeur in the ribs with the revolver. "Now!"

Santana kneeled to the ground, wiped away some loose wood scraps and rocks, and flattened onto his stomach. Braxton pulled a long plastic cable tie from one of the pockets of the oversized coat. He moved over the prone body and yanked back on Santana's arms. The driver let out a squeal.

Braxton bound the man's wrists, then duplicated the restraint at his ankles. He stepped back to admire his work. Quite a way from network security.

He went over to the pile of chauffeur's clothes and started to change. "What's your name?" he asked.

The driver rolled over and looked up. "Enrico Santana, *Señor.* Most folks call me 'Rico."

"Well 'Rico, just take it easy and you'll be fine. I've got some work to do this afternoon. When I get done I'll call the police and they'll come and get you. That's all there is to it."

Braxton knew he would never make the call, but also knew the driver wouldn't wait around. He was a resourceful, street-wise operator who would make quick use of the ample nails, hooks, and rusty metal straps in the old building. All Braxton needed was a couple of hours.

He finished changing and brushed the ashes off the uniform. It was too large but would have to pass. He left his filthy street clothes in a pile on the ground.

"When will Greystone want you?"

"Don't know, man. He calls me on the phone when he's ready. It's in the coat pocket."

Braxton found a small, folding cell phone in the chauffeur's jacket.

"*Señor,*" Santana called. "What you gonna do with Mr. Greystone? You gonna off him?"

Braxton turned. *What am I going to do? Could I kill him?*

So much had happened. All the lies. All the deaths. Greystone had to be stopped.

"That's up to him 'Rico. It's a personal thing."

Santana raised his head and nodded as if he now understood

Braxton's intensity. "I hope you do, man. He's one mean sonova-bitch."

Braxton drove into the limousine parking area at 11:15. He sat quietly in the soft leather seat, trying to stay alert despite the debilitating fatigue that encased him. He needed to rest but couldn't allow himself to drift off and enjoy the peace it would bring. He had one more obligation he had to fulfill; an obligation to Paul, to Susan, and even to Warren; an obligation to end the nightmare of the Cache.

He stared out over the parking lot, with its neat, parallel white stripes, and then beyond to the straight, chiseled lines of Union Station. More examples of the cold, logical order man imposed upon the world.

Soon his supposed friend and mentor, Robert Greystone, would call for his limousine. He would then pay for the horror of the previous night.

*   *   *

Greystone gingerly walked down the steps of the Capitol Building. His back was killing him. It was 2:30 and he had been sitting in the damn Senate gallery since nine-thirty that morning; in seats that reminded him of high school bleachers. The worst part was that there had been no reason for the appearance. It had been all Potterfield's show. The old bastard had huffed and puffed, growled and groveled, but finally had his way. The Bill had passed, essentially unchanged, sixty-five to twenty-nine.

The success would calm Flitterman's and Hajima's concerns and keep them off his back for a few more days. Ahead, the joint conference committee would be a major test. He decided to return to the office and gather some background on the more difficult Representatives.

The loss of Nicholson was unfortunate. This was normally a job he would have left to his colleague. He had been very useful, an internal source for many of the political battles they had worked, but there were other ways of getting information. Most of the government was connected electronically and poorly trained staff often left sensitive background data easily accessible.

Potterfield, however, was as much a liability as an asset. He had been sharp early in the session, but had become visibly weary by the afternoon. Nicholson's death was still having its effect. Potterfield was critical to the Bill's passage, and critical to Greystone's plan for Theater.

Greystone had a meeting with the Senator scheduled for Wednesday. Potterfield would need to be reminded of the successful handling of Lynch and Braxton.

His limousine was waiting at the foot of the limestone staircase. As he approached, the chauffeur opened the passenger door and Greystone slid onto the wide bench seat. The door closed behind him.

"What happened to Enrico?" he asked after the driver had settled behind the wheel.

"'Rico was taken ill, sir," came a voice from the front. "They asked me to take you back."

He was angry that Santana had the impudence to get sick, but it wouldn't be the first time that the Cuban had gotten into some trouble and had to be replaced.

Greystone didn't like surprises. And he really didn't like incompetence. The new driver looked like a bum. His uniform was too big and hung sloppily from his body. His cap sat forward on his head, partially obscuring the man's features. From what little Greystone could see, the face looked dirty with a short, scruffy beard. The transport company would hear about this later.

He relaxed back into the seat and pulled a manila folder out of his briefcase. Hajima had sent some new proposals by courier that morning. He would review them on the way back to Reston.

The documents were unbelievably complex. Takagawa's lawyers had learned all the nuances of corporate law in the United States. He scanned the changes quickly, then started again for a more thorough reading. Suddenly the vehicle swayed violently, throwing his briefcase onto the floor and knocking him against the door.

"What the hell!" He looked up and observed the scenery flashing by. This was not I-66 to Reston. It looked more like Rock Creek Parkway. "Driver, where are we going?"

"Just a short side trip, sir. We'll be there in a minute," the driver replied.

Greystone grabbed the passenger handle above the door for support and straightened up. He swept his hand across his lap to remove the loose documents and leaned forward to catch a glimpse of the driver in the rear view mirror. There was something familiar about the dark-haired man behind the wheel. The limousine tipped again and he grabbed for the lip of the control console at his side. He squeezed it tightly until he regained his balance then calmly leaned back in the seat and crossed his legs. The corners of his mouth turned up slightly, revealing a self-satisfied smile.

The limousine sped up the Parkway for another three miles, weaving dangerously in and out of the mounting afternoon traffic. Greystone sat silently in the seat, only the colorless knuckles on his left hand displaying any hint of concern.

The limousine lurched suddenly, throwing Greystone forward into the facing seat. He felt the wheels lock and heard the sound of squealing rubber on the asphalt. Sliding out of control, the car miraculously found a hole in the oncoming traffic and dove across the road into a rest area.

The area ahead was little more than a small dirt and gravel pull-off. There were no buildings to be seen, but a wooden picnic table had been placed just off the clearing by the Park Police for tired and hungry tourists. A foot path led from the table along the edge of the pull-off then disappeared down a slope into brush and increasingly dense woods.

The limousine's tires cut into the loose surface and threw a dense cloud of dirt and debris into the air. In the midst of the darkness, Greystone felt the car again accelerate as the driver steered into the narrow path. The vehicle flew over the ridge and landed hard on the downward slope. The impact threw both of the vehicle's occupants up to the roof then unceremoniously dumped them onto the floor. Fortuitous positions as the uncontrolled projectile careened another fifty yards down the trail before colliding with a 300 year old oak. A low branch of the aged tree speared through the front windshield and the privacy divider. Had anyone still been seated, they would have been gored by the thrust.

Ten minutes later, there was still no movement from the limo.

CHAPTER 71

Fowler paced the hall of the hospital like an expectant father. The past hours had confirmed his fears; he had been completely helpless to protect his friends from the dangers they had uncovered. Now one lay near death and the other was being actively hunted by his own department.

Where the hell is Braxton?

Fowler had been working the night shift and had heard the call at 12:45: *ambulance and backup needed at location of bombing.* He had rushed into Virginia, but it had still taken nearly a half-hour to get to the motel. When he had arrived, a Fairfax County cop had recounted the reports of the witnesses and paramedics. The most seriously injured survivor, a Susan Goddard, had already been transported to Fairfax Hospital.

The decimated motel unit had an all too familiar look and smell. This was *his* fault. He should have put them in protective custody, arrested them, anything but this. He had kicked at the charred and broken timbers in frustration.

The detectives on the scene believed there had been four people inside the apartment at the time of the explosion. How any of them had lived through the blast was the major topic of discussion.

Goddard had been found first and had occupied most of the paramedic's time.

An unidentified man had been found under a pile of rubble, declared in stable condition, and ignored while dealing with Goddard's injuries. After she had been sent to the hospital, the paramedics discovered the man had disappeared. A search of the surrounding area was underway.

The gruesome remains of another body had been found scattered throughout the debris.

Finally, forensics had found a trail of blood from another survivor. They were sure it was not from the paramedic's missing patient.

Fowler had joined the search for the absent witness; there was no question in his mind that it was Braxton, but he had eventually given up and had headed for the hospital.

Things hadn't gotten any better through the night. Goddard had now been unconscious for over twelve hours. The emergency room staff had treated her obvious injuries: broken collarbone, three broken ribs, collapsed lung, face and neck lacerations, hairline skull fracture, and assorted other cuts and scratches. Serious, but not necessarily life threatening. But they couldn't wake her. She had been taken to the intensive care unit and wired to every blinking box they could find.

Where the hell is Braxton?

Fowler hated hospitals. Too many of his friends had gone inside and never come out.

He remembered another night so many years before. He had brought Kenneth Lynch to a similar ER after the ex-Senator had driven alongside the Jefferson Memorial and put a bullet in his brain. Lynch had held on for six and a half hours but the damage had been too great. Fowler had volunteered to tell the family and had kept in touch through the ordeal, but there had been little he could do to ease the pain. Until yesterday, that had been the last time he had seen Susan Goddard Lynch.

The critical eight hour milestone had passed and she had still not regained consciousness. The mood in the ward was somber.

The doctor had told him it was up to her. Did she have the will to pull through the trauma?

What the hell did that man know? The kid had seen more pain than any ten people deserved. Maybe she was tired of fighting all the time.

Where the hell is Braxton?

He had ordered the floor nurse to get him if anyone called asking for Goddard's condition. Succumbing to the all-nighter, he had finally walked down to the cafeteria to get some coffee and a sugar fix. That was when Braxton had called, of course. The duty nurse had tried to keep the unidentified man on the line but she couldn't find the detective. The caller had hung up just as Fowler had appeared around the corner.

"Detective Fowler?"

He turned and saw a much-too-young man in green scrubs walking toward him. The front of the pullover was dotted with dark red spots. "I think you need to come with me."

*   *   *

Braxton awoke on the floor next to the front seat. He hadn't anticipated the steep slope behind the ridge and had lost control of the long limo as it dove into the ravine. His plan had been to drive just far enough into the woods to hide the limousine, then force Greystone out. What happened after that was up to the executive.

Braxton lifted himself to the seat, shoved open the passenger side door, and jumped the three feet down to the ground. Sitting down on a fallen tree trunk, he took stock of his situation. There didn't seem to be any serious injuries; his back ached and one leg felt sore, but otherwise he was all right.

The limousine was another story. It sat on the enormous limb looking like a huge skewered hog. The front end had been crushed and the hood was buckled nearly in half. Steam hissed from the mangled radiator.

They were in a small clearing about fifty yards down a slope from the rest area. The foot path had taken a sharp turn around the old oak; his limo hadn't.

For the moment they were alone. The rush of traffic on the Parkway was only a whisper in the background. No one could see them.

He heard movement in the car. He wasn't sure what condition he wanted Greystone to be in. If the executive were dead, it would be over; but he would never get the evidence to clear his name. If Greystone were still alive he would have to figure out how to get the information he needed. He reached down and felt the revolver still stuffed in his belt. Pulling it out, he checked the cylinder, then raised it toward the limousine's mid-section.

The door swung open, pushed by a long suited arm. Greystone emerged, negotiated the short drop, then brushed himself off and stood nonchalantly in front of Braxton and the gun. He put his hands in his pockets and looked as if he had had nothing more than a hard day at the office.

"Not a bad disguise, Adam," the executive said. "But then, you've had a time of it, haven't you? I must say you certainly are difficult to kill."

Greystone's casualness was unnerving. Braxton pushed himself up and walked closer to the man, keeping the revolver leveled at his chest.

"Why, Robert? Why? I thought we were friends. I thought I *knew* you! What happened?"

"Happened? Nothing *happened* Adam. You merely saw what you wanted to see. You don't get anywhere in this world by waiting for things to happen. You have to make them happen. That's what I have been doing.

"Your problem is that you always let things happen *to* you. Then you try to react. You're just like your father in that regard."

"My father! What about him? You were supposed to be his friend as well. He hired you; mentored you. What do you mean?"

"Of course he hired me, I was the most qualified candidate. I gave him all the background he wanted; exhibited all of the personal traits he valued. But eventually I couldn't protect him any longer. The business was changing and he couldn't see it. Wouldn't see it. I could. The Board agreed with me. That's why I had to take over for him."

"He said you had supported him. That it was the Board's plan. But it was you!"

Greystone maintained his smug smile and shook his head. Braxton wanted to fly into this traitor, take his throat in his hands and squeeze the life from him, but that was what Greystone wanted. He had to stay calm to get what he needed; to keep Greystone talking.

"We know all about the Cache, Robert. Warren left a journal; a log of all your activities. We have it all."

"Oh yes, a journal. It would be like Warren to keep such a thing. He even mentioned something about it once. I'm sure the press will be fascinated by how you constructed the story. Unfortunately you have absolutely no corroboration. Who will people believe, a psychotic failure who has already killed two people, or a successful executive and national leader? I'm afraid it's a little too Machiavellian, Adam. No one will believe you."

CHAPTER 72

Rock Creek Park, Washington, D.C.
Tuesday, 3:30 p.m.

Braxton knew Greystone was right. The journal was not enough. He had to keep Greystone talking.

He took another step forward. "Why all the killing Robert? You had the power, the knowledge."

"It was a part of the plan, of course. You have to exercise all of your options. I have a Japanese colleague. They understand that business *is* war. And in war there are casualties. Remember that Senator Lynch took his own life. We didn't kill him. He was not able to compete for his seat. We won and he couldn't deal with the result. It happens."

"But why me?"

"You were perfect, Adam. Unwittingly, you had created our next breakthrough. The diagnostic port would give us complete access to the Internet. Warren recognized the opportunity but we knew you would never have allowed it to be included in the final product. By removing you, we eliminated that obstacle. The back door works very well, by the way, but I guess you have realized that.

"I discovered Ramal quite by accident, but once I had I simply couldn't let him open the operation to scrutiny. You were an insurance policy. I couldn't be sure what CERT would do with Ramal's information. I arranged to have you placed there so we could follow the progress of the investigation."

"But it didn't work out the way you had planned, did it?"

"No. You surprised me, Adam. I thought you would just bumble along and finally give up. But you were much more tenacious than that. So I had to take appropriate measures."

"What about Warren?" Braxton felt a tremor in his outstretched hand. He tried to will it to stop but his arm would not respond.

"Warren was ill. He was becoming increasingly unstable. I decided to eliminate both of you at once. An unfortunate decision on my part, I should have been more direct. It's always the best way."

"When does it all stop, Robert? You had no right to kill Paul. To involve Susan."

"Your friend was a mistake by my contractor. He has become quite ineffective wouldn't you say? Even botched the explosion at your motel.

"Ms. Goddard, or should I say Lynch, was an unbelievable coincidence. Who would have thought that she would be associated with both Ramal and Potterfield? Or that the two of you would get together? Nick made the connection, by the way, only two days ago. I was quite upset when I heard you had killed him. He was a very effective colleague. So it was finally necessary to get rid of you both. That's why one always has to have contingency plans, Adam. You never know what will happen."

"You're insane," Braxton cried. He felt the tremor getting worse. "I have to kill you. I have to get rid of you and your abomination, this Cache."

Greystone's gaze briefly dropped to the wavering weapon. "The Cache? Such an amusing name. Warren thought it was quite clever. You don't really think I only had the two of them do you? You cannot imagine the extent of my power." His friendly, chatty tone suddenly turned cold. "You have led a charmed life, Adam Braxton. That incompetent assassin missed you twice. I won't make the same mistake. It's time to end this little conversation."

Braxton could no longer restrain his anger. The man in front of him had taken his whole life: his father, his best friend, the woman he loved. He tried to raise the revolver at Greystone's face but it shook uncontrollably in his hand.

"Don't stress yourself unnecessarily, Adam. You can't kill me; it's just not in you."

Braxton felt sick. This had to all stop; he couldn't listen to any more. He thought of Susan and all she had meant to him; of all Greystone had done. He willed his arm to straighten and his finger to close on the trigger.

"Braxton! No! Don't do it!"

The shout came from up the rise. He turned and saw Fowler running down a path toward them. His gun was raised.

"Susan is all right," he yelled. "I was at the hospital. You don't have to do this!"

Braxton shook his head. Why couldn't he concentrate? If Susan was alive he had to see her. What was he doing here?

He was about to call to the detective when an explosion echoed through the woods. Fowler doubled over and dropped to the ground motionless. His gun fell from his hand.

"I think you should drop your gun too, Adam."

Braxton turned toward the voice. Greystone was pointing a large, very lethal looking, automatic at him.

"*Now*, Adam," Greystone ordered.

Drained physically and emotionally, he couldn't challenge Greystone this way. Shooting someone, even the bastard standing in front of him, was not who he was. And would get him in even more trouble not less. Better to back off and wait. His arm dropped to his side and the revolver slipped from his hand.

"That's better," Greystone said. "Move away from the gun." He motioned Braxton back, then pulled a pair of light cotton gloves out of his pocket and slipped them on, alternating the weapon between his hands.

Braxton stepped to the side, his chest heaving. He remembered the confrontation with Nicholson. He didn't give up then and he wouldn't now.

Greystone picked up Braxton's revolver, stuffed it into his belt, and pointed for the consultant to walk toward the detective. When they reached the motionless body, he took the detective's gun, trading it for his own automatic. He kicked Fowler in the side and the detective's head snapped up.

"Bastard!"

"Detective Fowler. What a surprise. I didn't expect you to join us."

"Sam, how did you find us?" Without thinking Braxton moved closer, knelt over the detective, and tried to help him up. Fowler's right pants leg was soaked with blood. He wasn't going anywhere.

"I went to the hospital to see Susan." The words came between winces of pain. "When she regained consciousness this morning she told me about Greystone. I promised her I'd find you. I was driving down the Parkway when I heard a call about a kidnapping and guessed it might be the two of you."

"What call?"

"Oh, I forgot to tell you," Greystone cheerfully replied. "I have an emergency transmitter in the car. When I recognized you, I activated it. It sends a silent alarm to the police and also acts as a locator. All very high tech don't you think?"

Braxton heard the faint sound of sirens in the background.

"Soon we will be found by members of the very efficient Metropolitan Police," Greystone continued. He turned back to Fowler. "You came by sooner than I had expected, Detective. I can't be sure what you might have heard, so unfortunately your colleagues will find there has been a terrible accident.

"I was going to have to kill you in self-defense, Adam, but now Detective Fowler has come to my rescue. Alas, you will have fatally shot each other just as the Detective was saving me. You may even get a commendation, Fowler. Posthumously, of course."

"Go to hell!" Fowler tried to raise up but collapsed on his wounded leg. He was breathing hard, trying to hide the pain.

Braxton felt Greystone's eyes upon him, and he quickly tried to hide his thoughts from the killer.

"You're thinking of Ms. Goddard aren't you, Adam? She is quite attractive, isn't she? I hope the two of you had some fun together." Greystone's expression changed into a suggestive leer. "She will be easy enough to take care of. Hospitals are such dangerous places."

Greystone's face turned back into an expressionless mask, only a fearful dark glow from his eyes betraying any emotion. Had it been that coldness, the lack of connection to humanity, that had driven Greystone to computers in the first place? Had he seen their inherent logic as more suitable to his personality than the unpredictability and fallibility of his colleagues?

Braxton realized there was a piece of Greystone in him, that part that had tried to shut out the human world and withdraw into work or despair. Susan had finally brought him back from that void.

He couldn't let Greystone kill Fowler. The executive was only twenty feet away. He would make something happen; he would do it for Susan.

A frantic charge worked with Nicholson. Could it be successful again?

"Screw you, Greystone."

The executive glanced down at Fowler's outburst and Braxton saw his opportunity. He screamed and charged, preparing himself for whatever would happen.

Braxton's suicidal dash caught the executive off guard. The moment's hesitation was a fatal mistake.

The first flash was almost too quick to perceive. Braxton saw the spot of speckled red light cross Greystone's forehead, then return to settle midway between his dark eyebrows. Half a second later it disappeared, replaced by a slightly larger black hole.

Braxton pulled up, still six feet short of his adversary, and heard the report, a sharp crack that resonated through the trees behind him. He started to turn and look toward the sound but was mesmerized by the sight of his would-be executioner.

Greystone's body shuddered as if he had caught a chill, then fell slowly backward finally reacting to the momentum of the bullet. He hit the soft sylvan floor with hardly a sound, a look of surprise still etched into his face. A pool of dark red blood quickly spread in the leaves and pine needles, forming an ironic halo around his head.

Braxton stared dumbfounded at the body, then snapped around to locate the shooter but all he saw was a jungle of brush and trees. He was still standing, so he supposed the sniper had taken care of his target and disappeared. Whoever it was, they were certainly better prepared than he had been.

He heard a moan and realized he had forgotten about Fowler.

"Sam, can you hear me?" he said, kneeling down next to the detective. The leaves under his leg were floating in a pool of blood.

"Sam!" he cried, shaking the detective's shoulders.

"Yeah," the detective grunted. His eye fluttered open. He was going in and out of consciousness. "What happened?"

"A sniper killed Greystone. He saved my life." Braxton was still shaking from the confrontation with Greystone. His last hope to clear his name was gone, but he had to focus on Fowler. "What can I do for you?"

Multiple sirens broke through the quiet of the ravine. They were coming in his direction.

"Greystone's alert," Fowler whispered in explanation. "Get

away." He was having trouble speaking. Braxton had to do something.

"Can't, Sam. I've got to look at your leg." He found the bullet hole and stuck his fingers though the pants leg. "This might hurt a bit," he explained as he ripped the material open, exposing the wound.

Fowler screamed.

Blood continued to gush from the wound. He had to find a way to stop the flow.

Braxton unbuckled Fowler's belt, yanked it out of the loops and wrapped it around his leg above the wound.

"One more time, Sam. Sorry." And he pulled the belt tight.

Fowler yelled again, but this time less loudly. Braxton didn't know whether that was a good sign or not.

What else could he do? What did he have that would help? He rubbed his hands over the chauffer's outfit and felt a bump. Besides his watch, wallet and cell phone, he had transferred the flash drive to Santana's uniform.

The cops were on their way. He couldn't leave Fowler, but his situation after they arrived was not likely to be cordial. There was no telling whether they would listen to what he had to say.

The drive was the last copy of Chamberlain's file. He had to keep it safe.

Lights flashed over the rise. They would be here any second.

He pulled the drive out of his pocket. "Sam, can you hear me?" Fowler's eyes were glazed. He was conscious but only barely.

"What?" Fowler responded weakly.

"I'm putting the drive with Chamberlain's journal in your pocket. The key is 'the journal of the cache'. Can you remember that?" He slipped the piece of plastic into Fowler's jacket.

"Journal?" The word came out in a slur.

"Yes, Chamberlain's journal. You remember we talked about it. The key is 'the journal of the cache'. Repeat it for me."

"Journal of . . ."

Suddenly Braxton flew into the air. Then just as rapidly smashed to the ground. His face was mashed into the carpet of pine needles and decomposed leaves. A knee stabbed in his back and his arms were ripped behind him and locked in a nylon cuff.

"Adam Braxton," came an angry, disembodied voice. "You are under arrest for the murder of Barclay Nicholson and Robert

Greystone. And the attempted murder of Detective Sam Fowler. You have the right to an attorney, anything you say . . ."

*　*　*

The sniper made one final scan of the kill zone, then stood back from the crook of the tree he had used as a stabilizer. The cops had turned the scene into a circus. They would be so focused on the two civilians and the dead body it would be hours before they even thought of another shooter. Ample time to make his getaway. It was the treacherous client that he had wanted, no one else. That score had to be settled.

It had worked out mostly as he had planned. Both Braxton and Greystone had been very predictable. The second arrival was a surprise, but Greystone had neutralized him and he hadn't presented any additional difficulties. The trip down Rock Creek, on the other hand, had taken all of his skills. Braxton had driven like a maniac and he had had trouble keeping up with him. Maybe he was getting too old.

It was time to retire, time to take his family to the quiet ranch outside Jackson Hole that he had purchased years before. A caretaker lived there now, keeping the home clean and the livestock managed. His boys would like the small herd of cattle, and the stable of riding horses. His wife would complain at first, and it would take some time for her to get used to his regular presence, but she would eventually succumb to the open air and breathtaking scenery. It would be a good life, and a fitting rest.

He slid his modified Remington M24 rifle into the case, bent down to pick up the spent casing, and dropped it into his pocket. One final look around to check for anything he might have left behind.

Then Harding limped back through the trees, disappearing into the ravine.

CHAPTER 73

BRAXTON HAD BEEN dragged through the ravine by two beefy
D.C. cops, thrown in the back of a cruiser and driven, full lights and
sirens, to Police Headquarters where he had been immediately led to
a claustrophobic interrogation room, dropped into a waiting chair
and left, his arms still handcuffed behind his back.

The room had originally been painted a sickly green, but now
there were more stains than paint covering the floor and walls.
Braxton couldn't decide which was more disgusting. Sitting there
alone, he tried not to think about the mix of bodily fluids that had
caused the spots.

He was seated in a cracked wooden chair. Directly in front of him
was a dented government-issue metal table, then two more chairs and
finally a small mirrored window stuck in the opposite wall. He
wondered how many cops watched from behind that wall.

A long fluorescent fixture with half its lens missing provided the only
light, and a small video camera was perched on a bracket in the far ceiling
corner, blinking its electronic eye at him with distracting regularity.

He sat in silence, a thousand thoughts flashing through his
head, but unable to bring any in focus enough to prepare him for
the forthcoming questioning. The Army had provided rudimentary
interrogation training, but he had paid little attention at the time.
In retrospect, a big mistake.

Adding to his anxiety, his arms ached and the plastic restraint
was having the expected effect on his psyche. He tried to breathe
deeply and relax, but the pounding in his chest refused to respond.

A door on his right opened and two men entered. Neither was in uniform. One man was tall, thin and completely bald. He wore dark trousers and a wrinkled blue shirt. The clothes of a working cop. His face was hard, like it was chiseled from a block of stone. And like a rock, his expression never changed.

The shorter man was stocky, with military-cut brown hair, hazel eyes and a dark stubble. His shirt was white, but no less unkempt. He, unlike Stone Face, had very expressive features, and from Braxton's position, the expression was one of pure hate.

"I am Detective Davidson," the shorter man began. "And this is Detective Frankel." Stone Face nodded. "Cooperate and you might get out of this alive.

"We've got your gun, two dead bodies and a critically-injured cop. My ex-partner by-the-way," Davidson added with a venom Braxton felt to his toes. "Now I don't give a damn about that Chamberlain guy, that's Massachusetts' problem. If they ever get their hands on you, which I doubt they will." Stone Face shook his head and agreed.

"No, you're mine until I say otherwise," Davidson continued. "We are not leaving this room until we get the truth. It will go a lot easier on you if you just tell us what happened. So why kill the aide to a Senator?"

*   *   *

And that was the way it went. Again and again. Davidson screaming questions, Braxton explaining what happened. Always giving them the truth. Never what Davidson wanted to hear.

It didn't matter what Braxton said, the questions were always the same. Sometimes Stone Face joined them, sometimes not, but it was always Davidson.

They had to have the ballistics reports by now. It would show he didn't shoot Greystone, Nicholson or Fowler. Why was Davidson insisting that he did?

Braxton struggled with his strategy. He could always just request a lawyer. The questioning would stop, but he would then be photographed, booked, thrown in a cell and forgotten. He didn't know any lawyers and there was no chance a public defender would believe him. He would be in the same position but buried deeper in the legal system. As painful as it was, he'd take his chances with Davidson.

They made every effort to wipe out his sense of time, but Davidson had forgotten to remove his wristwatch and Braxton had been able to sneak an occasional look. Between eight and nine his arms finally failed and he had slumped over in the chair; Davidson had removed his wrist constraints. It took fifteen minutes to get feeling back in his hands. At ten he had requested a bottle of water; it was provided. This was repeated at midnight and two. A bio-break was routinely requested, and routinely refused.

At three o'clock Davidson again appeared. Braxton hoped he didn't look as bad as the cop. His sweat-stained shirt reeked, his eyes were set into deep black craters and his cheeks had a pasty pallor that flushed red when the cop talked. The cop's deterioration was one of the incentives that kept Braxton going.

Davidson strode to the opposite side of the table, leaned forward and put his face three inches from his suspect.

"Okay, Braxton. Now it's really over." His rancid-coffee breath flooded over Braxton and made his stomach turn.

"You're a murderer and a liar," Davidson screamed. "You killed a D.C. cop and I'm not going to let you walk out of this room until you admit it!"

Killed a cop? What was he talking about? Had something happened to Fowler?

"What cop?" Braxton pleaded.

"You know damn well what cop. Sam Fowler is dead. I'm personally going to see you rot in hell for that!"

Braxton felt his heart explode. He couldn't breathe.

Fowler couldn't be dead. It had just been a leg wound. There was no one to corroborate what happened at Rock Creek. No one to explain the journal. He had no more proof of his story.

The exhaustion and despair finally struck him like a tidal wave. He nearly fell off the chair. He had never understood how innocent people could confess to a lie just to sleep. Now it seemed so obvious.

The door to the room opened and two men in dark suits entered. Davidson spun around.

"Who the hell are you?" he screamed. "Get out of my interrogation room!"

Braxton looked up and saw the intruders stand their ground. Even in his brain-dead state, they looked vaguely familiar.

The taller man spoke in a calm and clear voice. "You've had your chance, Detective Davidson. Time to give it up." He pulled a wallet from his pocket and flashed a badge. "Special Agent Brooks, FBI. This is Special Agent Salisbury. We're here to take custody of Mr. Braxton on behalf of the Federal Government."

"Bullshit," Davidson said, stepping in front of Brooks. His face glowed bright red. "This is murder of a D.C. cop! No way you put one more foot in this room."

Brooks flashed a condescending smile and turned his head. "Captain Rodgers, I think you need to rein in your pit bull before he gets himself in serious trouble."

A uniformed black man slid from behind Brooks. "Time to step down, Wes. These gentlemen have jurisdiction now." He turned toward Brooks. "*Everyone* needs to take a breath and calm down."

The room became deathly silent. Braxton watched as the politics of D.C. law enforcement fought the blood-red ties of police brotherhood. He felt like a piece of carrion being fought over by opposing packs of wolves.

Davidson made the first move. He turned, picked up his files from the table and headed directly for the door. Rodgers stepped aside but Brooks stood his ground as Davidson plowed forward. Their shoulders met with a force that would have been painful on a football field, but Davidson's momentum carried him through.

Rodgers followed his detective. "He's all yours, agents. I'd appreciate your leaving as quickly as possible. I can't be responsible for the actions of the rest of the Department."

The two agents picked Braxton off the chair, ground a new pair of handcuffs into his wrists, and led him out of the room. They walked him out of the building to a waiting black Escalade, and shoved him in the back seat.

He never imagined a car seat could feel so soft. He was asleep before the car pulled away from the curb.

* * *

He awoke with a start when Brooks opened the car door and yanked him out. It felt like he was in a cave: the space was cold and damp, lit only by flickering fluorescent lights. As his eyes grew more accustomed, he saw other cars and the acrid smell of gasoline and exhaust fumes bit at his nostrils. It was an underground garage.

"Where are we?" he asked groggily.

"You'll find out," Brooks replied and dragged him into an elevator at the end of the aisle.

They went up, the doors opened and he was led down an empty hallway with closed doors on each side. There were no descriptions on the doors, just numbers. Were they taking him to a cell?

He had initially felt the appearance of the FBI agents was a rescue, but now he feared they were simply taking him to a deeper level of hell.

They stopped and Brooks opened one of the doors. Braxton's heart was racing and he could feel his arms and legs shaking from the adrenaline. What were they going to do to him?

They entered a room not unlike the interrogation room at D.C. Police Headquarters. The space contained a plain metal table in the middle of the room with a chair on each side. Brooks pushed him into one of the chairs and he realized it was bolted to the floor as was the table. He was facing a large mirror, better for observing the condemned he imagined. To his surprise, Salisbury undid the hand-cuffs. Braxton brought his hands to the table, rubbing the raw red bruises on his wrists.

The walls were a pale yellow. In the corners of the ceiling above the two-way glass were large plastic bubbles; more sophisticated video monitoring equipment. At least the place was cleaner than his previous cell.

He heard a click and turned his head to see a new player enter the room. The man was tall, over six feet, with broad shoulders and a trim waist. He was dressed in an immaculate pin-striped suit, with a starched white shirt and bright yellow tie. His dark black hair was slicked back with not a strand out of place. A black leather folio was in his hand.

He looked like he was on the way to a White House state dinner. *How could anyone be this elegant in the middle of the night?*

Brooks closed the door and the two agents took positions out of sight behind Braxton. Whatever was going on, he sensed Brooks and Salisbury weren't happy about it.

The new man paused on the other side of the table, gazed down at Braxton, then sat in the chair facing him. His eyes were dark and emotionless.

"Where am I? Braxton repeated.

The man looked surprised that his prisoner had the audacity to speak. Then he replied with all the warmth of a rattlesnake, "FBI Headquarters, Mr. Braxton. The Hoover Building."

Braxton felt a wave of relief. At least it wasn't some CIA black site. If the man was telling the truth.

"My name is Craig Wheeler," he began. "I'm an assistant in the Attorney General's office."

Braxton's face furrowed. Did D.C. really have an Attorney General? Who was this guy?

Seeing Braxton's confusion, Wheeler added, "The Attorney General of the United States."

That certainly got Braxton's attention.

"This," Wheeler pulled a thick document from his folio and placed it in front of Braxton, "is a National Security Confidentiality Agreement. Think of it as your get-out-of-jail-free card.

"It states that under no circumstances will you ever disclose or discuss the so-called Saracen Incident with any one, in any way, at any time. If you do, you will be in violation of the listed sections of the United States Code and you will be prosecuted to the fullest extent of the law." Wheeler paused to let the threat sink in. "More likely, however, you will simply disappear.

"In return for this cooperation, all charges associated with your actions surrounding the Incident will be dropped. You will be free to go."

Braxton stopped breathing. He was being given a way out. He stared at the document. All he had to do was sign and it would be over.

Wheeler reached into his jacket, extracted a gold ball-point pen and laid it on the document.

Braxton began reading. Most was impenetrable legalese, but he was able to discern that everything involving the Incident had come under a National Security Finding and had been classified top secret. And it did offer complete Federal and State immunity for everything he had done.

The cover-up had started. That meant that someone knew what really happened. Knew about the mole, about Ramal and the Cache. Had Sam passed along the drive? But Davidson said he had died.

"How is Detective Fowler? Did he die?"

Wheeler hesitated for what seemed like hours. He wasn't used to being asked questions. Finally, he spoke. "The Detective will recover. He had significant blood loss and required surgery, but he is now out of danger."

Braxton had opened his mouth for another question when Wheeler continued. "Ms. Goddard had a broken collarbone, three broken ribs, a concussion and numerous cuts and bruises, but she is also in stable condition. The doctors expect a full recovery.

"That is all the information you get, Mr. Braxton. Time to decide."

"What if I don't sign?" Braxton asked.

"Believe me, you do *not* want to go there, Mr. Braxton," Wheeler replied with an unhidden enmity.

Braxton believed him. He knew he never wanted to face this man again. In court or otherwise.

He picked up the pen and signed the document.

Wheeler reached for the papers, stacked them neatly against the desktop, placed them back in the folio and stood up. "Have a good life, Mr. Braxton. You have some very influential friends. I expect to never see you again."

He nodded to Brooks and walked out of the room.

Brooks and Salisbury lifted Braxton out of the chair, only a bit more gently than before, and led him out the door and down the empty hallway.

* * *

Five minutes later, he was sitting at the top of the steps to the Hoover building, watching the pink glow of dawn brighten the dark D.C. sky. A Ziploc bag with his wallet, wristwatch, and seventy-five cents in change sat in his lap; a gift from Special Agents Brooks and Salisbury as they escorted him from the building.

Unknown forces had nearly taken his life. Now he apparently had his life back. But at what cost? Paul was dead, Susan and Detective Fowler were lying in hospital beds. All because he couldn't let go of a damn puzzle.

What should he do now? Where could he go?

The answer was surprisingly easy.

He walked down the steps to Pennsylvania Avenue and hailed a cab.

"Where to, bud?" the driver asked.

"Fairfax Hospital."

EPILOG

Tysons Corner, Virginia
Three months later, 9:30 a.m.

B RAXTON PULLED HIS shiny new Aztec Red Grand Cherokee into the Tysons Tower garage and spun his way to the last available space on the last available level. That's what he got for sleeping in.

He had considered other makes of car, but had finally decided that he owed Jeep an unpayable debt for getting him out of Chamberlain's property alive. He hoped his new baby didn't get a complex from sitting in the sea of Audis, Lexus and Mercedes.

He walked down to street level and crossed to the Tower under a cloudless blue sky and bright yellow morning sun. Most days he would have walked up the additional ten flights to his office, but today his briefcase was heavy with completed proposals and he decided to reward himself for the previous night's efforts.

The elevator door slid open and an attractive young woman stepped out. Freshly-scrubbed, blown-dry and bedecked in a trim conservative suit, she was fully prepared to do battle for her chosen beltway bandit. The twenty-two story Tower soared over the rest of the Tysons Corner landscape and was a high-visibility address for defense contractors who had outgrown their aging Crystal City offices. Whatever her destination, her outfit made Braxton feel like a vagrant in his sports coat and open-collared oxford.

He smiled, said a quick "good morning", and pressed the button for the tenth floor. As the door closed, he couldn't help but smile at his turn of fate over the past three months.

In spite of the National Security Finding, he had been able to glean something of the events following his release. Wheeler had been a diligent G-Man, visiting Susan, Sam, and nearly everyone at CERT/CC in the next two days, securing their signatures on non-disclosures. Information on the last location he had received from Flanagan who had kept in frequent contact.

Of course no one could speak openly about the Incident, but people did talk and they couldn't throw you in jail for innocuous references to Internet activities could they? At least he hoped not.

According to Flanagan, even though there was never any public disclosure of the rogue, the Incident had energized CERT's, and J. Timothy Rydell's, quest for a larger piece of the federal budget. He seemed to be having some success.

CERT/CC had, of course, dropped all investigations. Braxton was sure that the details on the mole were now in the capable hands of the CIA and NSA. He really would have liked to know whether they had ever informed Century of the problem, or kept it safely locked in the vaults of Langley and Ft. Meade to be leveraged at some future time in the name of national security. His gut said the latter.

Rumors, on the other hand, had spread among the Internet security *cognoscenti* like an out-of-control software virus. 'Government secret' was, after all, the ultimate oxymoron. White hats and black hats alike were burning up blogs and forums with outlandish speculations and bizarre conspiracy theories.

For his part, Braxton had received an unending stream of job offers, from commercial organizations as well as government agencies, promising both fame and fortune, but somehow he just couldn't bring himself to take any of them. At least directly.

He had even received a friendly email from Megan, alluding to his latest "adventure". It sounded like she was doing well on the Left Coast.

Staying in Cambridge had simply been too painful. He had left his apartment, and his past, in Massachusetts, and moved south. He now had a small but comfortable apartment in Reston and a suite in Tysons Corner's newest office building.

He had then conscientiously followed up with each of his would-be employers, politely turning down their offers, but dangling the carrot of cost-effective consulting services. They had responded with more contracts than he could handle, and he was now trying to figure out whether to bring a partner on board.

He stepped out of the elevator and walked down the hall to the offices of Cerberus Consulting. The irony of his company's initials was not lost on him.

Karen Chu, his new secretary, was typing furiously into her computer, probably searching for a better price on next week's flight to Berkeley. Chu was a sharp-tongued, Gen X wife and mother who had burned out teaching math in the Fairfax County school system and wanted to apply her considerable analytic abilities to a new profession. After a ten minute interview, Braxton had hired her on the spot.

"A little late this morning, Adam," Chu scolded as she looked up from the monitor. "Heavy date last night?"

"You got that right," he replied hefting his briefcase in the air.

He walked past her desk, gave a quick salute, and continued into the inner office. The space wasn't large, but comfortably held his desk, an old couch, a wall-full of overloaded book cases and a large window overlooking the sprawl of Fairfax County. When potential customers visited, he used a small conference room around the corner he shared with an aggressive young Virginia architect.

He dumped his briefcase on the sofa and moved to his desk, staring over a mound of unread reports and contracts. Email notwithstanding, the paper-less office had yet to arrive.

Despite the overflow of documents on his desk, Chu had managed to clear an open space and leave a stack of mail with his daily appointment card on top. Smart phones were great, but there was something emotionally satisfying about a carefully-annotated index card.

It looked to be an easy day: only two meetings, both in the afternoon.

Highlighted at the bottom of the card was a note to be sure to pick up his tuxedo for Sam Fowler's retirement party that evening. The doctors had said the detective had completely recovered, but the injury had been a stark reminder of Fowler's mortality. He had given twenty-six years of his life keeping the District safe and it was past time to find a new line of work. His wife Pat couldn't have been happier.

Braxton settled behind his desk and, as had become his habit, started the day by scanning the latest stories on the CNN web site. He had been waiting for one particular story to appear, and he found it on the third screen:

```
Lexington Named New Virginia Senator @Washington
Post
```

(Abridged)

```
Virginia Governor Howard Benedict today named
Wilson Lexington, a prominent Richmond attorney and
former Virginia legislator, as interim senator
filling the post left vacant by long time Virginia
politician, David Potterfield. Potterfield, the
Senior Senator from the State and Chairman of the
Senate's Committee on Technology and Communication,
resigned unexpectedly following continued allega-
tions of illegal conduct on the part of his former
Chief of Staff, Barclay Nicholson. Nicholson was
killed in an apparent mugging several months ago.
Potterfield could not be reached for comment. "Mr.
Lexington is honored that Governor Benedict has
selected him to represent the Commonwealth," stated
Susan Goddard, Lexington's Media Relations
Director, "and he promises to work diligently for
the people of Virginia, continuing in the strong
tradition of his predecessors."
```

[Press Release][Full Article]

Braxton clicked on the "Press Release" link to see what changes had been made since the version Susan had shown him a few nights before. He was pleased that some of his suggestions had been incorporated.

Their relationship had drifted to the platonic after the urgencies of the Incident had passed and new opportunities had presented themselves. He was neither surprised nor hurt; such was the way of life. Still, they were close friends and he knew they would always be there for each other.

Scanning the other stories, he read that the *Promoting Freedom and Democracy Bill*, now called the *Rasmussen Bill* after the new Chair of the Senate Foreign Relations Committee, was locked in a conference committee, while staffers, lobbyists and associated other Hill jackals fought over modifications to the Bill's encryption standards.

Hawthorne Systems in particular had been flooding dollars into the discussion. Just last week, he had read they had signed an agreement to partner with Takagawa Communications for the development of a new command-and-control platform. If they could tilt the specifications toward their technology, it would be a colossal windfall for both Hawthorne Systems and Japan.

Oddly, one of Braxton's job offers had come from Akira Hajima, CEO of Takagawa. He had written a very personal, and extremely generous, offer letter that had ended with an effusive "thank you".

But "thank you" for what? Braxton knew the Japanese were polite but he was still puzzled by the tone of the communication.

He turned back to his proposals, vowing from now on to stick to simple technology problems: bits and bytes; hardware and software. He would never get involved with politics and politicians again.

ACKNOWLEDGEMENTS

The Saracen Incident is a work of fiction, but much of the described Internet history is based in fact: CERT was formed after the appearance of the Morris Worm, the Phone Phreaks did exist, and 6.251 was definitely a celebrated course at MIT.

The story draws on the memories and experiences of many more individuals than I am able to name. My thanks to you all. Some names, facts and times have been changed to fit the storyline. All errors are mine.

First, a special thanks to Prof. J. Craig Wheeler for your encouragement and assistance. You kept me motivated when the muses were silent. I hope you don't mind being a shadowy Fed.

Thanks to Andrew Carleen and the MIT News and Registrar's Offices for your help in supplying important details about the Institute.

Thanks to Ken Lord for sharing your personal insights of life in our crazy business.

Thanks to my daughters Lisa and Jennifer, for your patience and understanding under a seemingly never-ending barrage of odd questions, usually without any obvious context. You always had the answers I needed.

And finally, a special thank you to my wife Sharon, for reading every word, finding all my slips, and most importantly, just being there.

Keep reading for an excerpt from

the next Adam Braxton adventure

The Liberty Covenant

coming in the Spring of 2016

CHAPTER 1

Southeastern Tennessee
Saturday, 10:00 p.m.

IT WAS TENNESSEE and he was Terry.

The ten men knelt in a clearing of the dense Appalachian woods. Wind whistled above their heads, a reverent chorus to their silent prayers. They were in a circle, with hands joined and heads bent; a confusing mix of dirty jeans, stained T-shirts, and well-worn camo fatigues. Each had his revolver of choice holstered on his belt. They already knew their own parts of the mission, there would be no need for further instruction or explanation.

Terry watched the ritual from beside a battered old oak tree, about twenty yards from the group. It would have been inappropriate to join, even though it had been his command that set the night's operation in motion. The temperature had fallen to the forties, still comfortable for physical activity but with just enough bite to keep everyone alert. Moonlight filtered through wispy cirrus clouds; enough light to provide guidance but not identification. God was smiling on them tonight.

He would have to commend Shepard for the use of the circle. For centuries, no millennia, the shape had been a symbol of supernatural power. The Druids had discovered its magic in the forests of primeval Britain and integrated it into their rituals and constructions. Their greatest achievement was Stonehenge, the mystical ring of stones that still rose majestically on the Salisbury Plain. He had once stood there, alone in a biting English winter night, to immerse himself in its strength. What uncountable secrets remained hidden within its circumference?

The shape had subsequently appeared everywhere: King Arthur and his Round Table, Yin and Yang, the Circle of Changes. He had even used it, sparingly of course, in the blistering sands of the Middle East to bind his men to their duty.

What would be his civilization's legacy three millennia hence? Rap music? The liberal rhetoric of equality for misfits and sodomizers? Tonight would mark the beginning of a new course for his country. A return to the values on which their civilization had been based.

After over two minutes of silence, one man broke the chain. Pete Shepard was just past forty, short and stocky, with silver-gray hair shaved close to his scalp. He had lived in this part of Tennessee his whole life. A faded red bandana encircled his neck, and a pearl-handled Colt M1911 hung prominently at his side. Terry couldn't help but smile at the selection of weapon. The old .45 was archaic compared to modern automatics, but its combat mystique alone was enough to command the respect of the gathering. Despite the fact that this particular one was purchased at a derelict pawn shop in Nashville.

Shepard rose to face the group. His voice cut through the cold air.

"We ask you, Lord, to be with us tonight, as we do your work. To protect us, our families, and the Covenant. Amen."

The circle echoed the blessing. Their leader gave a nod and the men disappeared into the night.

"Nicely done," Terry said as he approached Shepard.

"Thanks, Terry. The boys'll get in line when you lay it out square."

"They'll follow through all the way?"

"It was tough. They've got families too. But yes. They will."

"You've always known how to lead, Pete. That's why we came to you."

"I'm mighty proud. You'll tell 'em that?" Terry nodded understandingly. "Don't know what happened with Will. He always was a little slow, but never did nothin' to hurt anyone. I figure his wife put him up to it."

"That's probably it. But he talked to that reporter. Talked about *us*." Terry turned away and looked into the darkness. "You're sure everyone is in there?"

"Yup. Kappy's been watchin' all day. They're all there. You figure we have to do 'em all?"

"You have to send a message, Pete. For all of us. We can't have anyone breaking the Covenant." He put his hand on Shepard's shoulder. "Von Clausewitz said that 'Out of a thousand men who are remarkable, . . . perhaps not one will combine in himself all those qualities which are required to raise a man above mediocrity in the career of a general.' I know how tough it is to be a leader. You can become that general. You know what's at stake."

"Yessir. I do. We been waitin' for this all our lives."

"I know, Pete. We're gonna change this country. Beginning tonight."

A soft tapping broke the stillness of the night and the men's eyes moved down to an invisible log cabin nestled at the edge of the woods. There was nothing to see yet, just the sound of wooden wedges being driven into jambs.

"Have you started on those plans yet?" Terry asked.

"Yup. Got the boys goin' on 'em yesterday. We should have the molds in a week or so. What do ya want with those things, Terry?"

"That's great, Pete. Really great."

At first it was just small bursts of light, like window candles welcoming a tired traveler. The traitor had built the home himself. It had taken him three years to construct it for his family. The inferno reduced it to ashes in less than three hours.

The screams from inside had only lasted a few minutes.

* * *

Back in his motel room, Terry hunched over the small Formica-topped desk and slowly pecked the message into his cell phone. His joints ached from standing in the cold, damp evening, but he shrugged the pain away. His employer demanded prompt updates.

When he punched "Send", the custom iPhone app encrypted the message with AES and sent it into the Cloud.

The Advanced Encryption Standard was the latest cryptographic magic used to keep Uncle Sam's top secret messages safe. Ironic that the Commander was using the same technology to protect his own communications.

Sanction completed. Tennessee is secure.

ALPHA teams in place. Coordinated action possible.

Operation HALFTIME initiated.

CHAPTER 2

Tyler, Georgia
Sunday, 5:00 p.m.

THE AFTERNOON SUN was slowly disappearing over Providence Ridge filling the Georgia sky with broad brush strokes of sparkling crimson. FBI Special Agent Charlie Thomas squinted in the light, then collapsed his secure cell phone and settled back into the make-shift blind he had constructed in a depression on the hillside. He grimaced as another scrub pine needle jabbed into his backside. The damn needles had left permanent puncture marks in the most uncomfortable of places. It would make for interesting discussions with Laurie if he ever got back home.

When were they going to let him off this goddamned mountain with its prickly pears, voracious fire ants, and carnivorous flies, to do some real investigation work?

It seemed like all he had done on this assignment was wait. He had spent the last week camped on the side of the ridge, watching the activities in the valley below. The object of his attention was a nondescript Georgia farm, which, according to one of the Bureau's informants, had become a center of local militia activity.

Thomas's initial research had been intriguing. Halfway between Atlanta and Columbus, the property was convenient to both cities, yet remote enough to assure privacy. Four hundred acres of pristine Georgia farmland, about half cleared, the other half in heavy pine woods. Seemingly perfect for farming, yet apparently unused for years. And its ownership was a lawyer's delight, a nexus of interlocking corporations that, so far, even the Bureau's investigators couldn't untangle. These results had prompted his supervisors to give him the go-ahead for the next stage—surveillance. Unfortunately, in the Georgia countryside, you couldn't very well just sit in an air-conditioned rental and take pretty pictures.

So here he was, legs aching from fatigue, sitting on the hillside, huddled under camouflage netting and broken branches, taking his notes. He had cataloged visitors to the farm—there didn't seem to be any permanent residents—and mapped the movement of people and materiel among the old farm structures. There was no question the informant had been correct: there was a local militia cell using the property as a base of operations. He had watched as lines of pickup trucks brought fatigue-dressed males to late night meetings and crack-of-dawn exercises.

Binoculars in one hand, pen in the other, he had recorded the movements of people he knew only by their physical appearance: Gimpy, an old veteran with a bad right leg, Beau Brummel, with a swagger and perpetually ironed fatigues, Baldy, whose head reflected the sun like a mirror, and Walrus, the overweight apparent leader of the group. They had become his distant friends, these faceless creatures: his only contact with the rest of the world.

He prayed for the call that would let him escape from his woodsy prison, meet his adversaries face-to-face and find out what was really going on. Before the goddamn chiggers ate him alive.

* * *

"How was your weekend, Mr. President?"

Joseph Matthews looked up from the State Department's latest Mid-East advisory and saw Chad Dawson, his Chief of Staff, taking his seat in one of the Oval Office's plush, easy chairs. Dawson had requested the late afternoon meeting only a few hours before.

"Excellent, Chad. Excellent." Matthews closed the files, rose from his desk, and walked toward the sitting area. "Having the kids come down from school was wonderful, but they drove Margaret and me crazy. Maybe being President of the United States isn't the toughest job in the world."

Dawson began to respond but Matthews raised his hand as he sat across from his Chief of Staff. "Let's hold off for a minute. I've asked Steven to join us. I'd like to get his opinion on the results. I trust that isn't a problem?"

"Uh, of course not, Mr. President," Dawson replied flatly. "I have an extra copy of the report here."

Matthews smiled at his aide's obvious discomfort. Dawson was the ultimate facilitator and detail man. He had no time for the brusque, sweeping pronouncements of General Steven Carlson, the Director of National Intelligence. Still, the conversation affected them both. They could manage to put up with each other for a few minutes.

Carlson appeared at the famous "invisible door" and marched into the room. His uniform had changed from dress blues to custom-made silk suits, but the ex-Marine looked just as prepared for battle as he had been at the height of his military career.

Matthews had known Carlson since their days at Annapolis. They had both come from Mountain states and found they shared many of the same goals and values. They had toughed-out plebe initiation by drawing strength from each other, then sailed through the next three years finishing first and second in their class—Carlson had gotten the final nod based on his unequaled physical prowess.

After their initial tours, Matthews had jumped and returned to the family ranch in Wyoming where he executed well-funded campaigns for State Rep, then Governor. The clear-speaking, good-looking veteran then attracted the attention of the Republican National Committee and continued his ascension first to the Senate and now the Presidency.

Carlson had stayed in the Marines, advancing to a four-star, before retiring to a comfortable position at a Fairfax beltway bandit—at least until his newly-elected friend had nominated him for Director of National Intelligence.

Over the years, they had shared their lives: loves gained and lost, enemies engaged and vanquished, positions offered and accepted. Matthews relied on Carlson's counsel for nearly everything. The Marine was his sounding board, his advisor, and his confessor. But most importantly, he was the monitor of Matthew's political health.

The DNI strode across the tufted Presidential Seal to the sitting area. Even at sixty, he looked like he could play tight end for the Redskins. His five foot ten inch frame was straight as a spear, his gray hair still military-short, and his neck and shoulders thick with muscle. His face was as craggy as the Rockies, and the jagged scar along his jawline only gave it that much more character. He had gained a bit of girth, but Carlson still pitied any man that got in the General's way.

"Good afternoon, Mr. President," Carlson said cheerfully, pulling over another of the chairs. "You too, Chad."

"Good afternoon, General," Dawson replied without looking up from his papers. "Here are the results from J.T.'s latest poll. He just sent them over." Dawson handed a folder to Matthews, then one to Carlson.

Matthews thumbed through the results. J.T. Wells was the administration's political analyst. In reality, their head pollster. Matthews' existence was dictated by polls: What did the populace think about his legislative agenda? About his trip to Mexico? What he had for dinner? It was a never-ending game of chasing their own tails.

And now it would get even worse. Just two weeks ago, at a noisy, obscenely-expensive New York City national convention, he had been named as the party's candidate for the upcoming election. The selection had been a foregone conclusion, so he had been spared the pain of primary battles, but now the cold, hard political winter would start. Ironically just as D.C.'s sultry August rolled in.

God, he hated the battles that he knew were ahead. The negative publicity, the begging for more and more money, the backroom deals and equivocations. Three and a half years of debilitating work reduced to three months of sound bites, sore hands and empty smiles. But he had no choice, there was still so much he needed to do. And he knew *he* was the one to do it.

The two men before him were here to make sure it happened that way.

"Mr. President," Dawson began once Matthews' eyes had lifted from the papers, "These results show you are in a very strong position entering the general election. Approval ratings on trade and the global environment are all well over seventy-five percent. The public is pleased with your handling of the Turkey intrusion and foreign terrorism concerns have abated." He paused and managed a nod to the DNI. "Fiscally, as long as Jamison keeps the Fed in line, we should have no problem in this area as well. Finally, the signing of the intelligence exchange agreement with NATO in a few weeks will be an outstanding PR event. All in all, a very rosy report."

Dawson stopped and all eyes turned to Matthews. It sounded like an enviable position, but Matthews hadn't gotten to the Oval Office by believing everything his staff told him.

"Thank you, Chad. That does sound quite positive. Steven, any comments?"

"Actually, yes, Mr. President," Carlson replied, stretching even taller in the sofa. "Chad has summarized the positive findings very well. But I believe there must be some negatives. Politics are never this rosy. Is there a 'however' we should be aware of, Chad?"

"Chad, is there more?" Matthews asked.

Heads now turned to the Chief of Staff.

"Yes, Mr. President," Dawson answered. "There is one area that requires some attention. I believe it has ramifications for the re-election campaign. The polls suggest you are vulnerable on domestic policy."

"How can that be?" Matthews responded. "We've nearly balanced the budget and still kept taxes flat."

"Ah, that's *fiscal* policy, Mr. President." Dawson's voice exhibited a well-developed deference. "It's the quality of life that seems to be the problem. With the threat of foreign terrorism reduced, the population begins to worry about more mundane issues like employment and public safety. Your continuing education plan was soundly defeated in the House, the crime rate has started up again, and Henneberry is crowing about the drug problem. These are not positive trends."

Senator Mitchell Henneberry was a decorated veteran and Chairman of the Senate Judiciary Committee. He had been a constant thorn in the side of the Republicans ever since the Democrats regained majority in the senior chamber.

"It seems to me that Morgan has been handling things quite well," Matthews said.

"Mr. President," Carlson interrupted, ignoring Dawson and turning to Matthews. "As much as I respect the man's experience and contributions, A.G. Kahler is a wet fish. He has the charisma of a telephone pole. The American people want a dynamic, energetic individual as the nation's top cop. Someone who represents our best and brightest."

"That's not a particularly positive phrase, do you think?" Dawson asked. "It didn't work very well for McNamara."

"Thank you for the history lesson, Chad." Carlson scowled at the Chief of Staff. Bulging veins and tendons strained against his starched collar. He turned his attention back to Matthews. "Nonetheless, Mr. President, the latest results show a significantly lower acceptability rating on the domestic side. Approval in our target constituencies has dropped ten points since the last poll. Fifteen points in the conservative Democrats. This could become a rallying point. There's no question Henneberry could very effectively stake out this territory."

Dawson rapidly shuffled through the pollster's report. "General, where did you get those figures? They're not here."

"Oh, sorry," Carlson replied. "J.T. faxed me a copy earlier this morning. I reviewed the details with him an hour ago."

Matthews let the animosity cool before responding. "Even if I accept your premise, Steven, what would you have us do? I will not replace Morgan."

"Of course not, Mr. President. That would be a definite sign of weakness. I am only suggesting that we incorporate these findings into the campaign strategy for the next three months. Wherever possible, we should look to minimize any negative domestic publicity and highlight foreign policy successes. And make sure we place our best people on any issues when they arise."

"That is an excellent suggestion, General," the Chief of Staff replied. The edge on his voice was unmistakable. "We will make every effort to see that we don't put stupid people in prominent positions." He turned back to his boss. "But really, Mr. President, we *should* thank J.T. for the poll. Your domestic approval is nearly fifty percent. Combined you have an unbeatable position. Your record is exceptional and the people realize it. I don't think we need to go around worrying that the sky is falling."

Matthews waited for Carlson's retort, but the DNI refused to take the bait.

"Thank J.T. for a very thorough analysis," Matthews finally said to Dawson. "I'll review the results in detail tonight. I don't think any immediate changes in policy are called for. Let's talk again in a few days."

"Yes, Mr. President," Dawson said with a nod. "We really must prepare for the Congressional Caucus meeting now."

"I'll leave you two for that," Carlson said, abruptly rising from his chair. "I've got to get ready for tonight's call with the Australian security Ministers. Thank you for the review, Chad. Mr. President."

Matthews watched as his friend headed back over the Seal.

When he had first taken office, Matthews had carefully stepped around that circular section of carpet. He had felt guilty putting a foot on it. Now, he and his staff trod across it regularly, just as thousands of others routinely trampled across all the other trappings of his office. It was metaphor he tried not to dwell upon.

Carlson was a man that commanded attention, from friends and foes alike. His thoughts on defensive responses might be very enlightening. "Oh, Steven?" Matthews called.

Carlson spun back to face the voice. "Yes, Mr. President?"

"If you have any specific suggestions in these domestic areas, I'd be very interested in reviewing them with you."

"Certainly, sir. Thank you."

Carlson disappeared through the door and Matthews waited for the inevitable analysis.

"I'm sorry, sir," Dawson began as Matthews knew he would, "I know General Carlson is your friend, but sometimes he just gives me the creeps. I never know if he means what he's saying."

Matthews had to tread carefully. His friendship with Carlson was well-known and had compromised his relationship with other members of his staff on more than one occasion. It was a difficult line to walk but one he would not sidestep.

"You're not alone there, Chad. However, Steven is a valuable resource for all of us. I value his counsel."

"Yes, sir. I know. But he's so . . . well, *private*. I never see him relax. Does he have any family?"

"No one close. He never married. His first family was the military. Now I think he's adopted us."

"Do you really trust him? Some of the things he says, . . . well they don't sound like he's your ideological soul-mate."

Matthews couldn't hold back the grin. His Chief of Staff didn't miss a thing. "He is a self-possessed professional, Chad. Just like the rest of us. Do I agree with everything he says? No. Do I respect his opinions and ideas? Absolutely. Sometimes I need someone who can say things that I can't. Think of Steven as our lightning rod. Just be careful you don't get too close.

"Look at it this way, would you rather have him working for the opposition?"

"I don't know, Mr. President. Can we be sure he isn't?"

ABOUT THE AUTHOR

Jack Bowie was born and raised outside of Cleveland, Ohio, then headed to Cambridge, Massachusetts to attend MIT. After graduating, he held technical management positions in public and private sector organizations in Massachusetts, Virginia and Connecticut.

A lifelong reader of classic science fiction and espionage thrillers, Jack's writing began as a break from professional duties and grew into a passion for storytelling.

Drawing on his career as a researcher, engineer and high-tech executive, Jack's novels describe the subtle, and sometimes not so subtle, interplay of technology with personal passions and egos.

For more information on Jack, check out www.JackBowie.com, or follow him on Facebook at facebook.com/jackbowieauthor.